Praise

"A smart [...] wrecks galore . . . Boyle proves his mettle by [...] from the strange-crime annals into a life-and-death story of evolution, shipwrecks, and dominion over the earth. . . . Character, science, and history co-evolve marvelously here in a tale of fanaticism gone literally overboard. Boyle devotees will find everything they expect in the way of manic plotlines, flamboyant obsessions, and cool comeuppance outlandishly delivered."

—Barbara Kingsolver, *The New York Times Book Review*

"One stormy tale . . . Terrifically exciting and unapologetically relevant . . . Boyle's white-water prose propels us through sixty years of tumultuous history involving the Northern Channel Islands off the coast of Ventura, California. Long a master at scenes of quick-moving crisis, Boyle punctuates this plot with some of the best disasters of his career. . . . Gripping as all that stormy drama is, though, it also emphasizes the larger theme of *When the Killing's Done*—the chaotic randomness of the natural world, a world that human beings control but must ultimately submit to."

—Ron Charles, *The Washington Post*

"*When the Killing's Done* falls in nicely with the mood of Margaret Atwood's vatic sci-fi tales or Jonathan Franzen's recent, naturalistic *Freedom*. . . . It's an exciting narrative, incorporating tragedy, anger, and a satisfying amount of natural history, with the entangled moral complexities so difficult to unravel that the reader may find himself saying 'just tell me what to think.' Boyle doesn't, but one can feel his pleasure in dramatizing the inherent paradoxes of issues that do finally seem insoluble."

—Diane Johnson, *The New York Review of Books*

"*When the Killing's Done* centers on a face-off between a biologist and an animal rights advocate with strongly opposing views on what's best for the creatures of the Northern Channel Islands. The subject is far from frivolous, but Boyle deals with it in his dependably unpedantic, entertaining, and often very funny fashion."

—John McMurtrie, *San Francisco Chronicle*

"There's nothing reserved about T.C. Boyle, the maximalist whose never met a scene he couldn't spin into a fireworks show.... The opening shipwreck scene will leave you wearing a life jacket in the bathtub.... *When the Killing's Done* may be the world's first island-biogeographical thriller."

—Bruce Barcott, *Outside*

"Boyle's finest novel yet.... [He] aims high with his drama of human hubris matched by nature's indifferent savagery, and it works.... Predation, destruction, survival, and renewal: Human beings may interfere with this natural cycle, and one day they may damage it beyond repair. In this dark novel, itself a feat of creative engineering, Boyle tells us they will never master it."

—Wendy Smith, Salon.com

"A killer of a story ... A well-told tale about eating, animals, and conflict.... The ultimate joke in this riveting narrative is on us and our utopian attempts to get back to Eden.... Best of all, Boyle combines this strong commitment to the sheer entertainment of a well-told story with a fervent insistence that we think for ourselves."

—Mike Fisher, *Milwaukee Journal Sentinel*

"Read this engaging and lively and timely story, with the truths on both sides of the human arguments neatly dramatized, weighed, and balanced, and a wild homage to the power of the natural world."

—Alan Cheuse, *All Things Considered*

"The Pacific coast is anything but pacific. It's cold, rocky, harsh, fogbound, the perfect place for T.C. Boyle to bring together all his themes. . . . And he is at his best here, recalling the moral complexity of *The Tortilla Curtain*. . . . The surprise in *When the Killing's Done* is the mother-daughter stories, three generations of them, evoking birth, struggle, pregnancy, and death, providing a continuity that echoes the history of the islands."

—Betsy Willeford, *The Miami Herald*

"Boyle does so much right here: He poses the big questions, refrains from offering answers, and humanizes the argument without proselytizing. One thing remains certain in the end. There's a simple truth, that runs like an undercurrent through these pages. The presence of a single human footprint often proves to be the biggest menace of all."

—Don Waters, *The Portland Oregonian*

"Here Boyle is at the peak of his powers, emulating the five senses with cinematic clarity, modulating tone for sardonic effect, and nominating the perfect word for each particle of creation. . . . Boyle's brawny narrative shifts between perspectives, introducing tragic new details from the women's histories that recalibrate the balance of our sympathies."

—Joe Williams, *St. Louis Post-Dispatch*

"Boyle's intricate tale of two families fractured and yet knotted tightly by their experiences on and near the island hinges on a kind of chaos theory of biology. . . . He explores powerful, though not fully empowered, women, and their complex, dependent relationships with much weaker men. No matter whether one concurs with the morality of these outcomes, getting there is a ride the reader will want to tag along for, tantalized by Boyle's fine writing, perfectly paced and wryly voiced."   —Dana Coffield, *The Denver Post*

"A heartbreaking and complex tale of two conservationists working towards what they think is the betterment of life on the islands. . . . Equal parts cynicism and realism, Boyle's riveting morality play reflects the sneaking suspicion that, even in the remotest regions of the planet, man's good intentions eventually will become less like an improved road than like an invading virus."

—David Colner, *L.A. Weekly*

T. Coraghessan Boyle

When the Killing's Done

PENGUIN BOOKS

PENGUIN BOOKS

Published by the Penguin Group

Penguin Group (USA) Inc., 375 Hudson Street, New York, New York 10014, U.S.A.

Penguin Group (Canada), 90 Eglinton Avenue East, Suite 700, Toronto,
Ontario, Canada M4P 2Y3 (a division of Pearson Penguin Canada Inc.)

Penguin Books Ltd, 80 Strand, London WC2R 0RL, England

Penguin Ireland, 25 St. Stephen's Green, Dublin 2, Ireland (a division of Penguin Books Ltd)

Penguin Books Australia Ltd, 250 Camberwell Road, Camberwell,
Victoria 3124, Australia (a division of Pearson Australia Group Pty Ltd)

Penguin Books India Pvt Ltd, 11 Community Centre,
Panchsheel Park, New Delhi–110 017, India

Penguin Group (NZ), 67 Apollo Drive, Rosedale, Auckland 0632,
New Zealand (a division of Pearson New Zealand Ltd)

Penguin Books (South Africa) (Pty) Ltd, 24 Sturdee Avenue,
Rosebank, Johannesburg 2196, South Africa

Penguin Books Ltd, Registered Offices: 80 Strand, London WC2R 0RL, England

First published in the United States of America by Viking Penguin,
a member of Penguin Group (USA) Inc. 2011
Published in Penguin Books 2012

1 3 5 7 9 10 8 6 4 2

Map by Jeffrey L. Ward

THE LIBRARY OF CONGRESS HAS CATALOGED THE HARDCOVER EDITION AS FOLLOWS:

Boyle, T. Coraghessan.
When the killing's done / T. Coraghessan Boyle.
p. cm.
ISBN 978-0-670-02232-8 (hc.)
ISBN 978-0-14-312089-6 (export pbk.)
1. Women biologists—Fiction.   2. Businessmen—Fiction.   3. Introduced organisms—
California—Fiction.   4. Ecological disturbances—Fiction.   5. Channel Islands (Calif.)—
Fiction.   I. Title.
PS3552.O932W48 2011
813'.54—dc22
2010033604

Printed in the United States of America
Set in Minion Pro
Designed by Francesca Belanger

For Kerrie,
who tramped the ridges and braved the ghosts

And God blessed them, and God said unto them, Be fruitful, and multiply, and replenish the earth, and subdue it: and have dominion over the fish of the sea, and over the fowl of the air, and over every living thing that moveth upon the earth.

—Genesis 1:28

ACKNOWLEDGMENTS

I would like to thank Lotus Vermeer, Marla Daily, Kate Faulkner, Rachel Wolstenholme, Marie Alex, Jim Perry, Jay Brennan, Stephanie Mutz, and Mike DeGruy for their kind assistance with the research for this book. In addition, I would like to express my debt of gratitude to the historians and memoirists of the Channel Islands, whose accounts proved invaluable to the unfolding of this narrative, particularly those of Michel Peterson, Marla Daily, John Gherini, Tom Kendrick, Clifford McElrath, Margaret Eaton, and Helen Caire.

Portions of this book appeared previously, in slightly different form, in *McSweeney's, Orion,* and *The Iowa Review.*

Point Conception

Goleta

Goleta Point

<<< NORTHBOUND COASTWISE SHIPPING LANE

SEPARATION ZONE

Santa Barbara

SOUTHBOUND COASTWISE SHIPPING LANE >>>

SAN MIGUEL

SANTA ROSA

Santa Cruz Channel

Pacific Ocean

SANTA CRUZ

Santa Barbara Channel

West Point

Painted Cave

Scorpion Anchorage

Farney's Cove

Diablo Peak 2434'

Prisoners' Harbor

SCORPION RANCH

San Pedro Point

CHRISTY RANCH

China Bay

El Montañon

SMUGGLERS' RANCH

Smugglers' Cove

El Tigre 1484'

MAIN RANCH

Yellowbanks Anchorage

Anacapa Passage

Pacific Ocean

Malva Real Anchorage

Willows Anchorage

Coches Prietos

0 Miles 5

0 Kilometers 5

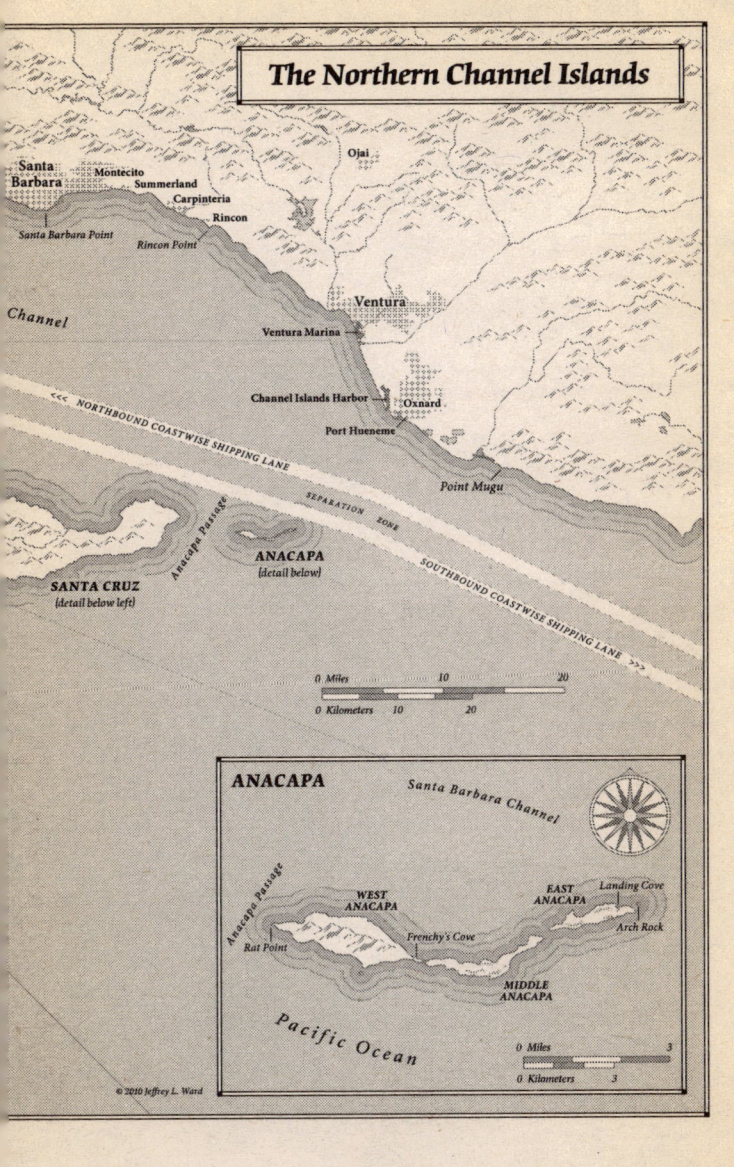

The Northern Channel Islands

Ojai

Santa
Barbara · Montecito · Summerland
· Carpinteria
· Rincon

Santa Barbara Point · Rincon Point

Channel

Ventura

Ventura Marina

NORTHBOUND COASTWISE SHIPPING LANE <<<

Channel Islands Harbor — Oxnard

Port Hueneme

SEPARATION ZONE

Point Mugu

Anacapa Passage

ANACAPA
(detail below)

SOUTHBOUND COASTWISE SHIPPING LANE >>>

SANTA CRUZ
(detail below left)

0 Miles   10   20
0 Kilometers   10   20

ANACAPA

Santa Barbara Channel

Anacapa Passage

WEST
ANACAPA

EAST
ANACAPA · Landing Cove

Rat Point

Frenchy's Cove

Arch Rock

MIDDLE
ANACAPA

Pacific Ocean

© 2010 Jeffrey L. Ward

0 Miles   3
0 Kilometers   3

PART I

Anacapa

The Wreck of the *Beverly B.*

Picture her there in the pinched little galley where you could barely stand up without cracking your head, her right hand raw and stinging still from the scald of the coffee she'd dutifully—and foolishly—tried to make so they could have something to keep them going, a good sport, always a good sport, though she'd woken up vomiting in her berth not half an hour ago. She was wearing an oversized cable-knit sweater she'd fished out of her husband's locker because the cabin was so cold, and every fiber of it seemed to chafe her skin as if she'd been flayed raw while she slept. She hadn't brushed her hair. Or her teeth. She was having trouble keeping her balance, wondering if it was always this rough out here, but she was afraid to ask Till about it, or Warren either. She didn't know the first thing about handling a boat or riding out a heavy sea or even reading a chart, as the two of them had been more than happy to remind her every chance they got, and Till told her she should just settle in and enjoy the ride. Her place was in the kitchen. Or rather, the galley. She was going to clean the fish and fry them and when the sun came out—if it came out—she would spread a towel on top of the cabin and rub a mixture of baby oil and iodine on her legs, lie back, shut her eyes and bask till they were a nice uniform brown.

It was only now, the boat pitching and rolling and her right hand vibrant with pain, that she realized her feet were wet, her socks clammy and clinging and her new white tennis shoes gone a dark saturate gray. And why were her feet wet? Because there was water on the galley deck. Not coffee—she'd swabbed that up as best she could with a rag—but water. Salt water. A thin bellying sheet of it riding toward her and then jerking back as the boat pitched into another trough. She would have had to sit heavily then, the bench rising up to meet her while she clung to the tabletop with both hands, as helpless in that moment as if she were strapped into one of those lurching rides at the amusement park Till seemed to love so much but that only made her feel as if her stomach had swallowed itself up like in that cartoon of the snake feeding its tail into its own jaws.

The cuffs of her blue jeans were wet, instantly wet, the boat riding up again and the water shooting back at her, more of it now, a shock of cold up to her ankles. She tried to call out, but her throat squeezed shut. The water fled down the length of the deck and came back again, deeper, colder. *Do something!* she told herself. *Get up. Move!* Fighting down her nausea, she pulled herself around the table hand over hand so she could peer up the three steps to where Till sat at the helm, his bad arm rigid as a stick, while Warren, his brother Warren, the ex-Marine, bossy, know-it-all, shoved savagely at him, fighting him for the wheel. She wanted to warn them, wanted to betray the water in the galley so they could do something about it, so they could stop it, fix it, put things to right, but Warren was shouting, every vein standing out in his neck and the spray exploding over the stern behind him like the whipping tail of an underwater comet. "Goddamn you, goddamn you to hell! Keep the bow to the fucking waves!" The ship lurched sideways, shuddering down the length of it. "You want to see the whole goddamn shitbox go down . . . ?"

Yes. That was the story. That was how it went. And no matter how often she told her own version of what had happened to her grandmother in the furious cold upwelling waters of the Santa Barbara Channel in a time so distant she had to shut her eyes halfway to develop a picture of it—sharper and clearer than her mother's because her mother hadn't been there any more than she had, or not in any conscious way—Alma always drew her voice down to a whisper for the payoff, the denouement, the kicker: "Nana was two months' pregnant when that boat sank."

She'd pause and make sure to look up, whether she was

4

telling the story across the dining room table to one of her suitemates back when she was in college or a total stranger she'd sat next to on the airplane. "Two months' pregnant. And she didn't even know it." And she'd pause again, to let the significance of that sink in. Her own mother would have been dead in the womb, washed ashore, food for the crabs, and she herself wouldn't exist, wouldn't be sitting there with her hair still wet from the shower or threaded in a ponytail through the gap in back of her baseball cap, wouldn't be teasing out all the nuances and existential implications of the story that was the tale of the world before her, if it weren't for the toughness—in body, mind and spirit—of the woman she remembered only in her frailty and decrepitude.

Of course, she felt the coldness of it too, the aleatory tumble that swallowed up the unfit and unlucky while the others multiplied. And if there were a thousand generations of shipwrecks in the same family, would their descendants develop gills and webbed toes or would they just learn to stay ashore and ignore those seductive unfettered islands glittering out there on the horizon? She was alive, in the crux of creation, along with everything else sparking in the very instant of her telling, and one day she'd have children herself, add to the sum of things, work the DNA up the ladder. Her mother's father was dead. And his brother along with him. And her mother's mother should have been dead too. That was the thing, wasn't it?

The month was March, the year 1946. Alma's grandfather—Tilden Matthew Boyd—was six months home from the war in the Pacific that had left him with a withered right arm shorn of meat above the elbow, nothing there but a scar like a seared omelet wrapped around the bone. Her grandmother, young and hopeful and with hair as dark and abundant as her own, broke a bottle over the bow of the *Beverly B.* while Till, restored to her from the vortex of the war in a miraculous dispensation more actual and solid than all the cathedrals in the world, sat at the helm and the gulls dipped overhead and the clouds swept in on a northwesterly breeze to chase the sun over the water. Beverly was happy because Till was happy and they ate their sandwiches and drank the cheap champagne out of paper cups in the cabin because the wind was stiff and the chop wintry and white-capped. Warren was there too that first day, the day of the launching, a walking Dictaphone of unasked-for advice, ringing clichés and long-winded criticism. But he drank the champagne and he showed up two weekends in a row to help Till tinker with the engines and install the teak cabinets and fiddle rails Till had made in the garage of their rented house that needed paint and windowscreens for the mosquitoes and drainpipes to keep the winter rains from shearing off the roof and dousing anybody standing at the front door with a key in her hand and a load of groceries in both her aching arms. But Till had no desire to fix the house—it didn't belong to them anyway. The *Beverly B.*, though—that was a different story.

She was a sleek twenty-eight-foot all-wood cabin cruiser, solid-built, with butternut bulkheads and teak trim throughout, a real beauty, but she'd been dry-docked and neglected during the war, from which her owner, a Navy man, had never returned. Till spotted the boat listing into the weeds at the back of the boatyard and had tracked down the Navy man's quietly grieving parents—their boy had been burned to death in a slick of oil after a kamikaze pilot steered himself into the *St. Lo* during the battle of Leyte Gulf—in whose living room he'd sat with his hat perched on one knee while they fingered the photographs and medals that were their son's last relics. He sat there for two full hours, sipping tepid Lipton tea with a bitter slice of lemon slowly revolving atop it, before he mentioned the boat, and when he did finally mention it, they both stared at him as if he'd crawled up out of the pages of the family album to perch there on the velour cushions of the maplewood couch in the shrouded and barely lit living room they'd inhabited like ghosts since before they could

6

remember. The mother—she must have been in her fifties, stout but with the delicate wrists and ankles of a girl and a face infused with outrage and grief in equal measures— threw back her head and all but yodeled, "That old thing?" Then she looked to her husband and dropped her voice. "I don't guess Roger'll be needing it now, will he?"

Over the course of the fall and winter, Till had devoted himself to the task of refitting that boat, haunting the boatyard and the ship chandlery and fooling with the engines until he was so smudged with oil Beverly told anybody who wanted to listen that he half the time looked like he was rigged out in blackface for some old-timey minstrel show. Her joke. Till in blackface. And she used it on Mrs. Viola down at the market and on Warren and the girl he was seeing, Sandra, with the prim mouth and the sweaters she wore so tight you could see every line of her brassiere, straps and cups and all. Careful, that was what Till was. Careful and precise and unerring. He never mentioned it, never complained, but he'd given his right arm for his country and he was determined to keep the left one for himself. And for her. For her, above all.

He had to learn how to make it do the work of his right arm and wrist and hand, punching tickets for the Santa Monica Boulevard line while people looked on impatiently and tried to be polite out of a kind of grudging recognition, the dead hand clenching the ticket stub and the newly dominant one doing the punching, and he learned to use that hand to fold his paycheck over once and present it to her like a ticket itself, a ticket to a moveable feast to which she and she alone was invited. At night, late, after supper and the radio, he'd let the hand play over her nakedness as if it knew no impediment, and that was all right, that was as good as it was going to get, because he was left-handed now and always would be till the day he was gone. And when they launched the *Beverly B.*, he was as gentle and cautious with his boat as he was with her in their marriage bed, the right arm swinging stiffly into play when the wheel

7

revolved under pressure of the left. The first few times they never took her out of sight of the harbor. Till said he wanted to get a feel for her, wanted to break her in, listen to what the twin Chrysler engines had to say when he pushed the throttle all the way forward and watched the tachometer climb to 2,800 RPM.

Then came that Friday evening late in March when she and Till and Warren motored out of the harbor on a course for the nearest of the northern Channel Islands, for Anacapa and the big one beyond it, Santa Cruz, because that was where the fish were, the lingcod as long as your arm, the abalone you only had to pluck off the rocks and more plentiful than the rocks themselves, the lobsters so accommodating they'd crawl right up the anchor line and dunk themselves in the pot. A man at work had told Till all about it. Anybody could go out to Catalina—hell, everybody did go out there, day-trippers and Saturday sailors and the rest—but if you wanted something akin to virgin territory, the northern islands, up off of Oxnard and Santa Barbara, that was the place to go. They'd brought along the two biggest ice chests she'd been able to find at Sears, Roebuck, both of them bristling with the dark slender necks of the beer bottles Warren assured her would have vanished by the time all those fish fillets and boiled lobsters were ready to nestle down there between their sheets of ice for a nice long sleep on the way home.

"We'll have fish for a week, a week at least," Till kept saying. "And when they're gone we can just go out again and again after that." He gave her a look. He was at the helm, the weather calm, the evening haze with its opalescent tinge clinging to the water before them and the harbor sliding into the wake behind, the beer in his hand barely an encumbrance as he perched there like some sea captain out of a Jack London story. "Which," he said, knowing how sensitive she'd been on the subject of sinking money into the boat, "should cut our grocery bill by half, half at least."

She'd made sandwiches at home—liverwurst on white

with plenty of mustard and mayo, ham on rye, tuna fish salad—and when they settled down in the cabin to take big hungry bites out of them and wet their throats with the beer that was so cold it went down like mountain spring water, it was as if they'd fallen off the edge of the world. After dinner she'd sat out on the stern deck for a long while, the air sweet and unalloyed, everything still but for the steady thrum of the engines that was like the working of a sure steady heart, the heart at the center of the *Beverly B.*, unflagging and assured. There were dolphins, aggregations of them, silvered and pinked as they sluiced through the water and raced the hull to feel the electricity of it. They seemed to be grinning at her, welcoming her, as happy in their element as she was in hers. And what was that story she'd read—was it in the newspaper or *Reader's Digest*? The one about the boy on his surfboard taken out to sea on a riptide and the sharks coming for him till the dolphins showed up grinning and drove them off because dolphins are mammals, warm-blooded in the cold sea, and they despise the sharks as the cold agents of death they are. Did they nose the boy's surfboard past the riptide and back in to shore, guiding him all the way like guardian angels? Maybe, maybe they did.

The last of the sun was tangled up in the mist ahead of them, due west and west the sun doth sink, the lines of a nursery rhyme scattered in her head. She lifted her feet to the varnished rail and studied her toes, seeing where the polish had faded and thinking to refresh it when she had the chance, when the boys were fishing in the morning and she was stretched out in the sun without a care in the world. The engines hummed. A whole squadron of dark beating birds shot up off the water and looped back again as if they were attached to a flexible band, and not a one of them made the slightest sound. She lit a cigarette, the wind in her hair, and watched her husband through the newly washed windows as he held lightly to the wheel while his brother sat on the upholstered bench beside him, talking, always talking, but in dumb show now because the cabin door was shut and she couldn't hear a word.

She finished her cigarette and let the butt launch itself into the wind on a tail of red streamers. It was getting chilly, the sky darkening, closing round them like a lid set to an infinite iron pot. One more minute and she'd go in and listen to them talk, men's talk, about the pie in the sky, the fish in the sea, the carburetors and open-faced reels and lathes and varnishes and tools and brushes and calibrators that made them men, and she'd open another beer too, a celebratory last beer to top off the celebratory three—or was it four?—she'd already had. It was then, just as she was about to rise, that the sea suddenly broke open like a dark spewing mouth and spat something at her, a hurtling shadowy missile that ran straight for her face till she snapped her head aside and it crashed with a reverberant wet thumping slap into the glass of the cabin door and both men wheeled round to see what it was.

She let out a scream. She couldn't help herself. This thing was alive and flapping there at her feet like some sort of sea bat, as long as her forearm, shivering now and springing up like a jack-in-the-box to fall back again and flap itself across the deck on the tripod of its wings and tail. Wings? It was—it was a fish, wasn't it? But here was Till, Warren bundled behind him, his face finding the middle passage between alarm and amusement, and he was stepping on the thing, slamming his foot down, hard, bending quickly to snatch the slick wet length of it up off the deck and hold it out to her like an offering in the grip of his good hand. "God, Bev, you gave me a scare—I thought you'd gone and pitched overboard with that scream."

Warren was laughing behind the sheen of merriment in his eyes. The boat steadied and kept on. "This calls for a toast," he shouted, raising the beer bottle that was perpetual with him. "Bev's caught the first fish!"

She was over her fright. But it wasn't fright—she wasn't one of those clinging weepy women like you saw in the movies. She'd just been startled, that was all. And who wouldn't have been, what with this thing, blue as gunmetal above and silver as a stack of coins below, coming at her like a torpedo with no warning at all? "Jesus Lord," she said, "what *is* it?"

Till held it out for her to take in her own hand, and she was smiling now, on the verge of a good laugh, a shared laugh, but she backed up against the rail while the sky closed in and the wake unraveled behind her. "Haven't you ever seen a flying fish before?" Till was saying. He made a clucking sound with his tongue. "Where've you been keeping yourself, woman?" he said, ribbing her. "This is no kitchen or sitting room or steam-heated parlor. You're out in the wide world now."

"A toast!" Warren crowed. "To Bev! A-number-one fisherwoman!" And he was about to tip back the bottle when she took hold of his forearm, her hair whipping in the breeze. "Well then," she said, "in that case, I guess you're just going to have to get me another beer."

She woke dry-mouthed, a faint rising vapor lifting somewhere behind her eyes, as if her head had been pumped full of helium while she slept. In the berth across from her, snug under the bow as it skipped and hovered and rapped gently against the cushion of the waves, Till was asleep, his face turned to the wall that wasn't a wall but the planking of the hull of the ship that held them suspended over a black chasm of water. Below her, down deep, there were things immense and minute, whales, copepods, sharks and sardines, crabs infinite—the bottom alive with them in their horny chitinous legions, the crabs that tore the flesh from the drowned things and fed the scraps into the shearing miniature shredders of their mouths. All this came to her in the instant of waking, without confusion or dislocation—she wasn't in the double bed they were still making payments on or stretched out on the narrow mattress in the spare room at her parents' house where she'd waited through a thousand hollow echoing nights for Till to come home and reclaim her. She was at sea. She knew the rocking of the boat as intimately now as if she'd never known anything else, felt the muted drone of the engines deep inside her, in the thump of her heart and the pulse of her blood. At sea. She was at sea.

She sat up. A shaft of moonlight cut through the cabin behind her, slicing the table in two. Beyond that, a dark well of shadow, and beyond the shadow the steps to the bridge and the green glow of the controls where Warren, with his bunched muscles and engraved mouth, sat piloting them through the night. She needed—urgently—to use the lavatory. The head, that is. And water—she needed a glass of water from the tap in the head that was attached to the forty-gallon tank in the hold that Till had made such a fuss about because you couldn't waste water, not at sea, where you never knew when you were going to get more. It had got to the point where she was almost afraid to turn on the tap for fear of losing a single precious drop. What was that poem from high school? "Water, water, every where/Nor any drop to drink."

The mariner, that was it. The ancient mariner. And he just had to go and kill that bird, didn't he? The albatross. And what was an albatross anyway? Something big and white, judging from the illustration in the book she'd got out of the library. Like a dinosaur, maybe, only not as big. Probably extinct now. But if albatrosses weren't extinct and one of them came flapping down out of the sky and perched itself on the bow right this minute, she wouldn't even think about shooting it. Uh-uh. Not her. For one thing, she didn't have a gun, and even if she had one she wouldn't know how to use it, but then that wasn't the point, was it? If the poem had taught her anything—and she could hear the high-pitched hectoring whine of her twelfth-grade English teacher, Mr. Parminter, rising up somewhere out of the depths of her consciousness—it was

12

about nature, the power of it, the hugeness. Don't press your luck. Don't upset the balance. Let the albatross be. Let all the creatures be, for that matter . . . except maybe the lobsters. She smiled in the dark at the recollection of Mr. Parminter and that time that seemed like a century ago, when poems and novels and theorems and equations were the whole of her life. She could hardly believe it had only been four years since she'd graduated.

Her bare feet swung out of the berth. The deck was solid, cool, faintly damp. She was wearing a flannel nightgown that covered her all the way to her toes, though she wished she'd been able to wear something a little sheerer for Till's sake—but that would have to wait until they were back home in the privacy of their own bedroom. She was modest and decent, not like the other girls who'd gone out and cheated on their men overseas the first chance they got, and she just didn't feel comfortable showing herself off in such close quarters with Warren there, even if he was Till's brother. She'd seen the way Warren looked at her sometimes, and it was no different from what she'd had to endure since she'd begun to develop in the eighth grade, leers and wolf whistles and all the rest. She didn't blame him. He was a man. He couldn't help himself. And she was proud of her figure, which was her best feature because she'd never be what people would call pretty, or conventionally pretty anyway—she just didn't want to give him or anybody else the wrong idea. She was a one-man woman and that was that. Unlike Sandra, who looked as if she'd been around and who'd shown herself off in a two-piece swimsuit when they'd run the boat down to San Pedro the week before—in a breeze that had her in goosebumps all over and wrapped in Warren's jacket by the time they got back to the dock. But thank God for small mercies: Sandra had been unable to join them this time around. She had an *engagement* in North Hollywood, whatever that meant, but then that wasn't Beverly's worry, it was Warren's.

She slipped into the head, used the toilet, drained her glass of water and then drained another. Her stomach was queasy. That last beer, that was what it was. She ran her fingers through her hair and felt all the body gone out of it, though she'd washed and set it just that morning. Or yesterday morning, technically. But she was at sea now and she'd have to make do—and so would Till, who expected her to be made-up and primped and showing herself off like one of the movie stars in the magazines. She cranked the hand pump to flush, rinsed her hands—precious water, precious—eased the door open and shut it behind her. As she slid back into bed she was thinking she'd just have to tie her hair up in a kerchief, at least till they got there and she could take a swim, depending on how cold the water was, of course. Then she was thinking of the mariner again and of Mr. Parminter, who wore a bow tie to class every day and could recite "Ode on a Grecian Urn" by heart. Then she was asleep.

When she woke again it was daylight and Till's berth was empty. She tried to focus on the deck but the deck wouldn't stay put. A great angry fist seemed to be slamming at the hull with a booming repetitive shock that concussed the thin mattress and the plank beneath it and worked its way through her till she could feel it in the hollow of her chest, in her head, in her teeth. On top of it, every last thing, every screw and bolt and scrap of metal up and down the length of the boat, rattled and whined with a roused insistent drone as if a hive of yellow jackets were trapped in the hull. And what was that smell? Mold, hidden rot, the sour-milk reek of her own unwashed body. Before she could think, she was leaning over and spewing up everything inside her into the bucket she'd kept at her bedside for emergencies—the last of it, sharp and acerbic as a dose of vinegar, coming on a long glutinous string of saliva. She shook her head to clear it, wiped her mouth on the back of her hand. Then she got up, fumbling for her blue jeans and a sweater, Till's sweater, rough as burlap but the warmest thing she could find, and how had it gotten so cold?

It took her a while, just sitting there and picturing dry land, a beach on the island, a rock offshore, anything that wasn't moving, before she was able to get up and work her way into the galley. She filled the percolator with water, poured coffee into the strainer directly from the can without bothering to measure it—she could barely stand, let alone worry about the niceties, and they'd want it strong in any case—and then she set the pot on the burner, but it kept tilting and sliding till she hit on the idea of wedging it there with the big cast-iron pot she intended to make chowder in when they got where they were going. If they ever got there. And what had happened? Had the weather gone crazy all of a sudden? Was it a typhoon? A hurricane?

She looked a fright, she knew it, and she'd have to do something about her hair, but she worked her way up the juddering steps to the bridge and flung herself down on the couch there—or the bench she'd converted to a couch by sewing ties to a set of old plaid cushions she'd found in her parents' garage. The bridge was close, breath-steamed, smelling of men's sweat and the muck at the bottom of the sea. Till was right there, just across from her, sitting on his bench at the controls, so near she could have reached out and touched him. The wheel jumped and jumped again, and he fought it with his left hand while forcing the throttle forward and back in the clumsy stiff immalleable grip of the other one. Warren leaned over him, grim-faced. Neither seemed to have noticed her.

It was only then that she became aware of the height of the waves coming at them, rearing black volcanoes of water that took everything out from under the boat and put it right back again, all the while blasting the windows as if there were a hundred fire trucks out there with their hoses all turned on at once. And here was the rhythm, up, down, up, and a rinse of the windows with every repetition. "Where are we?" she heard herself ask.

Till never looked up. He was frozen there, nothing moving but his arms and shoulders. "Don't know," Warren said, glancing over his shoulder. "Halfway between Anacapa and Santa Cruz, but with the way this shit's blowing, who could say?"

"What we need," Till said, his voice reduced and tentative, as if he really didn't want to have to form his thoughts aloud, "is to find a place to anchor somewhere out of this wind."

"That'd be Scorpion Bay, according to the charts, but that's"—there was a crash, as if the boat had hit a truck head-on, and Warren, all hundred and eighty Marine-honed pounds of him, was flung up against the window as if he were a bag full of nothing. He braced himself, back pressed to the glass. Tried for a smile and failed. "That's somewhere out ahead of us, straight into the blow."

"How far?"

Warren shook his head, held tight to the rail that ran round the bridge. "Could be two miles, could be five. I can't make out a fucking thing, can you?"

"No. But at least we should be okay for depth. There's a lot of water under us. A whole lot."

She looked out ahead of them to where the bow dipped to its pounding, but she couldn't see anything but waves, one springing up off the back of the other, infinite and impatient, coming and coming and coming. Her stomach fell. She thought she might vomit again, but there was nothing left to bring up. "What happened to the weather?" she asked, raising her voice to be heard over the wind, but it wasn't a question really, more an observation in search of some kind of assurance. She wanted them to tell her that this was nothing they couldn't handle, just a little blow that would peter out before long, after which the sun would come back to illuminate the world and all would be as calm and peaceful as it was last night when the waves lapped the hull and the sandwiches and beer went down and stayed down in the pure pleasure of the moment. No one answered. She wasn't scared, not yet, because all this was so new to her and because she trusted Till—Till knew what he was doing. He always did. "I put on coffee," she said, though the thought of it, of the smell and taste of it and the way it clung viscously to the inside of the cup in a discolored slick, made her feel weak all over again. "You boys"—she had to force the words out—"think you might want a cup?"

Then she was back down in the galley, banging her elbows and knees, flung from one position to another, and when she reached for the coffeepot it jumped off the stove of its own volition and scalded her right hand. Before she could register the shock of it, the pot was on the deck, the top spun off and the steaming grounds and six good cups of black coffee spewed across the galley. Her first thought was for the deck—the coffee would stain, eat through the varnish like acid—and before she looked to her burn she was down on her hands and knees, caroming from one corner of the cabin to the other like the silver ball in a pinball machine, dabbing at the mess as she went by with a rag that became so instantaneously and unforgivingly hot she burned her hand a second time. When finally she'd got the deck cleaned up as best she could, she fell back into the bench at the table, angry now, angry at the boat and the sea and the men who'd dragged her out here into this shitty little rattling sea-stinking jail cell, and she swore she'd never go out again, never, no matter what promises they made. "There'll be no coffee and I'm sorry, I am," she said aloud. "You hear that?" she called out, directing her voice toward the steps at the back of the cabin. "No coffee today, no breakfast, no nothing. I'm through!"

The pain of the burn sparked then, assailing her suddenly with an insidious throbbing and prickling, the blisters already forming and bursting, and she thought of getting up and rubbing butter into the reddened flesh on the back of her hand and between her scalded fingers, but she couldn't move. She felt heavy all of a sudden, heavier than the boat, heavier than the sea, so heavy she was immovable. She would sit, that was what she would do. Sit right there and ride it out.

That was when the water started coming in through the forward hatch. That was when her feet got wet and she began to feel afraid. That was when she thought for the first time of the life jackets tucked under the seats in the stern that was awash with the piled-up waves—and that was when she pulled herself along the edge of the table to look up into the bridge and see her husband and brother-in-law fighting over the controls even as she heard the engines sputter and catch and finally give out. She caught her breath. Something essential had gone absent in a way that was wrong, deeply wrong, in violation of everything she'd known and believed in since the moment they'd left shore. The ghost had gone out of the machine.

In the sequel she was on the bridge, trying to make Till and Warren understand about the water in the cabin, water that didn't belong there, water that was coming in through a breach in the forward hatch that was underwater itself before it shook free of the weight of the waves and sank back down again. But Till wasn't listening. Till, her rock, the man who'd survived the mangling of his arm and the fiery blast of shrapnel that was lodged still in his legs and secreted beneath the constellation of scars on the broad firmament of his back, sat slumped over the controls, distracted and drawn and punching desperately at the starter as Warren, wrapped in a yellow slicker and cursing with every breath, fought his way out the door to the stern while the wind sang through the cabin and all the visible world lost its substantiality.

Disbelieving, outraged, Till jerked at the wheel, but the wheel wouldn't respond. The boat lolled, staggered, a wave rising up out of nowhere to hit them broadside and drive down the hull till she was sure they were going to capsize. She might have screamed. Might have cried out uselessly, her breath coming hard and fast. It was all she could do to hold on, her jaws clamped, the spray taking flight up and over the cabin as Warren pried open the hatch to the engine compartment, some sort of tool clutched in one hand—Warren, Warren out there on the deck to save the day, but what could he hope to do? How could anybody fix anything in this chaos?

He was a blotch of yellow in a world stripped of color, there one moment and gone the next, a big breaching wave flinging him back against the cabin door and pouring half an ocean into the rictus of the engine well. Till snatched a look at her then, his face drained and hopeless. Warren, the figure of Warren, flailing limbs and gasping mouth, slammed at the window and rose impossibly out of the foam, the slicker twisted back from his shoulders— inadequate, ridiculous, a child's jacket, a doll's—and then he was down again and awash. In the next instant Till sprang to his feet, twisting up and away from the controls, the wheel swinging wildly, lights blinking across the console, the scuppers inundated, the bilge pump choking on its own infirmity. He took hold of her wrist, jerking her up out of her seat, and suddenly they were through the door and into the fury of the weather, the wind tearing the breath out of her lungs, the next wave rearing up to knock her to her knees with a fierce icy slap, and she wasn't sick anymore and she wasn't tired or worn or dulled. Everything in her, everything she was, howled at its highest pitch. They were going to drown, all three of them, she could see that now. Drown and die and wash up for the crabs.

"What do you think you're doing?" Warren, unsteady, hair painted to his face, made to seize Till's arms as if he meant to dance with him, even as Till shrugged him off and bent to release the skiff.

"It's our only chance!" Till roared into the wind, his legs tangled and rotating out of sync like a drunken man's. He flailed at the shell of the skiff, jerked the lines in a fury.

"You're nuts!" Warren shouted. "Out of your fucking

mind!" He was staggering too, fighting for balance, and so was she, helpless, the waves driving at her. The boat heaved, dead beneath their feet. "We won't last five minutes in this sea!"

But here was the skiff, released and free and riding high, and they were in it, Warren leaping to the oars, no thought of the life jackets because the life jackets, for all their newness and viability and their promise to keep men and women and children afloat indefinitely even in the biggest seas, were tucked neatly beneath that bench in the stern of the *Beverly B.* and the *Beverly B.* was swamped. Stalled. Going down.

Heavily, like a waterlogged post in a swollen river, the boat shifted away from them. They'd painted her hull white to contrast with the natural wood of the cabin—a cold pure unblemished white, the white of sheets and carnations—and that whiteness shone now like the ghost image on a negative of a photograph that would never be developed. Unimpeded, the waves crashed at the windows of the cabin and then the glass was gone and the *Beverly B.* shifted wearily and dropped down and came back up again. The decks were below water now, only the cabin's top showing pale against the dimness of the early morning and the spray that rode the wind like a shroud.

Beverly was there to witness it, huddled wet and shivering in the bow of the skiff, Till beside her, but she wasn't clinging to him, not clinging at all because she was too rigid with the need to get out of this, to get away, to get to land. No regrets. Let the sea have the boat and all the time and money they'd lavished on her, so long as it spared them, so long as the island was out there in the gloom and it came to them in a rush of foam and black bleeding rock. They rode up over two waves, three, and they were on a wild ride now, wilder than anything the amusement park would ever dare offer, and all at once they were in a deep pit lined with walls of aquamarine glass, everything held suspended for a single shimmering moment before the walls collapsed on them. She felt the plunge, the force of it, and all of a sudden she was swimming free, the chill riveting her, and it was instinct that drove her away from the skiff and back to the *Beverly B.* for something to hold fast to—and there, there it was, rising up and plunging down, and she with it. The wind tore at her eyes. The salt blistered her throat.

She didn't see Warren, didn't see where he was, but then she'd got turned around and he could be anywhere. And Till—she remembered him coming toward her, his good arm cutting the black sheet of the water, until he wasn't coming anymore. Where was he? The waves threw up ramparts and she couldn't see. He was calling her, she was sure of it, in the thinnest distant echo of a cracked and winnowed voice, Till's voice, sucked away on the wind until it was gone. "Where are you?" she called. "Till? Till?"

The waves took her breath away. Her bones ached. Her teeth wouldn't stop chattering. A period of time elapsed— she couldn't have said how long—and nothing changed. She clung to the heaving corpse of the *Beverly B.* because the *Beverly B.* was the only thing there was. At some point, because they were binding her feet, she ducked her head beneath the surface to tear off her tennis sneakers and release them into the void. Then she loosed her blue jeans, the cuffs as heavy as lead weights.

When finally the *Beverly B.* cocked herself up on a wave as big as a continent and then sank down out of sight, she fought away from the vortex it left in its wake and found herself treading water. The waves lifted and released her, lifted and released her. She was alone. Deserted. The ship gone, Till gone, Warren. She could feel something flapping inside her like a set of wings, her own panic, the panic that whipped her into a sudden slashing breaststroke and as quickly subsided, and then she was treading water again and she went on treading water for some portion of eternity until there was nothing left in her arms. Till's sweater dragged at her. It was too much, too heavy, and it gave her nothing, not warmth, not comfort, not Till or the feel or smell of him. She shrugged out of it, snatched a breath, and let it drift down and away from her like the exoskeleton of a creature new-made, born of water and salt and the penetrant chill.

She tried floating on her back but the wind drove the sea up her nose and into her mouth so that she came up coughing and spewing. Had she drifted off? Was she drowning? Giving up? She fought the rising fear with her spent arms and the feeble wash of her spent legs. After a time, she lost all feeling in her limbs and she went down with a lungful of air and the air brought her back up, once, twice, again. She thrashed for a handhold, for anything, for substance, but there was no solid thing in all that transient medium where the dolphins grinned and the flying fish flew and the sharks came and went as they pleased.

And Till? Where was Till? He could have been right there, ten feet away, and she wouldn't have known it. She closed her eyes, snatched a breath, let herself drift down and let herself come back again. Once more. Could she do it once more? She'd never known despair, but it was in her now, colder than the water, creeping numbly up from her feet and into her ankles and legs and torso, overwhelming her, claiming her degree by degree. *Water, water every where.* Just as she was about to surrender, to open herself up, open wide and let the harsh insistent unforgiving current flow through her and tug her down to where the waves couldn't touch her ever again, the ocean gave her something back: it was a chest, an ice chest, floating low in the water under the weight of its burden. A silver thing, silver as the belly of her fish. Sears, Roebuck. Guaranteed for life. She claimed it as her own, and though she couldn't get atop it, it was there and it sustained her as the wind bit and the sun rose up out of the gloom to parch her lips and scorch the taut white mask of her upturned face.

Rattus Rattus

She had never been so thirsty in all her life. Had never known what it was, what it truly meant, when she read in the magazines of the Bedouin tumbling from their camels and their camels dying beneath them or the G.I.'s stalking the rumor of Rommel's Panzers across the dunes of North Africa and water only a mirage, because she'd lived in a house with a tap in a place where the grass was wet with dew in the morning and you could get a Coca-Cola at any lunch counter or in the machine at the service station around the corner. If she was thirsty, she drank. That was all.

Now she knew. Now she knew what it was like to go without, to feel the talons clawing at your throat, the tongue furred and bloating in the tomb of your mouth, barely able to swallow, to breathe. There was ice in the chest—and beer, chilled beer, the bottles clinking and chirping with the rhythm of the waves—but she didn't dare crack the lid, even for an instant. It was the air inside that kept her afloat and if she lifted the lid the air would rush out and where would she be then? The bottles clinked. Her throat swelled. The sun beat at her face. But this was a special brand of torture, reserved just for her, worse than anything devised by the most sadistic Jap commandant, and she kept wondering what she'd done to deserve it— the ice right there, the beer, the sweet cold sparkling pale golden liquid in the bottle that would shine with condensation just inches away, and she dying of thirst.

She swallowed involuntarily at the thought of it, the lining of her throat as raw as when she'd had tonsillitis as a girl and twisted in agony with the blinds closed and the starched rigid sheets biting into her till her mother came like an angel of mercy with ginger ale in a tall cold glass, with sherbet, Jell-O, ice cubes made of Welch's grape juice to suck and roll over her tongue and clench between her teeth till all the moisture was gone. Her mother's hand reached out to her, she saw it, saw it right there framed against the waves, and her mother's face and the dripping glass poised in her hand. It was too much to bear. She gave in and wet her lips with seawater, though she knew she shouldn't, knew it was wrong and would only make things worse, and yet she couldn't help herself, her tongue probing and lapping as if it weren't attached to her at all. The relief was instantaneous, flooding her like a drug—water, there was water inside her. But then, almost immediately, her throat swelled shut and her cracked lips began to bleed.

To bleed. That was the secondary problem: blood. Both her elbows were scraped and raw and there was a deep irregular gash on the back of her left hand, the one the scalding coffee hadn't touched. How it had got there, she couldn't say, and she was so numb from the cold she couldn't feel the sting of it, though clearly it would need stitches to close the wound and there'd be a scar, and for some time now she'd been idly examining the torn flesh there, thinking she'd have to see a doctor when they got back and already making up a little speech for him, how she'd want a really top-notch man because she just couldn't stomach having her skin spoiled, not at her age. But she was bleeding in the here and now, each wave washing the gash anew and extracting from it a pale tincture of pinkish liquid that dissolved instantly and was gone. That liquid was blood. And blood attracted sharks.

Again the flap of panic. Her legs trailed behind her like lures, like a provocation, like bait, and she couldn't see them, could barely feel them. If the sharks came—when they came—she'd have no defense. She was trapped in a childhood nightmare, a vestigial dream of the time before there was land, when all the creatures there were floated free amidst the flotilla of shining jaws that would swallow them. She tried to hold her hand up out of the water. Tried not to think about what was beneath her, behind her, rising even now from the lazy depths like a balloon trailing across the sky at dusk. But she had to think. Had to terrify herself just to stay alive.

For as long as the ice chest had been there she'd maneuvered around it, straddling it like an equestrian as it rode beneath the clamp of her thighs, pushing it all the way down to tamp it with her feet and perch tentatively atop the tenuous wavering shelf of it, lying flat with its lid tucked between her abdomen and breasts so that her back was arched and her legs could spread wide for balance. Now she tried to huddle atop it, to kneel beneath the full weight of her limbs and torso as if she were praying—and she was praying, she was—struggling to hold her gashed hand clear of the water and balance there like an acrobat stalled on the high wire, but the waves wouldn't allow it. She kept slipping down while the cooler bobbed up and away from her so that she had to swim free and snatch it back in a single searing beat of white-hot terror, thinking only of a mute streaking shape lunging out of the depths to snatch her up in its basket of teeth.

She'd seen a shark only once in her life. It was on the Santa Monica pier, just after Till had come home from overseas. They'd walked on the beach for hours and then promenaded all the way to the end of the pier, her arm in his, the stripped pale boards rocking gently beneath their feet and the sea air deliciously cool against their skin. She was so alive in that moment, so attuned to Till and his transformation from the recollected to the actual, to the flesh, to the arm round her waist and the voice murmuring in her ear, that the smallest things thrilled her with their novelty, as if no one had ever conceived of them before. A paper cone of cotton candy, so intensely pink it was otherworldly, seemed as strange to her as if it had been delivered there by Martians from outer space. Ditto the tattooed man exhibiting himself in his bathing trunks in the hope of spare change and the eighty-year-old beauty queen in the two-piece—even the taste of the burger with

chopped raw onions and plenty of ketchup they ate standing under the sunstruck awning of the stand at the foot of
the pier was like that of no other burger she'd ever had.
Her feet weren't even on the ground. They were there in
the flesh, both of them, she and Till, strolling along like
any normal couple who could go home to bed anytime the
urge took them, day or night, or go get a highball and listen to the jukebox in the corner of some dark roadhouse
or drive slow and sweet along Ocean Boulevard with the
windows down and the breeze fanning their hair. It was
her dream made concrete. But then, right there in the
middle of that dream, was the shark.

There was a crowd gathered at the far end of the pier
and they'd gone toward it casually, out of idle curiosity,
people looping this way and that, little kids squirming
through to the front for a closer view, and there it was,
more novelty, the first shark she'd ever seen outside of a
picture book. It was suspended by its tail on a thick braid
of cable that held it, dripping, just above the bleached
boards of the dock. The fisherman—a Negro, and that
was a novelty too, a Negro fisherman on the Santa Monica
pier—stood just off to the left of it while his companion,
another Negro, took his photograph with a Brownie camera. "Hold steady now," the second man said. "Less have a
smile. C'mon, give us a grin."

A woman beside her made a noise in her throat, an
admixture of disgust and fascination. "What is it?" the
woman said. "A swordfish?"

The first man, the fisherman, smiled wide and the
camera clicked. "You see a sword?" he asked rhetorically.
"I don't see no sword."

"It's a dolphin," somebody said.

"Ain't no dolphin," the fisherman retorted, enjoying
himself immensely. "Ain't no tuna fish neither." He bent
close to the thing, to the half-moon of the gill slit and the
staring eye, and then cupped a hand over the unresisting
snout and tugged upward. "See them teeth?"

And there they were, suddenly revealed, a whole land-scape of stacked and serrated teeth running off into the terra incognita of the dark gullet, and it came to her that this was a shark, the scourge of the sea, the one thing that preyed on all the rest, that rose up in a blanket of foam to ravage a seal or maim a surfer and ignite an inflammatory headline out of La Jolla or Redondo Beach that everybody forgot about a week later.

"What this is, what you looking at right now? This a great white shark, seven feet six inches long. As bad as it gets. And this one's not much more than a baby. Hell, they five feet long when they come out their mother."

The crowd pressed in. Till's eyes were gleaming, and this was a thing he could appreciate, a man's thing, *as bad as it gets*. There was only one question left to ask and she heard her own voice quaver as she asked it: "Where did you catch it?"

A pause. A smile. Another click of the camera. "Why, right here, right off the end of the dock."

The image had stayed with her a long while. She'd asked Till about it, about how that could be, what the man had said—right off the dock, right there where she'd been swimming since she was a little girl—and he'd tried to reassure her. "They can turn up anywhere, I suppose," he said, "but it's rare here. Really rare." He gave her a squeeze, pulled her to him. "Where you really find them," and he pointed now, out into the band of mist that fell across the horizon, "is out there. Off the islands."

People died of shark bite. They died of thirst. Of hypothermia. She was dressed in nothing but bra and panties, naked to the water and the water sucking the heat from her minute by minute, and she clung there and shivered and felt the volition go out of her. Let the sharks come, she was thinking, dreaming, the cold lulling her now till she was like the man in that other Jack London story, the one who laid himself down and died because he couldn't build a fire. Well, she couldn't build a fire either because water wouldn't burn and there was nothing in this world that wasn't water.

She woke sputtering, choked awake, a cold fist in her throat. She was coughing—hacking, heaving, retching—and the violence of it brought her back again. Sun, sea, wind, waves. Sun. Sea. Wind. Waves. The ice chest bobbed and she bobbed with it. And then, all at once, there was something else there with her, something new, a living thing that broke the surface in a fierce boiling suddenness that annihilated her, the shark, the shark come finally to draw the shroud. She shut her eyes, averted her face. She didn't draw up her legs because there was no point in it now, the drop was coming, the first rending shock of the jaws, sadness spreading though her like a stain in water, sadness for Till, for her parents, for what might have been . . . but the next moment slipped by and the moment after that and still she was there and still she was whole, bobbing along with the ice chest, bobbing.

The next splash was closer. She forced open her eyes, tried to focus through the drooping curtains of her swollen lids. Her pupils burned. The blood pounded in her ears. It took her a moment to understand that this wasn't a shark, wasn't a fish at all—fish didn't have dog faces and whiskers and eyes as round and darkly glowing as a human's. She stared into those eyes, amazed, until they sank away in the wash and she looked beyond the swirl of foam to the sun-scoured wall of rock rising out of the mist above her.

Anacapa is the smallest of the four islands that form the archipelago of the northern Channel Islands and the closest to the mainland, a mere eleven miles from its eastern tip to the harbor at Oxnard. It parallels the coast in its east-west orientation, from Arch Rock in the east to Rat Rock on the western verge, and is, geologically speaking, a seaward extension of the Santa Monica Mountains. In actuality, Anacapa comprises three separate islets, connected only during extreme low tides, and it is of volcanic origin, composed primarily of basalt dating from the Miocene period. All three islets are largely inaccessible from the sea, featuring tall looming circumvallate cliffs and strips of cliff-side beach that darkly glisten with the detritus ground out of the rock by the action of the waves. As seen from the air, the islets form a narrow snaking band like the spine of a sea serpent, the ridges articulated like vertebrae, claws fully extended, jaws agape, tail thrashing out against the grip of the current. Seabirds nest atop the cliffs here and on the tableland beyond—Xantus's murrelet, the brown pelican and Brandt's cormorant among them—and pinnipeds racket along the shore. Average rainfall is less than twelve inches annually. There is no permanent source of water.

Beverly knew none of this. She didn't know that the landfall looming over her was Anacapa or that she'd drifted some six miles by this point. She knew only that rock was solid and water was not and she made for it with all the strength left in her. Twice she went under and came up gasping and it was all she could do to keep hold of the ice chest in the roiling surf that had begun to crash round her. All at once she was in the breakers and the chest was torn from her, gone suddenly, and she had no choice but to squeeze her eyes shut and extend her arms and ride the wave till the force of it flung her like so much wrack at the base of the cliff. Stones rolled and collided beneath her knees and the frantic grabbing of her hands, she was tossed sideways and had the breath pounded out of her, but her fingers snatched at something else there, sand, the floor of a beach gouged out of the rock. It was nothing more than a semicircular pit, churning like a washing machine, but it was palpable and it held her and when the wave sucked back she was standing on solid ground. She might have felt a surge of relief, but she didn't have a chance. Because she was shivering. Dripping. Staggering. And the next wave was already coming at her.

The foam shot in, sudsing at her knees, driving her back awkwardly against the punishing black wall of the overhang. She found herself stumbling to her left, even as the next breaker thundered in, and then she was crawling on hands and knees up and away from it, the rock pitted and sharp and yet slick all the same, up and out of the water and onto a narrow perch that was no wider than her berth on the *Beverly B*. She hugged her knees to her chest, clamped her hands round her shoulders, shaking with cold. Her hair hung limp in her face. The waves crashed and dissolved in mist and everything smelled of funk and rot and the protoplasmic surfeit of all those galaxies of wheeling, biting, wanting things that hadn't survived the day. She didn't think about Till or the boat or Warren, her mind drawn down to nothing. She just stared numbly at the wash as it stripped the beach and gave it back again, torn strands of kelp struggling to and fro, a float of driftwood, the suck and roar, and then she was asleep.

When she woke it was to the sun and the beach that had grown marginally bigger, a scallop of blackly glistening sand emerging from the receding tide, the teeth of the rocks exposed now and the wet gums clamped beneath them. She'd been in the shadows all this time, huddled on her perch, tucked away from the tidal wash and the sun too, but now the sun had moved out into the channel and the heat of it touched her and roused her. For a long while she sat there, absorbing the warmth, and if she was sunburned it didn't matter a whit because she'd rather be burned than frozen, burned anytime, scorched and roasted till she peeled, because anything was better than the cold locked up inside her, a numbness so deeply immured in her she might as well have been a corpse. She gazed out on the sea with a kind of hatred she'd never known, hating the monotony of it, the indifference, the marrow-draining chill. And then, abruptly, she was thirsty. Still thirsty. Thirstier than she'd been out there on the sea when she was thirstier than she'd ever been in her life.

In that moment her eye jumped to the gleam of metal at the near end of the cove. The ice chest. There it was, upright in the sand, its lid still fastened. She sprang down from the rock, slimed and filthy, her limbs battered and her tongue made of felt, and ran to it, threw open the lid and saw that the ice was gone and the bottles smashed— all but one, the precious last remaining dark brown sweating bottle with the label soaked off and sand worked up under the cap. Lifting the beer to the sun, she could see that it was intact, its bubbles infused with light and rising in a slow hypnotic dance. *Beer. Cold beer.* But she had no opener, no churchkey, no knife or screwdriver or tool of any kind. And where was Till? Where was he when she needed him?

She remembered how casually he would slam the neck of his beer against the edge of the counter or the workbench in the garage and how instantly the cap would fly up and away and the cold aperture of the bottle would come to his lips, all in a single fluid motion, as if the opening and the draining of the bottle constituted the same continuous physical process. Overhead, chased on a draft, a gull appraised her, mewed over her torn and abraded flesh, and was gone. She looked wildly around her for something, anything, to make a tool of, but there was nothing but sand and driftwood and rock.

Rock. Rock would do it. Of course it would. And then she was smoothing her hand over the wall of the overhang, feeling for a rough spot, a ledge, any kind of projection, and here, here it was, the cap poised just so and the weight of her burned hand coming down on it, once, twice . . . and nothing. She worked at it, frantic now, angry, furious, but the best she could do was flatten the ridges till the cap was even more secure than when she'd begun, and it was too much, she couldn't take a single second more of this—and then it was done, the neck shattered and gaping and she draining the whole thing in three airless gulps and if there was glass in it and if the glass cut her open from esophagus to gut she didn't give a damn because she was drinking and that was the only thing that mattered.

But the beer was gone and the thirst was there still, rattling inside her like a field of cane in a desert wind, and was it any surprise she was light-headed? She'd always been a capable drinker, proud of her ability to match Till beer for beer, but this one hit her hard and before she knew it she was down in the sand, sitting there cross-legged like a statue of the Buddha, as if that was what she'd meant to do all along. The sun seemed to have shifted somehow in the interval, dropping down close to the flattening gray surface of the sea where the fog could take hold of it and snuff it out like the burned-up butt of the cigarette she suddenly wanted as much as she wanted water. She stood shakily and went to the ice chest. It was right where she'd left it not ten minutes ago (or had it been longer? Had she dozed off?), but now the incoming tide was running up the beach to take it from her all over again. Seizing it by one corner, she dragged it awkwardly across the sand to the declivity beneath the overhang, then worked it up to her perch six feet above the beach. Inside, amidst the litter of broken bottles and stripes of sand and weed, there was a liquid that might have been a mix of beer and meltwater, that might have been potable, that might have quenched her thirst, but when she thrust a finger into it and licked that finger all she could taste was salt.

Dusk fell, aided and abetted by the fog, which closed off the beach even as the tide ran in, and though the water was up past her knees, she probed the scalloped ledges at both ends of the cove, looking for a way out. She braced herself, one foot up, then the other, straining for a hand-hold. Working patiently, her face pressed to the rock, she got as high as fifteen or twenty feet above the beach, but after she fell for the third time, coming down hard amidst the stones and the cold shock of the water, she gave up. It was no use. She was trapped. A single pulse of panic flickered through her, but she suppressed it. She wasn't afraid, not anymore—that was behind her. All she felt was frustration. Anger. Why had she been spared only to wash up here to die of thirst, hunger, cold? Where was God's hand in that? Where was His purpose? Finally, when it was fully dark and the fog settled in so impenetrably as to close off even the stars, let alone the running lights of any boat that might have been plying the channel looking for them, for survivors—and here she saw Till and Warren, wrapped in blankets in a gently rocking cabin, the glow of the varnished wood, lanterns a-sway, mugs of hot coffee pressed to their lips—she held fast to the ice chest and willed herself asleep.

In the morning, at first light, there was the sound of the gulls that was like the opening and closing of a door on balky hinges, but there was no door here, no bed or room or clothes or warmth, and she couldn't see the gulls for the fog. She shivered into the light, slapping at her thighs and shoulders and huddling in the cradle of her arms, and then the thirst took hold of her. It roused her and she rose to her feet, fighting for balance, the tide having receded and risen all over again, reducing her world to this rock and the wall above her. She wanted a pitcher of water, that was all, envisioning the white bone china pitcher in the kitchen at home, a hand-me-down from her mother she brought out for special occasions, and it took her a long moment to realize that there was a persistent cold drip tapping at her shoulder and that she'd been shifting unconsciously to avoid it. She lifted her face and saw that the cliff was wet, the fog whispering across the rock above her, condensing there, dripping, dripping.

What she didn't know was that forty years earlier a man named H. Bay Webster had leased the island from the federal government for the purpose of raising sheep, but the sheep had failed to thrive because of overgrazing and lack of water, and finally, in their distress, they had been reduced to licking the dew each from another's fleece in order to survive. Not that it mattered. All that mattered was this drip. She held her tongue out to it, licked the rock as if it were a snow-cone presented to her by the lady behind the concession stand at the county fair. And when one of the little green shore crabs came within reach, a flattened thing, no more than two inches across, she crushed it beneath her foot and then fed the salty cold wet fragments into her mouth.

It took her a long while after that to get her courage up, because she knew now what she had to do though her whole being revolted against it. She kept praying that someone would come for her, that the prow of a ship would ease out of the fog or a rope come hurtling down from above, anything to spare her getting back into that killing water. The funny thing was that she'd always liked swimming—she'd joined the swim team in school and trained so relentlessly her hair never seemed to be really dry her whole senior year—but now, as she climbed down from the rock, clutched the ice chest to her and fought through the surf, she hated it more than anything in the world. Instantly, she was cold through to the bone and thrashing for warmth, then she was fighting past the breakers and out into the sea.

Here was the nightmare all over again, but this time there was a difference because she was saved, she'd saved herself, and she kept close to shore, trembling, yes, exhausted, thirsty, but no longer panicked. There wouldn't be sharks, not this close in, not with the sea full of seals, armies of them barking from the rocks and sending up a sulfurous odor of urine and feces and seal stink. The sea was calmer now too, much calmer—almost gentle—and from time to time she tried floating on her back, head propped on the chest and elbows jackknifed behind her, but invariably she had to roll over and pull herself up as far as she could in an effort to escape the cold. Fog clung to her. Great fields of kelp, dun stalks and yellowed leaves, drifted past. Tiny fishes needled the water around her and were gone.

As the morning wore on, the world began to enlarge above her, birds uncountable lifting off into the fog and gliding back again like ghosts in the ether, the cliffs decapitated above skirts of guano, shrubs and even flowers so high up they might have been planted in air. She let the current carry her, periodically forcing herself to unfurl her legs and paddle to keep on course, telling herself that at any moment she'd come upon a boat at anchor or a beach that spread back to a canyon where she could get up and away from the sea. How far she'd drifted or how long she'd been in the water, she had no way of knowing, the cold sapping her, lulling her, killing her will, every seal-strewn rock and every black-faced cliff so exactly like the last one she began to think she'd circled the island twice already. But she held on, just as she had when the *Beverly B.* went down a whole day and night ago, because it was the only thing she could do.

It must have been late in the morning, the sun lost somewhere in the fog overhead, when finally she found what she was looking for. Or, rather, she didn't know what she was looking for until it materialized out of the haze in a cove that was no different from all the rest. A rust-peached ladder, so oxidized it was the color of the starfish clinging to the rocks beneath it, seemed to glide across the surface to her, and when she took hold of it she let the chest float free, pulling herself from the water, rung by rung, as from a gently yielding sheath.

The universe stopped rocking. The sea fell away. And she found herself on a path leading steeply upward to where the fog began to tatter and bleed off till it wasn't there at all. Above her, opening to the sun and the chaparral flecked with yellow blooms that climbed beard-like up the slope, was a shack, two shacks, three, four, all lined up across the bluff as if they'd grown out of the rock itself. The near one—flat-roofed, the boards weathered gray— caught the flame of the sun in its windows till it glowed like a cathedral. And right beside it, where the drainpipe fell away from the roof, was a wooden barrel, a hogshead, set there to catch the rain.

She was in that moment reduced to an animal, nothing more, and her focus was an animal's focus, her mind stripped of everything but that barrel and its contents, and she never felt the fragmented stone of the path digging into her feet or the weight of the sun crushing her shoulders, never thought of who might be watching her in her nakedness or what that might mean, till she reached it and plunged her face into its depths and drank till she could feel the cool silk thread coming back up again. It was only then that she looked around her. Everything was still, hot, though she shivered in the heat, and her first thought was to call out, absurdly, call "Hello? Is anybody there?" Or why not "Yoo-hoo?" Yoo-hoo would have been equally ridiculous, anything would have. She was as naked as Eve, her blue jeans gone, Till's sweater jettisoned, her underthings torn from her at some indefinite point in the shifting momentum of her battle against the current and the waves and the sucking rasp of the shingle. When she touched herself, when she brought her hands up to cover her nakedness, they were like two dead things, two fish laid out on a slab, and she fell to her knees in the dirt, hunched and shivering and looking round her with an animal's dull calculation.

In the next moment she rose and went round the corner of the house to the door at the front, thinking to clothe herself, thinking there must be something inside to cover up with, rags, a bedsheet, an old towel or fisherman's sweater. But what if there were people in there? What if there was a man? No man on this earth had seen her naked but for the doctor who'd delivered her and Till, and what would she say to Till if there was a man there to see her as she was now? She hesitated, uncertain of what to do. For a long moment she regarded the door in its stubborn inanimacy, a door made of planks nailed to a crosspiece, weather-scored and unrevealing. Beside it, set in the wall at eye level, was a four-pane window so smeared as to be nearly opaque, but she shifted away from the door, cupped her hands to the glass and peered in, all the while feeling as if she were being watched.

Inside, she could make out a crude kitchen counter with a dishpan and an array of what looked to be empty bottles scattered atop it, and beyond that, a sagging cot decorated with an army blanket. A second window, facing north, drew the glare in off the ocean. She tapped at the glass, hoping to forestall anyone who might be lurking inside. Finally, she tried the door, whispering, "Hello? Is anybody home?"

There was no answer. She lifted the latch and pushed open the door to a rustle of movement, dark shapes inhabiting the corners, a spine-sprung book on the floor, shelves, cans, a sou'wester on a hook that made her catch her breath, fooled into thinking someone had been standing there all along. It took a moment for her eyes to adjust, the shapes manifesting themselves all at once—furred, quick-footed, tails naked and indolently switching, a host of darkly shining eyes fastening on her without alarm or haste because she was the interloper here, the beggar, she was the one naked and washed up like so much trash— and she let out a low exclamation. Rats. She'd always hated rats, from the time she was in kindergarten and her mother warned her against going near the garbage cans set out in the alley behind their apartment building— "They bite babies," her mother told her, "big girls too, nip their toes, jump in their hair. You know Janey, upstairs in 7B? They got in her cradle when she was baby. Right here, right in this building." Her father reinforced the admonition, taking her by the hand and probing with one shoe in the dim corners of the carport so she could see the animals themselves, the corpses of the ones he'd caught in spring traps baited with gobs of peanut butter. In secret, in the dark, they would lick and paw that bait—peanut butter, the same peanut butter she ate on white bread with the crusts cut off—until the guillotine dropped and the blood trailed from their crushed heads and dislocated jaws. *Rats.* Disease carriers, food spoilers, baby biters. But what were they doing here on an untamed island set out in the middle of the sea? Had they swum? Sprouted wings?

The thought came and went. She flapped her arms savagely. "Get out!" she shouted, rushing at them, whirling, clapping her hands. "Get!" They blinked at her—there must have been a dozen or more of them—and then, very slowly, as if it were an imposition, as if they were obeying only because in that moment her need was stronger than theirs, they crept back into their holes. But she was frantic now, snatching the blanket up off the cot without a thought for the rattling dried feces that fell like shot to the floor and wrapping it around her even as she fumbled through the cans on the shelf—peaches in syrup, Boston baked beans, creamed corn—and the utensils tossed helter-skelter in a chipped enamel dishpan set on the counter.

She ate standing. First the peaches, the soothing thick syrup better than anything she'd ever tasted—syrup to lick from the spoon and then from her fingertips, one after the other—then the creamed corn, spooned up out of the can in its essential sweetness, and then, finally, a can of tuna for the feel of it between her teeth. Only when she was sated did she take the time to look around her. The empty cans, evidence of her crime—theft, breaking and entering—lay at her feet. She sank down on the cot, pulling the rough blanket tight round her throat, and saw, with a kind of restrained interest, that the walls were papered over with full sheets torn from magazines, from *Life* and *Look* and the Sunday rotogravure. Pinups gazed back at her, men perched on tanks, Barbara Stanwyck astride a horse. A man lived here, she decided, a man lived here alone. A hermit. A fisherman. Someone shy of women, with whiskers like in the old photos of her grandfather's time.

She found his clothes in the trunk in the corner. Two white shirts, size small, a blue woolen sweater with red piping and a stained and patched pair of gabardine trousers. Without thinking twice—she'd pay him back ten times over when they came to rescue her—she slipped into the trousers and the less homely of the two shirts and then stepped back outside to see if she could find him. Or one of the men who must have lived in the other shacks, because if there were four shacks there must have been four men. At least. And now, standing outside the door with her face turned to the nearest shack, some hundred feet away, she did, in fact, call out "Yoo-hoo!"

No one answered. The only sounds were the ones she'd become inured to: the sifting of the wind, the slap and roll of the breakers, the strained high-flown cries of the birds. She went to each of the shacks in succession, and though she found signs of recent habitation—a bin of rat-gnawed potatoes, a candle melted into a saucer, more canned goods, crackers gone stale in a tin, fishing gear, lobster traps, two jugs of red wine and what might once have been sherry turning black in the unmarked bottle beneath a float of scum—she didn't find anyone at home. It was as if she were one of the wandering orphans of a fairy tale arrived in some magical realm where all the inhabitants had been put under a spell, turned to trees or animals—to rats, black rats with no fear of humans. Finally, after searching through all four of the habitations and calling out in the silence of futility, over and over again, she went back to the first shack, opened another can of peaches, ate them slowly, one by one, the juice running down her chin, then stretched out on the cot, wrapped herself in the blanket, and slept.

There was so much she didn't know. How could she? She was marooned, she'd seen her husband go down in the grip of a rising swell in the open sea (though she wouldn't admit it to herself, wouldn't give up that slowly unraveling skein of hope, not yet), she'd never been to the islands before in her life and had no idea where she was or what to expect, and the shack she was in might have dropped down from the sky intact for all she knew. It was a shack and she was in it and it would provide shelter until she was rescued—that was all she needed to know.

Of course, the shack she'd chosen hadn't dropped down from the sky, though there was certainly something of the numinous in its manifestation there on the bluff in her moment of need. The fact was, it had been created by human agency, by people who had wants and aspirations and very definite monetary goals, as Alma knew full well. Because her grandmother's story was her touchstone, because she'd read through the newspaper accounts, researched the archives and written papers on the subject in high school and college both, she could say with absolute certainty that Beverly had washed up at Frenchy's Cove on West Anacapa, the largest and most westerly of the three islets. The shacks—or cabins, as they were originally designated—had been built in 1925 by investors from Ventura, who'd hoped to run a sport fishing camp on the location. They were constructed of board and batten, with simple effects, designed to suit the rugged sorts who might come out to the island for the fishing but didn't necessarily want to spend their nights in a cramped berth on a yawing boat.

Unfortunately for the investors, the rugged sorts never materialized, the venture failed and the cabins sat unoccupied until a squatter named Raymond "Frenchy" LaDreau moved in and took possession three years later. He lived there alone, making his living off the sea, entertaining the occasional visitor and begging water from every ship that anchored in the cove, whether it be a working boat out of Santa Barbara or Oxnard or a pleasure craft come across the channel for the weekend. What his thoughts and expectations were or whether he was lonely or at peace, no one can say, but he stayed on until 1956, in his eightieth year, when his legs failed him after he took a fall on the shifting stones of the path up from the beach and was forced to return to the mainland for good. He was the owner of the shirt and trousers Beverly was wearing and the cans she'd opened, and he would have been present and accounted for and happy to offer them himself, except that he was away on one of his extended trips to the coast at the time and had no way of knowing he was needed. When finally he did get back, all he felt was outrage over the violation of his space and his things, but it was nothing new—it had happened before, the shacks set there on the bluff like a provocation to the kind of people who think the world exists for them alone, and it would happen again. He would have to buy more peaches, that was all, more beans and creamed corn, and maybe, if he thought of it in the rush and hurry of the hardware store in Oxnard, a padlock.

Beverly woke that first day to the declining light and creeping chill of evening. She sat up with a start, uncertain of where she was, and there were the rats, gathered round, staring at her. They were leisurely, content, taking their ease, draped over the chair pulled up to the counter, nestled in the refuse on the floor, hunched over their working hands and the things they'd stolen to eat. Enraged suddenly, she shoved herself violently from the bed, casting about for something she could attack them with, drive them off, *make them pay*—and here it was, a shovel set in the corner. The rats fell back as she snatched it up and began flailing round the room, the heavy blade falling, digging, caroming off the walls. Within seconds, they were gone and she was left panting in the middle of the room, the shirt binding, the pants grabbing at her hips and the sea through the window as hard as stone.

She went out the door then, the rage still building in her, muttering to herself, letting out a string of obscenities she never until that moment realized she knew, and began tearing through the heap of driftwood stacked behind the shack. Without thinking, without regard for her unprotected hands or the sobs rising in her throat, she flung one log after another over her shoulder and onto the flat between the shacks. When all of it was heaped in a towering pyre and the sweat stung at her eyes and soaked her hair till the ends hung limp, she went barefoot down the path to the beach and scoured the sand for anything that would burn and she hauled that up too. There was newspaper, rat-shredded, in a cardboard box just inside the door of the second shack. The matches she found in a jar atop the woodstove.

She waited till it was full dark, hunched over her knees in the too-tight shirt and the blue sweater with the red piping that smelled of a strange man's sweat, eating pork and beans from the can and savoring each morsel, before she lit her signal fire. And when she lit it and fed it and kept on feeding it, the flames rose thirty feet in the air, visible all the way to the mainland she could just make out through the gauze of fog as a series of drifting unsteady lights, as if the stars had fallen into the sea. The fire raged, sparked, tore open the night. Someone would see it, she told herself, someone was sure to see it. That first night she even called out at intervals, a hollow shrill gargle of sound that was meant to pierce the fog, ride out over the sea and strike the hull of whatever boat might be passing in the night to see her fire and hear her call. The second night, she saved her breath. By the third night she'd used up nearly all the wood she could scavenge and thought of setting the shacks afire—or the chaparral. At the end of the first week, she was resigned. She scattered rats, ate from the cans, drank from the barrel. When she wasn't gathering wood she lay in bed, dozing, thumbing through the yellowed newspapers to weigh the news of events that had been decided years ago, politics, economics, war stories, and would the Allies take Monte Cassino and push through to Rome, would the Marines land at Guadalcanal, would Tojo triumph or turn his sword on his own yellow belly?

The rats persisted, gnawing, thieving, slipping in and out of their cracks, thumping in the night, and she persisted too—her fires, of necessity, smaller, but beacons nonetheless, urgent smoldering pleas for help, for release. She saw boats suspended in the distance with their tiny quavering sails and she waved her arms like a cheerleader, fashioned flags from sticks and the tatters of an old faded-to-pink towel and waved them too, but the boats never grew larger or drifted out of frame, as static as figures on a canvas tacked to the very farthest wall in the most enormous room in the world. No one came. No one landed. No one existed. And where was Till? Where *was* he? He would have come for her by now, if he was alive, and how could he possibly have died in America, aboard his own boat off the lobster-rich Channel Islands, when the Japs hadn't been able to sink him in the whole wide blinding expanse of the Pacific?

The answer was too hard to hold on to so she let it go. She let it all go. Even the rats. And then, on the first day of what would have been the third week of her imprisonment in a place she'd come to loathe in its changeless, ceaseless, ongoing and never-ending placidity and indifference and sheer brainless endurance, a Coast Guard cutter, free as a cloud, rounded the point and motored into the cove.

And what did the Coast Guard find? A sunburned woman unused to the sound of her own voice, her hair stringy and flat and her eyes focused on nothing. She was the wife of a drowned man, a widow, that was all. She climbed into the rowboat and the sea shifted beneath her and kept on shifting until the big boat, the cutter, sliced across the channel under the downpouring sun, until the shore, with its sharply etched houses, swaying palms and glinting automobiles, rose up to take her in and hold her as firmly and securely as she could ever hope to be held again.

The Wreck of the *Winfield Scott*

Though Alma is trying her hardest to suppress it, the noise of the freeway is getting to her. She can't think to slice the cherry tomatoes and dice the baby carrots, can't clear her head, can barely hear Micah Stroud riding the tide of his emotions through the big speakers in the front room. Normally, aside from the odd siren or the late-night clank of the semitrucks fighting the drag of the atmosphere on the long run up the coast, the sound is continuous, white noise, as naturally occurring a phenomenon and no different in kind from the wind in the eucalyptus or the regular thump of the surf at Butterfly Beach, and she's learned to ignore it. Or at least live with it. But this is rush hour, when every sound is magnified and people accelerate randomly only to brake half a second later, making use of their horns an estimated eighty-seven percent more often than at any other time of day—a statistic she picked up from the morning paper and quoted to everybody at work in support of her conviction that mechanized society is riding its last four wheels to oblivion, not that anybody needed convincing. And her condo—over-priced and under-soundproofed—occupies the war zone between the freeway out front and the railroad tracks in back, a condition she's been able to tolerate for its access to the beach and the cool night air, and the option, which she almost always takes, even when it rains, of sleeping with the window open and a blanket wrapped tightly around her through all the seasons of the year.

Today, however—tonight, this evening—she's on edge, denying herself the solace of a glass of wine. Or *sake* on the rocks, which is what she really wants. *Sake* out of the bottle she keeps chilled in the refrigerator, poured crackling over the ice cubes in a cocktail glass, one of the six special glasses remaining from the set of eight she inherited

44

from her grandmother, clear below, frosted above, with the proprietary capital *B* etched into its face. She swallows involuntarily at the thought of it, thinking *Just half a glass, a quarter.* The carrots—slick, peeled and clammily wet in the cellophane package—feel alive beneath her fingers as she steadies them against their natural inclination to roll out from under the blade of the knife. On goes the tap with a whoosh, the tomatoes tumbling under the spray in the perforated depths of the colander. A horn sounds out on the freeway, a sudden sharp buzz of irritation and rebuke, and then another answers and another. She pictures the drivers, voluntarily caged, one hand clamped to the wheel, the other to the cell phone. They want. All of them. They want things, space, resources, attention to their immediate needs, but they're getting none of it—or not enough. Never enough.

Of course, she's one of them, though her needs are more moderate, or at least she likes to think so. And no, the *sake* isn't a serious temptation—she can do without. Has to. Because if anything defines her it's self-control. And drive. And smarts. People look at her and think she's some sort of uptight science nerd—the people who want to tear her down anyway—but that's not who she is at all. She's just focused. Everything in its time and place. And the time for *sake*—in her grandmother's etched glass with the *B* for Boyd front and center—is after the lecture. Or information session. Or crucifixion. Or whatever the yahoos want to make it this time.

The anger starts in her shoulders, radiating down her arms to her fingers, the knife, the mute unyielding vegetables. Furious suddenly, she flings down the knife and stalks into the front room to crank up the stereo, staring angrily out the window at the off-ramp and the rigid column of invasives Caltrans planted there to mask the freeway from her—and her from the freeway, though she expects the pencil pushers in Sacramento didn't really have her welfare in mind when they ordered the hired help to plant oleander, in alternating bands of red, white and salmon pink, along both shoulders. If there's a bird or a lizard or a living creature other than *Homo sapiens* out there, she can't see it. All she can see, through the gaps in the bushes, is the discontinuous flash of light from the coruscating bumpers and chrome wheels and streaming rocker panels of the endless line of carbon-spewing vehicles inching by, thinking *Seven billion by 2011, seven billion and counting. And where are we going to put them all?*

While she's standing there, Micah Stroud cruising high on his Louisiana twang over a low-pressure system of furious strumming and dislocated bass, one of the cars detaches itself from the flow—or lack of flow—and rockets down the off-ramp right in front of her. It's a white Prius, humped, ugly, forgettable but salvatory, and unlike any of the other white Priuses on the road, this one contains her familiar—her boyfriend, that is, Tim Sickafoose—and he's staring right at her with a look of startled recognition, waving now, even as the car slides out of sight and into the drive.

By the time he comes through the door, she's back in the kitchen, keeping things simple: toast the pita, dice the carrots, slice the tomatoes, toss the salad. Hummus out of the plastic deli container, feta in a thick white slab so perfect the goat might have given birth to it. Somewhere on its farm. With all the other goats. *Naa, naa, naa.*

They are not the kind of lovers, she and Tim, who peck kisses when they enter rooms or hang from each other like shopping bags in public. They give each other space, time to adjust. Before she can breathe "Hey," the usual greeting, he's at the table, cracking a beer, his backpack splayed open on the floor beside him.

The view out the kitchen window is of raffia palms against a white stucco wall draped with bougainvillea, at the base of which a heavily mulched bed of clivia and maidenhair fern bows to an overwatered lawn of Bermuda grass so uniformly and unwaveringly green it pulls the color out of everything. Beyond the wall, a stand of eucalyptus that gives off a fierce mentholated funk in the rainy season so that everything smells of fermenting cough drops, and beyond the eucalyptus a gap for the railroad tracks, then the faded-to-pink roof tiles of the hotel that gives onto the ocean—the ocean she can't see from here and can just barely make out from the upstairs bedroom. This is a view that irritates her. A view that's as wrong as it can be, and not simply because it's wasteful and cluttered and composed entirely of alien species, but because it defeats the whole point of living within sight of the ocean.

"Music's pretty loud," he observes.

She turns around now, her hands arrested in the act of halving tomatoes. "I left my iPod at work."

He has nothing to say to this, though she knows he hates Micah Stroud and Carmela Sexton-Jones and all the other new-wave folkies she plays in random shuffle through most of the day at her desk. When they'd first met, the first week they were together, she'd put on a CD she thought he might like and he'd waited through the better part of a sixteen-ounce can of Guinness before passing judgment. "I don't know how to say this without being too blunt or anything," he said, giving her his mildest look to show that he was only trying to be sincere, "but how can you listen to this . . . whatever you want to call it? I mean, give me rock and roll any day, the White Stripes, the Strokes, the Queens of the Stone Age." It was a challenge, a testing of the waters, and she didn't blame him for it—in fact, it was to his credit, because people didn't have to echo each other like twins to get along in a relationship—but still she stiffened. "At least they're committed," she said, "at least they sing about something other than sex and drugs." "What's wrong with sex?" he'd countered, too quickly, the faintest shadow of a grin creeping across his lips, and she knew she'd been had. He counted off a beat, letting the grin settle in. "Or, for that matter, drugs?"

"I was just looking in the paper," he says now, raising

his voice to be heard over the music, "to see if there's an announcement about tonight."

Despite herself, despite her nerves, she can't help conjuring the name of the behavior he's just exhibited—the Lombard effect, which refers to the way people unconsciously elevate their voices to compete with ambient noise, the roar of the restaurant, any restaurant, serving as the most salient example—even as she moves away from the counter, crosses the kitchen and strides into the front room to kill the volume on the stereo. At which point the cars and trucks and honking horns rush back into her life as if there'd never been anything else. And why couldn't they put the freeways underground, deep down, and make a park out of all that recovered acreage on top? Or a walking path? A garden to feed the hungry? Trees, weeds, anything? If she had enough money—say, five hundred billion or so—she'd buy up all the property in town, raze the buildings, tear out the roads and reintroduce the grizzly bear.

"Here, here it is," he calls out.

The notice, a pinched little paragraph in the Upcoming Events section of the local paper, is squeezed between the announcement of a performance of selections from "Les Sylphides" by the Junior Dance Studio of Goleta and a lecture on Chumash ethnobotany at the Maritime Museum:

Lecture and Public Forum. Alma Boyd Takesue, Projects Coordinator and Director of Information Resources for the National Park Service, Channel Islands, will address concerns over the proposed aerial control of the black rat population on Anacapa Island. 7:00 p.m., Natural History Museum, 2559 Puesta del Sol, Santa Barbara.

She's leaning over the table beside him, the print enlarging and receding because she's left her glasses on the counter, a trim pretty woman of thirty-three, with her mother's—and grandmother's—rinsed gray eyes and the muscular, ever-so-slightly-bowed legs and unalloyed black hair she inherited from her father. Which she wears long, down to her waist, and which slips loose now from where she's tucked it behind her ears to dangle across his forearm as he holds the paper up for her.

"Just the facts," he says. "I mean, that's all you can expect, right?"

It's somehow surprising to see it there in print, this thing she's been wrestling with privately for the past week made official, set down for the record in the staid familiar type she scans every morning for the news of things. Here is the fact of the news revealed: that she will appear at the place and time specified to make the Park Service's case for what to her seems the most reasonable and obvious course of action, given the consequences of inaction. And if that action requires the extirpation of an invasive and pernicious species—killing, that is, the killing of innocent animals, however regrettable—then she will show that there is no alternative because the health and welfare, the very existence of the island's ground-nesting birds, will depend on it. The entire breeding range of Xantus's murrelet lies between Baja and Point Conception. There are fewer than two thousand breeding pairs. Rats, on the other hand, are ubiquitous. And rats eat murrelet eggs.

"Not much of a come-on, though, is it?"

"No," she admits, straightening up and then stretching as if she's just rolled out of bed, and maybe she should have a cup of green tea, she's thinking, for that extra little jolt of caffeine. She stands there stationary a moment, gazing down at him, at the back of his head and the curiously fleshy lobes of his ears, at the way the hair, medium-length and mink-brown shading to rust at the tips, curls over the collar of his T-shirt and the ceramic beads he wears round his throat on a string of sixty-pound test fishing line. ("Why sixty pounds?" she'd asked him once. "So they won't break in the surf," he told her, matter-of-factly, as if he were stating the obvious. ("They never come off?" "Never.") She lays a hand on his shoulder, the lightest touch, but contact all the same. "But then, when you think of what happened last week in Ventura"—she looks into his eyes now and then away again, her lips compressing over the memory, the wounds still fresh and oozing—"maybe we don't really want a crowd. Maybe we want, oh, I don't know, maybe thirty people who've read the literature—"

"Thirty ecologists."

Her smile is quick, grateful—he can always lighten the mood. "Yeah," she says, "I think that'd be about right."

He's smiling now too, suspended there above the perspective line of the table like a figure in the still-life painting she's composing behind her eyelids: the pita on the counter, the late sun breaking through to slant in through the window and inflame the stubble of his cheek, the freeway gone and vanished along with the mood of doom and gloom she'd brought with her into the front room. All is well. All is very, very well. "But I just wanted to be sure," he says, breaking the spell, "in case you want me out front for crowd control." He gives it a beat, reaching out to take her hand and run his thumb over her palm, to and fro, caressing her, bringing her back. "No rat lovers, though. Right? Are we agreed on that?"

On the second of December, 1853, the captain of the SS *Winfield Scott*, a sidewheel steamer that had left San Francisco the previous day for the two-week run to Panama, made an error in judgment. That error, whether it was the result of hubris, overzealousness or a simple mistake of long division, doomed her, and as the years spun out, doomed generations of seabirds too. She had been launched just three years earlier in New York for the run between that city and New Orleans, but in 1851 she was sold and pressed into service on the West Coast, where passenger demand had exploded after the discovery of gold in northern California. Built for heavy seas, some 225 feet long and 34½ feet abeam, with four decks and three masts, she was a formidable ship, named for Major General Winfield Scott, lion and savior of the Mexican War, a gilded bust of whom looked out over her foredeck with a fixed and tutelary gaze. On this particular trip, she carried some 465 passengers and $801,871 in gold and gold dust, as well as several tons of mail and a full crew. Where she picked up her rats, whether in New York or New Orleans or alongside the quay in San Francisco, no one could say. But they were there, just as they were present on any ship of size, then and now, and they must have found the *Winfield Scott* to their liking, what with its dining salon where up to a hundred people at a time could eat in comfort, with its galleys and larder, its cans of refuse waiting to be dumped over the side and all the damp sweating nooks and holes belowdecks and up into the superstructure where they could live in their own world, apart from the commensal species that provided them with all those fine and delicate morsels to eat. There might have been hundreds of them on a ship that size, might have been a thousand or more, for that matter—no one could say, and the ones that turned up in the traps set by the stewards were mute on the subject.

Captain Simon F. Blunt was a man of experience and decision. He was familiar with the waters of the channel, having been a key member of the team that had surveyed the California coast two years earlier, shortly after the territory was admitted to the union. Coming out of San Francisco the previous day, he'd encountered heavy seas and a stiff headwind, which not only put the ship off schedule but kept the majority of the passengers close to their bunks and out of the drawing room and dining salon. In order to make up time, he elected to enter the Santa Barbara Channel and take the Anacapa Passage between Santa Cruz and Anacapa, rather than steaming to the seaward of the islands, a considerably greater distance. Normally, this would have been an admirable—and expeditious—choice. Unfortunately, however, while dinner was being served that evening, fog began to set in, a frequent occurrence in the channel, resulting from the collision of the California current, which runs north to south, with the warmer waters of the southern California countercurrent, a condition that helps make the channel such a productive fishery but also disproportionately hazardous to shipping. As a result, Captain Blunt was forced to proceed by dead reckoning—in which distance is calculated according to speed in given intervals of time—rather than by taking sightings. Still, he was confident, nothing out of the routine and nothing he couldn't handle—had handled a dozen times and more—and by ten-thirty he was certain he'd passed the islands and ordered the ship to bear to the southeast, paralleling the coast.

Half an hour later, running at her full speed of ten knots, the *Winfield Scott* struck an outcropping of rock off the north shore of middle Anacapa, tearing a hole in the hull and igniting an instantaneous panic amongst the passengers. People were flung from their berths, baggage cascaded across the decks, lanterns flickered, shattered, died, and the unknowable darkness of the night and the fog took hold. No one could see a thing, but everyone could feel and hear what was happening to them, the water rushing in somewhere below and the ship exhaling in a series of long ratcheting groans to make room for it. As they struggled to their feet and made their way out into the mobbed corridors, terrified of being overtaken and trapped belowdecks—water sloshing underfoot, the hands of strangers grasping and clutching at them while they staggered forward over unseen legs and boots and the sprawl of luggage, spinning, falling, rising again, and always that grim hydraulic roar to spur them—there was an immense deep grinding and a protracted shudder as the hull settled against the rock. Curses and screams echoed in the darkness. A child shrieked for its mother. Somewhere a dog was barking.

The officer of the watch, his face a pale blanched bulb hanging in the intermediate distance, sent up the alarm, and the captain, badly shaken, ordered the ship astern in an attempt to back away from the obstruction and avoid further damage. The engines strained, an evil tarry smoke fanning out over the deck till it was all but impossible to breathe, the great paddle wheel churning in the murk as if it were trying to drain the ocean bucket by bucket, everything held in suspension—the captain riveted, the officers mouthing silent prayers, the mob thundering below—until finally the ship broke loose with a long bruising sigh of splintering wood. She was free. Trembling down the length of her, lurching backward, but free and afloat. It must have been a revivifying moment for passengers and crew alike, but it was short-lived, because in the next instant the ship's stern struck ground, shearing off the rudder and leaving her helpless. Almost immediately she began to list, everything that wasn't secured careening down-slope toward the invisible rocks and the dim white creaming of the breakers four decks below.

Captain Blunt, at war with himself—lives at stake, his career ruined, his hands quaking and his throat gone dry—gave the order to abandon ship. By the light of the remaining lanterns he mustered his officers and crew to see to an orderly evacuation, but this was complicated by the gangs of desperate men—prospectors who'd suffered months and in some cases years of thirst, hunger, exhaustion, lack of female company and the comforts of civilization to accumulate their hoards over the backs of sweat-stinking mules—swarming the upper deck, dragging their worn swollen bottom-heavy satchels behind them and fighting for the lifeboats without a thought for anything but getting their gold to ground. At this point, the captain was forced to draw his pistol to enforce order even as the stern plunged beneath the waves and ever more passengers emerged from belowdecks in a mad scrum, slashing figures in the dark propelled by their shouting mouths and grasping hands. He fired his pistol in the air. "Remain calm!" he roared over and over again till his voice went hoarse. "Women and children first. There's room for all. Don't panic!"

The boats were lowered and the people on deck could see, if dimly, that they were out of immediate danger, and that went a long way toward pacifying them. It was a matter of ferrying people to that jagged dark pinnacle of rock the boat had struck in the dark, a matter of patience, that was all. No one was going to drown. No one was going to lose his belongings. Stay clam. Be calm. Wait your turn. And so it went, the boats pushing off and returning over the space of the next two hours till everyone but the crew had been evacuated—and then the crew, and lastly the captain, came too. What they didn't realize, through the duration of a very damp and chilled night with the sea rising and the fog settling in to erase all proportion, was that the rock on which they'd landed was some two hundred yards offshore of the main island and that in the morning they'd have to be ferried through the breakers a second time.

It was a week before they were rescued. Provisions were salvaged from the ship before she went down, but they weren't nearly enough to go round. Fights broke out over the allotment of rations and over the gold too, so that finally Captain Blunt—in full view of the assembled passengers—was forced to pinion two of the malefactors, gold thieves, on the abrasive dark shingle and horsewhip them to the satisfaction of all and even a scattering of applause. A number of the men took it upon themselves to fish from shore in the hope of augmenting their provisions. Others gathered mussels and abalone, another shot a seal and roasted it over an open fire. When finally news of the wreck reached San Francisco, and three ships, the *Goliah*, the *Republic* and the *California*, steamed down the coast to evacuate the passengers, no one was sorry to see the black cliffs of Anacapa fade back into the mist. The ship was lost. The passengers had endured a night of terror and a week of boredom, sunburn and enforced dieting. But no one had died and the gold, or the greater share of it, had been preserved.

As for the rats, they are capable swimmers with deep reserves of endurance and a fierce will to survive. Experiments have shown that the average rat can tread water for some forty-eight hours before succumbing, can grip and climb vertical wires, ropes, cables and smooth-boled trees with the facility of a squirrel and is capable of compressing its body to fit through a hole no wider around than the circumference of a quarter. And too, rats have a superb sense of balance and most often come to shore adrift on floating debris, whether that debris consists of loose cushions, odd bits of wood planking, whiskey bottles, portmanteaux and other flotsam or rafts of vegetation washed down out of canyons during heavy rains. Certainly some of the rats aboard the *Winfield Scott*, trapped in the hold when the baggage shifted or inundated before they could scramble up onto the deck, were lost, but it's likely that the majority made it to shore. Of course, all it would have taken was a pair of them. Or even a single pregnant female.

In any case, as Alma is prepared to inform her audience, the black rats—*Rattus rattus*, properly—that survived the wreck of the *Winfield Scott* made their way, over the generations, from that naked rock to middle Anacapa and from there to the eastern islet, and finally, afloat on a stick of driftwood or propelled by their own industrious paws, to the westernmost. Only luck and the six miles of open water of the Anacapa Passage, with its boiling spume and savage currents, has kept them from expanding their range to Santa Cruz. And no one, not even the most inveterate rodent lover, would want that.

The Prius is aglow with the soft amber light of the dashboard as it slips almost silently along the streaming freeway, Tim relaxed behind the wheel and offering a running commentary on the news leaking out of the radio, his way of calming her, of pretending that there's nothing out of the ordinary about this little jaunt to the museum. As if they were going to stroll arm-in-arm through the exhibits, examining the Chumash *tomol* and the skeleton of the Santa Rosa Island dwarf mammoth for the twentieth time, drawing down their voices to laugh and joke and feel at home amidst the dry stifled odor of preservation. Alma would have driven herself, except that she likes to free her mind before speaking in public and has learned from experience that the focus required of driving—however minimal and however short the distance—distracts her. There always seems to be some sort of problem on the road, an accident, a lane closure for repaving or reshouldering or whatever it is they do along the freeway at night—or mayhem, simple mayhem, bad manners, cell phone abuse, people with their heads screwed on backward—and the delay upsets her equilibrium. When you see brake lights ahead you never know if you'll be stopped for five minutes or an hour. Or your life. The rest of your life.

Sure enough, half a mile from their exit, they run into a wash of brake lights and in the next moment they're stalled behind a pickup truck elevated up off the roadway on a gleaming web of struts higher than the dwarf mammoth could ever have hoped to reach. "Shit," she hisses, and she's biting her lip, a bad habit, she knows it, but she can't help herself. "I knew we should've gone the back way."

Tim shrugs, reaches out a hand to switch channels, the reporter's intimate placatory tones dissolving in the thump and rattle of timbales, congas and cowbells and the keening almost-human voice of a guitar rising up out of the deluge of percussion. "It's probably nothing," he says. "We've got twenty minutes yet. And Mission's the next exit. See it? Right there—under this moron's rear end?"

She doesn't respond. Just turns her head and gazes out the window on the auto mall in the near distance—more cars—and lets the air run out of her lungs in a long withering sigh. It's not Tim's fault and she doesn't mean to take it out on him. He's doing the best he can, and the quickest way, no question about it, is the freeway. How could he know this was going to happen? (Though she did argue for the back way the minute he flicked on the signal light for the freeway. *Isn't it rush hour still?* she'd said. *Or the tail end of it? Nah,* he assured her. *Not now. We'll be all right.*) So it was his call. And she went along with it. And here they are. Stopped dead.

After a while he says, "Must be an accident."

She's dressed all in black—pressed cotton slacks, patent-leather heels and V-necked top accented by a modest silver bracelet and necklace, nothing showy, nothing anybody could object to—and her notes are tucked inside the manila folder atop the laptop balanced on her knees. It took her a long while that afternoon to decide on what to wear, trying to strike a balance between the formal and the casual, the ecologist dragged in from the field and turned out with just the right degree of chic to be persuasive and sympathetic rather than intimidating, and she spent the better part of an hour combing out her hair and applying her makeup. Too much eyeliner and she'd look like a slut. Too little and they wouldn't be able to see the shape of her eyes and the way the light gathered in them and made people stop to stare at her on the street, because looking good, or at least stylish and interesting, was part of the job description. Who wanted to sit there in a stiff-backed chair and have some dowdy forest-service type rattle off statistics about the decline of this species or that? She was there to be looked at, as well as listened to, and she had no problem with that. If she could use her looks to advance her cause, then so much the better.

But damn them, damn them for making this so hard on her. And she should never have had that tea—the caffeine has her heart pounding in her ears and her nerves stripped raw, just as if she'd opened up her skin and taken a vegetable peeler to them. "I wish I was out on the islands," she says, turning abruptly to him. "Recruiting invertebrates. Banding birds. Anything. I'm fed up with this crap."

He's looking straight ahead, his face dense with the reflection of the pickup's brake lights. "You are the spokesperson, after all."

"Director of information services."

"Same difference. But what I mean is, spokespeople have to speak. It's what you do, it's what you're good at." He pauses, fingers tapping at the wheel, working through his variations. "And why is it 'spokespeople'—shouldn't it be *speaks*people? Or speakpeople. There they go, the president's speakpeople, all ready to start speaking." He turns to her, serious suddenly. "They'd be lost without you and you know it."

"Dave LaJoy," she pronounces carefully. "Anise Reed."

He waves a hand in dismissal. "Okay, okay—there are crazies everywhere. Especially when you—"

"When I what?"

"I don't know—do something controversial. Or defend it, I mean. Explain it. Explanations always leave you open to attack, as if you're apologizing after the fact. Or before the fact, I mean."

She can feel a flare of anger coming up in her. "I'm not apologizing. We've got nothing to apologize for. We're scientists. We do the studies. Not like these PETA nuts that come out to shout you down because they've got nothing better to do—and they're ignorant, baseline stupid, that's all. They don't have the faintest idea of what they're talking about. Not a clue. If they would only—"

"So educate them."

She throws it back at him, bitter now, bitter and outraged. "*Educate* them. Good luck. These people don't want facts, they don't want to know about island biogeography or the impact of invasive species or ecosystem collapse or anything else. All they want is to stick their noses in. And shout. They love to shout."

"I know," he says, "I know," and they're moving now, the string of brake lights easing off all down the line, the tires gripping the road, rolling forward, the exit rushing at them. "I'm on your side, remember? Just keep your cool, that's all. Be nice. But firm. And professional. That's what you are, right—professional?"

The freeway releases them onto city streets, cars parked along the curb, storefronts giving back the glare of the headlights, trees broadcasting their shadows. People are coming out of restaurants, flicking remotes at their cars, standing in groups on the sidewalk for no discernible reason, going to meetings. A bus lurches out ahead of them and settles into its lane, shuddering like a ship at sea. They pass a storefront offering kung fu lessons and she has a fleeting glimpse of robes, faces, synchronized gestures. It's quarter to seven. They will be there, barring further surprises, with five minutes to spare, and in a way that's better than arriving half an hour early and having to sit in the back room staring at the ten-foot mounted grizzly and fret and pace and watch the clock portion off the seconds. She raises her hands to push the hair away from her face, then drops them to the folder in her lap. The rain, which has been threatening all through the afternoon, chooses that moment to dash at the windshield and sizzle on the dark tongue of pavement before them. "Yeah," she says finally, long after it matters, "that's what I am. Professional."

She's surprised at the number of cars in the parking lot. Every spot seems to be taken, at least the ones close in, and people are circling in predatory mode, the rain heavier now, sheeting across the blacktop and giving back the sheen of the headlights in a polished waxen glow. "Looks like you attracted quite a crowd," he says, leaning over the wheel on both forearms to peer out into the night while waiting for the car ahead of them, a black BMW, its left rear blinker pulsing frantically, to make up its mind: left, right or straight ahead? The delay is maddening. The kind of thing that drives her over the line, indecision, inattentiveness, the laziness of people who won't drive to the end of the lot for fear they might have to walk an extra twenty feet, who sit back with a bag of potato chips in one hand and a Cherry Coke in the other and wonder why all of America is fat and getting fatter. She actually leans forward to reach across the console for the horn—*What is with these people?*—before snatching her hand back. She can't afford to be rude. Not here. Not tonight. How devastating would it be for the speaker, the guest of honor, to get caught up in some petty embroilment in the parking lot?

She says: "There must be something else going on."

"Uh-uh. Not that I saw in the paper anyway." The car ahead of them creeps forward, the frantic winking eye of the blinker dying out on the left only to reanimate itself on the right. Then the brake lights flare and the car stops. Again. Beyond it, she can see the illuminated forms of couples hurrying across the pavement, bowed beneath the weight of their umbrellas, and that's when it comes to her that she's forgotten her own.

"Tim? Did you bring an umbrella?"

He gives her one of his astonished looks, eyebrows rocketing, eyes blown open, lips scrambling for an expression, at once a parody of and homage to his favorite late-night TV host. He can be very funny, Tim, nothing sacred to him, no occasion too solemn or pressing for a gag. But this isn't the time. Or place.

"You didn't then?"

He shakes his head, still mugging, as if this were all a big joke, as if he could even begin to soothe her at this point. "No. Sorry. Uh-uh. You want me to swing around and drop you at the door? Or I'll carry you. Want me to carry you?"

"No," she snaps, thinking of ruined hair and smeared makeup, thinking of standing up there at the microphone looking as if she's just fallen off a boat. "No, I do not want you to carry me. Didn't you know it was going to rain? Didn't you think?"

Before she'd taken him to Scottsdale to meet her mother the first time, after they'd been seeing each other for a month, she'd given him a full accounting of her mother's character, habits and predilections, and while it was for the most part a loving portrait, it was unsparing too. Her mother was a shopper. An inveterate shopper. A shopaholic. There was nothing she didn't collect, from ceramic stringheads to Zuni turquoise, Fiesta ware, porcelain dolls, antique dustpans and Victorian furniture so dense and dark it squeezed all the light out of every room in the house. In the face of a dying planet and the exhaustion of resources, this would be shame enough for any daughter to bear, but for an ecologist who'd devoted her adult life to educating the public, it was crippling and inexplicable. And hurtful, deeply hurtful. She felt bad about it on so many levels, about mentioning it even, as if she were betraying her mother and her mother's love. And what was the first thing Tim said to her mother? "I can appreciate the hoarding urge," he told her, sinking into the couch in the living room with the gimlet she had just handed him, "whether it's environmentally correct or not. My mother—you'll meet her, she lives in upstate New York, but she comes out to visit maybe twice a year—my mother used to be like that. And then I told her, 'Look, going antiquing for women is like fishing for guys, I understand that. But in this age of conserving resources, most of us practice catch and release.' You know, you get the thrill of stalking the trout, flicking out the fly, pulling this mysterious beautiful thing out of the water, one in a million, precious as gold, and then you let it go. Same thing with my mother nowadays, because she's totally reformed—she goes to the store, finds a precious whatever it is, bargains like a fanatic, like she'll die if she pays a nickel more, then counts out the money, watches the guy wrap it up, and hands it right back to him. You know what I'm saying? Catch and release."

He doesn't respond. But he's begun inching forward, flicking his brights on and off by way of suggesting to the people in the BMW that their behavior stands in need of correcting. "Why don't they just park in the middle of the fucking street? Come on," he mutters, coaching them, "come *on*." Whoever they are—shadowy forms emerging suddenly in sharp relief, the back of a man's head and a woman beside him, in profile, her hair massed like an unraveling turban—they've begun to get the idea. There's a quick sharp movement of the man's shoulders, the wheel swinging right, and the car rolls grudgingly out of the way.

That's when the feeling comes over her—what is it, dread, mortification, hate?—and she doesn't want to know, doesn't want to look, staring rigidly ahead, as if she's been frozen in place, as Tim pulls even with them, right there, right in the operatic glare of the headlights of the next car in line. She can feel his eyes sweeping sourly over them, the engine of the Prius gurgling softly, the windshield wipers beating time and the faintest whisper of a voice leaking from the radio as he eases past, but she doesn't turn her head. She's shut them out, negated them, hide-and-seek, but not before the sticker on the side window leaps out at her, vermilion letters on an electric yellow background superimposed over the figure of a cartoon rodent's anthropomorphized face. *FPA*, it reads, and beneath it, in characters that seem to bleed away from the banner: *For the Protection of Animals*.

But then she feels the car accelerate and they're parting the curtain of rain, or at least the visible portion of it, wheeling down the long double line of parked cars and back up again on the far side. Before she can protest he's pulling up in front of the entrance, on the wide strip of macadam reserved for *Pedestrians Only*, skidding to a stop within inches of the snaking line of slickered, umbrella-wielding people waiting to purchase tickets in the rain, already leaning forward to reach across her for the door. "Go ahead," he says, the seat belt tugging at his shoulder and the smell of him—of his aftershave and shampoo and the hot fungal odor of the hair under his arms and between his legs, her leman's smell, her mate's—rising to her, primal and comforting and confusing all at once. For a moment she doesn't know what to do. "I'll park back there someplace at the end of the lot," he tells her, making a vague gesture at the expanding arena of shadow behind them, "and catch up with you later." The door swings open. She unfastens her seat belt, tucks her folder and laptop under one arm, and emerges to the breeze and the blown rain and the taste of it on her lips, sweet and rank all at once. He's watching her. Grinning. "Break a leg," he says.

Before she can respond—and what would she say anyway, *I'll try*?—here's Frieda Kleinschmidt, the museum's director, stalking up to her with a bright pink parasol, the lights along the walkway fuzzed with mist, people looming out of the shadows to hunch under the parapet, furl umbrellas and stamp and blow and brush the rain from sleeves, shoulders, hats. Tall, narrow-shouldered, her face clenched round the shine of her steel-framed glasses and the alarm in her magnified eyes, Frieda stands there rigid, staring at the Prius skewed across the pavement where no car has ever dared go before it. She shoots an anxious glance at Tim—*No*, he's not a terrorist, Alma wants to tell her, *only my boyfriend*—and then says, "You picked quite a night for it. Who would have thought?" She pumps the umbrella in evidence, then lowers it again to Alma's height. "I mean, it was clear an hour ago. Wasn't it? I thought it was anyway. Last I looked."

Alma murmurs something in response, and then they're striding across the courtyard, past the entrance to the auditorium and up to the door of the room where the unlucky grizzly (*Ursus arctos californicus*, declared extinct 1924) stands guard. "But all these cars—this isn't all for me, is it?"

"I don't know who else," Frieda throws over her shoulder, bending from the waist to manipulate a clutch of keys and let her into the cold too-bright room, brisk now, hugging her arms to her and revolving around the floor on the spongy soles of her running shoes as if she's about to dash off into the night. She's anxious, Alma can see that, anxious because of the size of the crowd and the subject matter and what happened in Ventura last week. "But you have everything you need, right? There's water out there on the podium—and we'll start a little late, I think, maybe ten minutes or so, just to let everyone get settled, what with the rain—"

"Yes," Alma murmurs, "that's fine. "I'll just need to plug my laptop into the projector. And the microphone—"

"I did the sound check myself. You'll take questions afterward?"

The grizzly, formerly on display but exiled to this back room for crimes unspecified, looms over them with its plasticized eyes and arrested teeth, snarling mutely down the ages. There are other artifacts here too—a great stiff comb of baleen propped up in the corner, cast-off mammoth bones aligned neatly on an oak desk and looking unsettlingly like the refuse at the bottom of a Colonel Sanders bucket enlarged to implausibility, Chumash arrowheads and shards of pottery in a dusty glass display case skewed away from the far wall at a forty-five-degree angle, museum clutter awaiting the donors' dollars to rescue it from eternal storage. "Yes. I mean, that's what they're here for. Most of them, I guess."

Frieda gives her a look. "If any of them get, well—I don't know, *contentious*—don't be afraid to cut them off, and I do have Bill Braithwaite at the door, just in case . . ."

This is the point at which she's supposed to say, *Don't worry, I can handle it—I've done it a thousand times.* But she says nothing.

Erect, her glasses shining and her pigeon-colored eyes in retreat, Frieda claps her hands together and spins halfway round with a faint squeak of rubber or plastic or whatever it is they're making running shoes from these days. "Well, I guess I'll leave you to your thoughts then. I'll come get you in"—she raises her wrist to squint at a flat gold watch on a band no wider than a shoelace—"say, seven and a half minutes?"

It's warm in the auditorium, very warm, all those people—standing room only, which means three hundred at least—bundled tightly together, post-prandial, variously digesting their dinners, processing proteins and starches and sugars, generating heat. And it's humid, the rain beating remorselessly at the roof and percolating through the downspouts with a peristaltic tick and gurgle. And, of course, since it's November, the museum's central air has been long shut down for the season. Sitting there in the middle of the front row while Frieda reads through a list of announcements—upcoming events, classes, fundraisers, opportunities to get in on museum-sponsored field trips, films and slide shows—she can feel the sweat rising from her pores, collecting at the nape of her neck beneath the thermal blanket of her hair, trailing down her spine to where the blouse has begun to stick to the small of her back. When she slipped in stage left and took her seat, she caught a glimpse of the crowd, surprised all over again by the turnout, especially on a rainy night, but she didn't look closely enough to individuate anyone, not even Tim, who must have been part of the contingent, mostly male, milling around in the rear without hope of finding seats. If she was nervous a few moments ago, in the green room with Frieda—and the grizzly—she's over it now. In fact, all she can think of—hope for—is that Frieda's introduction will be short and to the point so she can get up there and get this over with.

But Frieda is not short and to the point. After a shaky start, Frieda is coming into her own, riding high on the heady business of insinuating a single human voice through the wires of a foam-jacketed microphone and the distant speakers they feed in order to hold the attention of three hundred people without lapsing or slipping up or making a fool of yourself. The introduction—Alma Boyd Takesue, B.S. in biology from the University of Hawaii, M.S. and Ph.D. in environmental studies from UC Berkeley, three years in the field studying the brown tree snake on Guam and all the rest, right on down to a recitation of the titles of her papers in scientific journals, all of them, all the journals and all the titles—manages to be both uninspired and interminable, and by the time Frieda finally announces her and stands back to shield her eyes against the spotlight and extend a blind hand of welcome, the audience is restless. The applause patters dutifully as Alma rises from her seat and then cuts off abruptly, even before she finds herself up there under the glare of the spotlight, struggling to adjust the microphone the taller woman has left poised well above the crown of her head.

"Hello," she hears herself say, the amplification hurling her voice out into the void and then bringing it back to inhabit every crevice in a throbbing overwrought vibrato. "I want to thank you all for coming, especially on such a"—and here she pauses, searching for the right word, the one that will soften things, lighten them up, and what kind of night is it anyway?—"dismal night." Yes, dismal. There is a collective rustling, as if the entire audience were balanced on a taut continuous sheet of paper, and then she's bending to her computer, and the first image—of Anacapa at twilight, Arch Rock glowing iconically and the sea so multifaceted and calm it might have been painted in oils around it—infuses the big screen behind her. "This is Anacapa," she says redundantly, "one of the islands that comprise the Channel Islands National Park, the islands often referred to as the Galápagos of North America."

The Galápagos of North America. It's a tired phrase, but one she conscientiously works into all her press releases and talks, whether formal or informal, because it never fails to have its effect, people drifting off on a fugue of

National Geographic specials, of blue-footed boobies, frigate birds, vampire finches and marine iguanas presented in loving close-up while azure waves beat at crinkled shores, only to awaken to the connection she's trying to make—that these islands, *our* islands, are equally unique. And equally worthy of preservation. And not simply preservation, but restoration.

She lifts her head to gaze out on the audience, sweeping left to right as if she's speaking personally to each and every one of them, though with the spotlight in her eyes and her glasses on the podium beside her and the auditorium lights turned low, she can barely make out anyone beyond the second row. "Anacapa," she pronounces, giving each of its aspirated syllables a long lingering beat, "is, as I'm sure you all know, a unique and irreplaceable ecosystem that is home to endemic species of both plants and animals found nowhere else in the world, from the island wallflower and an autochthonous *Malacothrix*, of the chicory genus, to the shield-backed cricket and the native deer mouse, *Peromyscus maniculatus anacapae*, just as the other islands harbor unique species of birds, as well as the spotted skunk and"—here a click of the mechanical mouse to display the next picture, one that never fails to arouse a tongue-clucking murmur of approval—"the island fox. Which, through some sixteen thousand years of separation from the mainland, has evolved into a separate subspecies, featuring the dwarfism often common to insular populations. On average"—she looks to the screen behind her, the fox blooming in the darkness, ears erect, paws neatly aligned and gazing out into the audience with all the ferocity of a stuffed toy—"these little guys weigh four to six pounds, the size of a house cat . . . one that gets regular exercise, that is." This last, her icebreaker, always generates the first laugh of the evening, or rueful chuckle, at least, as the cat owners reflect on the overfed, kibbleized giants curled up asleep on the sofa at home.

She has them now, and never mind that privately she'd

like to see all free-ranging cats exterminated in fact and by law, because she's ascending into her rhythm, the Latin nomenclature rolling off her tongue as if she were a priest in training, every fact and figure at her command, no need at all to glance down at the notes she's printed in 22-point type so she can dispense with her glasses and give them the full effect of her eyes. As the images click behind her, she presents a quick overview of island biogeography, of how isolated species evolve to fill niches in the ecosystem and of how that balance, unique to each island throughout the world, can be upset by the introduction of mainland species. She talks about the dodo, perhaps the poster animal for island extinctions, a pigeon-like bird that found its way to an isle in the Indian ocean and subsequently evolved, in the absence of predators, into the waddling big-bottomed flightless bird made infamous by its very helplessness.

"The dodo was naive," she says, giving them a hard, no-nonsense look, because this is the reality, this is what it comes down to—the permanent loss of an irreplaceable species—and there's nothing funny or even remotely ironic about that. "That is, it had had fear and suspicion bred out of it, and so waddled right up to the first seaman to land on the island of Mauritius, who plucked and roasted it, then introduced pigs and rats, which fed avidly on the eggs of this ground-nester. Flight is expensive," she goes on, "in light of caloric resources expended, and so too is tree-nesting. Why fly, why nest in a tree, if you've evolved in a place where there are no predators? The answer for the dodo—the result, that is—as every school-child knows, was extinction."

The audience has settled in, the initial rustling, nose-blowing and fist-suppressed hacking fading away into what she'd like to construe as engaged silence rather than a collective stupor. But no, they *are* engaged: she can feel them, alert and awake and alive to the argument to come (key words: *rats* and *poison*) and the bloodletting of the Q&A that will follow. All right. Time to bring it on. She clicks the mouse and the next image to infest the screen behind her is of those very rats, eyes gleaming demonically in the sudden illumination of the photographer's flash, as they rifle the nests of gulls and murrelets, their paws and snouts wet with smears of yolk, albumin and chalaza.

"Rats," she announces, letting the final s sibilate on her lips till it buzzes back to her through the speakers, "are responsible for sixty percent of all island extinctions in the world today." A pause for effect. "And rats are killing off the ground-nesting birds of Anacapa Island." Pause the second, this time accompanied by the steeliest squint she can manage, considering that she can barely see the audience. "Which is why I am here tonight to tell you that we must act and act now if we want to save these endemic creatures from the same fate that met the dodo, the Rodrigues solitaire, the Stephens Island wren, the Culebra Island giant anole and dozens—hundreds, *thousands*—of others."

And now the rustling, the creaking of the chairs and the whisper of voices, excitement flashing through the crowd like an electrical charge: this is what they've come for. And it's what she's come for too, the moment of truth. She straightens up, squares her shoulders. She has them in her power and now is the time to lean into the microphone, hold them with that squint, and say: "Which is why we have, after long deliberation and with the full backing of the National Park Service's biologists and the California Department of Fish and Game as well as the scientific community at large, decided to go to the air with the control agent brodifacoum to suppress the invasive rodent population, which, incidentally, is threatening the native deer mice in addition to the murrelet, the pigeon guillemot, the western gull and the cormorant." She clicks the mouse to display a close-up of a tiny Xantus's murrelet with its black head and mask over a white throat and underbelly, looking stricken as the snaking dark form of a rat gnaws the egg out from under it. "And let me assure

69

you that this agent is quick-acting and humane, and that if we were presented with any other alternative we would gladly have taken it, but given the urgency of the situation and our confidence in the method of control, we have, have . . ."

The crowd has fallen silent. They've become aware of a presence she's just now perceived at the periphery of her vision, the figure of a man risen from a seat at the far end of the front row, his hair in rusty dreadlocks, his head bowed, muscles rigid, his jaw clamped in fury. She knows him. Of course she does. And of course he's here and of course he's interrupting her and behaving like a brownshirt, like a, a—

"Bull," he pronounces, and his voice echoes from one end of the auditorium to the other. "Propaganda and doublespeak." He swings round on the audience suddenly, his arms raised like a prophet's. "Did we come here to listen to the party line like a bunch of drones under some communistic dictatorship, or is this a public meeting? Do we want our questions answered? Our point of view represented? Or is this show for mutes only?"

A groundswell of applause, a scattering of voices, male and female alike, calling out encouragement and then a chant starting like the rumor of a distant wind and blowing stronger with each repetition, "Q and A, Q and A, Q and A!"

And now she's raising both her hands, palms out, in a gesture for silence, patience, simple common courtesy, and a rumble of voices arises in support. "Sit down," someone calls from the darkness. "Button it."

"All right," she hears herself say, her amplified voice coming at them like the voice of a god, stentorian, omnipotent—she has the microphone and they don't— "we'll address all your concerns and take your comments in a minute. As for you, Mr. LaJoy"—he's still standing there, his arms crossed in defiance—"your opposition to our goals is well documented, and you will have your chance to comment, but I'm going to have to ask you to sit and wait your turn." And then she adds, superfluously, "All things in time."

The applause now is definitely on her side, on the side of civility and restraint, and it continues until Dave LaJoy sinks back into his seat and she's had a chance to take a sip of water from the glass Frieda has left for her on the ledge beneath the lectern, and is her hand shaking as she lifts it to her lips? No. It's not. It's definitely not. Determined not to let them ruffle her, she sets the glass firmly down and picks up where she's left off, describing—and yes, minimizing—the effects of the control agent and once again bringing home the point, in ringing terms, that there is absolutely no alternative to the proposed action, even as the final image, of a murrelet tending its nestlings against a soft-focus background of clinging plants and dark volcanic rock, crowds the screen behind her. She takes the applause graciously, bows her head and waits till Frieda has mounted the stage in her rangy unhipped slump-shouldered stride and thrust herself into the spotlight. "*Now*," Frieda projects into the microphone on an admonitory blast of static, "*now* Dr. Takesue will take your questions. In turn. And one at a time, *please*." She waits a moment, as if daring anyone to defy her, shields her eyes against the glare, and calls out into the void, "Up with the house lights, Guillermo. We want to see just *whom* we're addressing."

Immediately, Dave LaJoy is on his feet, his hand rocketing in the air—and there she is, Anise Reed, seated beside him in her cyclone of hair, her eyes burning and her hands clenched in her lap. Alma, her glasses clamped firmly over the bridge of her nose now, ignores them and flags a woman ten rows back. Red-faced, with a corona of milkwhite hair and a pair of rectangular wire-rimmed glasses that could have come from the same shop as Frieda's, the woman unfolds herself from the chair and in a thin sweet aqueous voice asks, "What about the mice? Won't the poison hurt them too?" then drops back into the chair and the anonymity of the crowd as if to stand for one second more under the public gaze would crush the breath out of her.

"Good question," Alma purrs, congratulating her, relieved to field a query from someone who's come to be informed, to learn something rather than suck up attention like a parasite, and that's exactly what Dave LaJoy is, a parasite on the corpus of the Park Service and the museum and Frieda and everyone else who works to improve things rather than tear them down. "Our field biologists"—her voice is soft now, honeyed, the pleasure of the exchange erasing the tension that settled in her stomach and migrated all the way out to the tips of her fingers till they tingle as if they've been frostbitten—"have taken the mice into account and we've trapped a representative population for captive breeding and release after the rats have been extirpated—and we expect them to repopulate very quickly in the absence of competition from the rats."

"And the birds? What about the birds? Isn't it a fact that there'll be a massive kill-off?" A man on her left—a confederate of LaJoy's?—has popped up out of nowhere, unrecognized. She sees a goatee, the glint of gold in one ear, the glaring blue unbreachable eyes of the fanatic, and for an instant she thinks to ignore him, but immediately relents—if she doesn't answer she'll look as if she's evading the issue.

"The bait is colored bright blue, a hue that doesn't fall within the range of anything the avifauna might be expected to consume. And, of course, we're going to do the aerial drop now, in winter, when bird numbers are down." She raises a placatory palm and lets it fall. "We expect very little collateral damage."

"Little?" It's LaJoy again, again on his feet. "The loss of a single animal—a single rat—is intolerable, inhumane and just plain wrong. Why don't you tell them—*Dr.* Takesue—about what this poison does to any animal unlucky enough to ingest it, whether that's a rat or one of your precious little birds? Huh? Why don't you tell them that?"

She can see Frieda stirring in the chair she's taken in the front row, Frieda the watchdog, her neck craned, glasses shining militantly. And where's Bill Braithwaite—wasn't he supposed to provide the muscle here? And Tim? Where's Tim?

"The agent is quick-acting and humane," she hears herself say.

"More doublespeak." LaJoy is swinging round to incite the crowd, juggling his arms and flaying the dreadlocks round the stanchion of his neck. "The fact is that this poison—call it by what it is, why don't you?—this poison causes slow death from internal bleeding over anywhere from three to ten days. Ten days! You call that humane?"

The audience breathes out, massively. Chairs creak. A soughing murmur of opposed voices starts up. She's losing them.

"Listen, Mr. LaJoy," she says, her voice as sharp-edged as one of the arrowheads in the back room, and she'd like nothing better than to run him through, pull back the bowstring and let fly, "I'm not going to debate you here—"

"Then where are you going to debate me? Name it. I'll be there. And then maybe people can get around to the truth of this thing, that you and your so-called scientists—"

"Frankly, nowhere. We've had your opinion. Thank you. Now—yes, you, the man in back, in the plaid shirt?"

But LaJoy won't give it up, just as he wouldn't the week before in Ventura when he had to be escorted from the room, spewing threats and curses. "You're no better than executioners," he shouts over whatever the man in plaid is trying to say. "Nazis, that's what you are. Kill everything, that's your solution. Kill, kill, kill."

Suddenly Frieda is there beside her, the microphone riding up to the level of her irate face. "Now that will be enough. If you can't be civil—"

73

He throws it right back at her. "How can you talk about being civil when innocent animals are being tortured to death? Civil? I'll be civil when the killing's done and not a minute before. Those rats—"

Alma feels the heart go out of her. She's standing there at Frieda's side, feeling helpless and exposed, trying to keep her shoulders from slumping, the scepter of the microphone taken from her and the crowd too, even as Frieda glares at the rear of the auditorium and calls for order. "Bill," she cries, "Guillermo. Will you please have this gentleman removed from the hall?"

And here they come, Bill Braithwaite, all two hundred fifty ventricose pounds of him, and the tech person, Guillermo Díaz, head down and a hundred pounds lighter, making their way up the right-hand aisle, looking grim. "Those rats have been there for a hundred and fifty years!" LaJoy calls out, edging down the row to box them off. "What's your baseline? A hundred years ago? A thousand? Ten thousand? Hell"—and he's out in the far aisle now, facing the crowd—"why not just clone your dwarf mammoth and stick him out there like in *Jurassic Park*?"

"Bill," Frieda pleads in a long expiring sigh of exasperation that bleats through the speakers like a martyr's last prayer. "Bill!"

Everybody seems to be standing now, voices caroming off the high open wood-beamed ceiling, no bringing them back, another night lost—or at least the most instructive part of it. And why couldn't the informed people speak up? Or the schoolchildren who want to know about the fox's habits or what the spotted skunk eats and how it got so small? Why the controversy? Why the anger? Why the hate? *Jurassic Park.* That was a low blow, the demagogue's trick of confusing the issue, and she wants to snatch the microphone back and let him have it, but she can't because she's a professional, she abides by the rules, she has taste and manners and truth on her side, and getting into a shouting match with a sociopath just isn't the way to advance her agenda.

She looks out into the audience, LaJoy already at the exit, a good half the crowd between him and Bill Braithwaite and Guillermo so that she won't even have the satisfaction of seeing him thrown out. He's taking his time, all hips and shoulders, his head swaying cockily, carrying himself like a wrestler marching into the arena. He's almost there, the crowd at the door parting to make way for him as they would for any embarrassment, any pariah, but at the last moment he jerks himself up, swings round to shoot a withering glance at the podium where she stands beside Frieda on the forgotten stage and lifts his chin to deliver the parting blow, loud enough for all to hear: "And who exactly was it appointed you God, lady?"

Afterward, over warm white wine and stale tortilla chips at the reception the museum board has arranged for her, a number of people come up to tell her how stimulating and informative her lecture was and how much they support what she's doing for the islands and how they deplore the sort of rude behavior and ignorance on display in the audience tonight. They mean to be kind, but a reflexive smile and a gracious "thank you" is the best she can come up with. Once LaJoy had been ejected—Anise Reed slithering off with him—Frieda managed to settle the crowd and the Q&A went off as planned, people genuinely interested and Alma taking advantage of the opportunity to educate them with all the graciousness and facility at her command. Which was plenty, especially considering the dramatic tension left hanging in the air—in a strange way, the outbursts made the audience all the more sympathetic and receptive. All things considered, she's weathered the evening well—and, more important, gotten her point across, nudging people toward the light in a calm and reasonable fashion that went a long way toward negating the distortions of the PETA fringe and the FPA and all the rest. Yes. Sure. And so why is she standing here balancing a plastic cup of tepid undrinkable wine on one palm while fielding the sort of looks usually reserved for the perky little gymnast who falls off the balance bar at the Olympic trials?

She's talking to a bony seventyish woman in a pink silk blouse the size of a football jersey about the feasibility of preserving island botanical specimens in mainland gardens, when Tim appears out of nowhere to take hold of her elbow—"Sorry," he mouths to the woman, "emergency"— and guide her to the door. "I just called Hana Sushi and they're serving till ten. You want that *sake*—that *sake* rocks, crisp on the palate, with the faintest nose of Hokkaido forest breezes and underlying hints of vanilla and pomegranate—or not?"

"But I need to say goodbye to Frieda—"

"With deep overtones of pineapple and, I don't know, wet schnauzer?"

"But Frieda—"

"Call her from the car."

"I can't do that," she's saying, but they're already out the door and into the night, where the parking lot stands all but empty and the clouds crouch low over a rejuvenant drizzle. She's thinking *I'll send her a note*, thinking she's had enough for one day, thinking of the sushi bar wrapped in its soft calm glow of the familiar, jazz softly leaking through the speakers and Shuhei and Hiro poised there to joke and gossip and whip up something special just for her, thinking of halibut and yellowtail and albacore tuna from the depthless sea, and *sake* in a clear beaded glass, with ice.

She's fifty feet from the car, its chassis moth-colored and palely glowing against the deeper darkness, when she realizes something's wrong. Everything seems blurred, even with her glasses on, but they're walking faster now, Tim aware of it too, and even when they're standing there right beside the car, she still can't make out what the marks are. They seem to be black bands of some sort— spray paint?

Tim, a shadow beside her, one facet of a deeper complication, lets out a curse, his voice strained with surprise and outrage. "Aw, shit! *Shit!* They graffitied the car!"

Great looping letters, coming into focus now as her eyes gradually adjust. *Die*, she reads. *Gook*, she reads. And, finally, *Bitch*.

The *Paladin*

If there's one thing he hates, it's a runny yolk. And toast so dry it shatters like a cracker before you can spread the butter. And rain. He hates the rain too. Three days of it now, making a mess of the streets and keeping shoppers out of the stores (pathetic numbers, absolutely pathetic, in all four units, and with the Christmas season coming on no less), depressing people, drooling like bilge down the plate-glass window at the Cactus Café, where he eats breakfast five days a week and they still can't figure out what *over fucking easy* means. His dried-out toast is cold. The coffee tastes like aluminum foil, and it's cold too, or lukewarm at best. And the newspaper has one stingy little article about what went down at the museum last night, tucked away in the Community Events roundup for Tuesday, November 20, 2001, the date in bolder type than the headline, as if to indicate that everything included beneath it would be just as mind-numbing and inconsequential as it had been the day before and the day before that. Under the headline "Protest at Museum Lecture," there's a scant two paragraphs that don't begin to get at the issue, and worse, don't even mention him or FPA by name, let alone set out the counterarguments he'd thrown right in the face of that condescending little bitch from the Park Service who was fooling nobody with her gray-eyed squint and her all-black outfit as if she were going to a funeral or a Goth club or something and all her tricked-up images of the cute little animals that just have to be saved in the face of this sudden onslaught by all these other ugly little animals, made uglier by somebody's Photoshop manipulations, as if the birds wouldn't last another week when a hundred and fifty years had gone by in complete harmony and natural balance with all the other birds and plants and the rats too, something Alma Boyd Takesue, Ph.D., didn't bother to mention.

Suddenly he's jerking his head around—and there's Marta, fat Marta with her two-ton tits and big pregnant belly that isn't pregnant at all, only just fat, bending over some other guy's table by the door, flirting with him, for Christ's sake—and before he can think he shouts out her name, surprising himself by the violence of his voice. Everybody in the place, and there must be thirty of them, half he recognizes and half not, looks up in unison, as if they were all named Marta, and what does he think about that? He thinks, *Fuck you, collectively.* He thinks he might have to find another goddamn diner where they know the difference between—

And here she is, her face drawn down around a mouth shrunk to the size of a keyhole beneath the flabby cheeks, coming to him as swiftly as her too-small feet can carry her, trying to act as if she cares. "Is everything okay?" she asks before she's halfway to him so everybody can hear her doing her job, even Ricardo, the cook, who's giving him a hooded look from behind the grill, a cigarette in one hand, spatula in the other.

"No," he says, still too loud, and they're still looking, all of them, because they're a bunch of sad-assed pathetic voyeurs with nothing better to do, and fuck them. Really, *fuck them.* "No, everything isn't okay. Because I come in here every day, don't I? And you people still don't know what *over easy* means? Shit, if I wanted sunny-side up, if I wanted a runny yolk, that's what I would have ordered."

She's already reaching for the plate, already apologizing—"Sorry, sir, I'll have the cook" and all the rest of the mollifying meaningless little phrases she dispenses a hundred times a day because the cook's a moron and to call her incompetent would be a compliment—but he can't help saying, snarling, and why is he snarling?, "Take it away and do it right or don't do it at all." And, to the retreating twin hummocks of her butt: "And the toast is like that shit they give babies, what do you call it—Zwieback—and I don't want Zwieback, I want toast." She's at the swinging door to the kitchen now, making a show of upending the plate in the trash while Ricardo shrinks into the Aztecan nullity of his face and everybody else in the place pretends to take up their conversations where they left off and he can't help adding, his voice lower now, the rage all steamed out of him though the heat's still up high, "Simple toast. Is that too much to ask?"

After breakfast, he heads out into the rain, picturing his umbrella back at home leaning up against the doorjamb, but it's not a problem because the moisture has the effect of puffing up his dreads, giving them body, frizzing them out—especially on top, at the roots, where he's been notic-ing a little too much scalp in the mirror lately—and this is more drizzle than real rain anyway. He pauses a moment outside the diner to shift the newspaper under one arm and pull up the collar of his black nylon jacket, feeling self-conscious all of a sudden, as if the upturned collar were an affectation out of the dim past and an old Clash concert at the Bowl. Which, he supposes, it is. Glancing up, he catches some balding geek giving him a covert look through the rain-scrawled window, but the show's over and he's not going to get himself worked up over runny eggs or this jerk or anything else, and yes, he took his blood-pressure medicine and no, he didn't take—will never take—the Xanax Dr. Reiser talked him into as a tool to combat the rage that seems to sweep up on him inex-plicably like a rogue wave on a flat sea, which really isn't anger so much as impatience with people and the multi-farious ways they can and will screw up just about any-thing, given the chance, over and over again.

The car is two blocks away, down a gently sloping street studded with meters and sloppily parked Volvos and Toyotas, mixed use, apartments and businesses side by side, the odd lawn, street trees, then around the corner to the cross street below. He's walking now, striding along in his business-as-usual gait, forty-two years old and as fit as the gym and Dr. Reiser's Lotensin and blood thinners can make him, ignoring the cars lined up at the light with their wipers clapping and the exhaust coiling out of their tailpipes in the last petrochemical gasp of the black stuff pooled up under layers of shale in Saudi Arabia and Nigeria and Venezuela, the death of the earth, the death of everything, smelling crushed worm, rotting leaf and the wet acidic failure of the newspapers stuck to the sidewalk where the Mexicans tossed them short of house stoops and storefronts in the grim desperate hour before dawn. He's walking, thinking he won't bother stopping in at any of the stores today—LaJoy's Home Entertainment Centers, with locations in Santa Barbara, Goleta, Ventura and Camarillo—because whatever might be happening or not happening there on a day like this is not so much his worry anymore as it is the problem and *responsibility* of the individual store managers and Harley Meachum, who's being paid more than he's worth to do just that: worry.

Semi-retired. That's his status and he's earned it, because he's done his scrambling and made his bundle and he's got his house in Montecito and his two cars and his boat and Anise too, time on his hands now, just the way he wants it—just like the bum he finds standing there by the Beemer when he turns the corner, a lean philosophical-looking white-haired bum planted there as if he's thinking of making an offer on the car.

And that's an automatic thing with him, calling a bum a bum instead of one of the homeless or less fortunate or needy or apartmentally challenged or whatever the phrase of the week is, Anise forever trying to correct him on that score, because his sympathies lie with the animals that *can't* help themselves—the pigs electroshocked into the killing chute, the chickens dismembered on the assembly line while they're still half-alive and conscious, the rabbits and donkeys and sheep the Park Service slaughtered on Santa Barbara and San Miguel and Santa Cruz islands without batting an eye—and not some white-haired upright primate who's had all the advantages of living in America instead of some third-world country and still just wants to plant himself in the grass and suck on a bottle all day long in infantile regression. Is this a fundamental inconsistency: pro-animal, anti-human? Let it be, because it's no worse than the way the eco-cops see things, and with what they're spending on brodifacoum and the helicopters to deliver it they could put up every bum in town at the Holiday Inn for a month.

His favorite bum, not that he'd ever actually give him anything and would be more than happy to see him put on a bus back to Echo Park or San Jose or whatever hole he dragged himself up out of, is a guy who must weigh three hundred pounds, always in a pair of shorts and workboots and a dirty white T-shirt the size of the sail on a Hobie Cat. He's got concrete pillars for legs and a gut that climbs up out of the shirt like a separate living thing all ready to set up on its own. His modus operandi is to stand outside whatever restaurant he's in the mood for, begging doggy bags off the pouchy sated half-looped tourists coming out the door. And don't try to hand him sushi when he wants Italian, uh-uh. Not this guy. He knows what he wants. He's discerning. He's a gourmet.

But this bum, the philosopher, has just become alerted to his presence as if he's awakened from a dream, eyes grappling toward him like fingers reaching for a ledge in the dark, and as Dave eases around the car to the driver's side, the bum, in a voice of carbon and phlegm, says, "You got a dollar?"

Key in the lock, rain on his dreads, collar turned up, and there is no anger here because he's got things to do, an appointment to keep, and no bum who isn't worth the time it takes to look at him, at his stunted eyes and deflected wrists and salvaged rain-wet black-and-red-plaid flannel shirt that droops away from him like shucked skin, is ever going to get a nickel from him, let alone piss him off enough—*You got a dollar?*—to tell him what he really thinks about the moral valence of this little interlude. He just holds up his hand like a stop sign, ducks into the driver's seat and lets the scene shift to leather and the glow of the dash and the sweet German-calibrated tune of the engine that sings the bum and the rotting newspapers and dead worms and all the rest to oblivion.

The traffic is backed up on State, but he turns onto it anyway, because he's in no hurry and he wants a look at all the stores with their newly erected Christmas displays— just, he tells himself, to get in the Christmas spirit and not at all to focus a trained eye on the hordes of shoppers and calculate who's doing what kind of business. His own stores—specialty shops for people with money who want the sixty-inch Sony LCD flat-screen wall-mounted TV and the top-of-the-line Linn electronics imported from England with the five mini-speakers and the big sub-woofer all set up for them in their media room so all they have to do is tap the remote to be engulfed in a truly theatrical experience—are never crowded, no matter the season. It's always been that way, even as he transitioned from the audiophiles of the eighties to the big-screen TV and surround-sound aficionados of the nineties and now the zeroes. No, his business is high-end, appealing to a need rather than a want, the society closing down day by day, people investing in home entertainment because they're increasingly reluctant even to go out into the backyard, let alone to the movie theater or anyplace else. His clientele is ready-made—they practically come to him—and he's always had the luxury of forgoing advertising and of locating in the more modest retail spaces off the main drag, where the rent's lower and you don't need all the bells and whistles.

Still—and he's looking at Macy's now, women parading in and out with their shopping bags strung from both arms, striding along the sidewalk with real satisfaction radiating from the play of their haunches and the no-nonsense strut of their heels—he has to admit the big displays are something, all that color and glitz, all that slick retail über-perfection that makes the shoppers want to attain über-perfection themselves, and in the easiest way possible, by spending money. Make me over. Make me well. Make my eyes bigger and my gut smaller, my calves harder and my hair fuller. Make me beautiful and success-ful and above all longed for, admired, loved. Sure, and how about a home entertainment center while we're at it?

It's just past ten but the colored lights girdling the palms are lit and softly shining against the long descend-ing backdrop of the rain-misted street, which sinks through the center of the shopping district and down through a maze of surf shops and eateries to the pier, where it intersects with Cabrillo, the Ocean Boulevard of Santa Barbara, famous as a tourist attractant and the earthly paradise of the peripatetic bum, broad, spacious, palm-lined, and stretching along the ocean from the cliffs at East Beach to the marina at its western verge, which is where he's headed. He stops for the red at the intersection, wipers intermittently snatching away the misting rain. Directly across from him is the fountain at the base of the pier, and for a moment he's distracted, thinking of the twenty-something bum in the top hat and scarlet jacket—and what is it with bums today?—who used to work the fountain with a generic Disney dog he'd dressed up in a crinoline tutu and taught to dance on its hind legs while the water leapt and flared in the background. King of the bums, that kid, the tourists lining up to empty their pock-ets for him. Of course, he's gone now, probably pushing a shopping cart down an alley someplace, the hat crushed, the dog dead, the rest of his life one long continuous road to nowhere.

And then he's thinking of the guy who could have passed for a board member of AT&T if you gave him a suit and a haircut, an industrious type who worked the sand just below the railing where beach and pier conjoin, fashioning boats out of discarded cardboard and handing them up to the tourists as they breezed past chattering in Korean, German, Swedish and New Yorkese. Nowadays the bums just spread a blanket in the sand with a cup located like a bull's-eye in the middle of it, then sit in the shade of the big pilings, passing a pint bottle of whatever it is they drink, till the tourists sink cup and blanket under a rising tide of quarters, dimes and nickels. Jesus. It's like crabbing or something. Like a sport.

A horn sounds sharply behind him. The light has changed. He looks to the rearview mirror—some asshole with his hat turned backward and his girlfriend and big yellow panting dog crowded in beside him in the front seat of an SUV—and then guns the car, shearing to one side before he rights it and rockets off down the street, not even angry, just . . . expeditious. There are two more lights to the marina, both in his favor, and at the first he slows just enough so that it goes red as he passes beneath it, trapping the asshole, who was trying to come up on him, trying to provoke him, and *Goodbye, friend. Suck on this.* A moment later he's out of the car and striding along the concrete pathway that runs along the waterfront, already digging out his card key. When he comes within sight of the wire-mesh gate erected at the entrance to the catwalk specifically to keep out unauthorized persons (read bums, and what was that story a couple years back where a sea-faring bum had got out to one of the yachts and took it for a joyride down to Ventura, where he wrecked it on the rocks?), Wilson is there waiting for him.

Wilson Gutierrez is twenty-seven, a first-rate carpenter whose mother came over from Copenhagen in the sixties and never left, and whose father, according to the check-one-or-more-boxes feature on the census form, is a white Hispanic from the west side of Santa Barbara via Culiacán, and he pronounces his name *Weel-soan*, something he's very particular about, edgy even. His eyes are blue, he wears a black silken goatee and a gold pin thrust through the auricle of his left ear that makes him look as if somebody's nailed him with a blowgun, he burns under the sun like anybody else, he's lithe as a weed but built in the shoulders, upper arms and especially forearms—"Like Popeye," he likes to say, "and it ain't from no spinach, man, but swinging a hammer all day long because I am am-bi-dextrous and you better believe it"—and Wilson is one of the three charter members of FPA, along with himself and Anise, going all the way back to its founding six months ago in direct response to what was happening out on the islands. At his feet are three visibly swollen black plastic trash bags. "What up, Dave?" he says, swinging round on him with an ear-to-ear smile that lights his face like the screen of an LCD in a darkened store window.

"Not much. You get the stuff?" And then, because he can't help himself, he's laughing aloud. "Shit," he says, bending forward to swipe his card, "it sounds like we're doing a drug deal or something."

Wilson, still grinning—or no, grinning wider: "We are."

"Sort of."

"Yeah, sort of."

And then the gate swings wide and they're hefting the bags—Wilson takes two and he takes one, because to this point they're Wilson's and he's in charge—and heading down the ramp to where the hulls of the boats wink and nod on the remains of the swell the storm has chan-neled into the mouth of the harbor. Black bags rippling and catching the metallic light in creases and crescents, noth-ing out of the ordinary, nothing anybody would think twice about, not even Mrs. Janov, coming up the ramp toward them from the *Bitsy*, a boat he hates not just for its name but for the people who own it, the type who never leave port but seem to have plenty of time to sit out on a deck chair with a drink in one hand and a pair of binoculars in the other, scoping out this thing or that and watching, always watching . . . for what? Normally he ignores her, just walks right on past no matter what inanities about the weather, the gulls, the gull shit or whatever else she spouts at him, just being neighborly and what kind of burr you have up your ass? But now, because he's feeling uplifted and right on his mark and maybe the smallest bit furtive, he treats her sealed-up face to a curt nod as he passes, the catwalk swaying beneath them and her flip-flops pounding the boards like twin jackhammers.

In the next moment they're on board the boat, sliding into the cabin like seals into a tranquil sea, and all is quiet and calm but for the faintest whisper of the drizzle on the cabin top and the salt-flecked windows of the bridge. Wilson sits heavily—or no, he throws himself down on the couch with a sigh—and announces, "Ten thousand tabs, like you said. Think that ought to be enough?"

The boat smells the way boats do when they've been sitting in a slip in the rain and cold, the head making itself known, wax and varnish and scale remover competing with the must of fungus and the damp grainy woody sea-stink the cold compacts and ferments and holds there till the sun—or the electric heater—comes to burn it off. He's already bending to flick on the heater, shifting himself around the table, adjusting to the reduced space that always makes him feel as if everything he's ever needed is right here at hand, just cast off the lines and head out to sea and forget all the rest. "You want coffee?" he asks, setting the pot on the burner. "I'm going to brew some anyway—man, that shit they served me down at the Cactus was like paint remover."

"Cream and sugar," Wilson says, flipping through a six-month-old copy of *National Geographic*. He's got his feet up. His eyes are half-closed. He is the type, when he's not working, that is, and he's definitely not working now, who can fall asleep anywhere anytime, whether it's ten-thirty in the morning on a gently swaying yacht in the Santa Barbara marina or five p.m. over a plate of deep-fried calamari on the deck at Brophy Brothers.

"I don't know," he says, easing two mugs from their hooks, "this is all just guesswork, of course. They estimate there's something like three thousand rats out there—"

"That all?"

He shrugs, a gesture that brings both mugs up to chest level, then drops them back to the counter. "Seems low to me too. But the environment's limited, I guess, not like here where you've got people. And garbage. But what's the deal with them—they're fat-soluble, right?"

"Yeah, right. Fat-soluble. B-complex and C are the water-soluble ones, meaning you piss them out. Which is why you get scurvy. Or sailors do. Or used to, in the old days. But this stuff gets stored in the body fat or the liver."

"So one shot should work? They eat this, they're protected?"

"Hell, I don't know. All I know is what I found on the Internet. Vitamin K_2, one hundred micrograms per tablet, totally natural. Says they're a 'biologically active form extracted from a fermented Japanese soyfood called *natto*.' You ever hear of *natto*?"

"No, can't say as I have." He sets the mugs down on the counter, just then noticing that one of them has a blackened ring worked into it about two-thirds of the way up. Which he chooses to ignore. "Sounds good enough to me, though. I mean, how complicated can it be—it's just a vitamin, right?" He can feel the first stirring of warmth from the heater. The kettle is just coming on to a boil. Outside, the rain has picked up again, drilling the deck, and he's suddenly transported back thirty years to the cabin of his father's boat anchored off Santa Cruz Island, a day like this, his mother at the stove making toasted cheese sandwiches—Swiss on rye with mustard and sauerkraut, her specialty—so that the air grew dense and sweet with the smell of them, and he with a cup of hot chocolate and a stack of comics, cozy, cozy and safe and enclosed. Like now. Like right here and now. "What kind of price did you get, by the way?"

Wilson sets down the magazine so he can cradle his head and stretch, his legs kicking out and the muscles bunching in his shoulders. "Thirteen bucks for a hundred, that was the come-on, but I found a site where if you buy quantity it winds up costing like three bucks off the low end of that. So an even thousand."

"You used your Visa?"

"No. A friend's. And I had it shipped to her house, in Goleta."

That sounds all right, not that anybody's going to trace it and even if they do, even if the whole thing blows up in their faces, they'll get it in the newspapers—and maybe save the rats too, because that's the bottom line here and no matter how loose-jointed he might get, that's what he has to remember: save the animals. He tilts the kettle over the brown-paper filter, fishes the half-and-half from the refrigerator. Back goes the kettle, then he's handing Wilson his cup and settling into the chair opposite him while the boat ticks and sways, making its minute re-adjustments beneath them. In that moment he's as calm as he's been since he walked into that lecture—*Alma's* lecture, and he hasn't forgotten her and what went down in the past between them even if she acts like she has, *Dr.* Alma, with all her tics and airs—and he realizes how much just being on the boat does for him. It's another world here, shut away from all the fights and hassles and the way people close in on you if you stop to take a breath. "I'll write you a check," he says.

"Whatever." Wilson shrugs, stifles a yawn.

And then he's leaning back, sipping coffee—real coffee—and thinking about the day he bought the boat ten months back—forget the cliché because it was a happy day then and it's happy now too. He got a deal, a real deal, because the people were desperate to get rid of it, the guy some sort of executive with PacifiCare, bloodless as a corpse, took it out exactly three times in the three years he'd owned it and very nearly ran it aground each time, or so the story went, the wife (once maybe, but no longer anything to look at) pursing her feather-veined lips over the details. Fatuous people. Jerks. They'd named the boat, talk of clichés, the *Easy Life*. But as he sat right here in this cabin listening to the wife go on in what was meant to be ironic fashion about the husband's seamanship, or lack of it, he knew what he would name her, as soon as the check was signed and the papers transferred, and he was thinking even then of today, of course he was, because how else was he going to make his intentions known, how else was he going to strike a blow for the animals when the animals were all the way out there across the channel where nobody could see them? And Anise—she'd been to college, but sometimes he wondered about the gaps, the yawning chasms, in her knowledge—asking, "Paladin? What's a Paladin?"

Next morning breaks clear over the water, the fog confined to a white ruff at the shoulders of the islands, the sea calm, the winds light, though the weather service is warning of another storm system moving in from the north sometime later in the day. Which might or might not affect them, depending on how long this is going to take. Or if anyone tries to stop them, which is always a possibility. Anise is asleep in the bow berth, the rhythm of her breathing punctuated by a light rasping gargle deep in the throat—a snore that periodically rises up over the throb of the engine and settles back down again. Wilson, the man who can nod off anywhere, anytime, is stretched out facedown on the couch, a blanket pulled up over his head. There's fresh coffee, for when they want it, and Anise-made sandwiches in the reefer. On the table, the three black plastic bags and the three backpacks that will receive and transport them. He hasn't got the radio on, preferring the silence. He sips coffee, watches the sea. The boat holds steady, barely a ripple on the surface.

Wilson's friend—her name is Alicia Penner and she makes the trip from Goleta all the way down the coast to Ventura five days a week to work as a secretary in the offices of the National Park Service on Harbor Way in the marina, where the sun sits in the windows and the NPS drones shuffle papers all day and think about what to kill next—has, in her humble role as a friend of the animals, pinpointed the day of the drop for them. It's not general knowledge. For all their lectures and Q&A sessions, these people aren't really interested in hearing what the public has to say—and they certainly don't want any interference, not at the museum, not in the parking lot, and especially not at the kill site, all the way out there across the belly of the gray lapping waves.

This is the day before Thanksgiving, a day when everybody's mind is on turkey and chestnut stuffing and football and champagne, and the islands, if they register at all, are nothing more than a distant blur in the mist. The Park Service plan is to hit East Anacapa first, while people are standing in line at Vons and Ralphs and Lazy Acres Market, ditching work to clink glasses at the downtown bars, nipping out to the airport to pick up Grandma and Aunt Leona, basting turkeys, geese, ducks, and then, two weeks later, when the very same people are busy Christmas shopping and planning their office parties, they'll bombard the middle and western islets. Secrecy. Privacy. Out of sight, out of mind. But what the pencil-necks in their swivel chairs haven't taken into account is that some people don't eat turkeys or geese or ducks, don't eat meat of any kind, because meat is murder and every living thing has an animating spirit and the same right to life as the humans who take it from them, butcher them, feed them into their gaping greedy jaws and toss the bones into the trash as if the thing that bore them never existed at all. And those people tend to pay attention. Real close attention.

When the island begins to climb up out of the haze and spread itself across the horizon to the south, fifteen minutes out and counting, he cuts the engine and ducks down into the cabin to nudge Anise awake. She's a heavy sleeper, a sprawler, as comatose as if she's been conked with a ball-peen hammer, and he bends to her gently, brushes the hair away from her face and leans in to kiss the corner of her mouth. Her lips are slightly parted, her lids closed on a faint stripe of eyeliner. In that instant he's involved in the heat of her, a rising radiant aura of flesh and fluids, the faint lingering scent of her perfume and the jojoba shampoo she uses, her breath sweet and moist and lush with sleep. "Hey," he whispers, "hey, Ankhesenamen, wake up. Imhotep's here."

It takes her a moment, coming back from very far off, and then her eyes ease open without a hint of surprise, as if she knew he was there all along. Her lips are warm, puffy, lipstickless. She's wearing an oversized T-shirt, pale blue to match her eyes, with her own name done up in freehand across the front and the dates and venues—Lompoc, Santa Maria, Nipomo, Buellton, Santa Ynez—of her last modest self-financed tour in support of her last modest self-financed CD scrolling down the back. "I want my mummy," she says, reaching out for him, and this is a routine that goes back to their first date, a trip to Paseo Nuevo to see the remake of the old Boris Karloff flick.

He holds the embrace just long enough, a morning hug, that's all, and then pulls away from her and straightens up. He can feel the caffeine working in him, the boat rocking like a cradle, sea air leaching in from above. What he's remembering is the first time he ever laid eyes on her, a Sunday afternoon in February or maybe it was March and she was playing at the Cold Spring Tavern high up in the San Marcos pass, opening for a grind-it-out blues band. She mounted the little five-foot-square stage with her head down, the guitar slung under one arm. He was at the bar with one of his buddies—Wilson maybe, or maybe not. Folk wasn't really his thing, but she was the whole package, a big wide-faced beauty with skin the sun had never touched and hair the color of honey hardened in the jar that reached all the way down to her knees, and—this really got him, as if all the rest weren't enough—bare feet. Those feet fascinated him, perfect, sleek, unadorned, the flexing toes and rising arch, the beat invested in the flesh. Her feet grabbed the stage and let it go, her lids fluttered shut and her head rolled back till her tongue found the words to ride out over the rhythm. She was like some kind of hippie princess resurrected from another time, out of sync, wrong, definitely wrong, but big-shouldered and confident and shining all the same. He began to listen, to tune out Wilson or whoever it was, and hear what she was projecting, a handful of covers and a skein of originals that went beyond cheating hearts and poisoned love to speak to the issues, to the way the sons of bitches were paving over the world, factory-farming animals, inserting their toxic genes into everything we drank and ate till they were inescapable. The songs weren't half-bad, he was thinking, and when she walked off the stage and disappeared out back he found himself having another cocktail and then another, and he might have forgotten all about her in the rush of conversation and the fumes of his Absolut rocks, but then the members of the blues band took the stage and halfway through the first set she appeared there in the middle of them as if she were a revenant made flesh and let her voice go on "Stormy Monday" till it made something ache high up inside him.

"Later," he tells her now, colder than any mummy, and then softens it. "Tonight," he says, "when we get back. And I'll take you to dinner. To celebrate. But right now we've got some business to do, remember?"

Stretching, her bare legs canted away from the sleeping bag and that warm, fleshy odor rising to him: "We almost there?"

He nods, already in motion. "Yeah," he says. "And

coffee's in the galley, hot, fresh and ready. I'm going to wake Wilson, okay?"

Breakfast consists of bagels, peanut butter and a fruit medley Anise put together the night before. They eat at the helm, she perched beside him on the seat, her bare legs tucked under her, spooning up fruit while he pushes the throttle forward and the boat skips over the waves. Wilson is down below, rattling around, singing snatches of something unrecognizable in a clear tuneless voice. The sun hovers and fades. Birds skew away from them and fall back in their wake. Full throttle, a bit of chop now, the bagels rubbery, too moist, the coffee setting fire to his stomach, each sliver of fruit dropping down his throat like a stone thrown from a cliff—is he going to be sick, is that it?—and then the island's right there in front of them, big as a continent.

The anchorage is on the north shore, near the eastern tip of the island, and as they motor into the mouth of the cove—rock right to the water, the cliffs wrapped around so tightly it's like heading into a cave with the top lifted off—they can see the Park Service boat moored to one of the buoys there, buoys reserved for the NPS and the Coast Guard, while the dock beyond them is for the exclusive use of the concessionaire that brings day-trippers out to the island. Everybody else has to drop anchor farther out and take a dinghy in to shore. All right. Fine. He has no argument with that—or maybe he does, because these sons of bitches act as if the place is their own private reserve when in fact it's a public resource, but that's moot now. What matters—what heartens him as he drops anchor and scans the cove—is that nobody seems to be around. No recreational boaters, no Park Service types, no Ph.D.s or birdwatchers. Just the mute black cliffs and a scurf of parched brown vegetation. And the dock, with its iron steps and railings winding up onto the plateau above.

Anise will stay with the boat, that's what he's decided. She's not going to be happy about it, but the breeze is picking up and even after he puts out the second anchor he realizes somebody's going to have to stay aboard in case of emergency—the anchorage isn't as protected as he'd like, and the last thing he wants is to come back to a boat blown onto the rocks. And he needs Wilson with him to spread the stuff, because Wilson has the mind-set and stamina to get the job done as quickly and efficiently as possible— before anybody shows up to ask what they're doing, that is—while Anise, for all her commitment to the cause, tends to dawdle, making a fuss over this plant or that or stopping to admire the view or a butterfly or the way a hawk soars and dips over the cliffs on wings of fire, already composing the song in her head. Besides, she's the most recognizable, especially with that hair and the long smooth white run of her legs no man could ignore, unless he's blind, and there aren't all that many blind park rangers, at least as far as he knows. All this comes to him as he stands on deck, scanning the shore with his Leica. Off in the distance, he can hear the barking of seals. The sea begins to slap at the hull. If it was flat-calm, dead-calm, it would be different.

Inside, in the cabin, Anise and Wilson are busy twisting open plastic bottles and upending them in the depths of the backpacks, along with a judicious measure of cat food, out of the twenty-five-pound bag, the tabs and kibble intermingled like chicken feed, not that he's ever seen chicken feed, but it's the principle, the scattering principle, he's interested in. Reach in and fling—that's what he's after. Vitamin K happens to be the antidote to brodifacoum and other anticoagulant baits, and the idea is that if the rats consume the poison pellets, well, then they'll eat the vitamins too—they'll want them, need them—and, once ingested, the vitamins will go to work neutralizing the blood-thinning properties of the bait. That's the hope, at any rate, because he's seen what the poison does and it's as cruel as anything he can conceive of—heartless, sickening—and people think nothing of it, not on the islands or in their own backyards.

He's never caught any of them at it, but his neighbors must sow d-CON like grass seed, judging from all the sick and dying animals he's found along the roads, birds especially. Jays, crows, sparrows, even a hawk. Any number of times, walking down to the post office or the beach or to have a drink in one of the bars along Coast Village Road, he's come across rats huddled on the side of the pavement, their eyes red, a bright blooming spot of blood in each nostril, quaking, suffering, unaware of him or anything else, and what of the raccoon or opossum—or dog—that comes along and scavenges the dying animal or even its corpse? They call that secondary poisoning, and he doubts if that's very pretty either.

"Okay," he says, bracing himself against the table as the boat rocks on the swell, "I don't see any helicopters, or not yet anyway—when they do the drop they're going to close off the island, and if we don't hustle out there, who knows how long before some Park Service honcho comes along and tells us we can't land at all." He hefts one of the backpacks experimentally. "Oh, and we're going to need to fit everything in just two of the packs." He glances at Anise, then drops his eyes. "The wind's up, baby. You're going to have to stay aboard. Like we discussed."

"Uh-uh. No way."

"Sorry."

"Shit," she explodes, jerking her pack across the table as if it's come to sudden vicious life before snatching it up and slamming it to the floor. "I don't want to be cooped up in here while you're out there, I don't know, *doing* things. I want to do my part. Why you think I even came?"

This is the kind of thing that goes right by him, because there aren't going to be any arguments, not here, not today, and he doesn't bother to answer. He props his own pack between table and bench, folding back the flap to expose the interior, which, he sees, is a little better than half-full. Without looking up, he bends wordlessly to retrieve her pack and invert it over his. There's a dry rattle as the tablets tick against the nylon interior, Wilson gliding forward to offer up his own pack so as to balance out the load. When they're done, when they've shrugged into the packs and adjusted their identical black baseball caps—Anise's idea, as are the black jeans and hoodies, a way of confusing their identities in the event anyone should spot them on the trail—he digs out a tube of sunblock and extends it to her. "It's not fair," she mutters, squirting a dab of the stuff in one palm and leaning forward to work it into his face and neck in a firm circular motion, her hands cold, fingers wooden, making her displeasure known.

What can he say? That he's sorry, that he'll make it up to her, that someone has to be in charge? That life is imperfect? That's she's not in kindergarten anymore and neither is he? He gets to his feet while she's still applying the stuff, impatient, nervous now, in danger of losing it, and all he can say is, "If the boat breaks anchor, you just start the engine and keep her away from the rocks till we get back. All right? You got it?"

Then they're in the dinghy, the waves jarring them like incoming rounds even though they're in the lee of the boat, and Anise is handing down the backpacks while he yanks at the starter cord on the little 20-horsepower Merc, thinking *Please God, do not let them get wet. Not now. Not after all this.* He can picture the thing flipping, the vividest image, the shock of the water, the crippling waves, he and Wilson clawing and blowing while the swamped boat slews away from them, a thousand bucks' worth of vitamin K_2 spread across the bottom of the bay and every rat on the island bleeding out its mouth and ears and anus. The wind tastes like failure, like defeat and humiliation. *It's over*, he's thinking, *over before we start.* But Wilson is sure-handed, Anise adept, and the engine catches on the second try. He shifts into gear as the dinghy drifts free on a whiff of exhaust, twists the accelerator and noses the boat toward shore.

Because of the cliffs, the only place to land is at the dock, where they'll be plainly visible, but the dock is deserted and the sky is closing in, and he wonders if the Park Service will risk flying their helicopters in weather like this. Maybe not. Maybe he and Wilson can get out in advance of the poisoners, give the rats a head start. Save them. Rescue them. Champion them. Nobody else is going to do it, that's for sure, nobody but him and Wilson and Anise, FPA, For the Protection of Animals. All animals, big and small. No exceptions. The wind's in his face, flapping the hood of the sweatshirt round his throat, the dock coming up fast—action, he's taking action while all the rest of them just sit around and whine—and he can feel the giddiness rising in him, the surge of power and triumph that rides up out of nowhere to replace the bafflement and rage and depression Dr. Reiser and his pharmaceuticals can't begin to touch. This is who he is. *This.*

There are something like a hundred and fifty steps up the cliff and onto the plateau above, and his hours on the StairMaster hold him in good stead here, he and Wilson climbing stride for stride and flinging out handfuls of kibble and rat vitamins as they go, taking pains to hit even the most inaccessible spots, and so what if the tabs tend to dribble down the rock faces? No place is off-limits to a rat. When they get to the top—humped and treeless, nothing in sight but the lighthouse and a couple of white-washed outbuildings, one of which features a plaque that says *Ranger Residence*—they decide to split up, Wilson taking the loop trail to the right and he to the left. "Okay," he says, the wind beating at him and the blood surging through him till he feels as if he could take right off and hover overhead with the gulls, "remember to hit the cliffs all along the way, not just the trail—"

Wilson is watching him from beneath the pulled-down brim of his cap, looking as if he's just heard a good joke. Or told one. "Yeah, you already said that. About six hundred times."

"And we'll meet in the middle"—the trail was an easy hike, mainly flat, two miles or less—"and cut across on a diagonal, just to make sure we cover as much territory as we can."

Wilson holds his grin, brings one fist up for a knuckle-to-knuckle rap of solidarity, and then they're going their separate ways. The sun is in retreat now, the clouds twined across the horizon to the north like weathered rope, the wind coming in gusts strong enough to rake the pellets out of his hand, and before long he's tossing the stuff as high as he can and letting the wind do the work. It's exhilarating. Like being a kid at play. The vitamin tabs are a pale yellow, the kibble rust-colored, blood-colored, and he doesn't want to know what it's composed of, doesn't want to think of offal, bone, the leavings of the slaughterhouse floor—it's enough to watch the stuff fly from his hand to loop and twist away from him like confetti.

Up the path, head down against the wind. And what if it rains? Will they postpone the drop? Will the vitamins dissolve, the kibble rot, stink, fester? He doesn't know enough about the properties of either compound to make that determination—besides which, it's too late to go back now. And even if the mix does break down, the most likely scenario has the rats eating it anyway—they're rats, after all, born to scrounge and hoard and eat till their stomachs swell like balloons—and it'll stay with them, fat-soluble, buried deep in their tissues. Who knows, maybe they'll find it so satisfying they'll ignore the cascade of blue pellets the Park Service plans to unleash on them. That's what he's thinking as he makes his way along the ridge, detouring when necessary to heave the mixture right out to the edge of the cliffs, lost in the rhythm of it—clutch, lift, release—and he begins to feel better, begins to think everything will work out after all.

He's in the moment, breathing deep, working his legs, the scent of coastal sage in his nostrils, birds hovering, lizards licking along ahead of him. Before long, he finds he's actually enjoying himself, twenty million people strung along the coast across from him and the island as deserted as it was when it rose up out of the sea. Except for Wilson, of course. And whatever Park Service types came out on that boat. And—lest he forget—the resident ranger, who's no doubt sitting on his ass in his little white house with a view to die for, reading crime novels, boiling spaghetti, blinding himself with gin.

He's off the path now—clutch, lift, release—thinking of the almost unimaginable degree of evil it must take to be a scientist in some big chemical company lab, Monsanto, Dow, Amvac, devoting all your talent and energy, your whole life, to coming up with a compound as deadly as brodifacoum and finding just the right mix of ingredients to make it irresistible, a kind of rat candy, rat cocaine, when his feet get tangled in the brush and the air goes suddenly still. It happens so fast he can't get a grasp on it, the cracked and veined earth vanishing beneath the thrust of his elbows as he pitches forward, dust in his eyes and the stones sifting away from him, flying stones, stones raking down the length of the chasm that opens up before him like a movie gone to wide-screen. *Warning: The cliffs are unstable. Stay on the path.* And then what's beneath him, beneath his torso and flailing legs, is going too, dropping away, and he with it. There's a brief moment of weightlessness and the panic that seizes him with an electric jolt, and then the blow he catches from the ledge ten feet down.

He lands on his right side, on his rib cage, the air punched out of him and the backpack wrenched askew. At first he knows nothing, and then what does he know? That he has fallen from the cliff, the unstable cliff, the friable, loosely compacted and stony cliff, and that he has not plummeted—that's the word that comes to him, a word he wouldn't use in any other context—to his death. On the rocks below. Where the sea, riding in on the swell of the storm, thrashes and foams and pulverizes. For a long moment, he's unable to move. And then, like a cat waking from sleep, he flexes each of his muscles in turn, reacquainting himself with the mode of their functioning, thinking, *Anise isn't going to believe this*, thinking, *What if I have to be rescued? What if the helicopter, the Park Service helicopter, the poisoners' helicopter—?*

The ledge, this projection of volcanic rock bristling with the spikes of xerophytic plants that has broken his fall—saved him—is one of many, a series of jagged battlements projecting from the cliffs as if to impede an invasion. He sees this, can trace the pattern that is no pattern at all up and down the rock face in both directions, as he very gingerly shifts his weight. It takes him a moment, forty-two years old and with high blood pressure and a knifing pain in his right side, before he's able to work his feet beneath him and rise, inch by staggered inch, hugging the rock. When he's fully erect and can see above him to the place where the ground gave way, he becomes aware of the shag of plants to the near side of him, *Dudleya* mostly, succulents that would snap in two, pull right out, send him *plummeting*, but something with a woody stem too, *Ceanothus* or scrub oak maybe, right there, just inside the limit of his reach. He takes hold of it. Tries it. And then, pressing himself so close to the rock that he will later find pebbles, sand, bits of leaf and twig worked under his belt and into the seams of his underwear, he lifts himself, snatching at the next handhold while the toes of his hiking boots dig for traction. Twenty seconds later he's on top, his legs churning at the loose dirt, the pack binding, his blood howling in his ears, and then he's safe, scrambling fifty feet into the brush before he collapses.

The next thing he remembers is looking at his watch. And this is the astonishing thing—only five minutes have elapsed. Five minutes. Not an hour, just five minutes, three hundred seconds, from what seemed certain death to resurrection. He is sweating, though the wind is cold, the T-shirt beneath the hoodie wet through. There's a deep blue bruise on the back of his right hand. His ribs ache. But he gets to his feet, digs out his plastic water bottle for a long hissing squeeze of the filtered water from the reverse-osmosis tank he installed in the kitchen at home, *aqua vita*, then tucks it away and starts back up the trail, mechanically scattering pellets. The decision has already been made: he will tell no one, not Anise or Wilson or Dr. Reiser, about what has just happened. Or almost happened. Why should he? He feels like enough of an idiot as it is, and as he settles back into his rhythm—clutch, lift, release—he can't help wondering how much more an idiot he would have felt if he'd had to have been rescued. Or worse: a posthumous idiot, splayed on the rocks with a crushed skull and his hips reverted, forever a totem of the Park Service, just like the pygmy mammoth. *Remember that clown? What was his name? The one that splattered himself all over the rocks trying to spread vitamin K?*

Despite the sweatshirt, he's begun to shiver by the time he spots Wilson coming along the trail toward him. The sky is uniformly dark now, the wind stronger, colder, the brush whipping, bits of chaff and seed beating past him on gusts that seem to come from every direction at once. He keeps pitching handfuls of the vitamin mix into the air, though he's beginning to understand that there will be no drop today, no helicopters hovering overhead, no rats bloodied, no authorities to dodge or confront. He's thinking he should have paid more attention to the weather report, should have been more flexible—but then he's the kind of person who makes a plan and sticks to it, which is why he's been so successful in business, never crap out, never say die, never, above all, admit you're wrong. Wilson, loping along, his right arm shooting out rhythmically to toss one handful after another of the mix over his shoulder, gives him a grin as he closes on him. "How's it?" he calls when they're still twenty feet apart. "You got any stuff left? Because I'm just about out."

They stand there together a moment, backs to the wind, and Wilson digs a pack of cigarettes out of his inside pocket. "Freakin' cold, eh?" Wilson says. "They say the weather's changeable out here, but this is"—he tucks a cigarette into the corner of his mouth, cups a hand and puts the lighter to it—"this is brutal. You know it was going to be like this? I mean, could you even guess?"

He's not complaining, just commiserating in the way of a comrade-at-arms. "Yeah, colder than shit," is all Dave can manage in response, though he appreciates the sentiment. The shock of the fall is fading, and no, he's not going to mention it, not now, not ever. It's like when he used to play football in high school—somebody blindsides you, you just get up and walk it off. The coach's face comes to him then, a joyless ego-glutted overworked sinkhole of a face above a gray sweatshirt and a shining silver whistle on a red lanyard. *Walk it off.* That's what the coach would say, even if you'd separated your shoulder or dislocated your knee.

Wilson looks to the sky from beneath the pulled-down brim of the baseball cap. "I don't know, man—feels like rain to me."

"Yeah. Me too. But at least it's going to keep the bastards out of the sky. At least for today."

"I was wondering," Wilson says, kicking the toe of one boot into the dirt at his feet, the smoke of the cigarette torn from his fingers, his eyes squinted against the blow, "if, you know, it does rain, like what is that going to do to this stuff? What if it really rains. I mean, like buckets, like the monsoon, because it's that time of year, you know. Are we wasting our time here? Is this all just going to wash away?"

If it is, he's not about to admit it. "Nah, I don't think so. And the fact that they're obviously not going to do the drop is okay too. It gives the animals a chance to store up, and even if the stuff gets wet, they're not going to care. You don't think a rat's that particular, do you?"

Wilson just shrugs. He's looking out across the water to where the horizon dissolves in a cauldron of cloud. "Shit, I don't know—that's your department. You're in charge, you tell me." A drag on the cigarette, the butt end glowing. "You're the one that wanted to come out here, right?"

"Right."

"Okay, well here we are, so let's stop gassing like a pair of old grannies in their rocking chairs and get this over with so I can sit by that heater you got and crack the champagne. Long live the rats, right?"

It takes another half hour to cover the plateau, he and Wilson branching out at a forty-five-degree angle, the wind, if anything, getting worse. When he's done, when the backpack is empty and his fingers numb and his ribs throbbing as if he's being kicked with each step he takes, he makes his way back to the trailhead to find Wilson there waiting for him, hunkered down on the steps with a paperback and another smoke. "We out of here?" Wilson asks, glancing up at him. "Yeah," he says, and then they're both bouncing down the steps, the cove expanding beneath them to reveal the Park Service boat still tied up to the buoy, and the *Paladin*—not that he was worried— still at anchor, nose to the wind and the waves streaming round it like creases on a sheet.

It isn't till they get halfway down to the landing dock that they spot the figure there, a man in a teal shirt with his back to them, busy going up and down the ladder to secure his gear in a white Zodiac inflatable tied up next to the dinghy. Since there's only one other boat in the cove and only somebody escaped from the asylum would take that thing across the channel in weather like this, he has to conclude that the man is attached to the Park Service boat. "Don't look now," Wilson says, but he's already shushing him. "No worries," he says, striding across the dock as if the man on the ladder doesn't exist.

Up close—and the guy turns around on them now, as if he can sense their presence, or, more likely, feel the reverberations of their tread radiating along the boards of the dock—he's startled by the certainty that he's seen him somewhere before. The guy hoists himself up onto the dock, no smile, and he's tall, six-three or -four, giving them an expectant look, as if he's been waiting there for them.

If it was up to him he'd just brush right by without a word, not *What's happening* or *Looks like rain* or *Fuck you*, but Wilson takes it upon himself to be their ambassador of goodwill. "Nice day," Wilson says, rolling his shoulders side to side and showing off his grin, all lips, no teeth, as if that much pure white enamel would blind anybody with its radiant power.

Still no reaction from the man in the teal shirt. Who just stands there, arms folded, as if he's waiting for something, still waiting. His shoulders are narrow, his back slightly stooped. He looks to be in his mid-thirties, his face unlined and with something of the college frat boy in it, the tight cartoon slash of a mouth sketched in under the exaggerated nose that cants ever so slightly to the left, as if it's been reshaped. Green eyes. Mud-colored hair, whipping round his head with the wind. And one more thing: a plastic nameplate, like cops wear, on the breast of his teal shirt. *Sickafoose*, it says.

So there's the wind, the dinghy jerking back on its painter, waves slapping at the pilings of the landing dock, the smell of rain on the air, the *Paladin* sitting right offshore and this jerk standing in their way. "The island's closed to the public," he says finally. "Will be closed for the next three weeks. Maybe you didn't see the sign?"

"No," he hears himself say, and he's not going to get worked up here, he's not. "No, we didn't see any sign."

Sickafoose measures out one of his long big-knuckled fingers and directs their attention to a white enameled sign the size of a regulation backboard, the squared-off admonitory letters stamped there in take-no-prisoners red. How had he missed it? Not that it would have mattered. This is public land, reserved for the public, owned by the public.

"So what are you," Dave says, "some kind of cop?"

"I'm a biologist."

"Congratulations."

Sickafoose ignores him. He's got something in his hand, in the palm of his hand, which opens in a kind of slow phalangeal striptease on a spatter of rust-red cat kibble and pale yellow vitamin tabs, even as Wilson tugs at the brim of his cap and says, "Well, we got to be going, see you later, man," and starts for the ladder.

"One minute," Sickafoose says. The hand thrusts forward. "You know what these are?"

He can feel it now, the quickening pulse of that rage the drugs can only snatch at, and it's all he can do to stop himself from spitting at the guy's feet. "Uh-uh," he says, the voice threshed in his throat. "Never saw them before."

A beat. Wilson has his hands on the ladder, ready to kick down into the boat, in retreat, and that's what he should do too—just get out of here and forget it. "You know it's against the law to feed the wildlife in a national park?" Sickafoose says. "If that's what you were doing. This is food, right?"

Another beat. Longer. Much longer. He's thinking of the rat he saw along the road one sorrowful morning, huddled there in the tight binding robe of its agony, a perfect being, perfectly made, every detail of it alive in his memory, the pale exquisitely shaped fingers and toes, whiskers brushed back as if they'd been groomed, the suppleness of the nose, the dark bloodied holes of the nostrils and the pits of the suffering eyes, all of it senseless and wrong, wrong, wrong. All he says is this: "You going to step aside or what?"

Then they're in the dinghy. Then the boat. Then the rain comes, washing across the surface in a series of sweeps that bring the waves to a boil, and forget the champagne, forget the whole thing, because the engine selects this moment, out of all the myriad others since he's owned, maintained and piloted the *Paladin* up and down the coast and out to the islands and back in every sort of weather and the most violent of seas, to fail.

Boiga Irregularis

In the mid-1950s, when the indigenous birds of Guam began to dwindle in number, and then, in the sixties and seventies, to disappear altogether, no one could trace the cause. Researchers serially suspected DDT, herbicides, habitat loss and disease, but it wasn't until the early eighties that Julie Savidge, a graduate student doing field work for her Ph.D., focused on a hitherto little-noticed reptile that first appeared on Guam just after World War II. The brown tree snake, native to Australia, Malaysia and New Guinea, was thought to have arrived as a stowaway in a crate of munitions, the engine compartment of a military vehicle or perhaps the wheel well of a Navy transport plane. Its appearance had been duly recorded but very few people came into contact with it. Nonetheless, having eliminated the other possible causes, Savidge decided to plot the snake's spread from the main port at Apra to the southern, eastern and northern verges of the island, and found that she was able to correlate its expansion with the progressive topographical decline of the island's avifauna. The mystery had been solved. The problem remained.

In fact, when the brown tree snake reached the island, it found itself in an ophidian paradise. The only other species of snake on Guam, an innocuous thing the size of an earthworm, was no competition at all, and there were no predators to limit its numbers. The food supply, consisting of some eighteen species of birds found nowhere else in the world, was rich and abundant, and the birds, in common with other insular species, suffered the sort of naïveté to predation that had doomed the dodo and its ilk. *Boiga irregularis* lives in equilibrium with the other species in its native environment, and isn't particularly impressive or dangerous as snakes go. For one thing, its venom, distributed through fangs located at the back of the throat, is relatively mild and only marginally a threat to humans. For another, it is nocturnal and thus rarely seen, and so reedy—no thicker around than a man's index finger until it reaches a length of three feet or so—as to pale in comparison with some of the snakes of the continental tropics, the cobras, boomslangs, mambas and water moccasins that slither through the herpetophobe's nightmares.

Still, it has proven to be one of the most insidious and successful invaders on record, reducing those eighteen species of unique birds to eleven, of which two—the Guam rail and the Micronesian kingfisher—exist only in captivity, while six are considered rare and three uncommon. The snake's density—up to 13,000 per square mile—is among the highest recorded densities of any snake anywhere, and it has proven infinitely adaptable, feeding quite happily on the island's native frogs and lizards in the absence of the birds, as well as snapping up introduced geckos, skinks, cane toads and just about anything else it can work its jaws around. It grows to some ten feet in length. It appears in toilets, showers, infants' cradles. Since 1978, 12,000 power failures have been attributed to its climbing electrical poles and shorting out the carrying wires—unintentionally, of course, but knocking out lights, computers and refrigerators all the same. Above all things, it is a climber. A great and undaunted and increasingly voracious climber that has adapted its diet to include pet food as well as pets—in one documented case, a three-week-old golden retriever pup—and anything, alive or dead, that carries the scent of meat. Or blood.

Alma is reminded of all this by the printout—"The Use of Acetaminophen in Controlling *Boiga irregularis* Among Insular Populations"—spread open beside her laptop on one of the gently rocking Formica tables in the main cabin of the *Islander,* bound for Anacapa. Sipping coffee from a paper cup and staring into the computer screen as the neatly marshaled lines of type hypnotically rise and descend along with the tabletop and the deck and hull beneath it, she's not yet aware she has a headache coming on, but every sixty seconds or so she looks reflexively away from the screen and out over the water so as to refocus her eyes. Then she comes back to the text, hits the backspace key and inserts a new phrase or extends a line, her lips silently forming the words. She's frowning but unaware of it.

The boat's carrying capacity, both in the cabin and on the upper and stern decks, is a hundred-fifty or so, and today, eighty-five of the spots have been reserved for NPS employees and assorted biologists, including Tim, who are part of the Anacapa Recovery Program, as well as a collection of journalists from the AP, the *Los Angeles Times* and the *Santa Barbara Press Citizen*, a dozen local politicians and tastemakers and a television crew from the local NBC affiliate. In the ship's hold are three big coolers chock-full of marinated chicken, turkey sausage and tofu burgers for the barbecue grill, various salads, whole-grain breads, a pot of chili and rice, a fourth cooler of bottled water, soft drinks and dessert, and a fifth reserved exclusively for champagne. Two cases. On ice. Medium-priced California stuff, as befits the Park Service budget, but champagne—or, more properly, sparkling wine—all the same.

The sea is flat, the fog already lifting. The captain has just slowed for a pod of dolphins, and most of the passengers—NPS people, tourists, backpackers, a sugar-and-hormone-fueled group of sixth graders under the rapidly eroding control of two harried teachers—have gone out on deck to watch the glistening cetaceans slash through the water like shadows come to life. When she glances up she can see Tim out there amongst them, a paper cup of coffee in one hand, binoculars in the other.

It's early June, ten in the morning, just over one and a half years since the initial drop of the control agent, and the purpose of this little jaunt is purely celebratory—while the journalists tap at their keyboards and the photographers manipulate their digital cameras and the TV crew homes in, Alma will lift a glass of champagne in faultless synchronization with Freeman Lorber, the park's superintendent, and declare all three islets that compose Anacapa one hundred percent rat free. At the moment, she's busy polishing her press release, while the article, by Robert Ford Smith, the herpetologist she'd worked under on Guam, awaits a free minute. It came to her via e-mail from the field station at Ritidian Point on the northernmost tip of the island, where the beaches are soap-powder white and the vegetation gnarled and snake-haunted, before she left her office at seven-fifteen this morning, and she's as eager to get to it as a child with a new video game, but duty calls, always calls, and always takes precedence.

The press release, which she's been tinkering with for the past two days, will inform the assembled journalists, and through them the public, that the rat-eradication project has been an unqualified success. No rat sign has been detected anywhere on Anacapa since the release of the control agent, neither nests nor scat or tracks or any evidence whatever of predation, and the dummy eggs the consulting ornithologist has slipped into the nests of various birds have not been disturbed, whereas formerly they would have been scrimshawed with tooth marks. Careful monitoring over this period has led her to be able to declare with absolute confidence that all the target animals have been eliminated. And the result has been swift and dramatic. The seabirds have rebounded, not to mention the Channel Islands salamander and side-blotched lizard—whose numbers have doubled—as well as the native deer mouse, the population of which is estimated at 8,000, the highest count on record. And more: Tim Sickafoose, consulting ornithologist, resident humorist and all-around prince of a man, has discovered the first pair of Cassin's auklets nesting on Rat Rock in living memory, a place which, she imagines—and yes, this will be the sly and triumphal joke to insert in an otherwise by-the-numbers text—will soon have to undergo a name change. How about Auklet Rock? she's thinking. Do I hear any takers? Or what about Sickafoose Point? Will that fly?

Jokes aside, she can't help worrying over the small details—punctuation, paragraphing, the drum-beating phrases that seem increasingly fatuous every time her eyes fall on them. Or not just fatuous: asinine. Right here, right in the first paragraph, for one. She calls Lorber "a monument of preservation," which conveys a modicum of truth, but doesn't it make him sound like something static, like one of the carved heads at Mount Rushmore or a blade dulled by use? Or worse: dead. And here's his epitaph: *Loving husband, loving father, and* a monument of preservation.

"Hey," Tim breathes, sliding into the seat beside her. The boat has begun to move again and the passengers are trooping back into the cabin, all but the sixth graders, who will linger along the rail until they're soaked through and shivering and in dire need of the hot chocolate, popcorn and microwave burritos the galley dispenses. "You done with that thing yet?" he asks, his voice oily with insinuation. She gives him a sidelong glance. He's right there, invading her personal space—which is the prerogative of a lover, she has to remind herself—and holding his lopsided grin. "Because there's a point you reach where you're just going to tinker it to death, right? And isn't this supposed to be a party, or am I wrong?"

She's on the verge of snapping at him, but she catches herself. For a long moment she stares into his eyes, the spray flying beyond the windows, the squeals and shouts of the sixth graders rising round them like the cries of the raptured. "Yes," she admits finally, and she can smile now too, relax, celebrate, because he's right—the worst is behind her and this is a day for looking ahead, not back. "Yes, you're right."

And it works. The air's been cleared. Her headache—the incipient headache she's just begun to become aware of—extends its tendrils and begins to recede all in a single moment. She shifts the mouse, shuts down the laptop and dips forward to reach into her pack and dig out a bag of trail mix, just to keep her energy level up. Party or no, she'll still have to make a speech after distributing the press release, and she'll have to oversee her assistant, Wade, who's in charge of the food, and shine with glowing interest as Freeman gives his own speech replete with awkward pauses, furious lip-tugging and jokes amusing by definition only. But this *is* a party, or the very beginning of one, and she slips her laptop into its case with a definitive shrug of her shoulders and a business-like chafing of one palm against the other, then cracks the Ziploc bag of trail mix. She sifts a handful into her mouth and works her molars over a cud of sunflower seeds, dates, raisins and M&M's, the sugar rush almost instantaneous, before offering it to Tim, who takes it absently. He's giving her a dubious look, as if he's thinking about something else altogether, as if he's anticipating her, worrying for her. "You better hope the printer out there's going to work—"

Her smile is richer now, spreading across her lips till she can feel the tug of it in the muscles at the corners of her mouth, and what are they called? Zygomaticus major. Or minor. Or both. That sounds about right, but it's been a long time since she took anatomy, and if she remembers correctly something like seventeen different muscles are required to achieve a full smile. But that doesn't matter. The important thing is she's smiling because this is Tim smiling back at her and they're getting a rare day off together, if that's what you can call this.

"He don't know me very well, do he?" she says, reaching down to pat the backpack at her feet. "I brought my own along. Just in case." Before he can respond, she's holding up a hand to forestall him. "Yes," she says, "yes, I know. And paper too."

She'd gone to Guam seven years ago because the opportunity presented itself, because Julie Savidge was one of her enduring heroes and because she'd just broken up with Rayfield Armstrong, who played his guitar in the bars and coffeehouses around Berkeley when he wasn't working on his dissertation assessing the impact of a species of introduced crab—the European green—on the local invertebrates in San Francisco Bay, and whose chest, shoulders and back were so intricately and finely muscled from all the hours he spent in the water he looked like a living mosaic. She'd moved in with him, and that was a commitment, the first real commitment of her life, but as the months wore on he depleted her patience and her hope and goodwill too. He was never home, always diving, strumming his guitar under the gaze of a spotlight in some bar or coffeehouse somewhere or riding a Greyhound bus to play in towns nobody had ever heard of, and when he was home he was so self-absorbed—crabs and guitar, crabs and guitar—he didn't seem to have much time for her. And so she moved out. And took a job in the field. In Guam.

What she expected to find there was something like the environment she'd known in Hawaii, only less developed, more primitive, closer to the edge, and she wasn't disappointed. The roads, hacked out of the bush, were congested and deadly, the architecture tended toward reinforced concrete block (out of necessity, as a way of surviving the typhoons in this corner of what meteorologists dubbed "Typhoon Alley") and everything, even the inside of the plastic bleach container she kept under the sink in her bunker cum one-room apartment, smelled of the festering explosive microbial life of the tropics. The jungle was lush, but many of the native trees, destroyed during the war, had been replaced by a South American import, the tangantan-gan, and it was eerily silent in the absence of the birds. With the birds gone, the insects had bred out, with the attendant result that the spiders—palm-sized, with iridescent yellow stripes on a gleaming black body—had experienced a population explosion, draping understory and canopy alike with the great trembling tents of their webs so that it was impossible to move through the jungle without having the stuff cling to you like a second skin. Not to mention the spider itself, presumably disappointed at being displaced from its web to your sleeve, hair, face.

The local people—Chamorros and Filipinos, mainly—never gave her much more than a vaguely curious glance. They saw her as Asian, or some variant thereof, and so, despite her Big Dogs running shorts and T-shirts touting Micah Stroud and Carmela Sexton-Jones, less an anomaly than someone like Robert Ford Smith or his wife, Veronica, both from Lancashire, with great beaky English noses and skin as blanched and lusterless as potato meal. She felt at home, as she had in Hawaii and at Berkeley, and perhaps she would have felt differently if she'd gone to lily-white Wisconsin to study the effects of cat predation on woodland birds or to Salt Lake City to monitor the grebe population on the Great Salt Lake, but she hadn't.

Robert—not Bob or Rob or Robbie, just Robert—was in his mid-fifties and had been working to undermine the brown tree snake since the time of Julie Savidge, who'd since moved on. He was funded by the U.S. Department of Agriculture as part of the Brown Snake Research Program and his primary objective was to devise barriers to keep the snake away from the shipping containers at the port and the planes at the airstrip, the fear being that it would hitchhike to one of the neighboring islands—or worse, Hawaii. That was the first step—to limit its spread—but the second, and larger initiative, was to find some biological agent, a bacterium, virus or parasite, that could control its numbers so that the captive-bred native birds could be reintroduced. To that end, he trapped snakes and experimented on them. And her job, both in daylight and at night, with a headlamp and a stick to clear away the spiderwebs, was to check the traps and return to the lab with her clutch of snakes—there were always plenty—so that she could dissect them and determine what they'd been feeding on. It was solitary work—"creepy," as Tim, no fan of snakes, would describe it—but it got her out of doors,

114

which was the whole point of working in wildlife management to begin with.

There were three hundred sixty-five days in a year, that was incontrovertible, but in the three years she was on the island it seemed as if time had become elastic, stretching like a finely gradated bungee cord till a single day felt like two or even three. She learned to do without culture—American culture anyway—and while she did make several Guamanian friends and attended their various family gatherings and fiestas and came to relish octopus *kelaguen* and breadfruit stewed in coconut milk, she never went native as so many of the others at the field station invariably did. Her time was for the most part solitary and she moved through the bush like a native creature herself—smallish, with abundant pelage, keen observational powers and a reflexive ability to duck branches draped with spiderwebs. She trapped snakes in a wire basket in which a second much smaller wire basket held a white mouse and its ration of chopped potato, stuffed them in a sack and brought them back to the field station, where she removed, euthanized and dissected them or fitted them with miniature radio collars and let them go again to see exactly what they were up to.

The snakes were whips of muscle, powerful enough to raise three-quarters of their length up off the ground and hold it there for minutes at a time, but her muscle, a primate's muscle, was superior. She killed thousands of them. She was bitten half a dozen times. She became intimate with the peculiar dry pickled odor of the brown snake's intestines. And she found, contrary to popular opinion or the first law of amateur snake collectors, that this snake did not require live prey or even prey at all. It was so adaptable as to be frightening. When the birds were gone, it ate rats and lizards. And when it couldn't find a rat or lizard, it came into the yard and the house and snapped up what it could, whether animate or not. Twice, while slitting open the bellies of snakes, she came across pale greasy twists of the plastic raw hamburger is packaged in. And once, in an image worthy of Buñuel, she discovered the stained white tube of a used sanitary napkin, saturated in blood. Even now, when she closes her eyes at night, she can see the snakes in the twilight of her consciousness, erect and weaving their heads, looking for the purchase to climb.

Tim chatters. The boat hydroplanes. Her stomach flutters around the fragments of trail mix and the coffee she's washed it down with, but she doesn't get seasick—she never does. It's a question of mind over matter—or rather, mind over peristalsis. And reflux. Some people can control it and some can't. Tim, for instance. Tim's a rock. He could eat a seven-course dinner and ride the roller coaster at Magic Mountain all day long and it wouldn't affect him in the slightest—in fact, if it weren't for the centrifugal forces involved he could probably tuck in his napkin and chow down *while* on the coaster. A number of the passengers are a bit more delicate, though, including at least one of the journalists this little jaunt is meant to win over, and Alma can't help feeling a prick of anxiety. Toni Walsh, of the Santa Barbara paper, which to this point has been less than enthusiastic over the rat issue and the ensuing question of pig control on Santa Cruz, came aboard looking as if she'd had a rough night, and as soon as they left the harbor she settled in at a table by the window and put her head down, feigning sleep. Now, when they're no more than a mile out, she rises abruptly and staggers outdoors to the stern, where the wind can carry off whatever she's had for breakfast. Not a good start. And of course, just to needle her, Tim lifts his eyebrows and whispers, "There's a shitty write-up in the making."

As the boat slows and they cruise into the dock, the sun cutting through what's left of the mist in great rectilinear columns, the cliffs rearing, birds squawking, everyone seems to come alive. People who've been silent the whole way across are suddenly gabbling in high excited voices, the sixth graders are uncontainable—What are *they* getting out of this, she wonders, besides sugar and sunburns?—and the faces of her office mates have that rare look of release she sees only on Friday afternoons. She's right there in the middle of it, helping people up the ladder, making small talk, bantering, even drawing a smile from Alicia, the pale shy secretary who seems locked up like a box without a key, and then she's shaking hands with Fausto Carrillo, the mayor of Oxnard—he's all smiles—and guiding a shaky Toni Walsh to the levitating rungs of the ladder.

There's a brief conference with Wade, then out come the coolers, lifted from the hold and propelled across the sun-blasted planks of the dock with a whoosh of molded plastic, all the details settled, the picnic in its nascent stages and nothing left to do but distract everybody with what she hopes will prove to be the highlight of the day, the nature walk. While Wade and some of the others go on ahead to light the charcoal and set up the portable picnic tables in the courtyard of the visitor center—a spot calculated to move even the palest driest desk-bound cynic with its views across the channel—she and Tim, as planned, begin working their way up to the bluff to lead the group hike along the loop trail. She reminds herself to go slowly, especially up the steps, pausing at each landing to flag one plant or another and give the less fit a chance to catch their breath. Once they get to the top, where the walking is easy, she'll have ample opportunity to score points for the principles and rationale of island restoration, indicating the nests of the western gull and other recovering birds while subtly but unfailingly bringing home the point that all this has been made possible by the rat-control project, which, incidentally, was funded by a court judgment against one of the gross polluters of the ecosystem—Montrose Chemical Corporation, responsible for pumping over a hundred tons of DDT-contaminated waste into Santa Monica Bay between 1947 and 1982—and so cost taxpayers virtually nothing.

In her detail-oriented way, she's reminded each of the guests through repeated e-mails to dress appropriately for what should be a moderate two-mile hike in changeable weather conditions, and most seem to have gotten the message. She sees hiking boots and windbreakers, daypacks, water bottles and the like, but Toni Walsh, bringing up the rear in a pair of blood-red espadrilles, cropped crepe pants in a jungle print and a spandex tube top—sans jacket or sweater—is already hugging her arms to herself and looking as if she's in need of a cigarette. Or no, Alma corrects herself, that's cruel and judgmental—she doesn't even know if the woman smokes. But then all writers smoke, don't they? And drink? And sit in front of computer screens till their arteries clog and muscles atrophy? Tim has the floor at the moment, telling those gathered round him something of the nesting habits of the gulls, how they pair for life and defend the same patch of ground year after year and will attack and even kill any chick from a neighboring nest that might blunder onto their turf, so she gives him a truncated wave of her hand and makes her way back down the trail, thinking she'll offer Toni Walsh the extra windbreaker she's brought along for just such a contingency as this.

The trail is half an inch deep in dust the consistency of waffle mix. The sun has burned off the mist by now but there's a wind out of the north that brings the chill factor down into the low fifties, she guesses, and as she eases past people ("What's with you, Alma," the mayor jokes out of a flushed moon face, his eyes exophthalmic and his tongue licking for air, "giving up so soon?") and down a gentle incline to where Toni Walsh seems to be struggling to put one foot in front of the other, she's already got the windbreaker out of her pack and bunched in her hand. Though her intention is obvious, the reporter—what is she, forty,

forty-five?—just stares numbly at her. "You okay?" she asks.

"Me?" Toni Walsh hasn't bothered with makeup, not even lipstick. Her shoes are coated in dust. Her hair, dyed an unnatural shade of red, hangs limp at her shoulders, over-processed and dry as the bunch grass at their feet. "Oh, yeah, I'm fine. Just not used to boat rides, I guess. In the morning anyway."

"You look cold." Holding out the windbreaker now. "I've got this if you want it. It's extra, so—"

There's something in the woman's face that warns her off and she feels embarrassed suddenly, as if she's been attempting in some unconscious way to bribe her, or at least curry favor, but that's not the case. She's just being accommodating, that's all, because everyone here is in a sense her guest, and a good host . . . or just common courtesy . . .

"No, no, thanks," Toni Walsh says, and she's fishing in her purse for—yes—a cigarette. Which she puts to her lips and lights in a windblown puff of smoke. There's goose-flesh on her upper arms. Her eyes are red-veined. The ends of her hair, split and eroded, flail round her throat.

Alma drops her arm awkwardly, the rejected garment catching the wind till it flaps like a pillowcase on a clothes-line. "If you want, you can just go back to the visitor center and have a cup of hot coffee—Wade'll have the fire going by now—or wine, if you want a glass of wine. We won't be long."

Toni Walsh looks over her shoulder to where the white monolith of the lighthouse rises up out of the scrub against the broad bright pan of the ocean, the light spanked and coppery, the thin distant sail of a yacht like a scrap of cloth blown on the wind. The rest of the group has begun to move off now, Tim, his shoulders slumped, loping on ahead of them, talking all the while. "Yeah," Toni Walsh says finally, puckering her lips to exhale a lungful of smoke and watch the breeze snatch it away, "that sounds cool. Think I'll just do that."

Later, after she's caught up to the group to add her comments and exhortations to Tim's running monologue and the hikers have had an opportunity to absorb something of the island's rare solace and beauty on their own, she begins to forget herself, trying to imagine the experience through their eyes, as if she were seeing the place for the first time. It's not all that different geologically from what they'd find along the coast opposite, where Highway 1 bends away from Port Hueneme and the cliffs stagger back from the breakers under a mantle of coreopsis and coyote brush, except that there is no highway, there are no roads or buildings or trash. And it's quiet, as quiet as the world must have been before the invention of the internal combustion engine, the sea and the wind providing the backdrop to the barking of the seals and the mewling of the birds. Sometimes, when she's out here alone, she can feel the pulse of something bigger, as if all things animate were beating in unison, a glory and a connection that sweeps her out of herself, out of her consciousness, so that nothing has a name, not in Latin, not in English, not in any known language.

Today, of course, she's too wound up to get to that point or anywhere even close. Yet still everything looks fresh and eternal at once, wildflowers in bloom, the views unencumbered, the gulls cooperative, lizards exploding underfoot as if to underscore the point that the rats are gone and all is well. The hikers are enjoying themselves, she can see that, the hands-on experience of the place worth a thousand press releases. And isn't this what she took the job for to begin with—to familiarize the public with the specialness of these islands and by extension all the dwindling retreats of the world made so much more precious by their rarity? To turn them on? Make them advocates? Engage them in the fight against the land-grabbers and developers and people like Dave LaJoy, who might mean well, or think they do, but act solely out of ignorance and vindictiveness?

She's left her hair loose and the wind takes hold of it, flinging it across her face, and when she shakes her head to settle it, any thought of Dave LaJoy and the rest of the self-appointed saviors is gone. She shuts her eyes, lifts her face to the sun. This is perfect. A perfect day. She feels like a conqueror, like a queen, like the first Chumash woman come ashore ten thousand years ago. She's soaring. High on the moment. And the feeling sustains her for a whole thirty seconds—until she thinks to glance at her watch, that is. How did it get so late? They're ten minutes behind schedule, ten minutes at least.

She feels a familiar stab of unease, swings round and maneuvers herself to the front of the group, beside Tim. He's made a platform of a rock the size of an ottoman and he's standing atop it, arms akimbo, sunglasses dangling from one hand. The frayed baseball cap he hung on the bedpost last night so as not to forget it is pulled down tightly over his brow, leaving the lower half of his face to incandesce in the sun. At the moment, he's delivering a synopsis of the burrowing owl's habits and predilections, and the hikers have gathered round him to reflect on the cored-out habitation of the creature itself, which proves to be absent. She clears her throat to get their attention. "Anybody getting hungry?" she asks. "Because I sure am."

Well, they are. Of course they are. There is an unspoken quid pro quo here. Whenever she leads a group hike for PR purposes, there's always the promise of a good and bountiful free lunch and the chilled wine to go with it. One of the hikers, a stout woman in an unfortunate straw hat that whips round her face in the wind till it's like one of those plastic hoods the veterinarians use on dogs—and is she the mayor's wife or his special friend?—looks particularly ready, so Alma focuses her smile on her. "All right then. Follow me."

Then she's leading them down the trail and back to

where Wade and his helpers, Alicia among them, have set out the meats, salads and other dishes on a long table made festive with a crisp white cloth and a vase of wild-flowers. Beyond the table, in the near distance, the light-house stands burnished and welcoming under the sun, the sea fanning out in a dazzle of color beneath it, everything companionable and inviting. Like a party. Exactly like. The hikers break ranks as they approach, what had been single file giving way to drift, people talking in low voices, chug-ging from water bottles, joking in the spirit of camarade-rie a shared experience of nature always seems to bring out. Alma's eyes flit critically over the scene, not keeping score exactly, but noting who's elected to stay behind and trying to get a quick take on their various moods and postures—do they look hungry, bored, pleased? That sort of thing. It's almost a reflex with her.

She spots Toni Walsh standing on the far side of the fire pit, a glass of wine in one hand, cigarette in the other, chatting up Alicia. Alicia? But then Alma can't con-trol everything and whatever Alicia—dark-eyed, stylish, twenty-something, about as talkative as a stone—can tell Toni Walsh probably won't amount to much and certainly can't hurt the cause. Alicia's a secretary, that's all, and she's stolidly efficient, if bloodless, but she's had no train-ing in restoration ecology except what she's picked up by osmosis, and Alma doesn't doubt for a minute it'd be all the same to her if she worked in industry or service or for the polluters themselves.

In fact, she's remembering a time when she and Alicia were alone in the office, working late on a paper the super-intendent was going to deliver before a gathering presided over by the secretary of the interior, Alma reading proof aloud and Alicia checking it against her own copy. It was fairly dull going—Freeman was no Rachel Carson—and at some point they took a break and went out on the deck to watch the fog tangle itself in the shrubs. Alma found herself doing the talking, trivial things mostly, nothing to do with work, and if Alicia didn't want to open up, even then, when things were more relaxed than during regular working hours and the boss-employee dynamic might have constrained her, Alma could understand that. But to get the girl to say anything, about her boyfriend, her parents, a movie she'd seen—the weather even—was all but impossible. With her it was always yes or no or uh-huh—if she had any opinions, she kept them to herself. And yet on this occasion—just this once—she did speak up, apropos of nothing. Or, as Alma later realized, of a minor point Freeman was making with regard to biological control in closed ecosystems.

"I don't know why we have to kill everything," she said, studying her nails, which had been done in two colors, aquamarine and raspberry, and speaking in a voice so soft it was barely audible. No eye contact. Eye contact would be confrontational, assertive, and Alicia, if anything, was non-assertive, more the vessel than the substance that fills it. "What if we just left everything alone like the world was before us—like God made it. Wouldn't that be easier?"

Alma had been stunned. To think that this girl, this young woman, this locked box of a personality, had been working and breathing and thinking amongst them since she left community college, and she'd absorbed nothing? Zero? Zilch? And maybe she could have responded more gently, more in the tutorial mode, in the way of the educator she ostensibly was, but that was the end of the conversation and of Alicia's attempt to reach out and engage the issues, because Alma, her voice gone flat, said, "But that's exactly wrong, don't you see? Because we're the ones who put the animals there, the sheep and cattle and pigs on Santa Cruz and Santa Rosa, the rats on Anacapa and cats and rabbits on Santa Barbara, and it's our obligation, our *duty*"—and then she was lecturing, she couldn't help herself, and Alicia never raised her eyes from the nest of her hands and never said another word that wasn't yes or no or uh-huh.

At any rate, she reminds herself yet again, this is a party and she should just let go, at least for today. She tries out a smile and a little wave for Toni Walsh and Alicia, clasps hands with half a dozen people and casts a quick glance over the table. Wade—with Alicia's help—has done his job well, as usual, and everything's ready to go. Beautifully. Swimmingly. And if there's a detail that's escaped her, some niggling thing she feels sure she's forgotten as if she's trapped in one of those early-morning dreams where she's late for class or the airplane or can't find her blouse or brassiere or jeans, it'll just have to remain undiscovered. Determined, she lifts an empty glass from the table and wades into the crowd, going from one group to another to encourage them to step up to the buffet, the smell of roasting meat shifting with the wind in promise of what's to come, and there's nothing more primal, more celebratory, the animal itself plucked out of the bush and offered up to the tribe. People are beginning to form a ragged line now, taking up plates and silverware and the paper cups she insisted on rather than plastic because plastic is the devil's polymer, but that's another issue, and she erases the thought from her mind as soon as it arises.

She waits and watches, the anticipation building in her as people work their way through the line, filling their plates, pausing to chat in groups of three and four or exchange pleasantries with Wade and some of the others dishing up the food. As soon as the last couple (the mayor and his wife, definitely his wife, and what's her name—Yolanda?) have entered the line, she snatches a dripping bottle of Piper Sonoma from the ice as if it's a living thing, raises it high and begins rapping a spoon against the base of it in a sharp peremptory way. "Attention, everybody!" she calls, whirling about to draw their eyes to her. "The time has come to gather round for champagne"—holding her grin, watching their faces—"because we've got some toasting to do here."

And now Wade's beside her, furiously untwisting the

wire from one bottle after another, the corks jumping in succession and people crowding in with their paper cups as the bottles go round. Laughter rings out. There are sallies, quips. Freeman, a plate in one hand, glass in the other, makes his way to her. The TV camera, shining and insectoid, moves in. Smiles abound. When all the glasses are full and she's feeling a rush of triumph and vindication as purely satisfying as anything she's ever known, she lifts her glass and Freeman follows suit. She holds it there for one climactic second, and then, grinning so furiously she can barely form the words, she sings out, "To Anacapa, one hundred percent rat free!"

On Guam, there was no champagne, because Guam wasn't snake free and never would be. There were too many species involved, too much vegetation, too many invasives, too perfect a pest. Half a dozen times Robert teased himself into thinking he had a solution, the last being a virus able to survive only in cold-blooded creatures, and he busily inoculated snakes with the pathogen and set them free, but the pathogen didn't take and there was no noticeable change in the population numbers. He used to joke that the only way to eliminate them would be to nuke the island, and even then it was his bet that some would survive, hidden in a crack in a wall or coiled in a lead pipe. Once, when she was working in the field with him, they discovered a length of PVC tubing no more than half an inch thick and there were six snakes wedged in it, aligned like the wires of a conduit. And now, according to the article he'd sent her, he had a new hope: acetaminophen. Simple, cheap, the active ingredient in Tylenol. A blood thinner, like brodifacoum, but far more selective in what it kills.

Early experiments had been promising. Two three-hundred-milligram tablets, delivered in the carcass of a dead mouse, would kill a brown tree snake, through internal bleeding, in three hours. Yes. But how to deliver it? Robert and his colleagues had air-dropped a thousand

Tylenol-laced mice over a carefully cordoned-off section of forest, but most had become hung up in the branches and gone to rot before the snakes could discover them and there was the further question of what the bait would do to non-target animals. Plus, how many mice would it take? How many drops? There were estimated to be upward of two million snakes on the island and even if the staggering amount of funding for that kind of operation could be raised and even if the agent was found to be non-reactive with other animals, the chances that all the snakes could be eliminated was, roughly—or no, exactly—zero. They were there for good. And so the native trees would continue to decline because there would never be birds sufficient to broadcast their seeds, and the spiders and insects would thrive, and in a hundred years, fifty, Guam would no longer be Guam.

The sun is in her eyes and she has to pinch them shut to tip back her head and allow the cool affirmation of the wine to trickle down her throat. She will give her little speech, hand out her press release, lie back on a blanket with Tim and watch the birds slip overhead against a sky drawn back to the infinite. This will be her reward, her peace, her joy. She has been an instrument of good, striking down the invaders that plagued her grandmother in her distress all those years ago and for all the years hence wrought havoc on the eggs and unfledged chicks of the birds that evolved to roost and breed in a ratless world. Well, she's given them back that world. Given them a chance. And now, as she's about to avow publicly on the raising of the next glass, she is prepared to move forward, undaunted, with the aid and guidance of Freeman Lorber and all the other incomparable people of the National Park Service, Channel Islands, to the far bigger challenge of Santa Cruz.

"Santa Cruz!" she'll call out, the bludgeoning trochee rising from deep inside her like a war cry while they lift their glasses in unison, in support and encouragement and as a mark of their commitment to the cause, right-thinking people, educated people, caught up in the intoxication of the moment in this place she's come to love more than any other on earth, more than Hawaii, more than the Berkeley Hills, more even than Guam. "On to Santa Cruz!"

And then it's the next morning, a Sunday, fresh-squeezed orange juice, bagel with cream cheese, the newspaper. Tim's habit is to sleep late whenever he can and today is no different. When she slipped out of bed at her usual time— six-thirty—he was hunched under the blankets, breathing lightly, looking as if he'd sleep till noon, and she saw no reason to wake him. Let him sleep. Her life isn't like one of those soft-focus movies where couples moon at each other over poached eggs and coffee out of cups the size of salad bowls and then stroll hand-in-hand along the beach— no, it's real, and she has a real relationship with a living breathing man who likes to sleep later than she does. And so what? Good for him. Tim has his life, she has hers. And when they intersect, so much the better.

Outside, the fog is already lifting, the sun emerging as a pale presence among the trunks of the trees, till suddenly, in a single burst, it slices through the window to illuminate the kitchen, taking hold of the stainless-steel knobs of the oven and the glass lens of the clock on the far wall. The yard jumps to life. The begonias fire. Morning in Montecito. She's had a lazy glance at the headlines—Bush and his war—and filed the dishes away in the dishwasher. There won't be anybody on the beach this early but for a handful of dog walkers and joggers, or at least that's her hope, and so she slips on her sneakers and heads out the door and into the morning.

On down the block, past the hotel and its Lucullan expanse of lawn, the air cool and fresh still and no cars moving along the access road out front. Cutting diagonally across the blacktop, she takes the direct route to the stairway down to the beach. She doesn't follow the tide charts—no time to bother, and besides she'd rather be surprised—and so she feels a little lift to see the expanse of wet sand running out to the flats cobbled with the slick dark mounds of boulders rubbed smooth by the twice-daily shifting of the waters. Low tide. When the tide's up full, the waves beat at the seawall and she's reduced to taking the sidewalk above it. This beach, directly across from the long tan smudge of Santa Cruz on the horizon, doesn't catch the big waves, which tend to run lengthways down the channel, and so isn't especially interesting as far as beaches go. It's pretty, no doubt about it, but there isn't much by way of tidepools and relatively little washes ashore. Aside from trash. And dogshit wrapped in neat little plastic bags. Does that drive her crazy? Yes, it does. That people should take something natural, waste, feces, the end product of an animal process, and seal it in plastic for future archaeologists to unearth from the landfill in a thousand years is pure madness. This world. This skewed and doomed world.

But here she is, on the beach, weighing her options—right or left?—before deciding to turn right toward the bluffs that wrap around to Santa Barbara proper and the pier beyond and all the mad crush of civilization that comes with it, thinking there might be something of interest among the slabs of rock that have successively peeled away from the cliff face over the years and come crashing down into the surf. When the tide is exceptionally low, as it looks to be now, a reef is exposed there, with some scattered pools hosting the usual suspects—mussels, barnacles, urchins, winkles, anemones and hermit crabs, in addition to the occasional surprise of a brilliant blue-and-white nudibranch or stranded octopus. The carcass of a juvenile gray whale had washed up on the rocks there one spring—bearing what had to be wounds inflicted by a great white—and summer before last, during a dinoflagellate bloom, she'd come upon a crowd of people gathered round a seal pup, trying to urge it back into the water, when clearly it had drawn up on the beach to warm itself.

The animal was obviously undernourished—she suspected domoic acid poisoning as a result of the toxin concentrated in the plankton working its way up the food chain and delivered in its mother's milk—and when she reached it, a shaven-headed young Latino in a wife beater was attempting to drag it over the rocks and back into the sea. Before she could think, she was on him, furious, snatching at his arm and trying, for all his bulk, to pull him away. There was a screaming in her head—here was yet another well-meaning animal lover doing exactly and precisely the wrong thing, the fatal thing—and she could feel the blood rush to her face. "Let it go!" she barked, rigid with anger, locked there—her hand fixed to his arm as if it were mechanical, made of nuts and bolts and titanium tubing—until he obeyed her. And then, as the pup fell away from his grasp and he gave her a look of such confusion she almost felt sorry for him, she added, in a voice of steel, "Stay back, all of you."

She'd maneuvered herself between him and the seal, which was scrabbling at the rocks in a panic, but too weak to do much more than that, rising on its flippers and falling back again, and the man came to life in the flicker of that instant, thrusting his face in hers. "Who the fuck are you?" he demanded. He had a slim faded blue tattoo on the inside of his left wrist—a dolphin, leaping—and his breath smelled of tangerines, as if he'd just worked his way through a citrus grove.

It was an interesting question: who was she? It went to a point of authority—what gave her the right to interfere when he'd got there first and was only trying to do the obvious, flexing his muscles and his will for the benefit of his girlfriend and maybe his buddies and the crowd too, a true Samaritan motivated not by love of self but by love of all things? Even now, with a twinge of embarrassment, she remembers the answer she'd offered up: "I'm a scientist."

Well, all right. At least she'd saved the animal, punching in the number of the Marine Mammal Center on her cell while the crowd stood back and the seal settled into its skin and the angular blades of its bones. Now, making her way toward the bluffs, the memory of the incident rises up and fades away again, because she's spotted a pod of Risso's dolphins—five, six of them—working the shoreline two hundred yards out. These are among the biggest of the dolphins, ten to twelve feet long and as much as eleven hundred pounds, normally a deepwater species but feeding in close this morning, and she takes their appearance as a rare treat. She's walking briskly, trying to keep the animals in sight as they move toward the bluff, when she spots a figure up ahead, a man coming toward her with a pair of dogs. The dogs—airbrushed skulls, plunging pelvises, skin painted to bone—are greyhounds, she sees that now, and she's thinking, *Good for him, he's rescued the animals from one of the racetracks in Florida*, until she focuses on him and sees her mistake. There's the set of the jaw, the wide shoulders and disproportionately long neck, something in his stride—but none of that gives him away. There are plenty of people, plenty of men, built like that, men who kick out their legs as if they're trampling something or somebody with every step they take. No, it's the dreads. Sand-colored dreads that fan out from his head as if he's striding through a wind tunnel.

She feels a beat of panic. He's seen her, she's sure of it. Does she need an ugly confrontation now, this morning, when all she wants is a walk on the beach and a chance to savor the moment? She thinks to turn away, to walk in the opposite direction, retrace her steps—she can explore the reef anytime, tomorrow, the next day—when he calls out her name and she freezes. "Hey, Alma!" he shouts, the dogs fanning away from the bare struts of his legs like interceptors. "Alma Boyd! Alma Boyd Takesue!"

What she's never told Tim—he never asked and he wouldn't believe it anyway; she can barely believe it herself—is that once, for one disastrous truncated evening, she dated Dave LaJoy. Or had dinner with him. Or tried to. She'd met him at one of the music venues downtown, a coffeehouse that featured new young singer-songwriters. She was there alone one night—she was new in town, just weeks into the job she'd felt so lucky to get, six months away from meeting Tim—and here was this good-looking guy in his thirties sitting with another guy at the table next to hers. He was wearing a concert T-shirt with a likeness of Micah Stroud, guitar in hand, imprinted on the back of it, and that was an immediate plus in her eyes because in those days Micah Stroud was known only to those in the know. She liked his smile, the way he held himself, his hair—his hair made a statement. You didn't see too many men his age in dreads. She figured him for a musician or an artist, maybe a writer, a photographer, someone independent anyway. "You look lonely over there," he said. "Want to join us?"

And she did. And it went well. And when the weekend came he called and asked her to dinner, her choice, anyplace she wanted to go. She wasn't really looking to get involved, not after Rayfield and her three years on Guam, where she'd got used to entertaining herself, and since she knew nothing about him except his own version—he owned some electronics stores, had done well, liked the outdoors, was currently unattached—she decided on a place she knew in the lower village. Pricey, but what wasn't? The cuisine was nouveau Italian and she'd been there often enough, either alone or in the company of one of the girls from work, as to qualify as a regular. Often enough in any case to rate special treatment from Giancarlo, the owner and maitre d', and to feel comfortable dining there, under his auspices, with a stranger. Who could turn out to be the love of her life. Or a disaster.

Things started out well enough. He showed up at her apartment on foot, with lilies from the flower girl—woman, actually—around the corner, and he made small talk while she put them in a vase, grabbed her black lace shawl and led him out the door. They walked up the street, across the bridge over the freeway, and into the lower village, the getting-acquainted banter running along smoothly—he had a house just up the hill, not more than half a mile away, and he went right by her place all the time, and how long had she been here? Three months? How had he missed her? He couldn't believe it. She didn't have a dog, he guessed, because if she'd had a dog he would have been sure to run into her on the bluff or the streets or beach. No, as he'd seen, she didn't have a dog, though she loved dogs, but she was hardly settled yet and her business took her out to the islands a lot and dogs weren't allowed there for fear they might spread disease to the resident foxes and skunks. *The islands?* he'd said. *I love the islands.*

Giancarlo greeted them at the door and showed them to a table by the window and then the waiter—Fredo, a tall saturnine Chileno who assumed the air and accent of a Neapolitan for the sake of authenticity—presented them with the wine list. "What do you prefer?" LaJoy had asked her. "Red or white?"

She shrugged. "I like red," she said.

"Yeah," he said. "Me too. But of course it depends on the dish. And the occasion."

"Actually," she confessed, "I'm not that much of a sophisticate. Three years on Guam'll do that to you." She gave a deprecatory laugh. "When you're on Guam you drink what you can get. *Sake*, mostly. And whiskey. Or as they say, 'Wheesky. Wheesky-soda.' And gin, of course. G and T, the old reliable."

He didn't have much to say to this. His head was lowered to the wine list, the dreads falling forward to reveal the pink tessellations of scalp beneath. He was running a finger down the columns of offerings until finally he summoned Fredo. "Let me talk to the sommelier, will you?"

Fredo, funereally proper, stood over them, hands clasped behind his back. "I am afraid," he pronounced, fighting his accent, "that we do not have a sommelier as such—"

"As *such*?" LaJoy—Dave—was giving him a look of

hostile disbelief. "What the hell is that supposed to mean? Do you or don't you? Or are all the wines on this list ordered, cellared and poured by the tooth fairy?"

"I," Fredo began, "or Giancarlo—"

"Get him over here."

Fredo gave a small bow and vanished. While he was gone, LaJoy, gnawing a breadstick as if it were made of wood, lifted his eyes to her. "Amateurs," he said. "I hate amateurs."

She said his name then, slowly, reprovingly. "I'm sure they'll do the best they can. This place—I don't know if you've eaten here before—but this place is really topflight, as good as any restaurant in town." She paused. "What were you looking for? Exactly, I mean?"

He ignored her. He was staring beyond her to where Giancarlo was making his way across the crowded room, people beckoning to him, reaching out to shake his hand and bathe in his smile, congratulating themselves because they were on intimate terms with the owner. And Giancarlo more than fulfilled his role—fifty-two years old, born and raised in Turin, tall, open-faced, wearing a slate-gray Italian silk suit, his hair swept back like a don's. He was smiling when he came up to the table. "Alma," he said, repeating her name again, before bending to take her hand and kiss it. "What can I do for you and your gentleman friend?"

"You're the sommelier?" LaJoy seemed to be glaring at him. "I'd like a bottle of the Brunello di Montalcino Riserva, 1988—the Castello Ruggiero, the one here," pointing to the bottom of the last page of the leather-bound wine list. He raised an admonitory finger. "But only if you've got more than one on hand, because there's nothing more disappointing than ordering a top-end wine and getting to the bottom of the bottle only to have the waiter try to substitute something else."

"Yes," Giancarlo said, in answer to both questions. "This is one of our rarest and finest wines, and we do have at least a few bottles on hand, I'm quite sure." And then he attempted a witticism, which was lost on LaJoy: "If you should consume them, I would be more than just happy, perhaps even rhapsodic, and I will personally drive back to the house and get you yet another from my own personal cellar."

Through all this, Alma had held on to her smile, but she'd begun to view LaJoy—Dave—in a new light. He was agitated, she could see that, but why? Was he trying some sort of power play, putting down Fredo and now Giancarlo himself, as if this would impress her? But Giancarlo was gone now to fetch the wine—wine, she saw, glancing at the list she eased from the table—that cost three hundred and twenty-five dollars a bottle, and she tried to let the moment pass. "I'm sure it'll be good," she said, forcing a different kind of smile altogether, a smile that was two parts reassurance and one of unease.

All he said was, "It better be. At these prices."

And then Giancarlo was back, taking on the burden himself, presenting the bottle against a snowy cloth. He held it out for LaJoy's approval, then uncorked it and discreetly slipped the cork onto the table beside his plate. LaJoy snatched it up, sniffed it with a sour look, and set it back down again. Then there was the ritual of the trial pour and LaJoy's lifting the glass to his nose, holding it up to the light and swirling the wine to aerate it—it was as dark and viscous as the blood at the bottom of the polystyrene tray steak comes in at the supermarket, the steak she hadn't seen or consumed since she was a teenager because it was against her principles—and then, finally, tasting it.

She watched his face expectantly. Giancarlo was watching too, solicitous, more proper than proper, waiting for the command to pour the glasses full. But LaJoy's expression was pained. He took a second sip, rinsed his mouth and spat it back into the glass. "Rotgut," he pronounced.

Giancarlo said nothing. He stood there erect, the restaurant—his life's blood, his pride, his being—opening up behind him to the gracious tables of murmuring diners, the paintings spotlighted on the deep ochre walls, the potted palms and lacy ferns.

She didn't know what to do. Certainly she couldn't demand to taste it herself—or even request it. LaJoy was the expert here. He was the one paying—this was a date, a dinner date—and she had to defer to him. But he was rude, no doubt about it, unnecessarily so—no, boorish. Absolutely boorish. He didn't say anything in extenuation, not *Excuse me, I'm very sorry, and I know this rarely happens, but please bear with me here* or even, *It must have turned in the bottle*—he merely flicked his wrist as if brushing away an insect and dropped his eyes, once again, to the wine list.

This time he ordered a French wine—the second priciest bottle on the list—and this time it was Fredo who presented the bottle and assisted, in his rigidly decorous way, with the ritual of the uncorking, the examination of the cork, the pouring of the sample taste. And this time, without even glancing at the waiter, LaJoy, his lip curled and his gaze locked on hers, said only, "Vinegar." And when he did look up, his eyes burning with the kind of fanatical hatred you saw in the eyes of revolutionaries, he pronounced his words very carefully, fighting for restraint, "Bring me the list."

It was then that she began to gather her things, her purse, her shawl, the glasses she'd raised briefly to her eyes in order to glance across the table and match price to wine on the list LaJoy hadn't thought to offer her, as if her opinion—the opinion of a *sake* drinker—counted for nothing, first date or no. She was pushing back the chair even before Giancarlo glided across the room, looking grave, to inform them—to inform *her* as well as this peevish show-off of a smug insensitive tightly smiling man she unaccountably found herself sitting across from—that he was very sorry, but he just couldn't keep on opening bottles of wine, his finest wines at that, only to have them sent back.

Shoulders slumped, face burning, she made for the door even before LaJoy—not Dave, just LaJoy, as she would ever after think of him—said, "Well fuck you then. We'll just go someplace else. Someplace that's the real deal. You know what I mean? A place"—she pictured him gesturing over the table, the napkin slipped from his waist and trailing behind him as he rose to his feet—"with some class. Where they know what wine is." She pushed through the door and out into the night, turning right, away from her apartment, taking the opposite direction from which they'd come, moving quickly, finding the shadows, cursing under her breath and praying that he wouldn't try to catch up with her.

But here he is, on *her* beach, coming toward her with that same hateful gloating look on his face, and she's not going to let him spoil her morning—she'll ignore him, that's what she'll do, walk right past him as if he didn't exist. He's fifty feet away, thirty, ten, and the dogs, tight lariats of skin, are sniffing at her, poking the long tubes of their overbred snouts into the folds of her jeans. "Nice write-up in today's paper," he says, and he's stalled there, right in front of her, gloating, gloating. "Don't tell me you didn't see it? The one about your little celebration yesterday? No? Hey, don't turn away, I'm talking to you."

She's past him now, her heart pounding—article, what article?—focusing on the bluffs ahead, fighting to keep her pace steady because she's not going to give in, not going to give him the satisfaction of seeing her run or even quicken her pace.

"Hey!" he shouts, whirling round to throw his words at her back. "Hey, Alma Boyd Takesue, *Dr.* Alma—don't you want to hear what I have to say? Are you in denial or what? Just look in section B, nice article by Toni Walsh. Hey, nice headline too—'The Real Pests of Anacapa.' Catchy, huh?"

A hundred feet separate them. The sand is damp beneath her feet, the waves drawn all the way back and gentle as bathwater. Shorebirds run on ahead. Another dog walker solidifies in the distance. Her morning is ruined, she knows it. All she can think of is to get home and find that article, the nail in the coffin of her efforts to woo the *Press Citizen*. As she will soon discover, the real pests of Anacapa, in the august Toni Walsh's estimation, are the members of the Park Service in general and Dr. Takesue in particular, the kind of people who think they can manipulate nature and make a theme park out of the islands. And Sickafoose, Tim Sickafoose, consulting ornithologist, whom you would think should know better, wrapping a gloved hand round an auklet chick for a cheesy photo op.

"I'm going to bury you!" he shouts, and she would have laughed at the cliché, but there's nothing funny about this sick and hateful man and his agenda and the battle to come. "You'll never get away with it on Santa Cruz! We'll fight you in court, you wait and see!"

And now she swings round. He's standing there, pumped up in his T-shirt, bristling, red-faced, taunting her like a bully on the playground. The dogs have drifted away from him, sniffing at an exposed rock at water's edge, preparatory to marking their territory. A pair of female joggers—matching white shorts and sunshades, their limbs blurred, faces annulled by the sun—close on him from behind while their own dog, a shaggy white-whiskered golden, bolts on ahead of them to confront the greyhounds. She shouldn't get into this, she knows it, but she can't help herself. The mention of court, that's what does it. Court. He means to sue, just as he'd sued over the rat control on Anacapa, but it's an empty threat because the justices know who's in the right—who's serving the public interest—and who's the crank.

But she *will* see him in court, in two weeks' time. And she won't be the one squirming—she'll be a spectator, there to watch Tim testify against him and see justice done. Because finally, after all the motions and delaying tactics his lawyer could dredge up out of the depths of the legal books, after every avenue has been closed to him and there's no escaping the consequences of his actions, he will go up before the federal magistrate on the two misdemeanor charges against him and attempt to explain exactly what he was doing out on Anacapa Island on that gray wind-shorn day when Tim stopped him, and the park ranger, with the Coast Guard providing backup, stepped in to make the arrest.

"That's right!" she shouts out, ignoring the startled looks the joggers give her and the way the dogs, all three of them, glance up sharply at the vehemence in her voice. "See you in court!"

Coches Prietos

On the back side of Santa Cruz Island, the side that faces out to sea, there are any number of snug anchorages—Yellowbanks, Willows, Horqueta, Alamos, Pozo, Malva Real—but the one he prefers, especially on a weekday when nobody else is likely to show up, is a horseshoe-shaped cove with a buff sand beach called Coches Prietos. That's where he's heading now, Anise in the galley fresh-squeezing limes for a batch of margaritas (which he won't even sample till they're past the shipping lanes—he can't count the times he's been motoring along without a thought in the world only to glance up and see one of those big implacable seven-story container ships coming straight at him like a floating mountain), the chop moderate and the sun burned clear, for two days of R&R. He's been making an effort to get the boat out of the harbor at least once a month, because what's the use of owning the thing if you're just going to park it in a slip like the Janovs and all the rest of the slip hogs who like the idea of having a boat a whole lot better than the reality of sailing it, but with one thing and another there are long stretches when the *Paladin* sits idle. The motor has been rebuilt, top to bottom, and he's twice had her out of the water to be scraped, sealed and repainted, there's a new refrigerator with an ice maker and a seriously upgraded stereo-video system (put in by his best installer from the Goleta store), and she handles beautifully, *como un sueño*, as Wilson would say. So yes, he is making the effort to get his sea legs under him and motor out to the islands whenever he can find the time.

It's not that easy, actually. There's always something in the house that needs fixing, he can't seem to stay out of the stores no matter how much he's paying Harley Meachum to do his fretting for him and the FPA business is staggeringly time-consuming, what with fund-raising, e-mail campaigns, mass mailings and the website. Then there are the endless meetings with his lawyers, not only over the various lawsuits going forward but the final and ultimate hassle of the upcoming bench trial to answer the charges from that fiasco two years back when the engine failed him and he had to sit there at anchor while the Coast Guard came aboard with Tim Sickafoose, bird-watcher and first-class snitch, and Ranger Rick Melman of the National Park Service. That was a sad day all around. Within minutes of getting back to the boat it had begun to rain hard, the sea coming up fast and nasty, and he'd had no choice but to radio for help. Help came, all right—the Coast Guard wound up towing them back to the harbor, but not before arresting him and Wilson on the utterly asinine charges of feeding wildlife and interfering with a federal agency.

Wilson had been ready to fight. He'd been opposed to radioing for the Coast Guard to begin with—"What do we need those motherfuckers for, because you know they're going to want to poke through everything and how many life jackets do you have and like where's the fire extinguisher and what's with the empty cat food bags at the bottom of the trash when you don't even have a cat aboard?"—but there was nothing either of them could do about the engine and even if they sat there for a day and a night and another day till the weather cleared, what were they going to do, paddle back to Santa Barbara? The champagne was in the refrigerator, untouched, and Wilson was fuming. Finally, he did come around—and Anise was vocal here, since she had a gig the following evening at the Night Owl and there was no way in hell she was going to miss it—but when the Coast Guard cutter pulled up along-side and he saw Sickafoose and Ranger Rick there, his eyes went hard. "Don't let them on board," Wilson kept saying. "Shove the motherfuckers right the fuck over the rail."

When it came down to it, when they were actually

standing there on the deck in a tight little crowd and poking their noses into the cockpit and the cabin, Anise had gotten hot too. Ranger Rick was tricked out in one of those big black leather belts beat cops wore, replete with nightstick, dangling handcuffs and firearm. She wanted to know what right the Park Service had to board a private boat in public waters off an island owned by the people of the United States—all the people, not just the ones in teal shirts with nameplates on them—and he had informed her, in the sober monitory tones of cops worldwide, that if she didn't shut it he was going to have to think real hard about working up a conspiracy charge to go along with the misdemeanor counts against her boyfriend and his accomplice.

He was on the point of exploding himself—all this trouble and expense only to get arrested on his own boat in a bay eleven miles from the nearest reporter while the vitamin K was dissolving in the rain and he was utterly helpless to do anything about anything—but for once, he curbed himself. His focus was on keeping things from escalating. This was bad, sure it was, but he was already calculating how he could play it up for publicity, the charges clearly trumped-up, absurd—it's against the law to feed animals and perfectly fine to poison them wholesale? All he said was, "We're a vessel in distress, with a storm coming up. The rest of it, I never heard of. It's crazy. We took a hike, that's all. Tell me there's a law against that?"

Today, though, it's different. It's been a long time since the incident, time enough for everybody to forget all about it—except the court, that is, and the Park Service and Alma Boyd Takesue and all the rest of the vengeful sons of bitches—and his lawyer has put things off with one motion or another till finally he can put them off no longer. The trial—or farce, as his lawyer calls it—isn't till Monday next and at this point it's nothing more than a formality. Or at least he's ninety-nine percent sure it is. Or will be. Wilson's already pled to the charges and received a suspended sentence and a $200 fine—and since it made no sense for both of them to go down, Wilson stepped forward and stated for the record that he'd acted alone, that Dave LaJoy had no knowledge whatever of what he planned to do to save the lives of innocent animals and protect the planet from the people who would rather kill than preserve, that his friend was along merely to take a hike that day. How they'd missed the sign at the trailhead, he couldn't say. But it was windy, dust blowing in their faces, so they had their hoods up. And then it rained.

That's how things stand. So he's not sweating it. Or at least that's what he tells himself, because he's facing six months in jail and a $5,000 fine on each of the two counts, but today he's not going to think about it. He's here, out on the water, on an afternoon made to order, doing what he needs to do more of—and for now he's just going to push the off switch in his brain and open up and appreciate the world in all its glory.

The Anacapa Passage is a little rougher than he'd like, but nothing his stomach can't handle, given that he hasn't put anything in it except a slice of dry toast and two Dramamine, and the chop goes flat once he makes San Pedro Point and the big cliffs start knocking down the wind. He stays just offshore, in twenty to thirty feet of water, as they cruise along the southern shore, round the point off Albert's Anchorage and ease into the cove at Coches. Which, he sees to his satisfaction, they have to themselves. Every once in a while, especially on weekends, he's come all the way out here only to find that somebody else has beaten him to it, sometimes two or even three boats, but today, a Monday in early June while school's still in session and it's nose to the grindstone for the average wage-slave who can only dream about his two weeks off in August, it's deserted and looking as pristine as if he were the first to discover it, as if he were Juan Rodríguez Cabrillo himself, sailing for the Spaniards four hundred and fifty years ago. He's thinking about that, about what it must have been like when no one knew what was here, when the world was a mystery and the maps teemed with sea monsters and vast null stretches of terra incognita—anything could have happened, any miracle or horror, each new island more bizarre than the last, a fantasia of imaginary flora and fauna made concrete in the instant it took to record it on the retina—as he cuts back on the throttle and glides in on his own wake. In the next moment, when they're more or less in the middle of the cove, he swings the boat around to anchor stern-in so they can sit out on the deck and take in the view of the beach and the cliffs that frame it.

The anchor drops. The boat drifts tranquilly out to the end of the line and the line tightens. Satisfied, he settles into the deck chair, and Anise pads up barefoot from the galley and hands him the first margarita, the contemplative one, so cold there's a rime of frost on the glass. She's in her bikini, two little black strips of cloth that seem nothing more than an interruption in the blinding white spill of her. Her hair is up and she's wearing a wide-brimmed hat and retro shades that make her look like she's stepped out of an old black-and-white movie. "Nice," she says, easing into the deck chair beside him.

The margarita, the simplest recipe and the best—fresh lime juice, Herradura reposado, triple sec, shaken and poured into a salt-rimmed martini glass—is, he's thinking, the finest he's ever had. It kicks in right away on an empty stomach and as he lifts the glass to toast her he's feeling so relaxed he might as well be asleep. "Yeah," he says. "As nice as it gets."

Time compresses. There is no human sound, nothing, not the ticking of a clock or the murmur of a radio, no digital beeps, no sough and wheeze of appliances. He can hear the water trickling along the hull, the cartilaginous creaking of a gull's wings as it cranks past. The beach glows as if lit from beneath. The cliffs hold everything in.

"You want another?" she asks. "And maybe a sandwich?

I've got some of that Gruyère you like—on a ciabatta roll. How does that sound?"

He's put up the canopy to keep the sun off the deck because she's worried about her skin, milk-white, white as the flesh of the calves they deprive of light and iron so they can serve them up as veal for all the butchers and carnivores out there, and when she comes back from the galley with two sandwiches and the shaker of margaritas—and here's the first mechanical sound, the faintest click of the ice cubes dropping down out of the ice maker in the depths of the boat—he sees that she's removed the top of her bikini, and why not? It's not as if anybody's coming to lunch.

The sight of her—all that incandescent skin, the heavy ever-so-slightly asymmetrical load of her breasts—stirs him, and why wouldn't it? He'd have to be comatose not to respond to something like this, like Anise, all but naked. And that's the beauty of it—they've got all day, all night, all day tomorrow and tomorrow night too. No need to rush. "Nice," he says, the adjective of the day, as she hands him the plate and leans over him to pour the glass full, and he's thinking of the women's magazines she leaves lying around, a model all rigged out on the cover and the various come-ons, in neon letters, radiating out from her as if she were Kali of the supernumerary arms. *Love Secrets of the Stars, How to Please Your Man in Bed (Guy-Tested!), 63 Ways to Turn On Your Mate.* As if it was that hard. All you have to do is take off your clothes, baby, and if he's not dead he'll jump your bones.

So there's a nice little frisson going as he eats his sandwich with a hard-on, sips his second margarita, contemplates the waves and allows the sweet purr of her voice to envelop him as if she were singing, and maybe she is. Soon, when the mood takes him, he'll get up and slip the bikini bottom down her thighs and take her by the ankles, lift her legs and slide it off her. But right now he's savoring the moment. Like all women she can sulk and brood for days on end over some imagined slight or a thing so inconsequential—what somebody said to her at work, the color of the dress she knew she shouldn't have bought—as to make him question her sanity, but he's never seen her in a better mood than this, so pleased to be here on this deck anchored off her own special island at half-past twelve when everybody else in the world's at work, three-quarters naked and savoring the moment as much as he is. He hasn't touched her yet but she's wet, he knows she is, and he's thinking maybe they'll do it right here, right on the deck . . .

"You know what this reminds me of?" she asks, stretching her legs all the way out to flex her toes against the rail, the base of the cocktail glass balanced on her sternum, between her breasts. "I mean, out here all alone like this and nothing but open water all the way down to what, L.A.? Mexico?"

"What?" he says. "What does it remind you of?"

"*The Island of the Blue Dolphins.* You ever read that book?"

"I don't know. Sounds familiar."

"It's a children's book, I guess, or what they call young adult now. My mother read it to me when I was a kid, over and over—it was my number one favorite for a year probably."

"How old were you?"

"I don't know. Eleven, twelve maybe."

He holds on to that a moment, trying to picture her at that age, pubescent Anise, with her honey-colored hair and rounded limbs, breasts just starting to break through as if they'd sprouted from seed, which in a way they had, everything programmed in the genes, her smile, her voice, this gentle graceful irresistible flow of limbs and hair and lips and eyes holding him transfixed in this instant on this deck off the back side of this rocky volcanic island with its skirt of white foam and the cliffs that soak in the sun as if they were molten still. Natalie, his first love, was fourteen when she magically appeared at the desk across from his in Mr. During's third-period history class at Santa Barbara Junior High, a transfer from Plainfield, New Jersey, where she'd gone to Catholic school and learned to smoke Larks and the odd joint when the nuns were busy doing whatever nuns do. She didn't look anything like Anise—she was short, even as a newly minted adult of eighteen, which was when he married her, with her mother's Sicilian complexion that made her look as if she'd just stepped out of the tanning salon no matter the season. To him she was a real exotic, with her black hair and copper eyes and the way she pronounced things like fall and dog ("If it's dawg," he'd say, "then why isn't it lawg and fawg and bawg?"). Exotic can only take you so far, though, and when you marry that young—he was only nineteen himself—you're asking for disaster. Which was what he got. They lasted two years, during which he was working part-time and getting his associate's degree at the community college, and then he started up the business with help from his father and she was gone out of his life. "I'll bet you were sexy," he says.

"If I was, I didn't know it."

"Yeah, sure—tell me another one."

"I didn't. Really." She rotates the base of the glass, a pink circle of condensation left beneath it like a wet kiss against her skin, her hand balanced on the swell of one breast. "Too isolated. Way too isolated."

He doesn't have anything to say to this, but he's feeling the slow seep of the tequila settling in him, taking him out of himself, and he's going to get up, any minute now, and run his hand down her leg.

"Anyway, it's fiction, but it's basically a true story. About the last woman left out on San Nicolas Island? Indian, that is. Chumash. The Spanish padres took everybody off the island in the eighteen-thirties or forties or whenever, and she was left behind. And it's great, a great story, like Robinson Crusoe. How she survived."

"What'd she do, hide when they came to get them?"

He holds up his glass, examining it a moment in the light, then snakes out the tip of his tongue to get at the salt crystals caked on the inside of the rim. "That's what I would have done."

"No, she wasn't hiding—she wanted to go."

"Or was it like in those fables where she disobeyed her parents or snuck off to have a smoke or something? Maybe she was playing with herself. That must have been verboten, right? Or did the Indians encourage that sort of thing?"

"No, nothing like that. It was her little brother. They were all on the ship, just setting sail, when she discovered he wasn't there. He was only like three or four or something and he got lost in the shuffle. Or maybe he was hiding—I don't remember. I don't think the story gets into that. The point is, when she saw he wasn't there she jumped overboard and swam back to the island to rescue him. And since the wind was up, the boat couldn't come back for her." She pauses, takes a sip, levels her eyes on him. "Sad story, though—he died like a month later. The wild dogs got him."

"Wild dogs? On San Miguel?"

"Feral dogs, left there by the Indians years before. They're gone now, of course—"

"Yeah, of course. Probably picked off one by one by Alma Boyd Takesue."

"But anyway, she tamed two of them and she had a pair of pet ravens too. And that was it for company till she was rescued eighteen years later—they took her to Santa Barbara where she got sick and died within six weeks because she had no immunity, of course, being away from people for so long. You didn't get this in school?"

He shrugs. "Maybe. Yeah. I guess."

"I remember her dress," she murmurs, her eyes gone distant over the rim of the glass. He's watching her throat as she swallows, watching her breasts. "It was made of cormorant feathers so it shimmered in the light."

"Really," he says. "Feathers?"

She nods. "The pope has it now. In the Vatican. They took it to the Vatican—"

"Really," he says.

"Yeah, really." She's looking at him now, a soft slow unambiguous smile playing across her lips.

"I wonder," he says, rising from the grip of the deck chair, "what she did about sex?"

Two days and two nights, and then back to the coast, to real life and all the hassles that come with it, to the piss-poor numbers for the month of May at the Camarillo store for reasons no one can fathom, least of all Harley Meachum, and to the trial he's entitled to as a citizen of the United States of America who's been arrested on federal property on charges no sane law enforcement agent would have brought in the first place. He'd been hoping for a jury trial, a chance to speak to the underlying issues and maximize the press coverage, to explain himself, look people in the eye and let them know who the real criminals are, no mistake about it, until his lawyer, Steve Sterling—whom he's retained on the recommendation of Phil Schwartz, the wizard who handles whatever might happen to come up vis-à-vis LaJoy's Home Entertainment Centers, contracts, rental agreements, the odd lawsuit thrown at him by one litigious moron or another—disabused him of the notion. There will be no jury. No convocation of his fellow citizens from all walks of life and a grab bag of educational levels to weigh the evidence and sit in deliberation, because the counts against him don't carry a stringent-enough penalty to warrant it—that would require a felony, and he can only imagine what he'd have to do to wind up with a felony charge. Save something, he supposes. Pick up a rat, dust it off and set it back on its feet again.

No, this will be a bench trial. That is, a roving federal magistrate will come to the Santa Barbara courthouse to set up shop for the week and hear his case and whatever else they've got on the docket. According to Sterling, this is a real break—otherwise they'd have to trot all the way down to L.A.—and that's what he's been telling anybody who'll listen. A break. A real break. He does nothing more than go for a hike on property everybody in America owns in common, and he has to shout hosannas and kiss the sky for the great and all-sustaining break they're giving him: no L.A. "Isn't that something?" he tells Marta as she sets his two eggs over easy down in front of him, and Justin, the bartender at the Coast Village Grill, as he knocks back an anticipatory vodka cranberry. "Aren't I the lucky one?"

Sardonic comments aside, he's in a mood as he comes up the steps of the courthouse at seven forty-five a.m., Anise on one side of him, Sterling on the other. He was up two hours before the alarm rang, his stomach churning and his head cavernous and windy. He skipped breakfast— too tense to eat—downed two quick gulps of sulfurous coffee on his way to the car before upending the cup in the bushes, then got into it with Anise because he had to sit outside her apartment and lay on the horn for fifteen minutes before she hauled her sorry ass out the door. When she finally did appear, no hurry, no worry, she paused to frame her face in the passenger's side window and give him a look that didn't have a particle of contrition or even consideration in it, and for a second he thought she was just going to turn and walk away.

"Sorry," she said, sliding into the seat beside him with a cardboard Kinko's box wedged under one arm and a purse the size of a suitcase draped over the other. "I had to get the flyers together."

"I don't give a shit what you had to do!" He was already shouting, instantly shouting, slamming the car in gear and lurching out into traffic. "And why for shit's sake didn't you put the fucking things together last night like I told you? Huh? Tell me that!"

She didn't have anything to say to this. The flyers were

his idea. He'd chosen a heavy stock the color of pumpkin rind, for its visibility—you don't just crumple up and toss paper like that, at least not before you give it a glance and absorb the message, which was the whole idea—and downloaded a very clean close-up of a pure white hog he could have sworn was grinning, its skin as smooth and supple as a human's, its ears cocked inquisitively and its eyes lifted to the lens, which he'd enclosed within a red circle with a prohibitory slash through it and the legend *Stop the Slaughter* stamped across the top of the page. The rats were gone, the rats were history, but the pigs were next on the agenda.

"Because I'm the one facing jail time here, not you. And I hope you got your beauty sleep, because I was up all night. Shit. I mean, can't you think about me for a change? Even for one fucking minute? Even when everything's on the line—I could go to jail, you know that?"

She was sitting erect beside him, her posture flawless, her eyes secreted behind a pair of oversized sunglasses with lime-green frames. Her diction was very precise. "You're not going to jail."

And then, absurdly, and he knew he was making a fool of himself even as he turned to her, he was roaring, "The fuck I'm not!"

Now, his stomach in freefall, he stamps across the wide tiled entrance hall of the courthouse—wide enough to drive a truck through—and up the elaborate staircase, with its hand-painted tiles shipped all the way over from Tunisia, as if that's going to impress him, then around a turning to the right where the hall opens out to the grassy courtyard below, and finally down another enclosed hallway to Department 2. The door is immense, a great dark oiled slab laid to its hinges when they built the place back in 1929, and it opens on a courtroom out of another era, vaulted ceilings, wood paneling, high-crowned benches arranged front to back like pews in a church, the church of the law. He makes note of the court recorder perched at her desk off to one side of the room, of the dais in the center where, he presumes, the judge will appear in his own good time, of the bailiff, with his paunch and his swagger and his look of utter indifference, nobody innocent, nobody at all.

"This way," Sterling murmurs, guiding him by the arm, Anise half a step behind him, and he throws back his shoulders and strides down the center aisle to the front of the room as if he's walking the red carpet at the premiere of his own movie, and let them look, all of them, what does he care? The first person he lays eyes on is Alma, Alma Boyd Takesue, right there in the middle of the second row, wearing her executioner's face. She lifts her head to shoot him an abbreviated glare before turning to Sickafoose, who's propped up beside her like a stick man, and how he'd like to lay into him, just once, just sixty seconds behind a closed door or out in the alley, Jesus, yes, but then Sterling's leading him to the bench right in front where he'll have his back to the whole mob of them and he pulls away for just an instant before thinking better of it and sliding his butt resignedly across the slick burnished wood of the bench, Anise folding under the back of her dress to slide in beside him. And *she's* looking good, at least, her eyes done up, a blush of lipstick—not too much, because she doesn't need it—dressed all in white, the color of innocence, of exoneration and respect, the dress falling to the tops of her cherry-red vinyl boots and her hair raging round her like a jungle sprung to life. He feels a surge of pride in her. Anise Reed. The beauty, the lover of animals, the singer—he has her and they don't, not the puffed-up bailiff or Tim Sickafoose or Ranger Rick or the judge who sweeps out of a door in the back looking like the dictator of a third-world country nobody's ever heard of, and what is he, Mexican? Armenian?

There are preliminaries, of course, just like in a boxing match. Other cases, other people. Up and down, yes and no. And then they call the *United States v. David Francis*

LaJoy and he feels his heart seize, despite himself. Never show weakness, he knows that, and he checks off his muscles, one after another, fighting to keep his eyes locked and his expression frozen. The prosecutor, smirking, whip-thin, a preppie type with a preppie haircut in a checked suit half a size too small who could have been Tim Sickafoose's double, calls Ranger Rick to the stand and the court has to hear Ranger Rick go through a blow-by-blow account of how his suspicions were aroused by the consulting ornithologist and how ultimately he boarded the suspect's boat and made the arrest. Then it's Sterling's turn and Sterling rises from his chair to lay into Ranger Rick, going over the same ground what seems like a hundred times till the man creeps back into himself and admits that he couldn't specify what kind of shoes the suspect had been wearing on the day of the alleged incident, nor could he distinguish them from the shoes Wilson Robert Gutierrez had been wearing, and then it's Tim Sickafoose's turn to throw the dagger and on and on they go.

He has plenty of time for reflection (for one thing he never realized what a bore Sterling is, his voice like a TV announcer's—late, late-night TV, when they trot out the popcorn makers and Ginsu knives—his face as heavy as sleep and his posture so weak his bones might have been melting, his suit boring, his tie, but maybe that was a facet of his genius, maybe he meant to bore the judge comatose and how could a comatose man pronounce anything but a verdict of innocent?). Time drags. Every once in a while Anise reaches out to give his hand a squeeze, a gesture for which he should be grateful, but he only wants to lean over and throttle her because he doesn't need pity here or empathy or affection or whatever it is. Empathy's for the weak, for the guilty. Before long, even before Sickafoose has had his say and Sterling, boringly, tries to undermine the testimony, he's begun to feel sorry for himself. Begun to worry. He studies the judge's face as if it's a timetable at the railway station, complex, unrevealing, routed in a thousand different directions to a thousand different destinations. He's going down, he's sure of it.

And why? Because he believes in something, the simplest clearest primary moral principle: thou shalt not kill. There was a time when he was just like anyone else, feeding burgers into his mouth, hot dogs, roast beef, pastrami, the chops and steaks and chicken wings his father seared on the grill and his mother served up with salad and corn and fresh-baked rolls, and like everyone else he was oblivious to the deeper implications. He went through school eating the spaghetti with meat sauce, the burritos and tacos and carne asada the cafeteria ladies served up in neat tinfoil packets. In the commons at the community college he sat amidst the disarray of his books and sipped his Coke and chewed his ham and avocado on rye, and if the ham, stripped and cured and sliced, had once been the tissue of a living sentient being, he never knew or cared. On weekends, he pushed his cart through the supermarket with all the rest of them, humming along to the jingles and reprocessed Beatles' melodies tumbling through the speakers, the sanitized meat in its plastic wrapping as innocuous as if it had fallen off a tree, the lobsters in their murky sweating tank no more an object of concern or even curiosity than if they were carved of wood. Somewhere someone raised a cow and somewhere else the cow was killed and processed while another anonymous someone checked his lobster traps for the slow-witted crustaceans gathered there. And took them to market. And dropped them in the tank. And there they stayed, their claws pegged and their fate sealed, until someone else put down his money, took them home and boiled them alive. That was how it was. And he never thought twice about it.

His awakening came almost twenty years ago now, not as an epiphany per se but more a lifting of the veil, an infusion of light and clarity, and it transformed his life. He was twenty-six, putting in sixteen-hour workdays in the first of his stores, the flagship in downtown Santa Barbara, located back then in a transitional area three blocks off State, the building an anonymous cinder-block structure that could have housed anything from a muffler shop to a dental clinic. Three blocks away was life—tourists, bars, restaurants, retail—but there was nothing on his block but a taquería and a postage-stamp park populated exclusively by bums and the odd drugged-out high school kid and his pasty girlfriend. The sidewalk was pocked with dark blotches, there were empty bottles in the blighted shrubs along the street, stains of urine and worse in the alcove that gave onto the front door, tight black scrawls of graffiti scarring the pale stucco walls.

It was a sad state of affairs, as far as he was concerned, and it drove him crazy. His every thought was linked to the business, to attracting customers and upgrading his product line and, of course, it was all about perception as far as the customers were concerned—who, he asked himself, even the most diehard audio freak, really wanted to lay out his hard-earned money in a components store, however hip, that was located across from bum central? He worried over it, got into shouting matches with various burnouts and gimps, wrote letters to the mayor, the city council, the newspaper—Can't we clean this city up?—without any appreciable difference. But he was luckier than most. He worked hard. Offered a top product at a reasonable price. And because he knew what he was doing, an electronics freak himself, and his customers appreciated it, they came to him and came back again, and very gradually the business began to grow. Still, he wasn't exactly paying attention to the larger issues. He was absorbed. He was busy.

Then one afternoon a girl he'd hired to work the front counter while he was out doing installations handed him a slim pamphlet with an earth-green cover adorned with the old hippie sign for peace. He'd just come in the back door after fielding a complaint from a middle-aged woman with seriously sun-damaged skin who'd berated him because the remote wouldn't switch on the amplifier in the new system he'd installed for her just the week before (she was pointing it backward, he discovered, after wasting a good forty-five minutes checking out every possible glitch he could imagine) and he looked down at the pamphlet in disgust. "What is this?" he asked the girl, turning it over in his hand. He gave her a sharp glance. "I hope you're not handing this shit out in the store, because if you are—"

"It's not shit," she said, her voice so soft it was almost a whisper. "And I'm not passing it out to customers, don't worry." Her name was Melody Appelbaum—it comes to him in a flash while he sits there in the netherworld of the courtroom, Sterling droning on about something and the judge looking as if he's on the verge of passing out—and she was a student at UCSB. She shrugged. "I just thought you might find it significant, that's all."

Significant. He might find it significant. Not useful or eye-opening or revolutionary, just significant. Without thinking, he stuffed it in the back pocket of his jeans, and it wasn't until he was getting ready for bed that night that he discovered it there. Idly, he flipped it open. The title— *Animal Rights*—appeared at the top of the first page, the letters faintly blurred in the way of cheap reproduction. Beneath it was a quote from Arthur Schopenhauer: "The assumption that animals are without rights and the illusion that our treatment of them has no moral significance is a positively outrageous example of Western crudity and barbarity. Universal compassion is the only guarantee to morality." There was no author listed, and aside from a copyright symbol at the bottom of the page, no publication data at all.

He turned the page on a collage of photos that radiated out from the center like the petals of a black-and-white flower. It took him a moment before he saw what they were. And when he saw and understood, he experienced a jolt of revulsion and morbid fascination that was no different from what he'd felt when he was in junior high and came across the photographs of the victims of the Nazi camps in a claustrophobic carrel in the back room of the library. But the victims in these photographs weren't human—they wore the mute unrevealing faces of cattle, hogs, veal calves, of chickens, their wings flapping futilely against the clamp of the conveyor and the blade to decapitate them. He looked closer. One of the animals, a hog that had been strung up by its feet in the slaughterhouse amidst myriad others, stared back at him, fully conscious and headed for the eviscerator looming in the foreground.

On the next page, there was more of the same— turkeys, lambs, dogs in a pen at the animal shelter awaiting the burn of the needle. And then the text, which put numbers to the slaughter, eight billion chickens butchered each year in this country alone, a hundred million hogs, forty million cows (twenty-five percent of which had been carelessly or inadequately stunned and thus effectively skinned alive, their writhings as the skin is torn from their faces a regular feature of the assembly line). And the line never slows, not even when the hogs come to and break loose of the shackles to career in a panic into the pit below or when the shrieks of the ones crowding behind cause them to freeze in the chute till they're beaten and electroshocked into moving. He read of the conditions in the farm factories, of pigs raised in pens so small they can't even turn around, not once in their whole lives, of chickens debeaked and caged in warehouses with a hundred thousand others, knowing nothing but concrete and wire and the reek of death. Then there were the animal experiments—kittens having their eyes sewed shut to study the effect of sightlessness on development; rabbits subjected to the Draize test, in which a chemical irritant is dripped into their eyes by way of evaluating products in the cosmetics industry; dogs injected with plutonium; monkeys deprived in every conceivable way, tortured, mutilated; rats uncountable bred only to suffer and die, transgenic rats, oncogenic rats, rats upon rats.

He read the pamphlet through twice that night and in

the morning he brought it with him to the store and laid it down on the counter without a word, right next to the cash register. Melody Appelbaum, nineteen, pouty, fat-cheeked, expecting trouble, gave it a glance, then looked away. "Where'd you get this?" he demanded.

She shrugged as if to say it was nothing, no more consequential than an advertising flyer, that she hadn't meant any harm, that she'd take it back and never mention it again. "At school," she said finally. "From a PETA person? Actually, my boyfriend."

And he'd been so far out of the loop he had to ask what PETA was.

"It's a group, you know? Activists. People for the Ethical Treatment of Animals?"

He mulled that over a moment, watching her eyes, animal's eyes, no different essentially from the eyes of that hog or of dogs, cats, even fish and insects, organs of seeing and apprehension, windows to the soul. "Can you get any more of them?"

Another shrug. "I guess."

"A hundred? Five hundred?"

"I guess."

"Good," he'd said. "I'm going to want them right here, right by the register. And you hand them to anybody who walks in the door."

That was the day he gave up meat, cold turkey, and where did *that* expression come from? Of course, he still needed protein, especially since he was lifting at the gym, which was all about results, and so he continued to incorporate eggs and dairy in his diet, though he knew all about the battery hens in the egg-laying factories, how they're fed the remains of the male chicks, which are otherwise useless to the industry, how they're subjected to forced molting (that is, they're periodically denied food for six to ten days and then brought back on diet as a way of forcing ovulation), and how after a year they're played out and sent to slaughter. Anise is on him all the time about it—not to mention his cardiologist—but eggs are his one concession to the system, to cruelty. He means to change. He will change. Anise is a vegan and he's moving that way, he is, but it's hard, because through all his bachelor days from his divorce on up to the present, it's been eggs that sustained him. Omelets, especially. In fact, the first time he had Anise over for dinner, he made a green salad and a veggie omelet—his specialty—thinking it would be just the thing, till she sipped at her wine, picked at the salad, gave him the full chill of her glacial gaze and said, "Meat is murder. And so are eggs."

Now, sitting in the courtroom with her four years later, he comes out of his reverie to hear Sterling laying into Sickafoose, the tedious dead dry-as-dust voice come to life suddenly: "So you can't be sure then which of the two men you saw—at a distance of what, a thousand yards?—making throwing motions?"

And Sickafoose, shifting in his seat, knotting and unknotting his bony legs, drawn down to nothing finally, and finally, in a whisper, saying: "No."

"I'm sorry, I didn't hear you."

"No. I can't be sure."

Anise turns to him suddenly and she's huge, rippling, her face floating to his like an untethered balloon, the kiss, the squeeze. Is this it? Have they finally conceded, the sons of bitches, the killers, the—And then suddenly, unaccountably, he's back on the boat, the paradisiacal island rising up out of the sea before him. "Do you know why they call it Coches Prietos?" she's asking him, the postcoital margarita rocking gently on the rail.

"It must have something to do with cars, right. Coches? I don't know: dark cars?"

"There were no cars here back then." She's wearing a playful smile. A superior smile. This is her island, after all. "There are no cars here now."

"I don't know," he says. "Beats me. I give."

"Coches is slang for pigs. Get it? Dark Pigs Canyon. *La*

Cañada de los Coches Prietos. The dark ones, those are the ones that went feral back in the eighteen hundreds. They get big and mean and they're fast. The boars anyway."

"Right," he says. "That's why they have to kill them off. All of them."

"Yeah," she says, reaching for the frosted glass. She hasn't bothered with her clothes and he hasn't bothered with his either. "But we're not going to let them, are we?"

A week later, he's back in court, stomach churning all over again, in a mood, but he's forgone the tie and jacket. In their place, he's wearing a black T-shirt with the new FPA symbol—the pig in the circle—emblazoned on the front in aniline orange with the *Stop the Slaughter* legend, in the same loud shout of a color, done up in biker's script across the back. And why not? He's here to absorb the judge's verdict, and whether he's going down or walking out the door, he's going to do it in his own way.

What's happened in the interim is purely serendipitous and a whole lot better than he could have hoped for—the press has picked it up, his story, from his point of view, because the papers find this sort of thing irresistible. "Rat Activist on Trial," "Rat Lover Says He Acted to Save Animals," "Local Man Defies Park Service," "Stop the Killing LaJoy Says." And it's not just the local paper—the interest has blossomed beyond that to pull in any number of big-city dailies, the AP, even *USA Today.* He'd like to think people are on his side, that they see the value in every life, however small, but as Anise has been reminding him all week, there's the freak factor too. *Rat lover.* It's almost an oxymoron, for most people anyway. He's heard that two of the morning disc jockeys on the local oldies station have been making jokes about it—jokes, that is, at his expense, and yet still the word is getting out in a bigger way than he could have imagined. And that means money. Since the trial started, donations to FPA have gone through the roof—at last count nearly three thousand dollars came in in the last week alone.

Sterling—fifty, bald, with doughnut residue on his lapels and a steely smile imprinted on his face—swells beside him as the judge enters the courtroom and all stand. In the next moment they're sitting again, benches creaking, people coughing into their fists, blowing their noses, scuffing their feet. There's a delay of fifteen minutes at least as the judge shuffles papers, fools with his reading glasses and entertains one lawyer or another in private conference, the discreet murmur of their voices like background noise, the buzzing of insects or the whisper of a fan. While the judge—Karagouzian, definitely Armenian, with an accent and a moustache and a house in Glendale—is otherwise occupied, Sterling turns to him and gives him a sotto voce pep talk meant to impart serenity but which actually winds up scaring him more than anything that's gone down so far.

"There's no way the judge is going to convict," Sterling tells him, shaking his head back and forth like a metronome. "Not with how Sickafoose compromised himself on the stand—"

"Good," he hears himself say. "Great. But you said it was no sweat anyway, trumped-up charges, no evidence, right?"

"Yes, sure, but you have to understand Karagouzian's a ramrod for law and order and he has a reputation for ruling on the side of the authorities."

"But not in this case."

And here's where the scare comes in, and it hits him, as usual, in the stomach, in the stomach lining where the digestive juices, inflamed with caffeine, chew away at him, because Sterling wags his head even harder and says, "I'm ninety-nine percent sure, but then Karagouzian hates any kind of protest or press involvement, which isn't your fault, God knows, and it's legitimate, absolutely, but I just thought I ought to warn you in case we—well, as I say, I'm ninety-nine percent sure here."

He glances at Anise. She's chosen to sit on his left this time, so he and Sterling won't have to step over her when the judge gives his verdict. She looks great, a real presence, huge really, with her broad bleached face and big shoulders and her hair combed out and frizzed up so it spills over everything, her purse, her lap, the back of the pew and all up and down the left side of his body as if to hold him there beside her. Maddeningly, though, she's dressed all in black—a skirt that goes right to the floor and a leotard with a little embroidered vest over it, black on black. "Why black?" he'd demanded, stupefied, when she came down the steps of her apartment and dropped into the passenger's side of the Beemer. She took off her sunglasses to look him square in the eye. "I want to be ready for anything," she said, and though he tried to contain himself, his voice was as bitter as the sediment at the bottom of his coffee cup. "What the fuck is that supposed to mean?"

Now she gives him a tight smile. "I'll bake you cookies," she whispers.

"Very funny."

There's a rustling behind him, to his right, and he glances past Sterling to see Alma and Sickafoose squeezing into the far end of the bench. Neither of them will meet his eye, but they're wearing smug looks, as if no matter what happens they've got him where they want him, here in federal court, with a hanging judge up there squinting at his papers preparatory to coming down on the side of the law that protects the guilty and burns the innocent. But what a cunt, that night at the restaurant, the way she'd bailed on him—as if she was better than he was, as if he didn't know his wines—and wasn't she sworn by law to protect and nurture the resources of the national park instead of killing things off at random? Jesus. And she's looking Asian, real Asian, with that hair and the set of her jaw and the way she's holding herself like some little geisha, like the touch of the wood slab behind her would cripple her . . .

But now the bailiff's calling his name and Sterling's on his feet. He feels the muscles working in his legs as he rises, his chest swelling, and he's moving forward to stand there before the bench while all the reporters—is that what's her name, Toni, from the *Press Citizen*?—snatch at their pads and pencils and laptops. The room goes silent. Sunlight sits in the tall windows. There's a distant sound of traffic.

The judge—and there's another shithead he'd like to have five minutes alone with—squints at him over his glasses. He does something with his lips, a kind of preliminary licking or flexing, and then, glancing down at the paper before him, he begins to read aloud: "While there is a strong probability that the defendant did in fact commit the crimes with which he is charged, the evidence submitted and admitted does not serve to eliminate the doubt that remains. Further, since the Park Service eradication project was ultimately successful, the issue becomes moot."

And what's this? He can feel the mood shifting, the room coming to life as if a long collective breath has been expelled. He looks to Sterling, who's staring straight ahead at the judge, trying to keep his expression sober despite the first intimations of triumph compressing the crow's-feet rimming his eyes and radiating down to tug at the corners of his mouth. Everybody's watching. Everybody can see him. His T-shirt. His message. His meaning. He feels a hard hot surge of joy coming up in him and it's as intense as an orgasm: he's going to walk!

"Therefore," the judge pronounces over the steady retrograde tug of his accent, and yes, he could go right up there and kiss him, right now, "I pronounce the defendant not guilty."

In the aftermath, out in the corridor with Toni Walsh and the woman from the local TV affiliate, the fingers of his right hand entwined in Anise's and the camera trained on him, he makes a little speech, the lines of which he's been rehearsing in his head all week. "It's a sad state of affairs when our own federal government considers feeding wildlife to be a crime, while at the same time raining down poison indiscriminately from the sky is okay—legitimate, I mean." And what's even sweeter is that he's able to raise his voice and project it all the way down the long gleaming tiled hall at the very moment that Alma Boyd Takesue and Tim Sickafoose emerge slumped and tragic from the courtroom so that he gets to watch her turn her head to him and then turn away again as he winds it up with an inspired flash of rhetoric: "And if these people think they're going to get away with slaughtering some five thousand native pigs on Santa Cruz Island, well they've got another think coming."

He pulls back then, dropping Anise's hand to raise his own, two fingers spread in the victory sign. "Uh-uh," he says, shaking his head so that the dreads stir and rise in bristling affirmation, "not while the FPA's on the watch."

PART II

Santa Cruz

Scorpion Ranch

Rita was newly separated from a man who'd hurt her in so many ways she'd lost track of just how and why she'd ever gone with him in the first place, her car was in the shop with some sort of systemic failure she couldn't begin to fathom let alone pay for, her job was inadequate to her training and expectations, and she had a ten-year-old daughter to feed, clothe and educate. It was May of 1979, and all the good feelings—the vibrations, the groove—of the shimmering bright era that had sustained her through every failure and disappointment had dwindled and winnowed and faded till she was angry all the time, angry at Toby for leaving her, angry at her daughter, angry at her boss and the landlord who wanted two hundred fifty bucks a month for a dreary clamshell-gray walkup over a take-out pizza shop on Route 1 in downtown Oxnard, where the fog hung like death over everything and the trucks never stopped spewing diesel fumes outside the window, which might as well have been nailed shut for all the air it gave her. So when Valerie Bruns, her best friend from work, told her she knew of an opening—of a chance to get out, get away, change the scene as if this were Act II of one of the plays she'd been in in high school—she came back to life. Instantly.

"It's on an island," Valerie said.

"An island?" she echoed. "What do you mean, an island?"

"Santa Cruz."

She'd called Valerie because it was Friday night, thinking they could go someplace for a drink, listen to music, hang out, but Valerie was going to her mother's for dinner and didn't know if she could. Then they'd got to talking about work—they were both aides at Point Hueneme Junior High—and what an uptight bitch the assistant principal was, and Mrs. Paris, the special ed teacher, and how they'd both like to quit, when Valerie mentioned the job.

"I thought Santa Cruz was a city—we played there once, I think. They've got a college there, right?"

"No, Santa Cruz *Island*."

"Where's that?"

A long exasperated sigh. "You know Henderson's, in the marina? Where we went for margaritas that one time?"

"Yeah, I guess. Why?"

"Remember we sat out on the deck and we could see Anacapa? Remember I pointed it out to you and you made a big deal out of it?"

"Yeah, sure. Maybe." She'd been drinking too much lately, drinking out of rage and regret and boredom, and she had only the vaguest rattling recollection of the place—it was on the water, that much she remembered.

"Well, the island next to it, the big one—four times as big as Manhattan—that's Santa Cruz. It's like this brown blur most of the time? You've seen it. Everybody has. You probably just didn't notice, is all."

She was sipping vodka, no ice, from a glass she kept in the freezer beside the bottle, Absolut, her one concession to extravagance—that and smokes. It burned her lips, caressed her tongue. "So what's the job?"

"It's this friend of mine, Baxter Russell? He needs a cook out there. He's got a lease on a place they call Scorpion Ranch—sheep, he's raising sheep—and he needs somebody to cook for him and I think like six or seven other guys. Cowboys, or whatever you call them . . ." Valerie let out a laugh. "Sheepboys, I guess. If that's even a word."

And though the first thing she said was, "I'm no cook, I'm a musician," the idea of it—an island full of cowboys, and out in the middle of the ocean, no less—was already developing pictures in her mind, a whole montage of them, the wisteria-hung ranch house, the salt-sharp tang of the horses after they come in off the range, and *How you*

168

want your steak done, fellas? Their shoulders, their eyes, bandannas, broad-brimmed hats, tall men, sinewy, lonely. *Any way you like to do 'em, ma'am.*

"But I want to talk to him," she was saying, hasty now, afraid Valerie would shift the subject, drop a see-you-later into the conversation and head out for her mom's meat loaf and her stepdad's strawberry margaritas. "Definitely. Tell him I definitely want to talk to him."

So Valerie gave her his number and she liked his voice over the phone—a baritone with a ragged huskiness scraping the edges of it, a preacher's voice or a country singer's—and agreed to meet him the following day for a sandwich at a place on West Fourth Street, which was only five blocks away and didn't require vehicular transportation, and a good thing too because the car was as dead as the iron ore they'd dug out of the ground to give it shape. The sky was overcast—fog breathing up off the water like steam rising from a teapot, a million teapots, a hundred million, and why couldn't it ever rain? Or thunder. She'd settle for a good old-fashioned East Coast thunderstorm, anything to break the monotony. She watched herself shift, vanish and reappear again in the storefront windows, the trucks easing past like walls on wheels, pigeons and starlings scrabbling over the remains of a McDonald's Happy Meal splayed out on the wet pavement and the sad miniature plastic child's toy—Ronald, with his painted grin—cast away with it. Before she knew she was going to bend to retrieve the toy and slip it in her pocket she'd stopped to flick her hand at the birds and glance round her to see if anyone was looking, thinking of her daughter and the sitter she'd got in for an hour, just an hour, because how long could lunch take?

He was waiting for her in a booth by the window, a newspaper spread out on the table before him, and at first she didn't recognize him. *I'll be the one with the beard,* he'd said, but he'd also told her he was fifty-five (a quick calculation: twenty-four years older than she), which had her expecting a stringy old man with turtle skin and impacted eyes, white hair anyway, overalls, maybe a straw hat. But this man wasn't like that at all. He wore his hair long and it was streaked with blond where the sun had caught it and when he glanced up at her the look he gave her was anything but the look of an old man. "Mr. Russell?" she tried, still ten feet away, hesitant, uncertain of herself, because this couldn't be him . . . could it?

But it was. And he had a smile that was like an erasure, no worries, no fears. "Rita?" He pushed aside the paper and lifted his eyes to her (blue shading to gray with flecks of gold fracturing the field) over the lenses of his reading glasses. "Is that you?"

She'd dressed in jeans, flip-flops, a turquoise blouse with short sleeves and a scooped neckline, and she'd done her face and eyes, not knowing what to expect. She wore her hair up, thinking that was how a cook would wear it, and she made a point of getting there at the stroke of noon, rehashing in her mind the few recipes she knew, a handful of curry dishes their drummer had taught her, chicken cordon bleu, scallops in a wine reduction, but she really didn't think anything would come of it. If he asked her about experience she'd have to be honest with him and say that she'd never done anything professionally, just whipping up things for her daughter and her ex-husband and once in a while a dinner party, but if truth be told they wound up eating out about half the time, fast food, pizza, chicken wings—she was a fool for chicken wings. "Yeah," she said, giving back his smile, "it's me."

"Well, sit down," he said, folding up the newspaper and handing her the menu. He took a moment, realigning the silverware on the paper placemat that featured the name of the restaurant and a picture of the owner—a fat man, bald—printed on the front and puzzles for kids on the back. "Two things," he said finally, his voice a rumble, his cracked blue eyes fixed on her as if he was afraid she was going to get up and flit away like a bird. "Call me Bax. And

170

lunch is on me." Another pause. "And I have to say I didn't expect anybody so, so—what am I trying to say here?"

That was when she began to feel uneasy all over again: was he hitting on her, was that it? Was this just going be some sleazy proposition? An island? With cowboys? What had she been thinking? "I don't know," she heard herself say. And now she was the one toying with the silverware, fork, knife, spoon, shifting the mug and paper napkin like chess pieces. She looked up at him, trying to inject a little brightness into her voice: "What's good here?"

He seemed to have lost his train of thought, but he was still staring at her, reading her, giving her a look that was hard to mistake. It took him a moment. Finally he said, "I like the Reuben. But you aren't one of these types that don't eat this, that or the other, are you? I mean, meat or whatever?"

She shook her head.

"And you can cook?"

She began ticking off recipes—anything she could think of, from macaroni and cheese to lobster thermidor—before he cut her off.

"You don't understand. It's lamb we're talking about. In a stew, fricasseed, roasted, barbecued—with a pot of beans, raw onions, a stack of tortillas. Flapjacks in the morning, eggs, more lamb. There's seven of us. At shearing you can double that."

"Cafeteria style," she said, and he laughed.

Then the waitress was there and they both ordered Reubens and he asked for iced tea and she a diet Coke. They watched the waitress recede, looked up in unison as an elderly couple shuffled in the door as if concrete blocks were attached to their feet and settled into the booth across from them, heaving for breath. There was a counter running the length of the place, half a dozen disconsolate men there, propped up on their elbows and staring into the distance, truckers maybe, rejects from the naval base, the perennially laid off, people with time on their hands.

A chalkboard over the soft-serve machine advertised the spaghetti special, with tossed salad and garlic bread. She felt the tug of hopelessness.

"Three meals a day," he said, his tone business-like now, admonitory even. "Up before dawn, to bed at dark. What I'm hoping is to pick up a generator." He paused, dropped his eyes. "If not this trip, then the next one."

She let nothing show on her face. What she wanted was an adventure, what she wanted was out, but she could detect the makings of a long grinding disaster spinning out before her. What did she know about sheep, cowboys, ranches, islands, cooking even? "What about water? You have running water, don't you?"

He ducked his head, then lifted his chin and ran the fingers of both hands through his hair, which fell forward, thick and thickly greased. "We're working on it. It's all part of the plan. And if things might be a bit rough now, I tell you, it's worth it. I mean, if you like the outdoors—you do, don't you?" His eyes jumped at hers but he didn't wait for an answer. "And a cook—a cook is going to really help because it frees up a man so we can put all our energy into getting the place up and running. And improved. Livable, you know? Or more than livable: cozy. Cozy's what we're shooting for."

"O-kay," she said, very slowly, drawing out the vowels. "But we haven't talked salary."

He waved a hand as if to say nothing could be simpler or more amenable. She watched him lift the glass of iced tea and take a long leisurely drink. He was laughing suddenly, his eyes retreating into the hallway of some private joke. "Hell, we got Francisco cooking for us now—he's a sheepman and he smells like it too, no matter how many bars of soap I bring back for him, not to mention Old Spice. I gave him the biggest bottle I could find, but you couldn't tell the difference—I wouldn't put it past him if he drank it. The man burns everything—coffee, beans, meat. And I tell you, you lift your fork to your mouth and

172

it all tastes the same. I swear—and I've been meaning to do this, just for the satisfaction of it—you do a blindfold test and you wouldn't know if you were chewing lamb or a heel of bread or a sawed-off hunk of the cutting board."

"Sounds like a nightmare," she said, smiling now. "But what are you paying?"

"Does it really matter?"

"Yes," she said, "it does."

Another wave of the hand. "Minimum wage. But that's for eight hours and no overtime. Room and board. A chance to live in the most beautiful spot on the face of the planet and see the stars the way nobody sees them anymore, all the way to the deep white creamy heart of the Milky Way." He turned up the smile. "And all the lamb you can eat."

"I have a daughter," she said.

"I know."

"Valerie told you?"

"Valerie told me, yeah. But you can homeschool her—in an atmosphere which, let's face it, is going to be a whole lot healthier than where you are now, what with the gangs, drugs, teen sex and all that. Mexicans. Crime. You don't want her exposed to that kind of thing if you can help it, believe me—"

"You have kids?"

"Two girls, Marty and Fredda. They're all grown up now." He set down the glass. His hands were battered, the skin rough, the nails like horn. "I'm divorced. I used to have a drinking problem. Now I don't." In the next moment he was leaning back to dig something out of his pocket—a wallet—and she thought he was going to show her pictures of his daughters, but that wasn't it at all. He patiently extracted three bills and laid them on the table. Hundreds. Three one-hundred-dollar bills, as pristine as if they'd just come off the press at the mint back in Philadelphia. "Here," he said, his voice touching bottom, "you take this . . . Wait"—he groped in his pocket again until he came up with a set of car keys and slapped them down on the table—"you can drive a stick, can't you?"

She nodded, the bills splayed out between them like an insanely generous tip for the waitress who hadn't even brought their sandwiches yet.

"You know the Safeway up the street there?"—he was pointing down the length of the restaurant, beyond the counter, the dust-flecked windows and the macadam road glistening with moisture, his eyebrows lifted interrogatively. "Yeah? Well, take this and go buy us groceries."

"Groceries? What do you mean?"

"You're going to drop me down at the harbor is what I mean. I got about six thousand things to remember before the boat leaves . . . I mean, enough for a week or maybe a week and a half, and after that we'll take you back to shore and think about the long-term stuff, fifty-pound sacks of rice, beans, that sort of thing. You know the marina, right?"

"Well, I . . . I've been there, but—"

And now the waitress appeared with their sandwiches and they were both momentarily distracted as she set down the plates, extracted a bottle of ketchup from the pocket of her apron and asked if she could get them anything else. "A refill?" he said, rattling the ice in his glass. "What about you, Reet? Ready for another di-u-retic?"

There was a moment of silence as they both bent to their sandwiches and she felt as if she were already on the boat, out at sea, lurching with the waves, so hungry suddenly she could barely think. What was happening to her? Had she agreed to some sort of pact? And if so, when had that happened? She became aware of the music playing then—the jukebox, a tune she'd always loved, Neil Young's "Helpless," which she'd covered with Toby in a radically slowed-down version, their two voices enfolded on the chorus and Toby pounding down those chunky chords on the piano as if it were made of concrete, bliss, pure bliss—and she took it as an omen.

"So listen," he was saying, "eat up and then you can drop me at the marina—the boat's a friend of mine's, the *Side Pocket*. Just ask. Everybody knows it." He was wiping his lips, chewing. "Damn good sandwich."

She closed her eyes a moment, trying to picture things, the way they would evolve, because her mother was going to have to watch Anise, that was for sure, at least temporarily, at least till school was out, and she'd have to call in sick at work, maybe permanently sick—

"Oh," he said, waving the sandwich, which ran with its juices, his right hand slick with thin runnels of Thousand Island dressing and the liquefied fat of the Swiss cheese, "I just wanted to remind you—"

"But listen, I don't even know what I'm supposed to buy, and I can't, I mean, I have to—"

"Vegetables," he said, dabbing at his beard with the wet-through and stained remnants of his paper napkin. "Jug wine. Couple cases of beer—make that five cases, and the brand doesn't matter, whatever's on special. Condiments. You know," and he paused, deadpan, "whatever goes with lamb." And now the other hand came into play, held palm up so that the calluses shone with grease and the deep gouges of his lifeline leapt out at her like a map of her future. "But what I wanted to say, to remind you, that is, is that the boat leaves at five." He leaned into the table, leaned in close, and gave her a wink. "Don't you be late now."

And that was how she found herself hunched over the stained dried-out planks of the long sheepman's table in the mud-tracked kitchen of an adobe ranch house so far out from the coast and life and the morning paper she might as well have been marooned, propped up on her elbows and blowing the steam off a cup of coffee at the first turning of dawn some four and a half years later. Where those years had gone, she couldn't have said any more than she could have said where the wind went once it tired

175

of raking the canyon behind the house. Her hands were tough as wire cutters, her hair hung limp for lack of shampoo and she hadn't seen the inside of a restaurant of any kind in as long as she could remember. Not that she was complaining. She had Bax and Anise, half a dozen ranch hands and upward of four thousand sheep to keep her company, and she was so absorbed in the workings of the ranch—in the details, everything inhering in the details—that all the rest of the world seemed to dwindle down to nothing, as if she'd dreamed it, as if the whole town of Oxnard had been thrown up like a movie set or hardened in place out of a shower of fairy dust. And the news—what was the news anyway but a long continuous trumped-up shriek of impending doom and current disaster that just made everybody sour and distrustful and hateful of their fellow man? She didn't need it. Didn't miss it. The news for her, the news that mattered, was written on the wind and it dripped out of the fog and bleated from the throats of the sixteen hundred ewes about to drop their lambs in the rain-fed grass of the lower meadow that she could hear and smell and taste even as she got up to feed more wood into the stove.

The room was cold—warmer than it had been when she'd got up two hours earlier to make breakfast, but still below her comfort zone—and the heat of the stove felt good on her face. She poked the coals and laid a few sticks of driftwood over them and then topped that with splits of eucalyptus from the grove the owner's father or maybe grandfather had planted God knew when and which was forever shedding branches and bark, especially in winter when the rains came and the soft porous wood absorbed the weight of the water till it gave with a crack and a dull hurtling thump you could feel two hundred yards away through the soles of your boots. It was winter now—January—and there was a light rain ticking at the windowpanes, an installment on the twenty inches per annum they got if the currents, winds and barometer cooperated.

The last two years had been more than they'd bargained for, El Niño years, and the dry wash out front had become a riverbed overflowing its banks with a roiling brown tide sweeping the wrong way, into the ocean rather than out, and they'd lost the privy, the chicken coop, the corral and everything movable besides, including the ten or twelve cords of wood she'd patiently gathered, sawed, split and stacked through the long dusty unremittent season that stretched from April to the end of November. And then there was the mud, scrawled two feet high along the inside walls of the house, the mark there still like the rime on a dirty cup. Mud she didn't need, not this year. Let the rains come gentling down and the wash keep hold of the runoff.

It was just light enough to distinguish the colors of things outside the window—a pair of khaki gumboots hanging from a hook under the eaves, a once-red wheelbarrow overturned atop the heaped-up mound of the kitchen compost pile, the scored white hood of Bax's wrecked and wheel-sprung Jeep—when Francisco came in the back door to help her clean up the breakfast dishes and attack the mess on the pocked concrete floor. Francisco was a Basque with Mexican blood or a Mexican with Basque blood, depending on the company and his mood, and he'd been attached to the place through the last failed sheep operation and then as caretaker during the lonely years when the ranch house deteriorated from lack of care and money and the sheep forgot all about shearers, dogs and fences and scattered across the crags and ravines of El Montañon, the transverse ridge that separated this, the eastern ten percent of the island, from the western portion. Now he was with Bax. He was anywhere between fifty and eighty (no one could say and he wasn't forthcoming on the subject, preferring to speak in terms of eras rather than years, *el otoño de los vientos*, the epoch of the bone collectors from the university, the earthquake time or the drought time when he was a boy working cattle in the San Joaquin Valley and the *patrón* had hired a *chisera* to bring rain and she charged him a calf for her efforts, and then, after it had rained like Noah's deluge for two weeks running, demanded two calves to make it stop). He dressed in a faded blue workshirt, tattered bandanna, freshly oiled boots and jeans so saturated in blood, lanolin and dirt they could have been used to brace up the joists of the house in an emergency, and he wore the traditional sheepman's knife in a sheaf strapped to his thigh. How he'd ever translated his knowledge to Bax remained a mystery since he was about as communicative as a stone (unless he was drunk, when you practically had to gag him to shut him up), but he was as complete and efficient as one of the robots the future kept promising. What he said now was, "I take the Mister *su café*, Missus?"

The Mister—Bax, that is, the man whose late-life challenge it was to oversee these 6,800 acres on an inequitable profit-sharing basis with the owners and in whose bed she'd been sleeping since two weeks after her installation as cook, hence her status as Missus—was laid up. He'd been clearing debris out of the cratered road that angled precipitously up out of the valley on the far side of the wash, trying to preserve access to their makeshift airstrip, when the Jeep, which wasn't much more than animated debris to begin with, flipped on him. He was thrown clear. The Jeep rolled and kept on rolling, the windshield flattened, the steering wheel sheared off and the front wheels, fenders and hood permanently rearranged, till a boulder stopped it halfway down the side of the cliff. No one had any idea what had happened till the dark began to come down and Anise, looking up from her history homework, asked, "Where's Bax?"

He'd been lucky, or so he told it. The concussion was mild enough so he was able to keep the ravens off him, waving an arm when they got too close; it was his bad leg— the left one—that was broken; and he'd only cracked three of the twelve ribs a human being is graced with. "Forget all that Adam's rib nonsense," he'd told Anise that first night at the hospital in Ventura when she sat over his bed with her long worrying face on, "because men and women have exactly the same number. And that's a common misconception, that men have one less. You know what a common misconception is? Like a prejudice. An old wives' tale."

But he was laid up now, feeling his hurt, frustrated, angry, sixty years old a week ago and showing it. And he was a bear in the morning anyway. So she took the pot from the stove, poured a cup heavy with sugar and cream, and handed it to Francisco. "Yeah," she said, "that'd be great. You take it up to him. And don't tell him anything. Or no: you tell him I'm going to be out there with those ewes till every one of them has dropped. All day, all week, and next week too, if that's what it takes."

Francisco—his face was remarkably smooth for a man who'd spent his whole life under the sun, which was one reason why it was so hard to estimate his age, that and the fact that he carried himself like a far younger man, back straight, his stride long and his step vigorous—gave her a nod of accord. He said one word only—"*Suerte*"— and then he took the cup and ambled out the door and up the stairs to the room above where Bax lay flat out on his back reading through the pile of old *Life* magazines she'd picked up at a yard sale last time they were on the coast. There'd be a chamber pot to empty. And within the hour, after he'd had his first two cups of coffee, he'd want breakfast. Before that, though, there was a stew to prepare and set on the stove to slow-cook through the day, lunch and dinner both. That and the bread rising in the six pans arrayed on the counter behind her, which would go into the brick oven once the fire she'd banked there had burned down to coals.

She went to the drawer and took out her whetstone and put an edge on the butcher knife, all the while listening to the sounds of the house, the distant bleating of the ewes and the harsh avian cursing of the ravens that had gathered in their legions for the feast she meant to deny them.

Where they came from, she couldn't say—it was a mystery. There was always a resident population hanging round the slaughtering shed or the midden out back, but as soon as lambing season began they must have quintupled their numbers, flying in from the other islands or maybe even the coast. Francisco said they were the souls of the Indians, *las almas de los indios*, come back from the dead to plague the white men who'd displaced them, and maybe he was right. Certainly they were as smart as any Indian or anybody else for that matter. Step outside with a rifle and they'd vanish, only to reappear just out of range. Try it with a stick, even one you'd painted black for just that purpose, and they'd ignore you. She'd seen them work in pairs, one distracting the ewe while the other went for the lamb. And while scientists might make the claim that apes are the only tool-using animals aside from *Homo sapiens*, she'd seen ravens drop mussels on the rocks to crack them open or pick up a stone and hold it between their claws for ballast in a heavy wind. Souls of the Indians, devils, whatever they were: they weren't going to get at her lambs, not this year.

It was lamb at the chopping block though, one of last year's wethers fresh-slaughtered the night before, and if someone had tapped her on the shoulder and asked her if she saw any irony in that, she would have said no, just practicality—they were in the business of shipping wool and lamb on the hoof to the coast and sustaining themselves on what they could, and that was lamb and more lamb, just as Bax had warned her that gray socked-in day they'd sat in the diner in Oxnard and become acquainted for the first time. Sheepmen ate lamb and mutton because it was there and because they couldn't run out to Carl's Jr. for a burger when they felt like it or cruise up the avenue for a beer and a hot dog. If the diet was a crime of sameness, she'd learned to supplement it with the occasional hog one of the hands shot or the lobster and abalone she and Anise would dive for with mask and snorkel and two pairs of cracked blue rubber flippers, just for the change. The lobsters were a treat, as many as twenty or more of them set to boil in water she'd laced with salt, peppercorns, apple cider vinegar and bay leaves, but the hands—Mexicans, mostly in their forties and fifties—were suspicious of anything new. They ignored the drawn butter and lemon wedges she'd husbanded since her last grocery run, preferring to fold up the supple white tails in their tortillas, with a scoop of beans and rice and hot sauce out of the bottle.

She used her cleaver and the butcher knife to cut chops from the loin and separate the saddle to set aside for roasting, then to strip the meat from the bone and chunk down the rest, marveling at how far she'd come in her mastery of the details. When she was living in Oxnard after Toby weaseled out on her, she could barely slice an onion her knives were so dull—and before that, when they were on the road, waitresses brought them knives, the serrated kind, to cut their steaks or chops or prime rib, and where the knives came from and who put the edge to them was no concern of hers. But not now. Now she was an intimate of knives, her knives, and she had a knife for every purpose, sticking, skinning, boning, breaking, keeping them as sharp as when they'd come out of the box at the hardware store in a time when high-quality carbon steel was manufactured right here in this country.

She dredged the meat in flour, then browned it in lamb fat while she roasted green peppers and serranos in the oven and diced tomatoes, rutabagas, celery and onions with quick brisk efficient strokes, barely noticing Francisco creep back into the room to clear the breakfast dishes from the table and slide them into the washtub. Next, she dropped the vegetables in atop the meat, setting the roasted peppers and serranos aside to cool. Then it was half a gallon of Carlo Rossi red and enough water from the tap to fill the pot (yes, they had running water now, though they'd gone without for the first year and more, a gas pump bringing it up out of the well and into a reservoir on the rise behind the house, where gravity fed it through the pipes Bax had installed at her insistence, along with a water heater so they could experience the civilizing influence of a hot shower). She gave the whole business a few brisk turns with the stirring spoon, rapped it hard against the lip of the pot and set it down on the stove, and the silence she'd come to love and expect seeped back into the room.

She'd kept the radio off purposely because she wanted to be attuned to what was going on out there in the meadow, where since first light Anise had been sitting beneath a tarp propped up on the bifurcated ends of four bent eucalyptus sticks driven into the mud, with Bumper, the little black-and-white sheepdog, at her feet and her literature book spread open in her lap, and when the stew was going full boil, Rita was going to damp the stove, pull on another sweater and her rain slicker and go out there and join her. So the kitchen was quiet, the only sounds the hiss of the stove and the banked roar of the oven played against the murmur of Francisco's dishrag, the intermittent tap of the rain and the distant watery bleating of the lambs.

The hands liked their food hot, as in spicy, a taste she'd come to acquire herself, especially if there was plenty of red wine for lubrication and bread or tortillas to sop it up with, and she cranked the handle of the pepper grinder over the pot for a good slow count of fifty before turning to the cutting board and the mound of roasted peppers. She split each of the serranos in two, swept them off the scarred plank and into the mouth of the pot, then shucked the skins from the roasted peppers, cut them in strips and added them to the mix. Then it was sage from the herb garden, paprika, parsley, a handful of bay leaves, and finally, five fennel bulbs—the stuff grew everywhere the sheep couldn't get at it, as persistent as weeds—sliced and stirred into the simmering liquid to impart a faint hint of licorice at the very top of the palate. When she was done, she took the dented aluminum bowl full of scraps and cuttings and whatever had been left on the breakfast plates out into the rain-washed morning to toss it in the compost.

Strangely, it seemed warmer outside than in, the clouds rolling up out of the ridge to the south, bruised and fist-like, dense with tropical moisture. At her feet, new growth, shining with wet, the ground that had been barren so long exhaling low dense colorless clouds of vapor, as if it had been holding its breath till now. She felt the rain as cold pinpricks on her face, her scalp, the rigid plane of her extended right hand where it emerged from the turned-back sleeve of the wool sweater to clasp the rim of the bowl, and if the hand looked strange to her, like somebody else's hand, rough, work-beaten, too little acquainted with the bridge of a guitar, then that was how it was and how it was going to be because she was a sheepwoman now and proud of it.

There was a time when she slept till two or three in the afternoon, when she stayed up all night jamming and carried her hands around as if they were wrapped in cellophane. Then their first album came out and everybody thought the world was going to open up to them like a foil-wrapped present under the Christmas tree, and then Anise was there and they made the second album before things crashed and burned and she and Toby and Anise came out to the West Coast, where it was happening, really happening, or so Toby claimed, but then it wasn't happening and she'd had to start getting up early with all the rest of the wage slaves out there just to get to one shit job after another.

That was a long time ago and what she had then of ambition, of pushing out from herself to the world beyond, had settled deep inside her, gone inward, where it glowed like the last unquenchable ember in the stove. What did she love? Her people: Anise, Bax, Francisco. This place, where nature came at you in the raw, unmediated, untenanted, and you lived life in the moment. The flock. Bumper. And music. Music still. Music always. But when she played now it was for her daughter and her lover and the scored and weather-wrecked ranch hands, with their ruined teeth and wine-sweetened breath.

Behind her, the walls of the house were streaked with rain, dark veins of it pulsing against the pale skin of the stucco, the light from the kitchen window cutting a neat rectangle out of the wall below the smaller rectangle where Bax's reading light glowed in the second-story window. He was up there under his blankets and the big down comforter and she was out here. In the rain. With a full day of watching and worrying ahead of her. Not that it mattered, she told herself, not so long as he got better. And, in a way, as terrible as it sounded, his misfortune was her boon delivered up on a platter, an opportunity to prove herself, to take charge of the lambing while the others were out in the hills, mending fences and keeping the roads open with an eye to the roundup at the end of February, when the lambs would be docked and castrated along with any of the strays they'd missed the previous year. No need for them to hang around here when there was so much to be done up above. And really, there wasn't much to the lambing—the ewes did all the work. You just needed to keep watch during those first critical hours against some disturbance of the flock, a jolt of panic that would set them running and leave the newborns alone even for the space of a minute, because that was all it took for the ravens to come on.

This year she and Anise had posted *Keep Out* signs on the beach at Scorpion and at Smugglers' Cove over the ridge to the southeast, closing off the ranch to all visitors while the lambing was under way so there'd be no chance of any interference, intentional or not—unlike last year, when two jerks in a speedboat had buzzed the cove, taking potshots at anything that moved, the crack of their rifles repeating up the canyon in rolling crescendo till the flock scattered every which way. That had been a disaster. They must have lost fifty newborn lambs in the space of an hour, fifty lambs that wouldn't grow and thrive and be sent to market, and that took a real bite out of their profits. For weeks after, all she could think of was revenge, of standing those grinning idiots up against the wall of the house and shooting them with their own guns, see how they liked it. That was her fantasy, like something out of a John Ford movie, but even in her rage, even at her hardest, she knew it was just that. The only gun she'd ever touched in her life was the .22 Bax kept behind the front door to discourage ravens and the big golden eagles that carried the lambs off to their nests and dropped the empty sacks of hide to the ground when they were done, and she'd never fired it, wasn't even sure if she could figure out how.

She paused a moment to lift her face to the sky. The clouds were dark and tight-knit, the rain dancing off her skin: there wouldn't be any day-trippers coming out from the coast, not with this weather. She upended the bowl of scraps on the mulch pile, then took a minute to turn it with the pitchfork because it needed to be turned and she meant to deny the ravens these scraps too. It was then, the rain sizzling down and the working heat at the center of the pile giving up a plume of condensation and a curdled dank reek of decay, that she detected movement out of the corner of her eye and looked round to see the fox there in the lee of the Jeep, one paw suspended in mid-step.

Now here was an animal she could get behind—too small to annoy the sheep and always on the prowl for the mice that plagued the main house, their droppings ubiquitous, scattered over everything in dark little gift packets of filth and disease. She made a kissing noise and watched the fox's ears come erect. Then, very slowly, she bent to the pile to unearth the fresh scraps till she found a wet red fragment of bone and gristle and tossed it to him. It landed with a soft thump in the wet earth at his feet and he took it gingerly, as a dog would, but without fear or concern—people were no threat to him. He'd been here longer than they had and he went on eating his mice, insects, the occasional bird, and if people left food around (or variously, Francisco's briar pipe that went missing from the porch one evening, a half-burned candle, sweated socks hung out on the rail to dry and concentrate the salts of the body), he would oblige them by expanding the range of his diet. She watched him worrying the bone a moment, pinning it with his paws and working it with his teeth, his fur slicked with the rain and his eyes casting her adrift as if she had no significance at all, and then she went back in the house to see to the stew and slide the loaves into the oven.

Francisco had set the dishes aside to dry and was plying the mop on the concrete floor now, shifting the mud from one corner to the other in long yellowish streaks. The floor was always dirty, forever dirty, but that was a matter of degree—until she'd nagged Bax to have the supply barge off-load a hundred sixty-pound bags of concrete and until that concrete was loaded ten bags at a time in the back of the pickup and brought up here to be mixed in the wheelbarrow, poured, tamped and smoothed in place, the floor had been actual dirt, literal dirt, trodden and compacted by how many generations of sheepherders' boots she couldn't begin to imagine. The other substantial building on the property—the eight-room bunkhouse— was of wood-frame construction and as far as she knew had always had a pine floor, which was, if anything, even dirtier than the old dirt floor of the main house, but nothing to worry over. The hands took turns sweeping it and every once in a long concatenation of weeks even took a mop to it. They had their own communal room, a few rough chairs, a card table and a potbellied stove, but the main house was where they gathered for their meals and where they felt—at least in her presence—as if they'd come home, the talk at supper of mothers long dead, of haciendas that no longer existed in the mind-clouded valleys of Arizona, New Mexico and Old Mexico too.

She was enveloped in the sweet hot fragrance of the stew as soon as she stepped in the door, the windows steamed over, the big open space that served as kitchen, dining room and gathering place suddenly dense with it, the released molecules of the lamb she'd chunked and the spices she'd crumbled between her palms combining and rising and drifting till even Bax, frowning over his reading glasses in the whitewashed bedroom upstairs, must have been aware of them. Shifting the big pot to the right of the stove, she took out the frying pan, greased it and cracked half a dozen eggs in a bowl. She added a spot of condensed milk and a handful of grated cheese, beat the mixture to a froth and poured out the makings of two thin omelets, spiced only with salt and pepper. Then she laid out four slices of bread, slathered two of them with her own fiery homemade *pico de gallo*, eased the first omelet between them and poured out a fresh mug of coffee. "Francisco, when you have a minute," she called, and no irony intended here either, because things were easy on the ranch, "would you take this up to Bax?"

He nodded and gave her a grin. "Yes," he said, "sure, *no hay problema*." They were both aware of the subtext here: she was making use of Francisco as intermediary for the very good reason that if she'd taken the plate up herself she would have had to listen to Bax's dammed-up torrent of advice, complaints and animadversions, not to mention the mental list of chores, niggling worries and very pressing matters he was composing even now and had been composing ever since he took to bed.

She used ketchup on the second sandwich (Anise had been crazy for ketchup since she was a little girl, smearing it on anything, saltines, pretzels, bananas, fresh-sliced cucumbers and even, at least once she knew of, on a Hershey bar), wrapped it in tinfoil and filled the thermos with hot chocolate. Then she pulled on her rain slicker and the sombrero Francisco's cousin Manuel had brought her back from Tijuana the previous year after a week-long post-shearing debauch, and went back out into the rain. She skirted the wash, which had begun to flow now with the reanimated Scorpion River, and headed up through the grove of eucalyptus to the meadow beyond, where the sheep stood sodden and gray, like so many heaps of dirty rags scattered across the new grass as far as she could see. It was a scene out of some immemorial past and she couldn't help thinking of the first naked primitives who ran down the first wild ram and killed and cooked and ate it and sat round with swollen bellies thinking how nice it would be to have something like that tethered to the nearest tree so you could have meat and offal and a good warm fleece anytime you wanted it. Here was the ur-industry, as old as the tribes themselves. And Cain slew Abel because Abel followed the herds and Cain put seeds in the ground and what kind of sacrifice to the greedy God above was a mound of peas and squash compared to the haunch of a freshly slaughtered lamb?

Anise's tarp—fireman's red, or red-orange, a color you didn't find in nature, at least not on the West Coast—shone wetly on the far edge of the field. Rita could see her sprawled legs, her hunched shoulders, the black-and-white dog with his head in her lap, the book propped up against the dog's back and her daughter doing what she did all on her own without hassle or reminder, studying, learning, making herself a better person. Anise had already advanced beyond anything she or Bax could help her with, aside from guitar lessons, and the correspondence course, with its weekly standards and monthly planner, couldn't begin to keep up with her. She wasn't yet fifteen and she was already doing work equivalent to what they'd expect of a college freshman, and all on her own. Rita was amazed anew each time she saw her bent to her work—the discipline and determination she showed, which was nothing at all like what she'd experienced herself, not with academics anyway. She'd been too edgy, too eager to throw it all over and steal away to the Village and haunt the cafés and clubs, and what had that led to? To nothing. To a false life and false hopes. Anise was different.

Anise had a future. And the longer she stayed away from the trouble of the world, the better.

"Hey, Buttercup!" she heard herself call, rain on her hat like a spastic drumbeat, the ewes all around her licking their newborns, and here was Bumper, streaking through the grass to her even as her daughter lifted her head and gave her a faraway look.

In the next moment she was easing down beside her under the tarp and offering the egg sandwich, which Anise, setting aside the book, ignored in favor of the hot chocolate. There was a wet thrashing of paws and tail and then the dog was crowding in beside them, sniffing at the warm ripples of the foil. "You better eat that before it gets cold," she said.

"What is it? Not lamb?"

"Fried egg. With a ton of ketchup."

She watched her daughter unscrew the cap of the thermos and pour out a cup of chocolate, drop by drop, as if it were wine of rare vintage. And now she pushed the sandwich on her again and Anise took it and laid it in her lap, where it balanced precariously between the dog's probing wet nose and the damp sleeping bag she was perched on. Anise was tall, like Toby—already five-eight—and as she shifted position, she folded her legs under her, long legs, legs she could grow into, and rescued the sandwich at the last minute, as if it were an afterthought. Sipping, her eyes dropping to the glossy cover of the book (*Studies in the American Story, From Hawthorne to Hemingway*, $25.95, an amount they'd had to scrape to come up with), she murmured, "I really like this one story in my book? It's called 'Bartleby, the Scrivener.' You ever read it?"

It sounded familiar, but if she had read it, it would have been back in high school. "Maybe," she said. "But a long time ago in a galaxy far, far away. It doesn't have sheep in it, does it?"

"*Please.*" Anise froze up, irritated suddenly, and gave her a hard look. She could see her daughter was in a mood,

189

ready to open up on her about how bored she was and how much she hated sheep and sheep ranches and islands, and if you came right down to it, life, life itself. She watched that skein of complication run through her eyes in a cold accusatory flash, but then Anise just shrugged and let it go. "I mean, I don't know if you could care, but it's about an office and a scrivener—he copies things by hand, I guess, because they didn't have Xerox machines or anything like that back then. And whenever the boss asks him to do something he says, 'I would prefer not to.'"

"Uh-oh, am I in trouble here?"

Anise gave her a bitter smile, and yet her eyes lit with something like pleasure over the exchange. She needed to talk, to respond to someone in the flesh about what she was feeling, thinking, reading, and not the faceless instructor who graded her papers in a tight rigid hand and in lettering so minuscule he might have been copying out the warning label on a bottle of prescription pills.

Keep it light, she told herself. Go easy.

"Because if I ask you if you want to sit out here in the rain by yourself for a few more minutes while I go back in to take the bread out of the oven, you're going to say—what was it?"

"'I would prefer not to.'"

She wanted to help ease the burden—and she tried as best she could, tried to anticipate, cajole, keep things moving forward—but she was stretched to the limit through every minute of every day and right now the lambs needed her more than her daughter did. And there was bread in the oven and stew on the stove and Bax up in bed with his foul mouth and a temper like a nest of hornets somebody's just whacked with a stick. She didn't want to argue. She didn't want to nag. But she couldn't help herself. "How about eating that egg sandwich before it goes cold?"

"I would prefer . . . oh, shit. To go to the mall, to see somebody, anybody, except you and Bax and a bunch of stupid sheep. Like all my life. Like every day. I might as well be in prison."

And here came the guilt. The weight of it that was like a physical thing because she was guilty, guilty of everything Anise could throw at her and more. She shut her eyes to drive it away, but it did no good. She saw Anise as a little girl, the look on her face when she told her she was pulling her out of class three weeks before the close of the school year and taking her out to an island nobody had ever heard of. Fifth grade. Three weeks from the end. *What about all my friends? What about summer vacation?* We'll have our vacation on the island, she'd told her. You'll love it. Beaches—there's a beach right there, your own private beach right in front of Scorpion Ranch. *I'm not going.* And then she'd repeated herself—*You'll love it*—chanting it so many times it became a litany, and Anise, stubborn, unconvinced, adamant, throwing it back at her: *I will not love it, I'll hate it. And I don't want to go to any scorpion place, I hate scorpions. Don't you?* She'd wondered about that herself, but as it turned out there were no scorpions, or only the smallest little dull brown things you sometimes saw clinging to the underside of one of the logs in the woodpile, and she'd promised her—promised her and believed it herself—that it would only be for the summer. Yes, sure, and now Anise wouldn't know the inside of her old school—of any school—if it opened up right here in the pasture in front of her.

"You see any problems out there this morning?" she said, keeping her voice flat. She was staring off across the meadow now, and there were lambs everywhere, bright as cotton wool, and the ewes licking, licking.

"Uh-uh." And then, reluctantly, because they were both on the same page again: "Twins right over there, see—like right by that red rock. There? See?"

"Did she—?"

"Yes, she licked them both."

"And did you—?" With twins, it was a good idea to

bind them together so the stronger, dominant one, would pull the other along to the teat.

"I'm reading, okay? I have an assignment due. Not that you would care."

"Okay, babe, okay," she said. "There's plenty of time. We just don't want them to get separated, is all."

As if on cue, a raven began to croak from the screen of trees behind them, and then another joined in. A dark scribble of them marred the clouds overhead and there was a black patch on the ground a hundred yards away where two of them were trying to lure a ewe away from her lamb, but the ewe was having no part of it. "Keep your eye on that, hon," she said, pushing herself up. "And keep Bumper with you—we don't want him out there herding anybody, not this morning. I'll be back"—she twisted her wrist for a look at her watch—"in like twenty minutes. And then I'm going to walk the perimeter here all day, right till dark, and you can go back to your room and your books, anything you want. Okay?"

Her daughter's eyes, illuminated by the sheen of the rain, were as changeable as well water, the palest finest transparent gray shading to blue, not Toby's eyes and not hers either. She was trying to picture her own mother, her mother's eyes, but as hard as she tried to superimpose that vision on Anise, she couldn't quite manage it. Folding her arms round her knees and leaning forward, she watched as her daughter unwrapped a corner of the sandwich and lifted it to her mouth for an exploratory sniff. "Okay?" she repeated.

"Yes, already, *yes!!* I mean, what do you want me to say? What do you think, I'm like three years old? I'm here, okay? And if any of those frickin' birds even thinks about it I'm going to be on him like glue."

Frickin'. On him like glue. She heard Bax in the mix and maybe Arturo, the youngest of the hands, thirty-one and retired from rodeoing with a right leg that looked as if it had come out of a laundry wringer. She heard it and felt the guilt all over again, as if someone had switched on a circuit inside her—Anise needed to be with kids her own age, her peer group, kids she could go to the movies with and window-shopping in the mall and all the rest of it. Girlfriends. Maybe even a boyfriend. Or somebody to moon over anyway. She pushed herself up and ducked back out into the rain, which seemed to be slackening a bit. Or was it her imagination?

"You do that, honey," she said, thinking, even as she said it, of the kind of ache that would open up inside her if Anise ever did go back to shore, to Toby and Toby's mother in New York, where she spent a couple of weeks in the summer, at least when Toby remembered to send tickets for the plane. She'd already shifted toward the house when she swung round again, the dog looking up at her in expectation, Anise chewing her egg sandwich and regarding her warily. "And when you get 'em all glued down," she added, the rain drooling from the big bowl of the sombrero, "pluck out all their feathers for me, will you?"

Francisco was just coming out the door, wearing a heavy leather poncho over his workshirt and a faded red baseball cap that carried the legend *Trojans* in once-yellow letters across the crown, a legend that always made her think of the condoms she and Toby were so careful to use even when they both felt they were about to burst wide open with the fierceness of their need but which hadn't stopped her from getting pregnant at just exactly the wrong time. Twice. Once when the band (Tobrita, her inspiration, their names intertwined in the way of forever, as if forever meant anything) was just taking off and then again when the record company sent them out on tour. The first time he made her get an abortion. The second time she refused. That was Anise. And could she even imagine life without her? "I go to watch now," Francisco said. "*¿Todo bien?*"

She was standing there braced against the doorframe,

trying to kick off her muddy boots, the rain scent at her back, the dense complex odor of cooking coming at her through the open door. "I don't know," she said, her voice harsh in her own ears. "Jesus God, sometimes I just want to give up, throw it all over and go live in a motel someplace and collect welfare like everybody else, you know what I mean?" He didn't know. Sheep were what he knew, sheep and nothing else. One boot sucked free, then the other, and she reached out to steady herself against the wall. "But maybe you want to make a circuit and see what you can see—especially across from where Anise's set up." She gave him a softening smile. "You know me, always worried."

He would have smiled back at her, but he only smiled when he was drunk. He might have said yes or nodded his head, but he just stared at her, numb-faced, the cap already wet through with the rain.

She kicked her boots aside, snatched the sombrero from her head and beat it twice against her thigh to knock the rain from it. "Well, go on then, don't stand here gaping," she said, and then she smelled the bread and took it from the oven and set it aside to cool while she rotated the spoon round the depths of the stewpot and went absolutely still when Bax called down from above, "Rita? Rita, is that you?"

Ten minutes later she was back out in the field, striding through the grass to Anise and scanning the meadow for Francisco. A breeze had come up in the interval, sheeting the rain, and at first she couldn't make him out. She was almost to Anise when finally she spotted him, all the way across the field on the far perimeter, moving along briskly, his own variation of the shepherd's staff—PVC pipe, with a squared-off crook cemented to the end of it—bobbing along in front of him like a bleached white antenna. He would have been more comfortable on horseback—they used the horses at roundup and for day-to-day operations and just to get out in the hills and away from the ranch—but this morning Diablo, Moreno and Jonesy were back in the corral, rubbing their backsides against the rails or lifting their muzzles to snuff at the rain, because she felt it was better not to risk even the smallest, most usual perturbation of the sheep at a time like this. So Francisco was on foot. And so was she.

Nothing had changed. The sheep were in the meadow, the ravens in the trees, Anise and the dog where she'd left them, the rain holding steady. She was about to call out to her daughter, something silly and lighthearted—"Second shift reporting for duty" or "I would prefer not to see you sitting out here in the rain one minute more"—when the stillness was broken by the report of a rifle. It was a single sharp crack, as if someone had snapped a stick in two, but loud, impossibly loud, the sound charging out of the hills to chase itself across the meadow and then back again. Everything hung suspended for a single airless instant and then the second report rang out and the flock, as one, sprang into motion. She was already running when she saw the dark hurtling streak slicing across the meadow and the sheep flowing away from it, panicking now, bolting for cover, for the hills, and what was it, what was happening? Then she saw it—a hog, a boar, its head fused with the big neck muscles in a picture of flight, ears flat, legs beating so fast they slid out of focus—and before she could think the three men were there with their guns and their machines.

"Hey!" she shouted, her breath coming in gasps, the sombrero torn back and away from her head and lost to the elements. She was running full-out, arms pumping, knees high, but this was the thing, and she couldn't have been more astonished if a Martian probe had swooped in for a landing: the men were mounted on vehicles, three-wheeler ATVs that chewed up the wet earth and spat it out again in dark ropes of mud, and they weren't about to stop for anything. The boar was already gone, vanished into the scrub along the wash. And before she could do a thing—before she could confront them, demand an explanation, chase them off now and forever—the men were gone too, the pop and rattle of their engines fading away in the distance. She saw Anise running toward her, her face robbed of everything, saw Francisco jerking the staff over his head in agitation and Bumper veering for the nearest panicked ewe. And then she saw the ravens.

Off to her right, a hundred yards or more—and she was closing on it, flailing her arms and shouting—the first of them careened into a lamb, going for the head, always the head. Bewildered, abandoned, unsteady on its neophyte's legs, the lamb went down as if it had been struck with a club. And then the bird, implanted, rose up to stabilize itself on the cross trees of its wings and strike out the eyes, even as the next arrived to rip open the breast where the thin new tegument of skin was as yielding and soft as a vat of cream cheese. She bent to snatch up stones, still running, out of breath and ringing with hate and rage and panic, another lamb gone down and another, the ravens piling on and beating from one to the other like checkers jumping squares all across the meadow. She flung the stones. Bent for more. Ran like a terminal case, like brain damage, ran, because there was nothing else she could do.

Every time she closed on a mob of them they rose and flapped off to the next kill and she was left with the dead and dying stretched out like refuse at her feet, the barely formed limbs twitching still, eye sockets bloodied and vacant, the looping blue entrails exposed. They were in a hurry. They wanted the heart, the still-beating heart, and the liver and kidneys—the rest they could come back for. She got to the next lamb within seconds—it was right there, no more than fifty feet away—kicking at the black sheen of the wings and the quick reptilian stab of the slick bloodied beaks, but she was too late, the birds bounding away in short contemptuous hops till they got wings under them and glided off while the lamb thrashed in the grass. She watched it shudder along its length, attempting to lift its head, thrusting out its legs for balance, but its eyes were gone and the pale drum of its abdomen was sheeted in red. The sound it made—not a bleat, but a whisper, a choked gargle in the back of the throat—froze her for just that instant. And then she was on to the next while all around her the ravens plunged and screamed.

This one—just ahead and to her left—was untouched. It stood there weaving over its legs as if buffeted by a stiff wind, bleating weakly in its confusion. She grabbed it in stride and tucked it under one arm and then she had another one, this one with the umbilical still dangling and the ears and crown of the skull wet with afterbirth—and where was Anise? Where was Francisco? And Bumper? She spun around twice, shouting out her daughter's name. If she could only get her here, by her side, they could gather up as many as they could, make a stand . . . she heard the barking of the dog then but he was all but useless, chasing the ewes up and away from the meadow in a futile effort to turn them. "Anise!" she roared, the cords tightening in her throat. "Anise, damn it, where are you?"

There was nothing, nothing but the cacophony of the birds, until all at once her daughter's voice carried back to her—"Over here, Mom! Hurry!"—and she pivoted to see Anise stumbling toward her through the rain-slick grass, a lamb cradled in her arms. She was sobbing, her lips thrust back against her teeth, her mouth a hole carved out of her face, the wet hair hanging limp in her eyes and her eyes streaming. "I can't," she cried, her voice cracking, "I can't," and Rita saw that the lamb in her arms was bloodied.

She might have comforted her—should have—but she was caught up in the fury of the moment. "Put that goddamned thing down, will you? Can't you see it's dead?"

"It's not, Mom. It's not. It's still breathing." Anise was coming toward her, weak-kneed, stringy, a child still, the house and Bax and his lit window so far behind them they might as well have been in another country.

There was a smear of blood on the grass just there in front of her and the sight of it, the fact of it, lashed her forward. She meant to set the lambs down gently, but the rage jerked at her shoulders and she just dropped them there in the mud and trampled grass and flew at her daughter. "What in hell's the matter with you?" she demanded, snatching the thing out of her arms and flinging it aside like the refuse it was. She could have slapped her. Could have screamed in her face. Couldn't she see what was happening? Didn't she understand?

"You stand right here—and don't you even think about moving. I'm going to bring in as many as I can, right here, right here to you." Her voice was rising up the scale. A quick hot glandular jolt burned through her.

Anise just stared at her.

"Just keep the goddamn birds off them. Okay? That's all I ask."

Her daughter's face was blanched and small, as distant as if she were all the way across the field still. She was fifteen years old. She loved animals, loved her dog, loved the lambs, but this had nothing to do with love.

"Wake up!" she shouted, spitting the words at her over the rocketing surge of her blood, already turning away to scan the meadow for the lambs that had been spared, for the spindly inadequate legs and the rain-wet, blood-wet fluff of their coats, but all she could see was the ravens, dozens of them, piled up on the corpses like black blankets flapping.

Ovis Aries

No one knows when sheep were initially introduced to Santa Cruz Island, but the first flocks of any size appeared sometime in the 1850s, under the direction of the island's first individual owner, Andrés Castillero, or rather, his agent, James Baron Shaw, a Santa Barbaran he'd hired to manage the property. Castillero had been instrumental in negotiating a settlement after Alta California briefly seceded from Mexico in 1836, and for his efforts, the minister of the interior, by order of the president, granted him sole and exclusive ownership of the whole of Santa Cruz Island. From the point of view of the Mexican government, this was no doubt a reward of negligible value, since the Mexicans considered the islands too distant, arid and forbidding to be of much interest. Shaw erected a house and ranch buildings in the central valley, some three miles inland from Prisoners' Harbor on the north shore, and introduced cattle, horses and sheep. In the interim, the treaty of Guadalupe Hidalgo ceded all of California to the government of the United States, along with what is now Texas, New Mexico, Nevada, Utah and Arizona, and Castillero, who had understandably begun to feel insecure about the legitimacy of his title, placed the following advertisement in the *Daily Alta California* for May 25, 1858:

FOR SALE: An island containing about 60,000 acres of land, well-watered and abounding in small valleys of the best pasturage for sheep. There are no wild animals on it that would interfere with livestock. There is a good harbor and safe anchorage.

A year later, a consortium headed by Eustace Barron, the English consul at Tepíc, Mexico, purchased the island, keeping Shaw on as manager. The new owners set about establishing a sheeping operation on a large scale, going all the way across the Atlantic to acquire the finest pedigreed stock, merinos from Spain and Leicester longwools from England, breeds known for the superior quality of their wool as well as their hardiness and adaptability. Given a virgin range and no predators to interfere with them (not even the golden eagle, which was not then known to nest on the Channel Islands), the sheep throve. Within ten years, there were as many as fifty thousand of them roaming the island. Santa Cruz, formerly sheepless, was suddenly rich with sheep. So rich that Barron was able to sell his interest at profit to a partnership from San Francisco, but the new owners, who incorporated as the Santa Cruz Island Company under the directorship of Justinian Caire, a perspicacious French dealer in hardware who'd sailed west to take advantage of the gold fever sweeping the region, found the population unsustainable. Water sources had dried up. There was insufficient forage. Something had to give.

If rats are the single most devastating invasive species when introduced to a closed ecosystem, then goats and sheep, with their ability to seek out even the most inaccessible niches and their capacity to consume and digest practically anything short of the dirt itself, are a close second. The problem, of course, is overgrazing. Barron's sheep burned through the vegetation of the island like a wildfire, adapting their diet successively to include native succulents, shrubs and saplings once the grasses and forbs they preferred had been eliminated. The dry seasons lingered. The winds blew. And when the rains came on the shoulders of the monsoonal storms, the soil, no longer anchored by the roots of the devastated flora, peeled away like ineptly grafted skin. The seas darkened with silt. The native fauna, bereft of resources and shelter alike, died back and the pine forests of the high ridges thinned under the pressure of the relentless grazing so that there were fewer branches to collect and disperse the moisture of the fog, and the island became more arid still. So Monsieur Caire sent his lambs to market, sheared the flock in the *transquila* at the main ranch and sold the fleeces by weight, and then went out into the hills and shot what he couldn't use. Twenty-four thousand sheep, give or take a few, were eliminated. And still the coreopsis and live-forever, the silver mallow, the gooseberry, manzanita and monkey flower, the toyon and mountain mahogany and deerweed were grazed to the nub before they could bloom and set seed. And still the woodland skipper and the cranefly and the katydid and the slender salamander declined and declined again.

The solution to the problem of overgrazing, as far as Caire was concerned, was to diversify. He bought out his partners and took up residence on the island. Under his direction, fields were plowed for crops and feed, a vineyard and winery were established, beef cattle were brought in and satellite ranches constructed at Christy Beach in the far west and at Smugglers' Cove and Scorpion Anchorage in the east. The cattle grazed and so did the sheep, but their numbers were more or less kept in check by rigorous culling. A portion of the flock inevitably went feral and was hunted for sport, along with the wild hogs that infested the place like vermin, destroying fence, digging up the crops, raiding the vineyards under cover of night and leaving nothing behind but pulp and feces. Still, for all the fragility of the ecosystem, the Santa Cruz Island Company made a go of it, shipping lamb and beef, wool, hides, tallow and wine back to the coast, but it was the wine, especially, that made the coffers ring.

Caire had made his fortune catering to the needs of the forty-niners, dispensing picks and shovels and the like as they hit the pier running with maddened looks on their faces and hand-drawn maps of the Feather River drainage, Coloma and Dutch Flat clutched in their sweating hands, and offering them French porcelain, Sheffield china and fine cutlery when they returned flush with their profits, and this was all well and good. But his ambition was far grander. He saw himself as a *propriétaire* presiding over a château and cellars of his own, like those of Bordeaux or Languedoc. He had the *terroir*, now he needed *les vignes*. (And, not incidentally, a wife, a chatelaine to help him found the dynasty he was building in air each night as his head hit the pillow.) He sailed back to Europe first to acquire the wife—Maria Christina Sara Candida Molfino, of Rapallo, a district where the grapevines had woven their way across the terraced hills from time immemorial, a place where people knew grapes, where they knew wine, where their blood was infused with it and no meal, even breakfast, was without its medicinal touch—and then sailed again to bring back the finest French rootstock he could find.

He chose well, both in marriage, which was to produce nine children, six of whom survived into adulthood, and in matching his grapes to the *terroir*. The central valley, with the rich mineral content of its soil, its warm days and cool, sea-misted nights, presented ideal conditions for the growing of a suite of varietal grapes, and by the early 1890s the Santa Cruz Island label was shipping high-quality zinfandel, pinot noir, Burgundy, muscat de frontignan, Chablis and riesling up the coast to San Francisco. And when the *Phylloxera* aphid ravaged the Old World vineyards and laid waste to some 75,000 acres in California as well, Monsieur Caire's 600 acres of grapes were unaffected—neither the aphid nor the adult *Phylloxera* fly had the means of crossing the barrier of the channel. Wine was scarce. Prices went up. Even after the proprietor's death in 1897, the winery continued to prosper in the hands of his two sons, Arthur and Frédéric, right up until the unnatural disaster of Prohibition crushed it some twenty-two years later. Unaffected by such vagaries, the hogs continued their raids and the sheep grazed at will, until finally the sons dug out the vines and threw them on the dung heap for burning, so that all that remained were the deep horizontal furrows striping the flanks of the hills like the scars of an ancient wound.

The proprietor's will had divided the island into seven parcels, one for each of his children, and one—parcel 5, by far the largest, on which the main ranch and winery stood—for their mother, Maria Christina Sara Candida Molfino Caire, or Albina, as she was known, mercifully, for short. The division was contentious. Each of the siblings felt cheated. Arthur, the eldest son, for instance, was given title to Christy Ranch in the west, but there was no serviceable harbor there to make it useful, while Edmund Rossi, son of his deceased sister Amélie, was awarded the far more desirable parcel number 7, on the eastern end of the island, and Arthur's sister Aglae wound up with parcel 6, which included Scorpion Ranch and its excellent and protected anchorage. Litigation ensued. The original heirs began to die off and their heirs in turn took up the fight. Conditions deteriorated, the Depression intervened, the sheep kept on grazing.

Finally, in 1937, the main ranch and the four western parcels adjoining it were sold in large to an oil man from Los Angeles, Edwin Stanton, who attempted to revive the sheeping operation, bringing in domestic stock to interbreed with the remnant of the original flock and lure in the outliers. He soon gave it up when the whole of the flock, domestic and feral alike, scattered to the far ends of the island, making it too great a nuisance to round them up annually for shearing, docking and branding, and so he shipped 30,000 sheep to slaughter and focused on cattle, with mixed success. On his death in 1963, his son Carey took over majority ownership and ran the cattle operation until he himself died in 1987 and ceded the entire property to the Nature Conservancy, which hired a professional hunting concern to exterminate the remaining sheep, finally putting an end to the ovine occupation of the major portion of Santa Cruz Island.

But on the eastern two parcels, which remained in the

hands of Monsieur Caire's descendants, the sheep went right on ruminating, stripping the bark from the endemic oak, cherry and ironwood trees, grinding the bishop pine seedlings between their reductive molars, running every stamen and leaf and scrap of pith through the chambers of their four contiguous stomachs till the hills felt the pressure of them like a cinched belt, cinched and looped and cinched again.

By the time Bax took over the operation in 1979, things had fallen to ruin and the sheep were little more than an afterthought. The current owners, Pier and Francis Gherini, great-grandsons of the *propriétaire*, had come up with a scheme for developing their portion of the island into a resort, replete with marina, golf course, lodges and restaurants, but when the County of Santa Barbara denied them permits at the urging of the National Park Service, their interest flagged and whatever Scorpion Ranch once was, it was no more. It was Bax who brought it back to life. They hired him in an attempt to squeeze some profit out of the place, and he threw himself into the task, taking on new hands, repairing fence, rounding up as many of the ferals as he could and bringing in seventy prize Rambouillet rams to breed up the stock. Rita threw herself into it too. And Francisco. And Anise. They all did. But how could anyone hope to hold anything together when the world was as liable to fracture as Bax's ribs and the long white bone that was like the bone of a ghost on the sheeny black X-rays of his left leg? Bax was laid up, that was the fact, and trespassers were out there shooting their guns at will and scaring the ewes off their lambs.

Anise had been inconsolable. Once it was over—and it was over when the ravens decided it was, lifting themselves from the bloat and scatter like great winged slugs—Rita went to her. She found her crouched in the beaten grass with the lambs all gathered to her, the hair strung dripping across her face, her shoulders quaking and her clothes wet through with the rain and the blood. Some of the lambs were too weak to stand, their outsized ears fanned out in the grass, their bleating like some diachronic dirge. They needed their mothers—for protection, warmth, milk—and if they didn't get them soon the loss would go far beyond the seventy-three corpses Rita had already counted.

"Come on, honey," she said, struggling to control her voice. "Let's go back to the house and get into some dry clothes. I'll make you some tea. Or hot chocolate. How about some hot chocolate?"

Anise didn't respond. She sat hunched over her knees, rocking back and forth, the line of her clenched jaw as bloodless and jumpy as a diviner's rod. She didn't even lift her eyes.

Rita stood there in the rain, trying for her daughter's sake to be gentle, reasonable, calming, motherly, but she felt none of these things. The fact was that in that moment Anise looked exactly like Toby, Toby when he was down, when they played and nobody showed, when the A&R man at the record company told them he had reservations about some of the songs on their second album, that they were weak, worse than weak, that they were shit, pure and unadulterated, and Toby was the last thing she wanted to think about now. Toby with his tantrums, his cheating, his coke. *Cocaína*, he always called it. As in, *Let's do some cocaína.* Cute. Real cute. When they couldn't even pay the rent.

She made an effort. "There's nothing we can do," she said, the smell of the rain enlivening the odor of death that hung over the field till she felt as if she wanted to sink down in the mud—right here, right in front of her daughter—and cry herself dry. What was the use of it all? The worry, the deprivation, every penny put back into the flock and no satisfaction but in increase? "The damage is already done and all we can do now is let the mothers come back to their babies. Look," she said, pointing across the field to where Francisco and Bumper were working to bring them in, "they're already coming back. They're as worried as we are."

Anise's voice was small and bitter. "What about the ones that don't have anything to worry about? What are they going to do?"

"I know," she said. "I know, it hurts."

She was remembering the previous year when one of the ewes that had lost a lamb to a withered leg kept nosing at the remains of the carcass—the hooves, the head, the coat—long after the flesh had gone. That was a kind of heartbreak that jumped species, from *Ovis aries* to *Homo sapiens*, and here it was again, seventy-three ewes come back to bleat for the lambs that couldn't answer, and the ravens laughing from the trees.

"We have to get the police," Anise said in a steady low voice, and now she looked up, her eyes hard and fixed. "Make *them* pay, those jerks, those *hunters*. For every one."

"We will, honey, believe me." And here she felt the anger and hate and despair come up in her all over again. "I'm going to go straight in there to the radio and call the sheriff, because this is criminal trespass, and, I don't know, vandalism—"

"And murder."

There was a countervailing breeze coming up off the ocean—she could smell the sharpness of it, the iodine, the salty sting of scales and feathers and fins—and it loosened the grip of the rain till it began to fall off in random spatters. "That's right," she said. "That's what it amounts to." She held out her hand, impatient now. "Come on, get up, *move*. Let's get to the radio while there's still a chance of catching them."

Anise rose from the grass and smoothed down her wet jeans. The lambs she'd gathered just lay there looking into the wind, but already the ewes were trotting up to them, each instantly identifiable to the other by smell and a distinctive note of voice. "What good's the sheriff going to do? Even if he came, which he won't, it might be days from now and those guys are going to be long gone."

"I don't know," she said, already turning toward the house, "maybe we can get the Coast Guard on them." One of them, the one in front, was a big square-jawed blond who looked as if he could have been one of those phony TV wrestlers her father had liked so much when she was a girl back in New York. He hadn't even given her so much as a glance. And he wasn't carrying a gun, unlike the other two—they roared past, as oblivious as he was, rifles slung over their shoulders as they worked the handlebars of their machines and looked out ahead for ruts, obstructions, the retreating flanks of a black tusker boar. He must have thought he was the real deal, because he had a bow and a quiver of arrows strapped to his back. Big man. Big hero. "Because they've got to have a boat somewhere, you know that—"

Anise, rangy, tall, her back slumped under the weight of everything that was wrong, and her book, in its plastic sleeve, pressed to her chest, fell into step with her, and there was the house ahead of them, smoke rising from the chimney, Bax's light still on, and it was as if nothing had happened, as if all the clocks were frozen and the sun locked in place. "Where do you think they are—Smugglers'? Because we put signs there and they—they can't just say they didn't know . . ."

"Don't you worry, darlin'," she said, striding along as briskly as her legs would carry her, and was she quoting some song, was that it? Lyrics clouded her head, all the songs she'd heard and sung and would sing in the years to come when all this was over with, and she was already envisioning a new song, with a blues progression and a theme of final and uncompromising revenge. "Don't you worry," she repeated, the words like cold little stones in her mouth, "those sons of bitches are going to regret this, and you can take my word for it."

But they didn't. And they wouldn't. Because wheels were turning that she knew nothing about, and when she mounted the stairs to the bedroom she was surprised to see Bax out of bed, dressed in his faded flannel shirts—he wore as many as three or four of them, depending on the temperature—and his blue jeans with the one leg cut away for the cast. He was perched on the edge of the chair, attempting to pull on his socks, but when he tried to reach down to his good foot the ribs tugged him back as if his arm was attached to a bungee cord. He winced. Let out a curse. "Goddamn it," he rumbled when she came through the door, "will you help me with this? And my boots. Where the shitfuck are my boots?"

She slid his socks on over his cold white feet with their horny yellowed nails and splayed toes before she said a word and when she did she was already at the door. "You mean your *boot*, don't you? Because there's no way a boot's going to go over that cast, even if I slit it with a knife. And I don't know that you should even be up on it."

"I heard two shots," he said, swiveling toward her, the left leg swinging like a pendulum in its chrysalis of dirty white plaster. "What was it—day-trippers? Hunters?"

It was day-trippers who punched holes in their illusion of serenity anytime they chose to show up, day and night, from the diver who drowned within sight of the beach while taking abalone out of season so that Anise had to find him there at low tide with his facial features all eaten away and one rigid arm hooked up like an invitation to dance, to the bonfire builders and stranded fishermen and the six teenagers in their daddy's cabin cruiser out of Santa Barbara shooting up a pod of gray whales in the shallows off Scorpion Rock. You never knew, especially in summer, when somebody you'd never seen before would waltz right into the kitchen, as if the whole ranch was nothing more than a curiosity out of a museum. But this wasn't day-trippers. This was worse, far worse. "Hunters," she said.

He'd stopped just short of her, weaving on the pinions of the crutches, huge, big-headed, his hair gone white in the past year and his white-flecked beard fanning out across his collar and up into his sideburns as if a wind were spitting in his face. "Where? Not on ranch property?"

She tried to keep her voice level. "Right in Scorpion meadow. Right in the middle of it."

"Shit. The dumb fucks. We lose any?"

She just nodded. "Anise's downstairs trying to get the Coast Guard on the marine radio. This time we're going to make them pay."

"What'd they look like?"

And now she had to see them all over again. The way they'd come on, heedless, clueless, the sheep starting up. "I don't know. Like the average jerk. The one of them had a bow and arrow and he was all in camouflage like this was Vietnam or something."

Bax wedged himself through the doorway and she followed him to the head of the stairs, the kitchen opening up beneath them, the long table, the boar's head Bax had had stuffed presiding over the room with its meshed tusks and lopsided grin, as if death were a rare joke. "He didn't"—handing her the crutches so he could take hold of the rail and begin easing himself down the stairs, one step at a time—"have blond hair by any chance?"

"He did, yeah," she said, stepping down to him and forcing her shoulder up under his arm for support.

"Big guy? Forties?"

"Yeah, I guess. Why, you know him?"

"Shit, yes. That's Thatch." Another step down and then another, the room looming beneath them, opening up like a chasm, the stove, the oven, the dull glow of the battered pots and pans, a pit of domesticity and daily strife. She could hear Anise's voice at the radio—"Mayday, Mayday, Mayday!"—and the screech of static on the other end. *Who's Thatch?* was what she was about to say, but he was already spinning out the answer. "Doesn't he know the rules? They told me he was strictly to stay off the ranch and just hunt the hills."

"Who told you?"

He was breathing hard, sweating, though it couldn't have been more than fifty-five degrees in the house, and when they reached the bottom of the stairs he winced as she ducked out from under his arm and handed him the crutches. His eyes pulled away from hers. "The owners," he said.

"What do you mean? They didn't—?"

"Yeah," he said, his voice gone to the very bottom of the register, more a snort or growl than a human vocalization, "and I've been meaning to tell you about it for a couple of weeks now, but with the accident and all I just—"

She was furious, burning. "Just what? Lied to me? Kept me in the dark? Treated me like a hired hand, like a cook, instead of what I am, or what I thought I was anyway. You son of a bitch. You're worse than they are."

He dragged himself across the room to the door before he responded, and when he did, he was already reaching behind it for the .22 rifle, as if that would do any good against a band of pig killers with high-powered rifles and a longbow with a fifty-five-pound pull. "They gave them the hunting concession, all right? And I didn't want to get you all pissed off and raving because it's the owners' decision and there's nothing we can do about it except the deal was they'd stay off the property and up in the hills and now the deal's off." He swung his head round angrily and shouted down the length of the room to where Anise sat at the big Steelcase desk where they did their paperwork, crying "Mayday!" into the radio microphone. "Shut that goddamn thing off, will you? Anise! Shut it!"

Rita had a hand on his arm. He was grimacing,

tottering, trying with his two hands, two armpits and two shellacked and shining crutches to maneuver the rifle so he could hold on to it and throw open the door at the same time. "What are you going to do? Shoot them? You can hardly stand up."

He was outside, on the landing, and then he eased down the front step and into the wet, the rubber-tipped struts of the crutches sucking at the mud and already blackened. In the absence of the Jeep, their only vehicle was the geriatric Ford pickup one of their unnamed predecessors had left behind. He and Francisco had resurrected it, but it was balky in the extreme, and they spent as much time fooling with it as racecar mechanics. Shoulders hunched to the level of the crutches, his head dipping and rising with each labored step and the cast swinging wildly, he made straight for it. She was right behind him, outraged, as furious over this exclusionary secret he'd been harboring as she was over the slaughter of the lambs. He fumbled with the passenger door of the pickup, unequal to the task, then slammed the flat of his hand against the rusted sheet metal and jerked his head round, savage suddenly. "Open the goddamn door, will you. And then get in behind the wheel."

She pulled back the door and he clattered and groped his way in, cursing under his breath, the leg in its cast like a timber he was trying to fit in place, the rifle careening across the floorboards and the crutches tangled and banging, wood to metal. When she tried to help, he shrugged her off, jerking at the crutches as if he were trying to break them in two, and so she gave it up, ducked round the hood and slid into the driver's seat. She watched him strain and heave and jerk at the unyielding wooden struts, wanting to say something but fighting down the urge because he was going to do what he was going to do and no amount of advice or sympathy or sense was going to change that, then shifted into neutral, put one foot on the clutch and the other on the accelerator, turned the key and listened to the engine crank and then catch with a mufflerless farting blast of exhaust. He was in now, the crutches flung into the truckbed, the door slammed shut. She goosed the accelerator, dropped the stick into low and the truck lurched forward, shimmying over the ruts. "Where to?" she said, her tone low and nasty, and she was ready to lay into him, she was, but he forestalled her.

"Smugglers'," he said.

She pictured the ranch house there, run-down, uninhabitable, a kind of spook house she sometimes sat in to get out of the rain or just to listen to the phantom tread of the sheepmen who'd tromped the floorboards in a day gone by. That was where they'd be, she'd known that much herself —even Anise had known it. But what she hadn't known—what he hadn't told her—was that they had the owners' blessings. That the owners were branching out because the sheep operation was bringing in practically nothing and they wanted a return on their investment like anybody else. They lived on the coast, in nice warm houses, they ate out in restaurants and went to the movies and the yacht club or the symphony or whatever it was, and they had no idea of the kind of work and dedication she and Bax had put into the place. No idea. Not an inkling.

Suddenly she felt scared. Just three hours ago she was secure, serene, her every thought focused on the lambing, on life and giving and *increase*, and now she was trapped in a burning house and all the windows were nailed shut. She jerked the wheel, hammered the brake, pounded the accelerator. There was a moment of weightlessness succeeded by a grinding thump and a cascade of piss-colored water as they plunged into the Scorpion River and ricocheted up the far bank. The gear shift throbbed in her hand, the engine wheezed and ratcheted. Dropping down to first, she hit the ridge road at speed and they began to climb. Up they went, past the spot where Bax had flipped the Jeep, the road winding back on itself, higher and higher, till Scorpion Bay opened up beneath them and the ranch caught hold of the web of dirt roads that radiated out from it as if it were the center of all the world and the trees wove their fringe around it and the ewes, in the distance, were specks of non-color, licking their lambs. The rifle lay on the floorboards at their feet, sliding first to her, then to him, as she took the turns and beat in and out of the potholes. "So what are you going to do?" she asked him through her gritted teeth, her shoulders jerking, the seat bucking under her and Bax holding on to the door handle for his life.

He gave her a strained look. The ribs were killing him, she could see that, but at the moment she had no sympathy for him, not the smallest, fractured particle of it. "I don't know," he said, and the rifle slid all the way across the cab, barrel first, till she had to nudge it away from the accelerator with her foot. "I'm just going to go have a little talk with them, is all."

By the time they got to the top of the ridge the sky had begun to clear, the black clouds rolling off to obscure the coast to the north and a continuous thread of silver running along in their wake. The going was easier here, the terrain ironed flat across the mesa that separated the two ranches, but the road was soupy and there were displaced rocks and mudslides of one degree or another round every turning. Half a dozen times she had to climb down and roll stones out of the way or ply the shovel they kept in back for just such a happy occasion and all the while Bax sat there fuming. Even in the best of times the road wasn't much—every spring, after the rains, Bax and Francisco would take turns coaxing the old John Deere bulldozer to life and scrape it smooth of ruts, rocks and brush—but it seemed especially bad now that the Jeep, with its four-wheel traction, was out of commission and she had to negotiate it in the pickup. All the while, fishtailing across the mesa, she dreaded the prospect of winding her way down through the stacked-up switchbacks on the other side. That would be a trial, the sodden earth giving way, the wheels skewing toward the shoulder that wasn't a shoulder anymore but an edge, a precipice, a drop.

When they got to the top and the road began to dip down again, she and Bax had a view of Smugglers' Ranch and the grove of olive trees, gone wild now, that somebody had put in the ground when the place was a going operation and they planted hayfields for the cattle, picked grapes and pressed olives for their oil. Nothing looked amiss, at least not from a bird's-eye view, and she didn't dare take her eyes off the road for more than a hurried glance as she humped in and out of the gullies and kept so close to the inside she scraped whatever paint might have been left off the long run of the fenders and the battered door that was all there was between Bax and the gouged-out hillside. "Jesus," he said—twice—but that was all he said.

The wheel jumped like a fistful of snakes, the tires slipped and grabbed and slipped again. She snatched a quick glance out the window, and as far as she could see, there were no boats in the bay or drawn up on the beach, but when finally the road stopped pitching and she could lift her eyes from the hood for a better look, she saw the tracks the three-wheelers had left in the yard out front of the abandoned house. They ran in tight graceful arcs, looping in on themselves, weaving and interweaving, their message all too plain.

She pulled up in the yard, killed the ignition and set the brake with a jerk of her arm. The house was a two-story adobe, like the ranch house at Scorpion, but here the glass of the windows was gone, long since shattered by day-trippers practicing their marksmanship with stones and bullets alike, and the three parallel doors—one on each end and one set in the middle as if the place had been designed by kindergartners on a stiff sheet of construction paper—stood perpetually open on their ruptured hinges. It looked the way it always had: unoccupied, deserted, bereft. Heart leaping, she slammed out of the truck and went straight for the middle door, the one that gave onto the main room. If she saw Bax tugging at the dead weight of the cast and fumbling for his crutches, it didn't register because this wasn't about being polite or compassionate or even loving, and it was cold fury that propelled her. He shouted something at her back, but she was already inside.

The light faded to gray. Shadows fell away from the walls. She made out an irregular shape on the floor of the entryway, something that didn't belong, and it took a moment for it to cohere out of the dimness: a blue backpack, its flap flung back on a box of dehydrated meals in silver pouches. Beyond it, there was a jumble of clothes and equipment, manufactured things, shucked wrappers, crumpled cans, three twelve-packs of Tecate stacked haphazardly one atop the other in their flame-red jackets. The smell she remembered—mild and botanical, the odor of dry rot, mold, the dehisced seeds of the plants that drifted through the broken panes and settled in the cracks of the floorboards—was different now, coppery and hard, with an overlay of the mechanical, of oil, gun oil, and here were the rifles, two, three, four of them, propped against the back wall like an exhibit in a gallery.

The sleeping bags she found laid out on the floor of the main room, a pair of Coleman lanterns propped up beside them in a scatter of hunting magazines—*Oregon's Mule Deer Paradise, Ozarks Bear and More!*—and a yard-long ice chest, orange and white plastic, set like a bench beneath the lintel of the shattered window. She heard Bax call out her name, but didn't answer. Inside the ice chest, amidst a slurry of melting ice, were two plastic-wrapped slabs of meat, what looked to be a liver in one and four or five crudely cut steaks in the other. Behind her, at the door, there was the sound of a heavy footfall and then the thump and grate of the crutches. Bax's voice echoed through the emptiness: "Rita, where in hell are you?"

Still she didn't answer. She was too angry, each crumpled cigarette pack and balled-up wad of underwear or grease-stained rags infuriating her anew, and what did they think this was, a hotel? A flophouse? She took the stairs two at a time, cursing under her breath. At the top of the stairs was a door, and that was strange, because she hadn't remembered a door there at all. She couldn't be sure, but it looked as if it had new hinges, or at least they'd been newly oiled and scraped of rust. She lifted the latch and pushed the door open, and here she was surprised— or no, shocked and outraged—all over again.

The room had been transformed. The floorboards gleamed as if they'd been varnished, or if not varnished at least scrupulously swept and mopped. And the windows— there were two of them, set in the side and back walls— were covered in plastic sheeting, which had been carefully affixed to the window frame with duct tape. A camp bed stood against the far wall, complete with blankets, pillow, sheets and pillowcase. There were jackets and shirts suspended from nails driven into the wall above it, another backpack—this one in plain unvarnished khaki, as if it were military issue—set atop a slab of driftwood beside the bed, a crude desk and chair fashioned from produce crates squared off against the wall opposite. And worst of all, a fleece, a tanned fleece splayed out on the floor in front of the bed so the sheep killer wouldn't have to get his feet cold when he shucked off his boots, strung his bow, sharpened his steel-tipped arrows.

"Rita?"

She was frozen with hate. "Up here," she called. "I'm upstairs." She could hear Bax scraping around below, muttering to himself. And then, as if she needed anything more to provoke her, vinegar to rub in her wounds, a jab with a sharp stick, she saw what was on the table. There, beside a Coleman lantern and half a dozen paperbacks, was a hunting magazine turned back to a full-page ad. From a distance, it looked as if a huge pair of binoculars was staring out from the page, but when she snatched up the magazine, she saw that she'd been looking at two circular photographs, one of a boar flashing its tusks and the other of a ram, a Rambouillet ram, perched on a crag. The legend at the top read: *Eldon Thatch's Island Hunt Club*. There was a phone number and a Ventura address, followed by a price list: $750 for a razorback boar, $1,000 for a trophy ram and two meat sheep. *Meat sheep*. What went through her mind in that moment wasn't so much a thought process as it was an escalating flood of images, each more bitter and ironic than the last. Their sheep, their rams, the animals they'd paid for themselves and broken their backs over, nurtured, docked, dipped, were going to be hunted down—*were* being hunted down—at prices that were twenty times what they could get for them. And by strangers. Interlopers. Jerks.

In the next moment she was sweeping everything—bedding, paperbacks, the lantern, even the plastic sheeting she ripped from the windows as if she were ripping the skin from their backs—into one of the wooden crates, and in the moment after that, her breath coming so fast she might have been hyperventilating the way she had over the lines of coke Toby would chop and lay out for her any time of day or night whether she wanted it or not, and she did want it, she always wanted it, she was bumping the thing down the steps and yelling out to Bax, who was standing there at the base of the staircase gaping up at her, to get out of her way. "What in Christ's name?" Bax said. "You can't touch this stuff, this is private property, this is—"

She said nothing. There was no time for debate—she was in the grip of something here and it was going to play out whether or not he liked it or Eldon Thatch liked it or Pier and Francis Gherini or the commander of the Coast Guard himself. Down the stairs, across the floor and out the door to the yard, Bax clumping behind her. She overturned the box and dumped everything in the mud. Then she snaked past Bax, who was rumbling away at her in a language that was English, insistent and harsh, but might as well have been Mandarin Chinese for all the effect it had on her, propelling herself back into the house, to the main room now, stuffing the sleeping bags in the box, the backpack full of just-add-water meals, the magazines, the beer, even their rolls of toilet paper. She dragged it all outside and dumped it there, and if she heard the scream of the three-wheelers on the hill above or the harsh machine-gun clatter of the helicopter blades that could only mean that the owners were on their way to deliver their poisonous news in person, it didn't matter a whit. Because she squared her shoulders and went straight to the truck and the spare can of gasoline Bax kept behind the passenger's seat and in the next moment the sweet smell of benzene rose to her as she sloshed it over the whole mess and then reached deep in the pocket of her jeans for a match.

So it went up, all of it, before Bax or anybody else could stop her. And Bax did try to stop her because he was the peacemaker, the coward, the dog who would roll over on his back so the owners could scratch his belly and then sell the concession out from under him. She watched the flames rise, roiling and bright, the lanterns bursting with the violent release of their kerosene, the food pouches popping like firecrackers, cotton and leather and Gore-Tex shriveling away to nothing while the foam pads beneath the sleeping bags sent up an evil oily black smoke that forked into the sky and hung there overhead like a tattered umbrella. When Bax did get to her—scrape, clump, scrape—she swung round on him, furious. "Do you know what they're doing? Do you have any idea?"

"I don't care what they're doing, you don't come into somebody's house—"

"Somebody's house? This is nobody's house. This is *our* house. Part of our ranch, part of what we're paying through the nose to lease."

"—and destroy private property. It's not right. It's crazy. *You're* fucking crazy, you know that?"

"Yeah? And so what are you then? They're selling our sheep, Bax, our rams that we . . . for any jerk with a gun to just . . ." She felt herself giving way, all the jolts and frustrations of the day tearing loose inside her, and her eyes were wet suddenly. "A thousand dollars, Bax, they're killing our stock for a thousand dollars for one ram and two meat sheep. *Meat* sheep, for God's sake!"

She saw that register on his face. His eyes went wide, his jaw locked. He was in pain—just standing up was a trial—and this was like climbing up on his shoulders and kicking the crutches out from under him. She felt bad then—he hadn't known, or hadn't known the extent of it. "What are you talking about?" he said, his face lit freakishly by the flames, sick flames, chemical flames, the beer cans bursting with a long liquid hiss that was the sound of capitulation and defeat.

"Upstairs. In the bedroom. *His* bedroom. He's got an ad in *Field and Stream*, for Christ's sake. 'Eldon Thatch's Island Hunt Club.' Prices and everything."

It was then that the noise she'd been hearing off on the periphery grew in intensity, grew closer, and it wasn't the clatter of the helicopter that had appeared overhead like a big ratcheting bug and vanished over the rise in the direction of Scorpion, but the angry mechanical buzzing of the ATVs come home to roost. She looked up to see the three of them, in single file, working their way down the road from the mesa. Bax had seen them too. He was already in motion, moving faster than she could have imagined, and when they came roaring into the yard he was at the truck, propped up against it, and he had the .22 in his hands.

She didn't know guns, didn't want to know guns. She was in a transcendent state, the hate and fear burning in her in equal portions, and where were the peace and love she'd shaped her voice around through all those years when music was the means and brotherhood the end? She'd started the fire. She'd provoked this. Her throat clenched. Somebody was going to get hurt. Somebody was going to die.

She watched the three of them shut down their engines and dismount, their motions fussy and exaggerated, as if to show how purely cool and unconcerned they were, nothing out of the ordinary, just a bonfire burning in the yard and a .22 rifle leveled on them. Thatch removed the khaki cap he was wearing, shook out his hair—he had one of those layered cuts the hair bands favored to distract you from the fact that they couldn't play their instruments, and that said all she needed to know—then ambled across the yard, the other two trailing in his wake. "Hello there," he called, trying on a smile that was like the smile of a man stepping onto a used car lot for the first time, hopeful but expecting the worst. He wanted to know what was going on, what they were doing there, what the fire was all about. "For a minute," he said, trying to be friendly, trying to smooth things out, as if trespassing and sheep killing and cutting their living out from under them was just a little gaffe, nothing really, "I thought the house was on fire." But then he had a look at the piled-up mess of the fire and saw what it was and his face went hard.

"You're killing our animals," Bax said. "Livestock. You and these two clowns"—he had the rifle laid out across the hood of the truck and the truck was between them and him, and he indicated the two hunters, fat-faced types in their thirties or forties, with a jerk of his head—"are shooting up our sheep. That we paid for out of our own pockets. And that's got to stop."

She'd moved in beside him when the men had climbed down from their vehicles blinking against the light of the spreading sky. The mud sucked at her boots. A cold shiver ran through her. "And the lambs," she heard herself say. "What about the dead lambs? Seventy-three of them."

The big man—Thatch, and he must have been some sort of bodybuilder or something—just shrugged. "Talk to the Gherinis," he said. "I don't owe you shit. You owe me. You've got no right to destroy people's personal property, and I tell you you're going to pay every penny it's going to cost to replace it, or—"

"Or what?" Bax lifted the gun now, though it was puny, ridiculous, a child's toy compared to what the two fat-faced men had slung over their shoulders.

Thatch hadn't moved. He was twenty feet away. The bow loomed over the back of his head as if it were attached to him, a supererogatory limb sprung up out of the jointure of his shoulder blades. "I'll sue you. I'll have you evicted, that's what I'll do. You just try me. And I'm about a heartbeat away from coming over there and kicking your crippled ass, crutches or no." He shifted his gaze to her. "You too, you bitch."

The violence of the curse, the hate, the explosive freight-train rush of the moment—*Life and death*, that was what she was thinking, *life and death*—stunned her. Scared her. What had she done?

No one moved. No one said a word. Movie images flickered through her head, shootouts and quick draw, Technicolor irreality, playacting, and who were those people lying there in the dirt with the fake blood spurting? Extras, stuntmen, bad guys. Not Bax, not her. But where was the reality, exactly, where the restraint? The law? Normalcy, even?

Ultimately—and it happened before she could draw her next breath—there was only a single shot fired, and it was Bax who squeezed it off, a sudden sharp snap like the crack of a whip that kicked up a puff of dirt all the way on the far side of the house, and Bax wasn't aiming, maybe didn't even mean to pull the trigger, but it had its effect. The two fat-faces staggered back as if their knees had buckled and she watched the color drain out of Thatch's face.

Bax—she couldn't read him, couldn't tell if his own stone-cold look was the result of the pain of his ribs or a flare of anger or even surprise at what he'd done, what it had all come to—dropped his voice down to its fiercest pitch and said, "You cocky son of a bitch—who the hell do you think you are?"

And Thatch, white still, white as Gold Medal flour, his blood drained as neatly as if somebody had pulled out the stopper, fought to master his voice. "You think you can intimidate me?"

And Bax, check and checkmate: "You're damn right."

She could see it was going to be difficult getting back into the truck, Bax fumbling and exposed for the fatal space of one long moment while she twisted the key in the ignition and Thatch and his sheep killers did whatever it was they meant to do to get their own back, and so she started round the truck to the driver's side, saying loud enough for all to hear, "The hell with it. Let's just leave. Let's just get out of here."

Thatch made no move to stop them, though the look he gave her was death delivered. She had the truck up and running and blasting its exhaust, and the noise and her motions, the briskness with which she sprang into the seat, squared herself and jerked at the gear shift, gave Bax cover enough to juggle gun and crutches and heave himself into the truck, and she never gave Thatch a second glance as she pinned the accelerator to the floor and slashed away up the road until the ranch and the bonfire with the three puny figures in front of it was just a speck in the rearview mirror.

She'd never been so torn up in her life. Her hands were trembling, her feet were like dead things, and she could feel her stomach, the very bottom of it, as if it had been pinned to her with a tack. Bax roared out his rage all the way up the snaking muddy road to the mesa and she roared it right back at him. They made all sorts of resolutions, what they were going to do, what Bax was going to say to the owners and to the police and the Coast Guard and anybody else who would listen, but none of it did the least bit of good, because when they wound down the other side of the mesa and Scorpion Ranch appeared beneath them and grew larger and larger till the view out the windshield was filled to surfeit with it, they saw the helicopter there, inert in the yard, and the pilot and a man in suit and tie—the Gherinis' agent or lawyer or whoever he was—standing beside it and Anise and Francisco with them, looking grim.

Yes. That's right. Pull the plug and let it all wash down the drain, the blisters, the backbreak, the stock and the improvements, the gas-fired water pump and the saddle horses and all the rest, the taste of the dirt between your teeth when the sundowners are clipping over the hills and the deepest requited love of a place that was like the love of the soul of God, let it go. Because Mr. Gherini's agent, stepping delicately through the mud in his city shoes, said, "I'm very sorry to have to tell you this, Mr. Russell, but I have instructions to inform you that you've got two weeks to vacate."

Bax had thrown it back at him: "What are you talking about?"

The agent—erect, in command, though he couldn't have stood more than five feet five and his eyes were mortised with disgust—gave a little speech then, peppered with figures torn from a ledger sheet, forty thousand dollars total profit to the Gherinis in the business year just concluded versus the promise of some hundred and fifty thousand in annual revenues from sport hunting alone, and all that with the Park Service breathing down their necks and threatening a public taking of the property that had been in his clients' family from their grandfather's time for a compensation too mean even to mention. "Let's face it, Mr. Russell," he said, lifting one foot from the ooze and then, thinking better of it, setting it down again, "the world's moving on. Sheeping's something out of the old west and the old west is dead."

Bax, strung tight, trying to gesticulate and hold on to

the crutches at the same time, tried to reason with him, but the man kept shaking his head and interrupting him. "Two weeks," he kept saying. "I'm very sorry. My clients are sorry. Everybody's sorry." He moved forward then, very carefully, like a man wading through cake batter, removed an envelope from his breast pocket and handed it over. "Two weeks. You've been duly served."

It was as if the breath had been knocked out of her. She felt like the survivor of a shipwreck clinging to a scrap of rock as the seas rose and crashed. She was drowning on dry land. "What about the lambs?" she asked, angling toward him, her palms held out in extenuation. "We can't just—"

He looked at her now for the first time. His eyes were black, his hair close-cropped. He was a very little man in a very expensive suit and a pair of ruined shoes who'd come from another world on an urgent errand and that errand had been completed. "Leave them."

"For what? For those, those"—she couldn't find the word—"*people* to shoot them?"

"I'm not here to argue," he said.

Francisco was staring at the withered cracked upturned toes of his boots. Anise brought a hand to her face. From the distance came the long withering bleat of the lambs.

"But that's our profit," she protested. "Our increase."

And now, as if things weren't black enough, Bax turned on her. "You keep out of this," he said.

The man stared through her as if she didn't exist, his eyes on Bax.

"What about the lease?" Bax demanded. "You can't break the lease just like that. We could sue. Anybody could."

"No visitors," the man said.

"What? What are you talking about?"

"Your lease. It states, quite clearly, that you're to have no visitors here without express permission of the owners."

Bax did a little dance inside the cage of his crutches, every hope he had dying right there in the mud in front of him. "Visitors? We never had any visitors here—"

The agent had turned to wade his way back to the helicopter, the pilot—a pair of arms and legs, two eyes and a face as bland as the Los Angeles white pages—standing there looking on as if he were already gone, whirling overhead in his thunder machine, goodbye, so long, and this has nothing to do with me.

"Mr. Hazeltine?" Bax was stumping after him, a pleading tone come into his voice, an oiliness she'd never imagined in him, a begging, a soul-selling, and what was he doing? Who was he to plead? He should have been roaring, should have thrown down the crutches and wrung the little shit like a rag. "Mr. Hazeltine, we never—"

But the agent, on his high horse now, with all the lawyers and contracts and lease-breakers in his pocket, just swung round on them, and with a long slow rising gesture, pointed to Anise. It took her a moment—she was rinsed clean, blown clear of words, and so was Bax—before she could say, or no, bleat, because that was what she was doing, bleating, "But that's my daughter."

The man was at the door of the helicopter, the pilot already settled in at the controls. "Exactly," he said, looking back over his shoulder. "*Quod erat demonstrandum.* Case closed." He lifted himself up into the glass bubble, careful to dangle his feet outside the open door long enough to unlace his shoes—cordovans, in oxblood, with black rubber heel lifts—remove them, and rap them gingerly against the body of the machine. They stood there watching him in silence as if he were performing a holy ritual, a little man on a gray day on an island far from shore, beating the mud from his shoes. Then the big blades began to whirl and they stepped back away from the wash of them and the sudden shrieking assault of noise. "Two weeks," he mouthed over the roar, and then the door pulled shut and everything they knew and wanted and hoped for lifted off into the sky.

Sus Scrofa

From dreams of exhaustion—her dreamself so depleted she can't think, her legs gone to stone, her arms leaden, her two hands so weak she's barely able to fold back the blankets and crawl into bed—Alma wakes to the first hesitant gathering of light. It quivers on the ceiling above her, not quite ready to cohere, the trees beyond the open window dark still, gaunt, stiff-kneed. From the direction of the sea there's a soft continuous wash that's indistinguishable from the murmur of the freeway whispering at the wall behind her, broken only by the distant solitary cry of a bird suspended over the waves. She lies there, adjusting to the world, nagged by the feeling that something's out of place, until very gradually she becomes aware of a rich penetrating aroma wending its way through the hall to rise up the stairs, slip under the crack of the door and wrestle her back to her childhood: bacon crackling in the pan, giving up its salts and nitrates and heavy freight of animal fat.

It takes her a moment to understand: this *is* her childhood. As unlikely as it might seem, especially in a vegetarian household at—she squints in the direction of the digital clock—six thirty-two in the morning, a parental figure is stirring in the kitchen, sorting through pots and pans, adjusting the coffeemaker and toaster oven, laying thin strips of cured pig flesh in a cross pattern in the depths of a Farberware frying pan, sans top. There will be spatters of grease all over the stove, the floor, the teapot, and the smell of seared meat, like the odor of cigarette smoke in a non-smoking room, will linger in the corners, in the carpet, in the folds of the drapes, for weeks, months maybe. Before she's even pushed back the covers and set her feet on the floor, she's upset—or no, not upset, because this is her mother, after all, arrived unannounced with her stepfather last night at dinnertime, but put off her rhythm. Put out.

226

Agitated. Or—but what's the use? The facts are these: Tim's out on the island, her mother's in the kitchen, and she's got a breakfast meeting in Ventura at seven forty-five.

Katherine "Kat" Boyd—she dropped Takesue after the death of her husband and elected to keep her maiden name on remarrying, because that was who she was and what she felt comfortable with—is fifty-nine, short, square, suffering from adult-onset diabetes and a creeping addiction to vodka and diet tonic. She keeps her peach-colored hair cut in a pageboy, which makes her look younger than she is—people mistake her for fifty, or fifty-five, anyway—and she favors blue jeans and T-shirts, the uniform of her generation. For twenty-two years she taught third grade at Coeur D'Alene Elementary in Venice, before retiring to Scottsdale. She has an antipathy for the ocean, a fear and dislike bordering on hatred, and she's seen enough fog to last her a lifetime. Right now, she's got so much bottled-up energy she doesn't know what to do with herself, so she's cooking. Alma won't touch the bacon—she hasn't eaten meat since her conversion to vegetarianism in the seventh grade under the influence of her best friend, a girl from India whose parents were both doctors and who persisted in wearing a red caste mark on her forehead through the end of junior high—but Ed will. And she might have some herself.

Though she isn't really conscious of it, in a way she's laying claim to her turf, because why should she feel like a stranger in her own daughter's kitchen? She's rearranged the cups on the hooks beneath the cupboard, facing in rather than out, run the dishwasher, mopped the tile floor and then mopped it again to get rid of the streaks and adjusted the radio to a station she can hum along to. Cat Stevens—the Muslim apologist—is singing "Peace Train" at the moment, and he was preceded by the Carpenters and before them whoever did "Up Up and Away in My Beautiful Balloon." The bacon pops and sizzles in a gratifying way. She pokes it with a fork, then removes it piece by piece to drain on a paper towel. Turning down the heat under the pan, she mixes in tomatoes, peppers and onions for *huevos rancheros*, to which she'll add a generous shake of Tabasco once the eggs firm up. And then, when Alma has gone off to work and Ed is propped up in front of the TV with his eggs and bacon and his morning Bloody Mary, she'll preheat the oven and separate the eggs for the cake batter.

Upstairs, in the bathroom, Alma shucks her robe and steps into the shower. For a moment steam rises around her, but the shower's never hot enough, some glitch with the water heater, and now, suddenly, it goes cold. Lurching back and away from the icy spray, the shock electric, instant gooseflesh, she raps her elbow sharply on the aluminum handle of the shower door and lets out a clipped reverberant curse. Her mother must be running hot water, filling the teapot, or God forbid, switching on the dishwasher, in which case the rest of the shower will be an exercise in masochism, her feet cold against the tiles, cold spray splashing her ankles . . . she's about to pound the wall and shout out to her when the hot water suddenly comes back and she's ducking her head under the stream and spinning a quick pirouette to distribute the warmth. Though she does her best thinking in the shower—something to do with the calming effect of trickling water and the opening of the pores—she nonetheless strictly limits herself to five minutes, regulating the time on the diver's watch Tim gave her for her birthday last year. It's hardly enough to get her hair shampooed, rinsed, conditioned, rinsed again and combed out with the spray-on detangler—especially when the flow goes stone cold for fifteen seconds—but she won't waste water, not during the ongoing and eternal drought brought on by deforestation, global warming and user demand that grows exponentially by the day because the developers have to turn a profit and the condos keep on coming. Guilt—that's what defines her usage. Guilt over being alive, needing things, consuming things, turning the tap or lighting the flame under the gas burner.

The minute hand shifts, the seconds beat on, and she rinses for the second time and shuts down both handles with nine seconds to spare. Shivering, she towels off briskly before running Tim's electric shaver over her legs and digging out a dry towel to wrap her hair in. All the while, even through the steam and the cloying scent of the various perfumes the manufacturers have somehow managed to work into their allegedly unscented hair-care products, she smells incinerated flesh, and what do they cure bacon with anyway? Salt and carcinogens, what else? Faintly, through the misted-over slab of the bathroom door, she can hear her mother, in the kitchen, singing along with the easy-listening station.

The night before, just as she'd been sitting down to dinner with a film she'd picked up at the video store on her way home from work (keep it simple, stir-fry and brown rice, *Madame Bovary*, in the Jean Renoir original), the doorbell had rung. She'd hit the stop button just as Emma, busty, square-shouldered, with the little puckered mouth and razor eyebrows of the thirties, was coming on to the country doctor in a bucolic farmyard with its lowing cattle and a cadre of piglets straining at the teat, thinking it was somebody selling something, only to pull back the door on her mother and gaunt alcoholic stepfather, both of them cradling sacks of groceries. Her mother had insisted on cooking—"We're both of us starved and you know how I hate road food"—and ten minutes later the three of them were standing in the tiny kitchen, she with *sake* on the rocks and her mother and Ed with tall glasses of vodka adulterated only by a splash of diet tonic and a paper-thin twist of lemon peel while her mother whipped up a quick spaghetti sauce, "Vegetarian for you, hon, eggplant, peppers and mushrooms, with some turkey sausage on the side for your father. Or Ed, I mean."

It wasn't until they were seated at the dining cum

kitchen table and the third round of drinks had been poured, the stir-fry and rice folded into a Tupperware container and isolated in the back of the refrigerator for future reference and the pasta steaming on their plates, that her mother wondered aloud where Tim was. "Is he working late or what?" She cocked her head over the plate of spaghetti and gestured with her glass, the ice cubes softly clicking. "Everything okay between you?"

"Yes," Alma said, feeling as if she were somehow evading the truth or the essence of it, though she wasn't and she and Tim were, in fact, as close as they'd ever been, closer even. "Fine. He's out on the island this week."

Her stepfather—white-haired, bad-hipped, six years older than her mother but looking twice that—wound a skein of red-stained pasta around his fork, then set it down and asked, "How's all that going? Good?"

She answered automatically, conscious of her mother's eyes on her. "Yes, sure, of course. Never better."

"Did you get the article I sent you? From the *Sun*?" Her mother leaned in confidentially, her food untouched still, and this was her pattern, talk, drink, talk some more, and let the food go cold. The sausage she'd arranged to conform to the inner rim of the plate had been cut neatly in six or seven slices, but none of the slices had made the journey from plate to fork to mouth.

All at once, her mind went blank. Article? What article?

"The one about the protests? The picture showed your building—and you could see the window of your office there on the second floor—with, I don't know, picketers out there with their signs?" Her mother shot a look at Ed, then came back to her. "You were mentioned I think three times, or four—was it four, Ed?"

Ed gave a vague nod. He was somewhere else altogether, his question—*How's all that going?*—nothing more than an attempt to be sociable. He'd been the P.E. teacher at her mother's school and they hadn't married till Alma was a grad student. He barely knew her and knew Tim even more peripherally—he'd met him once, on one of his rare trips to the coast in the company of her mother, or maybe twice. He liked sports. Liked to talk about this team or the other, so-and-so's batting average, the Diamondbacks' need of pitching. Of birds, ecology, the ruination of the islands, the islands themselves, he knew next to nothing and what he knew was as vague and untroubling to him as what was going on in the former Yugoslavia or among the Dayaks of Borneo. She didn't blame him. He was like anybody else, living in the world of society, commerce, TV, oblivion.

Her mother's tone was defensive. "I circled your name. In blue. The blue pencil I use for my crosswords, I remember it distinctly. And don't tell me I didn't mail it—I'm not that far gone yet."

"You did, Mom, thanks. I'm sure it's around somewhere, probably at the office—I try to keep a file on each project, public response and whatnot, just for future reference. Not that anybody'd be interested."

A familiar sense of dread had come over her then, a feeling that things were out of control, that there was some specific task that wanted completing, the task that would make it all come out right, but she couldn't pin it down or remember exactly what it was. The fact was that the AP had picked up the story of the protests out front of the Park Service offices and every animal rights group in the country had jumped on that bus. Dave LaJoy—it was two years now since his public exoneration, and he still wore the triumph of it like a chest full of medals—had led the protest, marching out front of the looping circle of thirty or forty chanting protestors, most of them students from City College and UCSB. It had gone on for a month now and she'd taken to parking the car at the other end of the marina, where the restaurants and tourist shops were, just so as to avoid the rush they made at her when she wheeled Tim's Prius into the lot at the office.

In the morning, at breakfast, she'd be meeting in one

of those very restaurants—the Docksider—with Frazier Carter, of Island Healers, Annabelle Yuell, her counterpart from the Nature Conservancy, and Freeman—expressly to avoid the protestors and discuss the continuing implementation of Phase III of the pig eradication project in peace. Over omelets. Lattes. Super-sweetened Thai spiced tea. And a view that carried beyond the masts of the ships to where the channel opened out and rolled all the way to the feet of Santa Cruz Island, where Tim wasn't banding murrelets or doing counts or checking nests, but trapping eagles, golden eagles, for removal to the coast.

Her mother was saying something, and it was as if she'd just come awake. "I'm sorry, Mom. Thank you, I mean it. Thanks for thinking of me. It's just that this whole thing—this project—is complicated, that's all. And if I don't—I know I should call more, but . . ."

Now the fork bent to the plate and her mother dropped her eyes, rolling the long strands of pasta neatly round the tines with the aid of a soup spoon, then setting the whole business down again on the side of the plate. "I'm not saying that," she said. "I just want you to know I'm thinking about you, is all." She looked to Ed. "We've got a lot on our plates ourselves, you know—in a lot of ways, retirement's more hectic than teaching was. Committees, bridge parties, parties all the time. And golf. Did I tell you Ed's been teaching me golf?"

"Oh, yeah," Ed put in, coming fully to life for the first time since they'd sat down, "we'll have her on the women's PGA tour before long. Your mother's a real natural, did you know that?"

Her mother was smiling, her eyes warm, dimples showing. The vodka was silvery in the glass, like some rare reduced metal. She gave her husband a long buttery gaze, and they were complicit.

"No," Alma said, shaking her head side-to-side in an exaggerated gesture, smiling herself now, the burden gone, or at least lightened, at least for the time being, "I had no idea."

In the bathroom, in the present moment, she's wiping the mirror clear of condensation preparatory to putting her makeup on, the sound of her mother's voice—a sweet quavering contralto, honed through all the years of singing along with her third graders to "Lean on Me," "The Man in the Mirror" and "The Lion Sleeps Tonight"—oddly comforting. She even finds herself humming along as she dresses. This meeting, like all the meetings she arranges, is informal, and so she dresses as she would for any workday: tan Patagonia fleece vest over a Micah Stroud T-shirt, fawn-colored corduroy shorts and suede hiking boots. It's the end of October, the sun up now, no fog, but it's always chilly along the coast, and she wears the vest—or vests: she's got three of them, in tan, cranberry and rust—year-round, with a tee in summer, and in winter with a long-sleeved shirt or sweater. They're handy and practical both. Though she won't be going out to the island this morning or any day this week for that matter, she can be ready to take off at a moment's notice, the various flaps and pockets of the vest ideal for secreting sunblock, lip balm, her Leatherman, compass, maps, water bottle and the like. Finally, she unwraps the towel, combs out her hair and trips down the steps to the scent of bacon and the sight of her mother and Ed and a kitchen in disarray.

Her mother, amazingly resilient considering the vast quantity of vodka she put down between dinner and bed the previous night, sings out a cheerful good morning. "Coffee, honey?" she offers, waving the Pyrex pot in invitation.

"Okay, yeah," Alma hears herself say. "But I'm going to have to take it with me—I'm already running late—so put it in . . ." She's reaching for her special mug, the one with the picture of the gnashing razorback Freeman gave her as a joke, but it's not there. Her mother, for some unfathomable reason, seems to have rearranged things, not only the cups, but the toaster oven, coffeepot, microwave and radio too. The trash container has vanished. The pictures on the refrigerator are bunched haphazardly. And where's the calendar?

But here's the coffee and here's her mother pouring it and asking if she's got time for a bite and she's saying, "No, Mom, got to run," even as Ed—jaunty and athletic still, despite the hips—saunters across the room with his morning Bloody Mary to ease into the table where a plate of redolent bacon and a mound of scrambled eggs, Mexican style, awaits him. "Morning," he says.

"Morning, Ed." She tries for a smile and so does he.

But has she got everything? She sets down the mug and pats her pockets, then slips into the front room for her laptop, sunglasses and three-ring binder, and in the next moment she's making her getaway amid a flurry of regrets. "Wish I could stay and spend the morning with you," she says, easing out the door, "but I'll see you tonight. And, Mom, don't bother to cook because I wanted to take you to this seafood place, okay?"

She's belted in, her laptop and notebook on the passenger's seat, mug in the cup holder, the car fuming silently beneath her. Then it's out the drive to meld with the traffic coming off the freeway ramp, which is already backed up from the stop sign at the end of the block. To connect going south she needs to make a left at the intersection, go two blocks north past banks of condos on both sides, then across the freeway overpass to turn right on the southbound ramp. Just as she swings out onto the surface street ahead of a little yellow convertible going too fast, something darts across the road in front of her—a blur, a shadow—and she hits the brakes to the blare of the convertible's horn at the instant she feels the thump of mortality under the left rear wheel. In the next moment, heart pounding, she pulls to the side as the convertible slashes by, peering anxiously in the rearview to identify this thing she's hit, the creature, the animal—a squirrel, is it a squirrel?—writhing at the curb behind her.

There are other cars, three, four of them, easing past

as she fumbles for the emergency blinkers and steps out of the car. Across the street, incongruous in this neighborhood of condos, is a white colonial with dark trim, a generous lawn and a stand of junk trees screening it from the freeway beyond and below it. Oaks, she's thinking, there must be some oaks back in there or why else the squirrel? Squirrels are rare here, the native vegetation displaced by ornamentals and citrus trees, their niche taken by the roof rats that thrive on the avocado, orange and loquat the developers have planted for their delectation. But— she's moving toward it now, watching its eyes, bark brown and luminous with shock—this is definitely a squirrel, a western gray, *Sciurus grisens*, in the wrong place at the wrong time.

The weight of the car has crushed its rear legs and tail, pinning them to the pavement in a glutinous mélange of fur, gristle, bone and blood. Its head and neck are rigid and the front legs—the miniature paws with their shining claws black as pencil lead—scrape spasmodically at the unyielding blacktop as if to dig their way free. She tries to be dispassionate about it—she's at risk of being late for a meeting that will help determine the fate of any number of species interlocked in a unique ecosystem while this animal before her, this unfortunate individual, is superabundant in its range. But when she's standing over it and the eyes, trembling, liquid, unplumbable, are fixed on her and she examines the fine arrangement of the black-tipped hairs and the perfect cream white arc of the chest, she feels the emotion come up in her. This perfect thing and she's killed it. Or crippled it. Crippled it beyond hope. But what should she do? Nudge it to the gutter with the toe of her shoe? Wrap it in something—newspaper, the old pair of shorts Tim keeps in the trunk to wear under his wetsuit—and take it to the vet? Or animal rescue? Or just—put it out of its misery?

As it happens, the decision is taken out of her hands, because in that moment a kid she vaguely recognizes—a boy of twelve or thirteen, from the pricey condos that give onto the oceanfront across from the hotel—rattles up to her on his skateboard and lets out a low whistle. "Oh, man," he says, looking from her to the writhing squirrel, "gross. Did you hit it?"

"Yes," she says, and why is her voice reduced to a whisper? Why is she suddenly on the verge of tears?

Before she can say anything further, before she can think, the boy steps forward on his own initiative and grinds his heel into the animal's head till the gray and pink strands of the neural matter sluice free, like spaghetti.

She's chosen the Docksider for breakfast because it's close to the office, has unmatchable views and an upscale menu. Frazier—he's a Kiwi, having founded Island Healers back at home in New Zealand where the invasive species practically outnumber the native, a man's man who prides himself on his ability to handle anything, any terrain, any animal—would no doubt have preferred a coffee shop without the vaguest aroma of pretension, but there's no harm in elevating the ambience a little. Plus, while he might put on a rough exterior the way a bushman might wrap himself in a hide against a cold night, she's begun to notice that he's as conversant with a good wine, nouvelle cuisine and a snifter of Armagnac as anybody she's met in the committee rooms of Sacramento or the District of Columbia. As for Freeman and Annabelle, they're just happy to be out of their offices and looking at a tablecloth instead of a scored card table with a pot of coffee and a straw basket of stale bagels set in the middle of it.

Of course, everything's a bit off kilter from the first, because by the time she's found a parking spot, darted across the lot and up the outdoor stairway to the restaurant, she's thirteen minutes late and they're all sitting there waiting for her, cranked up on their second—third?—cups of coffee and talking nonstop. For a moment, watching their expectant faces as she propels herself across the room, notebook and laptop tucked under one arm and her hair flying out behind her like a deflated parachute, she considers making an excuse—telling them of the contretemps with the squirrel, the congestion on the freeway, the way the lights, every one of them, seemed to have been timed against her by an evil DMV bureaucrat tracking her Prius on a computer screen—but excuses are for children, kids like the boy with his skateboard and gory heel trying to explain the blood spoor on the carpet to his mother, and she opts simply to slide into the seat next to Annabelle and whisper, "Sorry."

But everything's relaxed, everybody on the same page, working toward the same goal without animosity or bickering or internecine competition. So what if Annabelle's constituency has possession of nine times the land the Park Service has? So what if the main ranch, sitting squarely on the Nature Conservancy property, is the jewel of the island and Alma would give her eyeteeth to be able to set up there in the old Stanton house and has to make do instead with Scorpion? So what if Carey Stanton, rubbed raw by some Park Service functionary twenty years ago, ceded the property to the Nature Conservancy instead of her and Freeman and the people of the United States of America? So what if Annabelle had pushed so hard to hire a concern out of Wet Bone, Idaho, over Island Healers that Freeman had twice stormed out of the room? So what? They're all in this together and they're all friends—old friends now—and they're sitting down to breakfast together in a place designed to make everybody feel good so they can hear what each in turn has to report about the progress from Phases I and II to this, the climax of the entire campaign: Phase III, the unleashing of the hunters, not to mention their dogs, ATVs, helicopters and lead-free bullets, which is already now in its fourth month.

Freeman is watching his waistline. He orders grapefruit, cottage cheese and coffee, "Black, no cream." He's not overweight, or not at least as far as she can tell, but he's one of those men who just seems big all over, big in the shoulders, arms, wrists, fingers, big right on down to his fingernails, his head massive, his neck thick as one of the stanchions under the pier. The only incongruous thing is his feet, which are disproportionately small, so that he always seems to be floating above them as if he's been pumped full of helium.

Frazier—forty-six and big enough in his own right, dressed in his khaki bush shorts and matching short-sleeved, multi-pocketed shirt, his silvering hair in a military buzz cut and his legs stretched out casually in the aisle—orders the Captain's Breakfast, crab-stuffed crepes, fresh fruit plate, eggs benedict and sourdough toast saturated in butter, with a side of fries and homemade cole-slaw. He upends the sugar container over his coffee, then fills the cup to the top with half and half. And smiles round the table. "Hard work chasing pigs up and down those canyons," he says. "A man's got to have *calories* to burn. Not to mention a beer or two and maybe a wee little nip of something at the end of the day."

"Wee?" Alma echoes, and she's grinning at him while the waitress hovers, all in good fun. "Wee" for Frazier translates to half a pint, minimum, which is what his engraved silver flask holds. She's seen him refer to it time and again as they tramped the fence line, looking for pig sign, and when they sat down to an evening meal at the picnic table out front of the ranch house at Christy Beach on the far end of the island, he was able to put away a six-pack all on his own—and never, not for an instant, had she detected any change in him. Half a pint of Mexican brandy and a six-pack of beer in a system all sweated-out, and no clumsy movements, no slurring of words, just a steady stream of Kiwi talk on every subject under the sun. She looks to the waitress, then nods to Annabelle, to see what she's having before committing herself to the strawberry crepes and crème fraîche.

Annabelle—she's Alma's age exactly—is a white blonde with see-through eyebrows and invisible lashes, dressed today for the office, in a blue silk suit and matching heels in a shade so close to the color of her eyes it's uncanny. How many shops did she trundle through to find that ensemble, Alma wonders, envisioning whole armies of sales girls paraded across the floor in consultation, the multifarious phases of light parsed against the sheen of the material and the narrowly focused hue of her eyes. Where does she find the time? Not to mention the money? Like Alma, she's unmarried, but unlike Alma she's currently unattached—and working for a nonprofit in service of the environment is hardly the way to worldly wealth. She must be a real bargain hound. Either that or she has family money. Alma watches her push the menu away with a languid flick of the wrist and lift her eyes to the waitress. "I think I'll have the spinach and goat cheese omelet with a side salad—the endive. It comes with a balsamic vinaigrette, right? Nothing creamy?"

The waitress—all of nineteen or twenty, with a ponytail that reaches to her waist and a skirt so short she might have come directly from early cheerleading practice—answers in the affirmative and then turns to Alma. "Have you decided, ma'am?"

"Yes," she says, handing over the menu and snatching a quick glance round the table, "I'll just have the organic oatmeal. With skim milk."

Phase I of the project—Administration, Infrastructure and Acquisition—involved securing the funds from their overlords in Washington and, in Annabelle's case, the Nature Conservancy, hiring additional staff to oversee the project, acquire equipment and supplies and take bids from the hunting and fencing contractors. Not to mention dealing with an inflamed press (*$7 Million Awarded to Foreign Hunters to Slaughter Santa Cruz Island Pigs,* read one *Press Citizen* headline) and an ongoing campaign of harassment from the Dave LaJoy–Anise Reed contingent, both in the courts and in the parking lot out front of their offices in Ventura. Phase II, the division of the island into five zones for the purpose of constructing forty-five miles of pig-proof fencing so that each zone can be sequentially hunted till it's pig free, was completed in the spring, which means that Phase III is well under way. Afterward, and the nearest estimate is that it will take up to six years to achieve an island-wide extirpation, Phase IV will be implemented, in which the fences will be monitored for an additional two years to ensure that the eradication is complete, after which they will be removed and the island will return to the way it was before humans began altering it. At least that's the plan. And the hope. The fervent hope of them all.

"Well, yes," Freeman is saying, his coffee cup held aloft and beating time to some inner rhythm, "we've posted signs and sent out the press release stating that the entire island, not just the TNC property, will be closed to the public while the hunt is under way. We're making it a public safety issue. And the promise is that once Zone One is cleared, we'll let people back in and open up the campgrounds at Scorpion."

"As soon as possible," Alma puts in, looking round the table. "We don't want to give people any more reason to gripe than they already have."

"Oh?" Frazier's giving her a sardonic grin. "Are they griping? I hadn't heard."

"You can't really blame them," Annabelle says, turning to him.

"I can," Alma says.

"Because they don't like to see violence—like me, like us. Life is sacred, I believe that. And yet—"

"And yet no matter how many times you explain it"—Alma's voice jumps up the register—"they just don't get it because they don't want to. Logic means nothing to these people. Long-term goals. Expert opinion." She can feel the caffeine working in her to the point of coffee jitters, of running at the mouth, of cutting people off—she needs to put something on her stomach, needs her steel-cut oat-meal and her skim milk. "But we've been through all this before and we're just going to have to grin and bear it. For the greater good. For the foxes."

"Or bear and grin it," Freeman says. Lamely.

"At least the courts are on our side." Alma can feel her smile bloom and then fade. She reaches for her coffee cup, then thinks better of it, pulling both hands down into her lap.

"For now," Annabelle says. "But you can't count on that. Every time one of these crazies sues for an injunction I tremble to think what's going to happen if we wind up with a judge that just doesn't get it."

"Amen," Alma says, "me too. I can hardly sleep nights thinking of what it would be like if they stop us now, when we've committed the funds, when weeks, days even, could mean the difference for the foxes. I mean"—looking round the table, caught in the grip of her emotions, so wired she can't find the off switch—"they've got money behind them. Have you seen their website? The ticker there show-ing how much people are donating? And the local paper. The editorials? They're just manipulating public opinion. Cynically. Stupidly. But it works. I mean, the pig in the bull's-eye?"

There's a silence, as if all this is too much to bear, espe-cially at eight-thirty on a morning made in heaven with the sun riding up off the water and the brown pelicans—brought back from the very edge of extinction because people woke up to the fact that DDT wasn't exactly a vitamin—gliding low to report on the health of the local anchovy population. This isn't a morning for fear or doubt, this is a morning for celebration, for eggs benedict and sweet cakes, for resolve and concerted action.

"This LaJoy," Frazier says after a moment, looking up from the nest of his folded hands, "does he ever go to work or what? The man seems to have a lot of time on his hands. Christ, it seems like every time I come down here he's out in the parking lot marching around with his bloody sign. And I tell you these bloody chants—'Nazi' and 'Animal killer' and the like—just put my teeth on edge." He pauses, patting his breast pocket for his cigarettes, Camels, a pack of which he actually removes before he catches himself. "Almost forgot: no smoking in a public place in this glorious state. But what I want to say is maybe Phase I should have been 'Eliminate Dave LaJoy.'" He raises his left arm and squints an eye to sight down it, squeezing off an imaginary round with the trigger finger of his right hand: "Pow!"

"Can I buy the bullets for you?" Freeman says.

"Not that I'm violent or anything, just that certain species—or individuals within that species—sometimes have to be removed for the salvation of all the rest, right, Alma? Euthanized. There's a term I like. As long as it's got a .223-caliber slug attached to it."

Well, of course. And there's general laughter, fellow feeling, comradeship, and then there's food, plates heaped high with it, and the sun picking out each individual mast in the harbor and setting fire to the rigging while the islands float somewhere out there on the horizon. All well and good. But Alma's the one who has to bear the brunt of everything LaJoy can bring—she's the one who has to stand up there in the public forums and explain as patiently as she can the rationale for the killing, she's the one who has to pick up the morning paper and see her own name there like a slap to the face, and it's wearing her down.

Restoring an ecosystem is never easy—maybe it's not even possible. She thinks of Guam, where it's beyond hope. Or Hawaii. Florida. Places where so many species have been introduced it's hard to say what's native and what's not. She'd attempted to boil it down for her mother the night before, because her mother was trying, she really was, and Alma wanted her to appreciate what she was doing—or at least what she was going through. She'd waited for a lull in the conversation—Ed got up to refill the glasses, the ice maker clanking philosophically, the tonic hissing with a rush of released gas—and said, "Take Tim, for instance."

"Yes," her mother said, "take Tim. You mean to say he's not even going to be here for your birthday? Because I don't know about you, but I intend to bake a cake first thing in the morning—devil's food, with mocha frosting. And what was that ice cream you like—Vanilla Swiss Almond? Ed's going to pick up a pint. Or maybe a quart. What do you say to a quart, Ed?"

"I told you, Mom, he's trapping the goldens. Which has to be done because we discovered that it's the golden eagles killing the foxes. You see, what most people don't realize—"

And she went off into her tutorial mode, unraveling a parable of cause and effect that might have seemed like a sick cosmic joke if it weren't so catastrophic. The whole thing started with Montrose Chemical dumping DDT during the war, the DDT working its way up the food chain and preventing the eggs of the native bald eagles from forming properly. The balds—aggressive, highly territorial and primarily piscivorous—died back, and the goldens, which prey on land animals, cruised in from the coast to colonize the islands, attracted by the bountiful food resource presented by the wild hogs, *Sus scrofa*, that should never have been there in the first place. But then—and here's where she paused to let the lesson play itself out—you can never foresee how a closed ecosystem is going to react not only to introduced elements but to their elimination as well. The sheep had overgrazed and that kept the invasive fennel down, but once the sheep were removed the fennel sprang up in all but impenetrable thickets ten feet high, which provided ideal cover for the pigs. "So," she'd said, her mother's gaze bright but fading, "you've got no balds to keep the goldens away and the goldens are nesting and hungry but with fewer and fewer pigs available. In that case, what do you think they're going to eat?"

Ed, who by this time had shifted to the couch, where he seemed to be monitoring two baseball games simultaneously with the sound muted, looked up and said, "Foxes. Cute little dwarf foxes."

It wasn't till one of the biologists began to notice a falloff in the population that they began to trap and radio-collar the foxes. In the mid-eighties the island-wide population was robust, in the range of three thousand individuals. By the late nineties it was a tenth of that and no one could determine the cause of the decline.

"We were in danger of seeing the fox go extinct. On our watch," she said. "Look"—she carried her laptop over and set it on the kitchen table, canting the screen so that Ed could see it too, and brought up the image of a single golden eagle chick perched proudly on its nest with the remains of twenty foxes scattered beneath it, some still wearing their radio collars. "That was our proof. We followed the radio signals and this is what we found."

So the eagles had to be trapped and removed, no easy task. First they tried netting them on the wing out of the door of a helicopter, but it was like trying to catch butterflies on a roller coaster, and even if they'd been successful, there was the problem of the eagles surviving the fall. It was Tim who came up with the idea of baiting the birds to a carcass rigged with a spring trap that when activated would shoot out a net to ensnare them, and that worked, to a degree. In the interim the biologists trapped as many foxes as they could and caged them for a captive-breeding program, which to date had produced eighty-five kits to be released once the goldens were gone and balds could be brought in from Alaska to reestablish a viable breeding colony. The thinking was that the balds would keep the goldens at bay and that the goldens would have no incentive in nesting on the island once the pigs were removed.

The question everyone asked at this juncture—the question Dave LaJoy asked endlessly, vociferously, in the press and on the pavement—and the question her mother asked then, was: "Why can't you just trap the pigs alive? And bring them back for, I don't know, for farmers or something? Or food? Think of all the starving people in the world."

"Believe me," she'd said, "we would if we could. But there isn't a federal agency that would allow it. The risk is just too great."

The fact was that these hogs—Santa Cruz Island hogs—were a discrete population that had had no interaction with outside populations in a hundred and fifty years, and thus could carry leptospirosis, foot and mouth disease, mutations of common bacteria and viruses that could burn through the American hog industry and leave it twitching in the mud. So there was no choice but to euthanize them. With bullets, two each, the first to the heart, the second to the head, according to the American Veterinary Association guidelines. Clean kills. As swift and final as fate. And the carcasses? All that wild-bred pork? The carcasses were to be left where they lay for the entertainment of the ravens and the benefit of the soil.

"The thing is," Frazier is saying, now dabbing at a bright smear of egg and hollandaise at the corner of his mouth, "with pigs you get ninety percent of them right off, but it's that remaining ten percent that gives you hell. And you can't run the risk of missing a single individual because that could be a pregnant sow for all you know and then the whole business just starts in over again."

The oatmeal goes down like a brick, the wrong thing to order, definitely the wrong thing. Her stomach is on fire suddenly—too much coffee, too much tension, dealing with her mother, hitting the squirrel, fighting traffic to get here—and she has to square herself in the chair and sit rigid a moment till the burning passes. Is she developing an ulcer, is that it?

"Aerial starts when—next week? That's what you're projecting?" Freeman asks, leaning into the table, the rind of his grapefruit at one elbow, coffee cup at the other. The pen in his breast pocket has left a dark blue Rorschach blot on his pale blue shirt and the silver points of his bolo tie are tarnished—or maybe they're smudged with ink. But his eyes are bright. He's attached to the notion of the park superintendent as a man of action, like the legendary Bill Ehorn, who flew into San Miguel to personally pull the trigger on the last pregnant jenny, thus ending the occupation of the island by introduced mules, and Alma knows he's angling for an invitation.

Frazier nods genially. "As best we can figure. Because we're already having good success on the ground, but we need to get up on the ridges and work our way down. And I tell you, you only do a kill if you can get the whole group. If there's a chance even one'll get away, you draw back. Because, you understand, these are very clever animals—they say they're smarter than dogs, smart as a three-year-old child for that matter, but for my money even the dopiest dog beats that . . . anyway, they'll communicate to the others and go into hiding. And that's a nightmare."

Alma catches the waitress's eye from across the room, thinking to expedite things and get the check now, but the waitress misinterprets her meaning and brings the coffee-pot back round. Frazier, gesturing broadly now, holds out his cup to be refilled, giving the girl a quick wink and then going on about how while aerial is indispensable the real hunt takes place on the ground, now that the dogs—his own dogs, from New Zealand—are out of quarantine. And then, Freeman and Annabelle edging their cups forward for refills while Alma lays a palm over hers and mouths, "Check, please," he brings up his Judas pigs, a concept so devious it gives her a thrill every time he mentions it.

Annabelle, who to this point hasn't been as closely involved with the details of the hunt as she herself has, gives him a bemused smile and drops her voice. "Judas pigs?" she echoes. Her look says, *Amuse me*.

And Frazier stops right there to take in that look and sweep his eyes over the restaurant, the retreating waitress, the view out the window, before he comes back to her. "Oh, yeah," he says. "Very effective in an operation like this. You see"—leaning in over his plate to pin her with his gaze—"we use their own sex drive against them, and if that seems unfair, well, dearie, I guess it is. But this isn't a game. This is war. All-out war. And wave goodbye to the little piggies."

"Okay," Annabelle says, flashing a smile, "we can all agree with that—but what do you mean?"

"What we do is trap as many as we can and hope to find a couple females in estrus—these things'll breed all year round in this climate, so it's not so hard as you might think, especially if you cage a boar with them for a day or two. Then we radio-collar the females and let them go." He's leaning so far over the table he's practically in her lap at this point and Alma has to remind herself, while sitting rigid and fighting down the gas pains, that it doesn't really matter to her one way or the other if he finds a little solace wherever he can. "And you'd be surprised," he says, "or maybe not, maybe it's just what you'd figure. But each of those females will wind up with a whole parade of boars around her, rooting and fighting and sniffing her up—even the wiliest old scarred-up paranoid razorback'll come charging up out of his hole for a chance at that—and it can bring in a whole bloody contingent of sows and juveniles too, whether they're in heat or not, just to be close to the action. Like a pig disco."

"And then?"

"Then we track them and move in."

He pauses to take a sip of coffee, all three of them playing that scenario over in their heads, the abrasive hides, the mobile snouts, pig sex. "And believe me," he says, "nobody gets out alive."

Afterward, after she's put the bill on her card and said her goodbyes all around, she finds herself in the deserted ladies' room, the light of ten o'clock in the morning suffusing the high glass-block windows. She should be at work. And she will be, she promises herself, in just a minute—she'll leave the car where it is and walk so she can get a little sun on her face and steal a march on the protestors, blending with the tourists and slipping in the service entrance before they even know she's there—but for the moment she just needs to clear her head. And breathe, breathe as deeply as she can. The pain in her abdomen hasn't gone away—in fact, it seems worse, as if she's swallowed some sort of corrosive, Drano, Emma Bovary's strychnine, brodifacoum. The image of a rat flits through her head, its feet churning, eyes fixed. It's the coffee, it has to be. And the oatmeal. Whatever possessed her to order oatmeal? She should have stuck to toast, dry toast, but then the thought of it—brittle, abrasive, crushed and wadded and stuck in her throat—sends her banging into the stall and suddenly everything's coming up, the coffee, the oatmeal, the dregs of her mother's pasta and the thinnest disembodied hint of Onikoroshi *sake*, too much *sake*, formerly on the rocks.

Immediately she feels better. She flushes twice, watching the water swirl in the bowl, but the smell lingers even as the outer door wheezes open and footsteps approach in a sharp high-heeled tattoo. Her first thought is of Annabelle, but that can't be because she watched her go down the steps in animated conversation with Frazier ten minutes ago. At least. The heels tap closer and she freezes while the handle of the stall briefly rattles and whoever it is pulls back the door of the adjoining stall and settles in with a sigh, followed by a fierce hissing rush of urine. Then she's out of the stall and at the sink, cupping her hands for a sip of water to rinse her mouth, wishing she had a toothbrush—or breath mints; she makes a note to stop in the place downstairs to pick some up—and though she'd like to take a minute with her lipstick and hair, she doesn't dare because the occupant of the other stall is noisily unraveling toilet paper and she doesn't want to be seen. Not now. Not after being sick. So she's out the door and down the stairs, thinking to freshen up in the restroom at the office, thinking she'll get herself a Coke and maybe a package of crackers to settle her stomach. And the breath mints, definitely the breath mints.

Just below the restaurant, on the promenade that wraps around the marina, there's a shop that caters to tourists and carries the usual cornucopia of things, from Dramamine, sunblock and cheap straw hats for the whale-watching crowd, to postcards, T-shirts and bobble-head dolls for the landlubbers, to the soft drinks, hot coffee, pre-packaged sandwiches, crackers and cheese in the shrink-wrapped single-serving portion, breath mints, candy and tabloid magazines everybody needs all the time. She's about to duck in the door—a drift of metallic balloons in a stand there, artificial poppies sprouting from a styrene ball in a papery blaze of red, T-shirts clothespinned to a wire like wash—when she catches herself. There's a young woman, a girl, seated at one of the white plastic tables out front, her back to Alma, and her hair—dyed a uniform copper red—trailing down her back in a spill of trained curls. But isn't it Alicia? Alicia doing what, taking her lunch break? She checks her watch. At ten-thirty in the morning?

Before she can think what to do—Is it Alicia? Is she really prepared to question her, discipline her, wonder why she's not at her desk in the absence of her boss, opening the mail, answering the phone, for God's sake?—the light shifts as if someone's put a hand over the shutter of a lens and a man comes backing out the door, a cardboard tray with two cups of coffee and a package of powdered doughnuts held out gingerly before him. But she knows him, doesn't she? The earring, the goatee, the incongruous shock of the blue eyes in a Latino's face, or part Latino, Chicano, mestizo, whatever you call it, and who—?

And it comes clear. Because he recognizes her in that instant and in that instant she knows him, knows him in a flash of recollection, even as Alicia turns her head to look over her shoulder to see what's keeping him. Alicia, her features gone slack and her eyes retreating. Alicia, shrinking. Alicia revealed. But he—Wilson, that's his name, *Wilson*—he's unfazed. He saunters up to the table, sets the tray down, and looks back to where Alma stands arrested at the door to the shop in which her Coca-Cola Regular, cheese and cracker combination and breath mints await. Then, so casually he might have been posing for a snapshot, he flashes her a smile—a beautiful, full-lipped, effervescent smile, as if they're the best friends in the world—and slowly pulls up the chair beside Alicia, puts an arm around her shoulders, and draws her to him.

Prisoners' Harbor

He's at home, glancing up from the morning paper in what he likes to call the sunroom to look out the window on the crew he's hired to lay sod over the desiccated remnant of the lawn. The whole operation has him conflicted—lawns are bad news for the environment, yes, but he's got to keep up property values, or his property's value anyway, and he did turn down two contractors who wanted to go the herbicide route in favor of this crew, amigos of Wilson, who dug everything up and then laid down plastic sheeting to stifle the weeds—but the bottom line is that the old lawn, the one he inherited when he bought the place back in 1993, was looking pretty ratty. Now, with the sod—and they've already rolled out two long dense sections of it, like carpet—he'll have a deep blue-green Kentucky-perfect lawn right out of one of those glossy magazines, and he won't have to wait for it to grow in either. And it's not a question of vanity or keeping up with the neighbors or anything like that—it's about protecting your investment, because this house is the best investment he's ever made, a Spanish mission–style beauty situated on a hill, two stories high with carved wooden beams in the main rooms and intricate wrought-iron grillwork everywhere you look, nearly five thousand square feet of living space set on an acre and a half, and now, twelve years after he bought it, worth four times what he paid. He couldn't have done any better investing in a gold mine.

The sunroom is on the second floor, facing south, and he can look out beyond the humped backs of the Mexican laborers—three of them, two bareheaded, one in an off-white baseball cap with *El Jefe* looped across the crown in what looks to be black Magic Marker—to the stucco wall in front and over the roof of the house across the street and out to the ocean, five blocks distant. Today—it's the end of

251

October, the air clear and sharp—he can see all the way out to Santa Cruz Island, the channel spread out beneath him like a placid little pond and the oil rigs like stepping-stones lined up along the shore. Of course, this time of year the winds can come up and make things hazardous out there in a heartbeat, everybody knows that, and if Anise doesn't show up soon he's going to have to call and remind her of that fact. But the forecast is for light to moderate winds and he's trying to reform his behavior, trying not to be so controlling, so quick to explode—she'll get here when she gets here, he's thinking, lifting a spoon of granola to his mouth and watching the faintest little rumor of a breeze finger the leaves of the trees along the road.

Her mother's in town—Rita, flown in all the way from Port Townsend, Washington—and while he doesn't care much about that one way or the other, Anise does, Anise certainly does, and when they arrive, if they arrive, if they can ever get their shit together and understand that winds rule the channel and sunset comes early this time of year, he will drive them down to the marina in his Beemer, hop aboard the *Paladin* and take them out to the island for the day. For pleasure. For a day off from walking the picket line outside the Park Service offices and for the not incidental purpose of testing the limits of the Park Service's authority: the island is officially closed to all comers because they want to do their killing in private.

But just the thought of it is enough to set him off. Down goes the spoon, the bowl, the newspaper, milk sloshing, the wicker table trembling under the violence of it, and he's on his feet and across the Saltillo floor, pacing now, because he just can't sit, can't eat, can't read. The dogs, conscious of trouble, get up from their beds in the corner and come to him, tails thwapping at their bony haunches, but he takes no comfort in them. It's as if deep inside him a hammer has dropped, the rush of hate and rage and frustration shooting from his gut right on up to the top of his head to inflame the roots of his hair till they ache, actually ache. Every lawsuit he's brought has been thrown out of court because the judges work for the system and the system is the National Park Service. And now they're closing the island in their typical imperious way, no matter what the will of the people says, no matter how many petitions come across their desks or how many protestors stand out there chanting, because they're confident no one's going to cross that channel when the water gets rough. With the Civil Rights Movement you could get on a bus and drive down to Mississippi, with Vietnam you could bring people to Washington in cars, buses, trains and jet planes. But not here. And don't they know it. The sons of bitches.

Just then—the workers out there unrolling the sod, the wind stirring the trees and his mind going up in flames— he sees Anise's car at the gate and Anise's pretty white bare arm reaching out to punch in the code that will roll it back on its wheels so she can enter, with her mother, and the day can begin.

It can't be more than fifty degrees out on the water, the wind chill dropping the temperature a whole lot lower than that, but Anise's mother insists on sitting out on the deck the whole way across. He tried to tell her it was going to be chilly before they'd even climbed out of the car, but she dismissed him. "You think I don't know these islands?" she said, her eyebrows lifting till they floated on the furrows that ran up into her hairline. Her face was a template of Anise's, uncanny, exact in every detail, as if her daughter had been cloned instead of generated in the usual way—the same broad forehead, the round face and strong chin, eyes that jumped out at you from ten feet away, the perfect shells of her ears and the sexy slight eversion of the upper lip, the whole of it framed by a whipping hurricane of dirty-blond hair that was going to gray in long electric streaks. She was tall, square-shouldered, leaner than Anise, but built, still built, though she must have been in her mid-fifties. At least. She was wearing jeans and cowboy boots, a short-sleeved blouse and a bandanna at her throat. The blistered leather jacket, fleece-lined, her concession to the weather, was knotted round her waist. She wasn't wearing any makeup or jewelry.

When she'd put her rhetorical question to him, she wrapped an arm round Anise and said, "Now that Bax is dead and probably Francisco too, I don't think there's anybody alive knows them—or at least the one we're heading for—better." She broke into a smile and turned her face to Anise's as if she were going to kiss her—and she did, on the tip of her nose, a quick compression and release of the lips that made him uneasy in a way he couldn't quite pin down. "Right, honey?"

But that's all right. Everything's all right. The water's a cloud and he's floating on it now, living in the moment, getting away, and he feels his mood lightening by the minute. There's not much chop. The sun's unencumbered by even the hint of a cloud or the slightest tatter of fog. The dolphins come gamboling. The engine never misses a beat. And if he hammers it all the way out it's because he's eager to get there if only to reconnoiter, but he's hoping—they're all hoping—to be able to land at Scorpion, or if not Scorpion, then Smugglers', so Rita can see for the first time in all these years what's left of the place. So she can reminisce, spin stories, talk about sheep and ravens and the way it was sitting round a bonfire on summer nights strumming a guitar and blending her voice with her rangy tall pubescent daughter's while the moon rose up full-bellied out of the channel and all the dwarf foxes and skunks pinned back their ears and howled. Or barked. Or whatever it was they were capable of. For the most part, Anise stays out on deck with her mother, the two of them chattering away, Rita's mood so airy she might have swallowed his entire bottle of Xanax, and he doesn't mind. It's his pleasure—his privilege—to escort her and if that involves hearing the old stories over and over, that's fine with him. If it makes Rita happy—and here he steals a look over his shoulder to see the two of them seated in deck chairs, their heads together and the wind at their hair—it makes Anise happy. And what makes Anise happy absorbs him totally. Or so he tells himself as he pushes the throttle forward and the cove at Scorpion heaves into sight.

He knows better than to anchor before he can sweep his binoculars over the pier and the beach and the beaten dirt trail that curves around behind the rock face on the right, because that's where the house is and that's where the rangers will be, if the rangers are here at all. Rita, windblown, flushed, is leaning way out over the rail as the boat swings round in the chop. She's got her own binoculars, a little 8 × 22 birdwatchers' pair she pulled out of her purse. "There," she cries, her voice pitched high with excitement, "isn't that the Jeep? Bax's Jeep?"

And now Anise is in on the act, a hand shielding her eyes till her mother passes her the binoculars. She takes a moment to focus, steadying herself over the flexion of her legs. "I don't know," she says, "is that a patch of yellow or just my imagination?"

From where he sits at the bridge he can see nothing but a rusting heap of old ranch equipment the Park Service dragged down away from the house and left there in the tall weeds above tide line. They'd probably meant to haul it all away, wipe the place clean, but then they would have had to bring a crane out to lift the wreckage onto a barge and transport it back to the coast, so some Park Service genius decided they ought to just leave it there as a curiosity, a historical artifact, a reminder of the times when people like Anise's mother were out here running sheep. Maybe he can make out something in the pile that might once have been a Jeep, but he'd have to use his imagination to force the lines to coalesce and he's too busy jumping the binoculars from one point to another, looking for authority figures, for hunters, guns, hounds, helicopters, to pay it more than passing attention.

So he decides to drop anchor and lower the dinghy.

What are they going to do—shoot him? He sees nobody, nothing, not a flicker of movement but for the shorebirds doing their thing in quick-footed runnels of color. The outboard fires up right away, a long smooth swell rocking beneath them, and in the next moment they're planing toward the pier, Anise and her mother riveted ahead, their faces tight with anticipation, and for a moment he sees them both as children, Girl Scouts maybe, and here's their field trip, their wienie roast and the return of the native all rolled in one. Of course, there's a sign there, posted on the face of the pier, right where the tourist boat bumps up against the crossbeams to offload, and it tells them what they already know: ISLAND CLOSED TO ALL ACTIVITIES/NO LANDING UNTIL FURTHER NOTICE. BY AUTHORITY OF THE UNITED STATES GOVERNMENT.

But they're right there now, thirty feet away, Anise demurring—"Maybe we shouldn't . . ."—and her mother, Rita, in a soft coaxing voice, saying, "What's the harm? I mean, do you hear any gunshots? Do you see anybody? If we could just—I just want to feel the dirt under my feet, that's all. For five minutes. That's all I ask."

And he's thinking: *The sons of bitches.* And shoving the tiller to swing the bow abruptly and chase along the beach. Shouting to make himself heard over the noise of the motor, he says, "Maybe if we pull up on the beach we can always say we didn't see the sign." Spray shoots up. He eases off on the throttle and then they're riding the gentle crest of a wave up onto the beach as he tips back the motor and there's a long shudder and groan of the sand beneath them, everything glinting in the wet, shells, stones, the tiny scrambling things that make their living in the wash.

Rita's already out of the boat, quick-limbed and agile, tugging at the braided yellow nylon line to pull them up and away from the sea. Anise springs out behind her and now he's on the beach too, all three of them scooting the inflatable across the sand.

"Wow," Rita says, hands on her hips, not even winded,

"just look at it!" What she's seeing goes back twenty years and more, but what he's seeing is the six-foot sign pounded into the sand, a duplicate of the one on the pier, made out of the same sheet metal as a road sign, and before he can register the next one down the beach and the one beyond that he's wondering if the convicts up at Soledad or wherever had to pound it out in metal shop. Strange twist if they did, forming those proscriptive letters behind bars to keep people out of a place with no bars on it at all.

It is then—Rita exclaiming, Anise following her up the slope toward the house, which is just visible from this angle, some five hundred yards off, adobe, white walls, green tiles anchoring the roof, the sun throwing javelins at everything—that the two jerks in Park Service regalia come hustling out the door. He's startled, despite himself, because this is just what he expected, isn't it? His voice is a bark, harsh, snapping like a dog's. "Anise! Hey, get your ass back in the boat!"

She's fifty feet ahead of him and her mother's fifty feet beyond that.

"Rita!" he shouts, and when she turns he stabs a finger in the direction of the men in the distance and then sweeps his arm over his head like a third-base coach waving the runners home. There's a moment of inaction, Anise's wide wondering face, her mother's stacked in duplicate behind hers, and then they're both running and he's running too, for the boat, for the line, to haul the thing back in the water and get off before he has to listen to yet another lecture—or worse, go through the whole sick charade of another arrest.

So what is it—a matter of seconds? The rangers, one of them with a mustache, the other without, won't deign to break into a run because that would somehow impeach their dignity, or that's how he figures it anyway, but they're doing double-time nonetheless. For her part, Anise flies. She keeps herself in shape at the club because being fit and looking good are part of who she is and what she does, and here she is beside him, the foam of the surf climbing up their ankles, the dinghy afloat now, the rangers gaining and the sun still throwing spears. The surprise in all this—and how can he examine it so calmly?—is Rita. For the space of a heartbeat he thought she was going to stand there and confront them, lay into them, let them know in the most exacting detail just who she is and what her rights are and how this is her island, not theirs, and if they so much as lay a finger on her the sky will open up and the seas erupt, but he's managed to trigger the flight response in her and she whips round and bolts for the beach.

The engine catches with an accelerating growl and a quick angry puff of exhaust. Anise is waving her arm like a search and rescue victim. The Park Service types are coming on, stiff-kneed—oh, they won't run, it's not in them, because they're the authority here, the stuff, the man—but Rita never lets them close on her. She can run. For an old woman, or late middle-aged or whatever she is, she's moving like a well-oiled machine, the cowboy boots—tooled in the pattern of two snakes entwined over the bridge of each foot, red and blue—pounding across the sand and then sloshing through the low wall of the surf, water to her knees, and here she is in the boat and the boat already a hundred feet from shore. Give it some gas, let it ride. He's breathing hard, the excitement pounding in him like joy, like the very form and definition of it, but the joy comes with an overload of rage and he pins the tiller wide to bring the dinghy back round in a tight arc just as the rangers reach the shoreline and he can see their faces clearly and see that their mouths are open and that they're shouting something, some official threat or malediction.

Let them. Let them shout all they want. Very slowly, with the greatest deliberation, he raises his right hand, the middle finger extended, just to let them know how he feels.

Dave LaJoy is not the type to give up easily. Or graciously. Or at all. Anise's mother wants to land, wants to hike

258

around her old property, and that is the issue here. He never stops to think what a shame it is that she didn't come out on the tourist boat a couple months ago when everybody on God's green earth was welcome to wander at will and even spend the night in the campground—if they had a tent and a permit, that is—or that she could come out in April or May or anytime but now, because now is when he's bobbing offshore in the *Paladin* and now is when he wants access. So what he does, after backing off from Scorpion Beach, hauling the dinghy back aboard and securing it, is head east for San Pedro Point, and the other ranch beyond it, at Smugglers' Cove.

Anise and her mother are in the cockpit with him, their hands fluttering and mouths going nonstop—"What a rush!" Rita keeps saying and they both break out in laughter—because they're riding the high of outmaneuvering the Park Service drones, *out-foxing* them, and how's that? He doesn't look back, though he can picture the two figures receding on the beach, maybe wringing their hands and telling each other how unfair the world is. What are they going to do now with their little summons books and their bright shiny new taxpayer-funded handcuffs? He feels for them, he does. But he's watching out ahead just the same, watching for other boats—for the Coast Guard cutter specifically—because these people do have marine radios, after all. The engine thrums. The weather remains clear. It's eleven-thirty in the morning and everything's fine, the cliffs keeping watch on the right, the ocean opening up ahead of them in all its struck-blue empty rolling immensity. "We're going to try Smugglers'," he says, and Anise gives him a look.

She's unwrapping a sandwich and handing it to her mother—hummus and roasted pepper, on oatnut bread, no meat, though Rita's an unregenerate carnivore—and she wonders aloud if that's a good idea. "Shouldn't we just quit while we're ahead?"

"Shit, no." He's not angry, not disappointed or defensive

either. He's just going to do what he has to do and no one can tell him different. "Don't you at least want to see what they're up to? I mean, *monitor* the situation? If we were really thinking, we would've brought Toni Walsh with us." There's the sweet suck and wheeze of the engine, the shush of the water parting along the hull. "What do you think, Rita?"

"Me?" She glances up at him, the spark of amusement in her eyes still. "I'm with the program, because this is just, I can't tell you—amazing. Really amazing." She shifts her eyes to lean forward and extract a beer from the cooler under the bench. Then she sits up, arches her back as if to relieve the stress of the chase and cracks the beer with a celebratory pop. "I'd love to see the house there," she says, a seductive note come into her voice. "You know, it was abandoned in our time—until the hunters set up there anyway. Did Anise ever tell you?"

She had, yes. She'd told him about the trauma of all that, the boyfriend—Baxter—half-crippled at the time and powerless to do anything about the slaughter, and the owners exerting pressure on the captains of the hauling barges to ignore Rita's calls to remove their sheep to market because he wanted them there so the sportsmen could come and put very expensive holes in them, the killing going on even then, but under a different cover. And then the three of them found themselves living in a one-bedroom walkup in Oxnard, right back where they'd started, and instead of six thousand acres to roam they had a backyard the size of a hogpen, and instead of seeing nobody her own age and not knowing the least thing about style or top-forty music or the TV references it took her a year to get, Anise found herself in a classroom. Several classrooms. With a roster of different teachers and a streaming tide of sneering adolescent faces all around her, and if she hadn't been a born-in-the-flesh beauty and the very incarnation of an adolescent boy's wet dreams (here he's extrapolating), she wouldn't have survived it. Rita got a job as a waitress. The boyfriend—he was an old man by then—mended. Mostly anyway. And he couldn't find work because there weren't any sheep ranches to run in Oxnard and his leg bothered him still so it was pitchfork hell to stand up on it for more than ten minutes at a time and he surely wasn't about to take a minimum-wage job in a hardware store or some such at his age, so he went back to drinking. And so did Rita. They lasted six months, and then he was gone, and Anise, very slowly—watchful, imitative, using her native smarts and the scars of her isolation and her voice and her guitar to her fullest advantage—became Anise.

"No," he says. "No, she didn't tell me."

Playfully, reaching out to give his calf a squeeze, Anise says, "You know I did. About six thousand times?"

"Yeah," he says. "Okay. But I want to hear it from the source."

He's got a sandwich in his hand, and—he checks his watch to see if it's edged past noon—a beer too. Why not? Why not enjoy himself, have a party if he feels like it? The waters are still free, even if the island's locked up like a prison cell, only with all the prisoners on the outside.

Rita's voice is husky with wear, but she recounts the story with a forced gaiety, as if none of it mattered anymore, as if she were over the pain of eviction and the separation from the boyfriend and ultimately her daughter, as if her life of inaction and bar talk in the backwater of Port Townsend were just what she'd always hoped for. He listens in the way of a historian, one hand on the wheel, the other alternately lifting a sandwich and the beer to his mouth, and then Smugglers' opens up before them at the very moment the Coast Guard boat, lights flashing, some jerk out on the deck, makes the far point and slides across the bay. He can't believe it. But down goes the sandwich, down goes the beer, and he's swinging the wheel hard to port as if it's been programmed in his genes and heading back the way they've just come, all innocence, as if they were sightseers skirting the island, boating enthusiasts out for a run on one of the last glorious days of the fall.

Is his heart pounding? You bet. "Talk about high blood pressure," he says, and tries to laugh. The women are looking back over their shoulders, all the exhilaration blown out of them. "Are they coming after us?" he asks, keeping his voice level.

He won't look, in the same way he won't shift his eyes to the rearview when a cop's behind him on the freeway, on the theory that if you're too hyper, they'll nail you. Be respectful, let them know you're aware of their presence, and keep the speed pinned at sixty-five, no hurry, no fears.

"No," Anise says, "no, I don't think so."

Straight out, easy on the throttle, the blistered back-running slope of San Pedro Point in bright definition out there beyond the bow. He doesn't say another word. Just watches the point come to them as he changes course ever so slightly, bearing north and east as if he's heading back to the coast, and that's just what Anise and her mother are thinking, that they're done for the day, outmanned, finished, heading home. And then the cove disappears in their wake and the Coast Guard cutter with it—the snitches at Scorpion must not have radioed after all—and when the point is dwindling in their wake he changes course again, bearing west now, retracing the route that brought them here from Scorpion.

Anise and her mother are deep in conversation, every last bump and spike and guano-spattered tumble of rock bringing on a flood of recollection, and they haven't noticed the change of course—or at least they haven't mentioned it. But now, when his intention is unmistakable, Rita looks up and says, "Where you heading? Back around again?"

He nods, conscious of Anise's eyes on him. "I thought we'd just go over and check out Prisoners' for a bit, on the TNC property. They can't be everywhere, can they?"

Prisoners' Harbor, the main port of entry on Santa Cruz, lies on the north shore, just past the narrow eastern neck that gives the island a fanciful look from the air, as if it were a big dun plesiosaur stretching out its blocky head in pursuit of some swift-finned creature of the deep. There's a long stretch of beach opening out from a tumble of hills and the valley that runs back three miles to the main ranch, where the defunct winery still stands, and where the ranch house, with its pool and gardens and outbuildings, gives the Conservancy a base of operations that feels like a remnant of paradise. He's been there, twice, in happier times, before the killing started anyway, and the way the ranch house is situated to take in the views of its own private valley in a spot erased from the memory of the world moved something in him. He felt a desperate stab of covetousness, as if after ranging all over the globe he'd found his one true home, only to discover it belonged to somebody else. He wanted it. Wanted to sell the house he'd bought, mortgage his life and buy the place so he could pull all the doors shut behind him and say screw you to the world. Sure. Close it down. Live like Adam. Or the wild man who rowed out from the coast at the turn of the last century with nothing but a box of apples, a slingshot and a couple of fishhooks and took up residence on the barren shit-strewn lump of Gull Rock, gobbling up gull's eggs and whatever he could bring down with a sling-propelled stone. He wore nothing but a ragged loincloth, winter and summer. Grew out his hair and beard. Watched the sky.

Of course, that's all just a dream, an adolescent fantasy. Everything, every square foot of everyplace, belongs to somebody, and any contemporary wild man—or entertainment center magnate with the flicker of an idea of even thinking about going wild—would be hunted down and hustled off to the bughouse in padded restraints. He's reflecting on that, on wildness, on peace and eternity and the natural state of man, as they round Coche Point and motor close in along the coruscating arc of China Beach, using the headland behind them as a screen in the event that the Coast Guard cutter does in fact get word and come looking for them, and between bites of his sandwich he turns to Rita to see what she has to say about it. "Did you ever hear any stories about the wild man that used to live out here?" He chews, swallows, picturing himself in a loincloth and shaking a spear over his head. "Years ago, I mean. Turn of the century?"

She considers a moment, her eyes drifting off to some other destination before sharpening with the recollection. "Francisco used to talk about him," she says, hunched forward over her knees, beer can in one hand, half-eaten sandwich in the other, her head gently swaying with the movement of the boat. "It was like a legend or something, only real. This was in the early days, by the way, back before Prohibition when they had the winery going and all that. His father—Francisco's father—told him the guy was a poacher, stealing sheep to eat what he could and leave the rest for the ravens."

"He wasn't right in the head, was that it? I mean, sucking gull's eggs and sleeping out in the open and all the rest of it, the loincloth—"

"He was a Dane, but the shortest Dane on record—only five feet tall. Or that's what they say. And not only was he poaching sheep, he killed foxes, skunks, the island blue jay, whatever he could get hold of, and, I guess, just cooked it over a driftwood fire and dug in."

"Roast pork," he says automatically, and he means to be funny, or at least ironic, but he can't bring himself to grin or even smile because the thought sets him off all over again. *They're out there now*, he thinks, *blowing away animals. And we're laughing about it.* In the distance he can make out the pier at Prisoners', a strip of nothing out there in the sun glaze, but no boats at least. And no helicopters.

"So he was a carnivore," Anise puts in, and she's wearing a sour grin, needling her mother. "Just like you, Mom."

Rita grins back at her, then digs in her breast pocket for a pair of opaque iridescent blue sunglasses and claps them over her eyes as if she's going into hiding. "That's right," she says, "because that's the way we were made." She pauses to take a sip of her beer. "And I just love the taste of lamb."

"Yeah," Anise says, the grin gone now, "and meat is murder."

"I think I've heard that one before."

"Well, it is."

"You didn't seem to feel that way when we were living at the ranch."

"Come on, I was just a child. I didn't know any better." She's fixed on her mother now, twin creases of irritation emerging between her eyes. "But you should. After what we saw out there, I mean just that one day with the ravens and those hunters? You might not have known it, but that was the biggest trauma of my life—"

"That and Oxnard Junior High."

"I'm not joking. I'm telling you: animals are conscious. They feel pain. They have the same right to life you have."

"I remember one time"—Rita says, ignoring the appeal and lifting one dripping boot to brace an ankle on her knee before settling back in her seat with a sigh—"during shearing, when those vaqueros came out and raised a little hell after all the wool was in and they roasted a kid—the head, remember that? They put the head right on the coals and then split it open for the brains—"

"I don't want to hear it."

"—and that good rich creamy pale fat you used to spread on a slice of oven-hot bread like it was butter. Did you know that, Dave? Anise used to be a regular little mutton glutton."

"Yeah, well, me too," he says, trying to play peacemaker. "Until I saw the light. But anyway, you know we've got to stop this pig hunt—I mean, it's crazy. Nobody, not even the guy that runs the slaughterhouse, would want to see animals hunted down for nothing. Or you either, right?"

What he's trying to ask is whether she's on their side

265

or not, but Anise jumps in to answer for her: "No, no way. She's as opposed to it as we are. Anybody would be."

They're both looking to her, the harbor running up on them, waves creaming along the shore and the chaparral above it patchy and parched and waiting for the rains, when she sets down the beer in the cup holder in front of her and raises her head to level a savage uncompromising glare first on him and then her daughter. "Of course I am," she says, spitting out the words. "It's a waste of good meat."

That night, after taking them both out for a very pricey dress-up dinner at a new French restaurant Anise seemed to have heard about somewhere, during which he got into an unfortunate debate with the waiter over the way his sole meunière had been prepared, which he'd had to send back twice, Anise clucking over the fate of the fish—"If you're going to commit to vegetarianism you can't go halfway, Dave, because that's just cowardly"—and Rita giving him a sour smile while lifting dainty slices of all-but-raw filet mignon to her lips, he drops them off at Anise's apartment without comment and drives home to inspect the new lawn. And if he drives too fast and if a cop he vaguely recognizes pulls him over and asks him how much he's had to drink and does he know the speed limit on city streets is thirty-five miles an hour and lets him off with a warning, it's all because the day has been, well, complicated. He's tracing the chain of events that blasted his mood to fragments—the frustration at Prisoners' Harbor when the helicopter appeared out of nowhere to buzz the boat till he swung round and nosed it out to sea, the blaring circumambient voice warning him that "THE ISLAND IS CLOSED TO ALL VISITORS, REPEAT, THE ISLAND IS CLOSED," Anise taking so long to get dressed they missed their reservation by forty-five minutes and had to prostrate themselves before a little frog bastard of a snooty maître d' before they got seated, and then the waiter, and

266

the fish and the way Rita sucked at her filet mignon as if she were draining it of blood drop by drop—when the gate pulls back and he glides into the driveway to the streaming welcome of the motion-sensor light mounted over the garage door.

It's past midnight. He's tired. He's aggravated. He's not thinking deeply. The car door eases open, the radio dies on a jam from some anonymous band he must have heard ten thousand times, and why, in Christ's name, can't the programmers come up with something different, something obscure and new and unfamiliar, the B sides, nothing but B sides, just to give everybody a break before they go out and shoot themselves? He steps out on the firm hardscape of the cobbled brick drive, feeling the familiar boater's illusion that the ground is moving beneath him. For a moment he just stands there, taking in the night chill, the stars, listening to the silence and the muffled drone of the freeway. And then, just as he's about to dig a flashlight out of the trunk and stroll out onto the lush new yielding carpet of the turf, to admire it and congratulate himself on his decision to go with sod instead of scattering grass seed and worrying over birds and weeds and bald patches till it comes in, he becomes aware of movement there, out along the perimeter of the yard.

His first thought—and here he steels himself, ready to call out a warning or better yet a threat—is for intruders, burglars, thieves, but then he sees the shadows there, two of them, humped close to the ground, and thinks of the dogs, but the dogs are in the house where he left them. It takes him a moment before he understands that these are nature's animals, wildlife, come to enjoy what he's provided for them. Very slowly, with exaggerated caution, he slides along the length of the car, and with both hands, one to turn the key and the other to keep the lid from springing all the way up, he quietly slips open the trunk. There's a wince of escaping light, and then he has the flashlight in hand, thinking, *Coyote? Or just a neighbor's dog?* as he eases it shut again, stifling the click of the lock with the pressure of his hand.

He forces himself to stand stock-still, listening, until the smallest sounds begin to drift to him out of the shadows. What does he hear? A soft wet swishing, the faintest tick of breathing or mastication, then a rustle, a soughing, then nothing. He's almost afraid to lift his feet and so he shuffles forward, an inch at a time, the darkened cylinder of the flashlight held out before him like a homing device—he wants to get closer before switching it on, wants to be as close as he can before the light explodes and the animals scatter. He can feel the excitement building in him, the lure of the strange, the recondite, the hidden world that prowls through the dead hours of the night. A step closer, then another. And then, at the edge of the lawn, shadows enfolding shadows as if there were infinite depth to the night, as if the night were an ocean, as if he were underwater, in a cave, feeling for signs of the blind cave fish, he flicks on the light.

Two raccoons, their eyes flaming as if they were the source of the light and not he, stare up at him, the gray gloves of their paws arrested and revealed for the fraction of a moment, and then they turn away from him as if he weren't there at all, and go on with their business. Which, he sees now, is digging. They bend forward, paw at the turf, then rock back on their haunches, feeding something into the dark absence of their mouths. He runs the light over the belly of the lawn, each individual blade of grass clutching its shadow, and sees, in fact, that the new lawn is already pocked with holes, moonscaped, as if it were the apron of a driving range. It takes him a moment—this is nature, these are wild creatures, he is the interloper here and they the inheritors of the hills that have run continuous up the coast all the way to Alaska from the time the glaciers lost their traction—before he shouts out. "Get out of that! Get!" he cries, trying to pin them with the beam and clap his hands at the same time, running now and

268

watching the two shifting golden forms pull back reluctantly and scoot over the ruined turf to the wall, which is no impediment at all.

In the morning, after a closer inspection of the damage, he dials the number of Bruce Diaz, the friend of Wilson's whose crew installed the lawn. He lets the phone ring eight times before hanging up—patience is not one of his virtues—and dialing again. On the fifth ring a woman answers in Spanish—"*¿Bueno?*"—and his mind goes momentarily numb until he can think to say, "*¿Quiero hablar con Bruce? ¿Por favor?*"

There's a shuffling and wheeze, voices mingling and separating, the muffled bark of a dog. Then Bruce's voice, too loud, comes hurtling at him: "Yeah?"

"Bruce?"

"Yeah?"

"It's Dave LaJoy."

There's a silence.

"You installed a new turf lawn for me yesterday?"

"Yeah, sure. Dave. Okay. Sure."

"Well, it's all full of holes. I mean, I get home at midnight, I haven't even had a chance to see the job yet, and I turn on the flashlight and all I see is holes and bunches of dirt and dead grass piled up."

Another silence.

"Bruce, you there?"

"Raccoons," he says finally, as if reluctant to pronounce the name of the guilty party. "They're after the worms—nightcrawlers, you know? Worms are part of the product, necessary, you understand? For aeration, fertilizer. You get rid of the raccoons, the holes'll grow over in a week, you won't even know they were there."

But here it comes, rising in him, and he just can't stop it. "You mean you're not even going to get your ass over here and take a look? This a new lawn, new. I didn't pay for any raggedy torn-up piece of second-rate *shit*." There's an unfortunate emphasis on the last epithet, because the pressure is ticking in him now, scraping away at the core of him like a thousand gray-gloved little claws. "I'll cancel that check quicker than you can spit."

The voice that comes back over the wire is so reduced he can barely hear it. "Ten-thirty," Diaz says. "But I tell you, it's raccoons. I could lay a whole new lawn tomorrow and it won't make a lick of difference."

Diaz—tall, with the build of a heavyweight gone to seed—appears half an hour later and stands with him on the lawn looking down sadly at the cored-out scatters of turf, the whole thing like a big green blanket the moths have got to, tells him he'll replace the worst two strips at no cost at all, and then lifts his head to look him square in the eye. "But on condition you get rid of the raccoons first."

"How do I do that?"

"Call Animal Control," he says, and then he's shuffling off to his pickup truck and the gate is opening magically for him and he's gone.

Animal Control—amazingly, they answer on the first ring—informs him, through the offices of some overblown sandpaper-voiced clown half a step removed from a rent-a-cop, that they don't trap raccoons. He's in no mood. In the interval between the departure of Bruce Diaz and this phone call, Anise called to wonder what he was doing because maybe she was mistaken but hadn't they agreed on eleven o'clock for him to come by for her and her mother to go wine-tasting over the hill in the Santa Ynez Valley, and he was maybe just a tad abrupt with her. But now, before he can respond—*Well, what the fuck are we paying you for then?* is on his lips—the person on the other end, the Animal Control officer, says, "But we've got the traps here and you're welcome to come down and pick them up on overnight loan. Or we can do long-term too."

This takes him by surprise. "By traps, what do you mean? They don't, I don't know, hurt the animal—do they?"

"No, no, no—these are Havahart traps, same as you use for rats and mice, only bigger."

"A lot bigger, I hope."

There's an odd aspirated sound over the line as if the man on the other end were stifling a yawn. Or a laugh. Maybe he finds this funny. Maybe he's in Animal Control for the sheer hilarity of it, just to get his rocks off. "You're going to need a pickup or SUV," the man says finally.

It takes him a moment, picturing it. And then, with the phone to his ear, already on his way out the door to back the Yukon out of the garage, he thinks to ask, "What about bait?"

"Peanut butter. Peanut butter'll catch anything. They love it, let me tell you. But if you want to get fancy, just open a can of sardines, and you'll have every raccoon in the neighborhood fighting to get in—and half the cats and opossums too."

Again he pauses, the connection breathing static in his ear. One detail remains, and it looms up now like a submerged log riding a contrail of swamp gas. "Okay, yeah, but once I catch them, what do I do with them?"

Wine-tasting. To his mind it's just a euphemism for getting shit-faced in the middle of the afternoon, the kind of activity tourists and busloads of retirees get a charge out of, but as it turned out he was glad of it. For a few hours, it took him out of himself, and after their second stop—at a place he loved, the cellars cold and dank, the great oaken casks standing in ranks like monuments to all those corrupted livers of the past—he really loosened up for the first time in what seemed like weeks. Not that he hadn't felt the tension lift when they'd motored out of the marina the previous morning, but by the time they got to the island he was twisted up inside all over again. So the wine-tasting was a nice break. And he enjoyed Rita—she seemed to like him, respect him even, unlike his ex-wife's mother, who regarded him out of her black Sicilian eyes as if he were the Antichrist and jumped up from her chair with a little gasp every time he stepped into the room, wailing, *Oh, God, does* he *sit here?*

They had a late lunch—supper, really—outdoors at a little café in the studiously quaint town of Santa Ynez, then drove back up 154 and through the San Marcos Pass in the decanted sunshine of the dying afternoon and wound their way down to Santa Barbara with the islands of Santa Cruz, Santa Rosa and San Miguel laid out before them as if on a tray, the perspective shifting and shifting again as they wound their way through the switchbacks and watched the night begin to gather in a gray tumble of thickening gloom up ahead of them while the islands rode off to the west in red streamers of illumination. Rita remarked on how pretty it was and Anise chimed in to agree. "Maybe I ought to write a song about it," Anise murmured, her voice gone whispery in collusion. "Call it 'Floating Islands,'" her mother said, and though he was calm, floating himself, on an even keel, he couldn't help working up a little venom: "How about 'Killing Floor'? Or no. That one's already taken, right?"

At home, still half-looped, he parked the Beemer in the garage beside the Yukon—"Let's go to your place, and then maybe walk down to one of the restaurants in the village," Anise had said—and he'd said that that sounded just fine, and he was feeling no pain at all. Then he remembered the cages and he led the women out onto the lawn in the fading light to examine the depredations of the raccoons and it became a sort of game to position the cages, set the triggers and smear peanut butter all over the bait trays. At one point Anise had gone into the house for a bottle of wine and he shouted to her to see if there were any sardines in the pantry—there were—and when she returned they laid three sardines atop the smears of peanut butter in each cage, then stood back, satisfied with their work, sipping wine while the night deepened around them.

And now, at dawn, he awakens with a lurch, because something's wrong, something's definitely wrong, but what is it? He's been dreaming . . . what? Of pursuit, terror, faces out of the past diachronically summoned to cluck over his failures and inadequacies. A height. A drop. Laughter as ragged as hate. He sits up. Shoves the dreads up out of his face. His scalp itches. His stomach curdles. He has a mild headache, a fact of which he's just becoming aware in a stealthy crepitating way. While he's at the bathroom sink, staring numbly at his reflection in the mirror and mechanically filling and draining two glasses of tap water, he remembers the traps.

Filled with purpose, he ducks back into the bedroom to pull on a pair of shorts and a sweatshirt and slip into his sandals—made of synthetic materials, not leather, because leather just allows the killers to profit all the more—and then he's out the door and into the cool of the morning, shutting the dogs in behind him so they won't run on ahead and mess with the traps. He doesn't really expect to have caught anything, not yet, not the first night, but he finds himself quickening his pace nonetheless. Yesterday, when he picked up the traps, the Animal Control officer—he of the blowhard's voice, hoarse, too-loud and far too pleased with itself—had answered the question he'd posed over the phone. "What do you do with them?" the man had thrown back at him. He was skinny as a breadstick, his eyes close-set and his hair slicked down over his scalp like the pelt of a sea otter. "That's your decision. But we can't take them here. And it's illegal to possess wildlife."

"So what do I do—release them somewhere? Up in the hills?" He pointed in back of him, to where the Santa Ynez Mountains rose up abruptly beyond the window to crowd out the sky.

"That's what people always think," the man said, "but when you displace animals like that it's very hard on them. They don't know the environment and they're disoriented.

Plus, it's ninety-nine percent sure that the available range is already occupied."

"What are you saying?"

The man shook his head slowly, side to side. "I'm not saying anything. But these are problem animals, right?" A sardonic smile took hold of the lower part of his face. His irises pinched inward as if the pressure of focusing were too much to bear. "You reported them. They're damaging your property—your lawn, you said. Right?" He paused to hold up his palms by way of disclaimer and then lifted his shoulders and dropped them in a baroque shrug. "Our feeling is it's up to you to dispose of them."

So here he is, stalking across the grass, which is still wet with dew. There's fog this morning, drifting insubstantial shreds of it snarled in the lower branches of the trees and rising up overhead to pull down the sky. He's chosen to go with two traps rather than one, reasoning that since there were two raccoons they'd be more likely to prefer their own cages, but then he's no animal behaviorist—or trapper, for that matter—and all he can do is hope for the best.

The near trap, the one he's set right in the middle of the lawn, is as gray and empty as the fog itself, or so it seems until he gets right up on it and sees the patch of fur shoved up against the steel mesh there. But the color is all wrong—it's white, not brown or golden or tawny even. He's thinking of the danger suddenly, of puncture wounds, festering cuts, rabies, and he's on his guard even as he bends forward to peer inside and recognizes the bloated overfed Angora from two doors down, the one he's forever chasing off the property for the cardinal sin of stalking birds. Its eyes are soft pleading puddles. It begins to purr.

For a moment he thinks of taking the thing, trap and all, back to its owners, an elderly couple who seem always to be unloading groceries from the trunk of their car as if they're expecting a siege, but then he thinks better of it, feels along the outside of the trap and lifts the door back up on its hinges. Instantly the cat bursts out as if ejected on a blast of air, but then it stops, preening, and gives him a long steady look before mincing off across the lawn, tail held high. The peanut butter, he sees, is still intact, but the sardines are gone. He's thinking he'll have to re-bait the thing—and wondering how he's going to avoid catching the same cat night after night—when he glances up at the second trap, which he tucked in against the far wall in just the place where he saw the raccoons rise up and flow over it. He can't be sure at this distance, but there seems to be something in the depths of the trap, a dark concentration of shadow, and he can see already that this is no cat.

Approaching warily—he doesn't want to spook it, whatever it is—he comes up on the cage from the rear, where the dropped metal door screens him from view. He becomes aware of the chatter of the birds then, as if an unseen hand has just switched on the soundtrack of the morning. There's a cool clean smell off the ocean. Everything is still. When he's just there, just behind it, he slides to his right so he can see down the length of the cage, and the shadows separate—there are two of them—before bunching again. Two raccoons, the very ones, their eyes fixed on him, hands clutching the wire like prisoners in a penitentiary. It takes a moment to understand that the larger, sitting up now so he can see her gray nearly hairless underbelly, is the mother, and the smaller the pup or kit or whatever you call them. But then he goes down to one knee for a better look and the animals bunch again and the larger one, the mother, shows her teeth.

What does he feel? Wonder, certainly—here are the mysterious shapes of the night made concrete, captured, under his control, their existence as tangible and traceable as his own. Satisfaction. Vindication. And a strange sort of power, of species superiority—they'd assaulted him, however unconsciously, however naturally—and now he has them and it's up to him to dispose of them as he chooses. For a long moment, poised on one knee, he simply watches them—and they watch him in return, as aware as he is that they're his now, that they've been caught by a larger, more gifted predator, that any hope they might have had of escape or even survival is nil. After a while his knee begins to stiffen and he eases down on the verge of the grass and folds up his legs under him in the lotus position, a posture he adopts wherever he might be—in one of the stores, on the rug in front of the big-screen TV, outdoors on the patio or the lawn—when he needs to take a moment to shut himself down, to go deeper, to focus and see, really see.

What he sees is blood: the gray-gloved claws of both animals' forefeet are stippled with it, bright flecks where the flesh has been abraded, and there are worn red gashes at the corners of the larger one's mouth. The enormity of it hits him with the force of a blow: they've been clawing at the steel mesh since the door dropped down behind them, all night and into the break of day, tearing their own substance, in pain, bleeding.

He's on his feet suddenly, pounding with urgency. All he wants now is to set them free, but where? He looks again to the mountains rising out of the fog. He sees himself lifting the cage by the handle on top—or dragging it; it'll be heavy—setting it in the back of the SUV while the animals scramble and hiss in terror, then driving all the way up to the road that cuts into the hillside, as high as he can go, to release them at one of the trailheads. They'll be tentative at first, like in the nature films, but eventually they'll emerge, unable in those first few seconds to grasp the radical change in their fortunes, and then, heads down, almost comical, they'll barrel off into the bushes. Yes. Only to starve or fight their battles with the established population, with the coyotes, pumas and whatever else is out there, mountain bikers, pyromaniacs, hunters— or come right back and dig up his lawn all over again.

It's a conundrum. He feels as if he's still asleep, still dreaming, the animals slipping in and out of the cage as they please, their snouts glistening with the oil of the sardines, the lawn restored and the earthworms burrowed deep. How long he stands there, he can't say. But the phone has been vibrating in his pocket for some time now, off and on, and he needs to snap out of it if he's going to get down to Ventura to do any good on the picket line, especially after blowing them off yesterday to go wine-tasting, and how frivolous that seems to him now. How idiotic. Irresponsible. And then he feels the sun breaking through to chase the fog, the warmth of it on his shoulders and the back of his neck, and something makes him lift his eyes from the cage and gaze out over the wall and the gate and the red-tiled roof of the neighboring house to where the long crenellated run of Santa Cruz Island suddenly fills the horizon, all its chiseled facets aflame in a solid sheen of early morning light.

He knows then that he's going to be late, very late, and that he'll have to call Anise and Wilson to let them know, a dozen things running through his head at once. He can foresee draping a blanket or maybe a painter's tarp over the cage to spare the animals, maybe stopping for a bagel and a cup of coffee, just to have something on his stomach. But no, no time now, no time for anything. If he calls at all—and he has to, he promises himself—it'll have to be from the boat.

The *Black Gold*

That night, she stays late at the office, propped up behind her desk long after the others have gone home. It's not that anyone would ever question her over her hours or that she feels any compulsion to clock in like a factory worker because she's her own boss and her schedule is flexible—but she's conscientious, that's all, and when four-thirty rolls around she never even glances up. The breakfast meeting was work, certainly, but it took a chunk out of her day and there are things she wants to catch up on. Vital things. Purchase orders. E-mail. The latest figures from Island Healers, who need to be paid in monthly installments. And, not least, Alicia's computer.

She didn't say a word when Alicia did finally come in, fifteen minutes after she herself arrived, and Alicia, tentative, red-faced, her eyes dodging away from the issue— apostasy, and nothing less—murmured only that she was sorry she'd decided to take an early coffee break but that she was starving because she'd overslept and left home without breakfast and since nothing was happening in the office anyway, she thought no one would mind. Alma, mortified herself, had only stared at her as coldly as she could manage. Then it was lunch hour and Alicia stayed anchored to her desk. Conspicuously. Rising only to go to the machine for a Diet Pepsi and then, half an hour later, to the ladies', answering the phone in her breathy nuanced voice, entering data, typing, her fingers in swift softly clicking motion as people came and went, telephones rang and the fluorescent lights hissed overhead.

Shadows lengthened, the afternoon fell back and finally dropped into the ocean. At five-thirty, quitting time, Alicia stood, fluttering briefly round her purse and backpack before murmuring, "See you in the morning," and pulling the door shut behind her as she left. A full hour drifted by, Alma absorbed in her own work, before she went to Alicia's computer, and it was another half hour before she shut it down. She was looking for irregularities, outside contacts, e-mails that might have tipped her secretary's hand, but there was nothing whatever beyond the usual business correspondence. And yet Alicia had been with Wilson Gutierrez—had been intimately engaged with him, his arm around her, his tray of coffee and cakes set down before her as if he were used to courting her, serving her—and that was beyond the bounds on every level she could think of. But was it a firing offense? Was there anything in the Park Service's contractual agreement with its employees that proscribed consorting with the enemy? On company time, no less? Or was that considered free speech or free association or whatever?

At any rate, when finally she does leave the office, it's past six and all traces of light have faded from the sky. The yachts sit patiently at their berths, muted amber lights showing in one cabin or another, the water as still as the boardwalk that parallels it. There's a faint echoing thump, a noise so soft it's been sealed and wrapped twice over by the time it reaches her, and she looks up to see a working boat—*uni* divers—gliding past the ranks of ghostly masts, lights slowly pulsing, in search of its berth. It's a moment stolen out of the day, a moment of tranquillity and surcease, but she doesn't linger. She's always been a brisk walker, always in a hurry, and she's moving quickly, ducking around children, exiled smokers, strolling couples. Just as she's passing the Docksider, she becomes aware of the music drifting down from upstairs, a cover band sloppily working its way through one of the tunes from her mother's day—and that's when she pulls up so suddenly the jogger coming up behind her has to swerve wide right to avoid her, very nearly colliding with a pair of oncoming women in the process. She sees the women's faces flood with alarm and annoyance beneath their flap-brimmed whale-watchers' hats, there's a murmured apology, a scramble of limbs—the jogger's legs glowing as if they were fluorescent—and then he's gone and one of the women calls out something, but she's not listening. She's rooted to the spot.

Her mother. In the confusion of the day she's forgotten all about her. Her mother's baking a birthday cake. She expects to be taken out to dinner, as promised. At this very moment she's no doubt sitting in the easy chair in the living room, with Ed, abusing vodka, the images of chaos on CNN drifting past like clouds in a flattened sky. Guiltily, Alma digs out her cell phone and dials her home number.

Her mother answers on the first ring.

"It's me, Mom. I just wanted to say I had to work late and—"

"On your *birth*day?"

"Well, yeah. Some things came up." She can hear the falseness in her voice, the amateur theatricality—and why does it always seem as if she's hiding something when she's speaking with her own mother? When, in fact, she's not? Because many things *have* come up, one of them—Alicia's duplicity—as disorienting and disturbing as anything she's been through in a long while. Aside from the protestors, that is. And they tend to give it up when the sun sets. "But I'm leaving now—I'll be home in half an hour, half an hour tops."

"I'm cooking."

"But I wanted to take you out, my treat—"

"I said to Ed, 'Ed, she's overworked, and I want to make it nice for her today of all days, no stress, know what I mean'—just like when you were a girl, and Ed agreed with me." A pause. "If you really want to, we can go out to that restaurant tomorrow, but it's *our* treat, definitely our treat." And then she muffles the phone with one hand and calls out to Ed for confirmation. "Right, Ed?"

"But tomorrow's the concert. Remember? Tim got me tickets?"

No response.

"You said you'd go with me because Tim's out on the island?"

"Who was it again?"

"Micah Stroud? I told you, I think you'll like him. He's"—she's about to say *Just like what you were listening to this morning, but not as soft-brained and poppy, because he sings with fire, real fire, and commitment*, but catches herself—"I don't know. But you'll like him. Trust me."

"Okay, fine. But forget the restaurant. The lasagna's already in the oven—meatless. Homemade. And both Ed and me are fine with a quiet night at home. Okay?"

She's about to chirp "Okay" into the receiver because it's been a long day and the idea of letting her mother baby her is beginning to enlarge for her, since what's the point of having your mother installed in your guest bedroom if you can't let yourself go? when she reaches the car and suddenly loses the ability to form a coherent sentence, to speak even. Because the car, parked in the shadows facing the artificial lagoon with its tethered boats and strolling tourists, has been defaced all over again. The fact of it, the discovery of it, after Alicia and Wilson Gutierrez and the muffled chants of the protestors that kept breaking through the pianissimo passages of the string quartets on the classical channel so that it became a kind of static in itself, is as much a shock as a sudden fender bender or the savage propulsive snarls of the dog at the window of the car beside hers. From the phone, clutched in the hand she's dropped to her side, the thin complaint of her mother's voice, lost to circumstance: "Alma, are you there? Alma?"

This time the color of the paint is red, or at least it shows red under the streaming yellowish illumination of the arc lights running along the promenade, and the message, though its import is the same, aims at a more general application. What it says, in the ballooning continuous letters of spray-can fluidity that loop up over the hood to obscure the view out of the windshield, is: *Pig Killer.* Only that. An epithet and accusation wrapped up in a single compound noun, which is, she has to admit, in her case at least, incontestable.

For a long moment, she stands there, feeling the sting of it. She *is* a killer, of pigs, of rats, of fennel and star thistle and of the introduced turkeys that will have to be removed in good time, a killer in the service of something higher, of restoration, redemption, salvation, but a killer all the same. Sadness, with its rotten edges, fills her—and weariness, weariness too, an exhaustion that saps her like the first withering assault of a winter cold—as she leans forward, and with the raised plastic wedge of her cell phone, begins to scrape the dark red paint from the glass.

The concert is at the Lobero, a restored downtown theater that ticks and groans with the decelerated rhythm of life three-quarters of a century ago, when the world was a bigger place with fewer people in it. Standing there with her mother on the Spanish tiles outside the tall wooden doors, Alma can't help thinking about that, about a world in which the population was less than a third of what it is now, all these surplus people absent, blown away like pollen to the far ends of the earth to let the rivers recover, the forests, the animals. Nineteen twenty-four, that's what the plaque out front says. She tries to picture it. Not the flappers and gangsters and all the rest, but people living close to the bone in the aftermath of war and the influenza it gestated and delivered, populations confined by geography and the limits of food production, jungles standing tall, mountaintops unconquered, the seas swarming with fish, mammals and invertebrates—that was the way it was when this theater was erected on the site of the old one, which dated back to 1873, when the world was bigger yet.

"You want another glass of wine?" her mother asks. She's dressed for the occasion in a powder-blue pantsuit and she's done her eyes and appropriated a pair of dangling earrings from the jewelry box in the bedroom. She's wearing heels and she's teased out her hair and sprayed it in place. She looks nice. And she's radiant in her pleasure over the evening out. Which is nice too.

"No, I don't think so," Alma says, shaking her head for emphasis. They each had a glass at home, to get in the mood, and a second glass—or plastic cup, which is what the wine is served in at the booth outside the theater—when they arrived. Alma likes to be on time, likes to be ahead of time in a way she'll be the first to admit is just a shade neurotic—she's not comfortable at the airport unless she's sitting at the gate with a newspaper before the display announcing her flight even appears on the monitor above the check-in desk—and she and her mother are first in line. Which is not to say that she isn't ready to unwind, enjoying the faint out-of-body sensation the second glass gives her while the cool of the night breathes around her, and more than happy to chat with the people behind them, two college girls who've come up from L.A. on the train because they're rabid Micah Stroud fans, but she's thinking ahead to the concert itself and the pressure on her bladder five or six songs in. So, no—no more wine now. "Maybe later," she says, even as her mother, with a restrained smile, ducks away to get a refill, mouthing (redundantly: the seats are reserved), "Save a seat for me."

At quarter of eight, the ushers push open the doors and she takes her mother's arm to guide her across the carpeted foyer. There's a small contretemps about the wine—one of the ushers gliding up to inform them that no drinks are allowed inside even as her mother drains the cup and hands it over—and then they're in the auditorium itself, her mother giving a little chirp of surprise over how elegant the theater is, as if she'd expected some barren rave hall or bottle-strewn dive. They stand there in back a moment, silently gazing out on the graduated rows of plush burgundy seats and the darkened stage beyond, before her mother excuses herself and heads off in the direction of the ladies' room. Alma finds her way to their seats on her own—decent seats, fifteen rows back, center section—and settles in to study the program in the pre-concert hush.

She feels herself relaxing, relishing the moment. The lights glow softly from the wall sconces, people's voices thrum with anticipation. She's seen Micah Stroud six times now, twice in San Francisco, three times in L.A. and once in Phoenix. This will be the first time for the girls who were behind her in line, and she envies them that, the rush of experience, the way the lights dim even as the hovering forms of the band members begin to take shape and drift through the shadows and then the spot comes up full on the naked mike and the drummer skims the hi-hat with his brushes and suddenly Micah's there, his voice floating up and over the anchor of his guitar till it insinuates itself into every last crevice of the house and all the people in it. That's how it's been every time. And now, expectantly, she leans forward, studying the stage. Taps one foot idly. Resists worrying about her mother.

Soon, the empty spaces around her have begun to fill, the lights quaver and she's just turning to look over her shoulder for her mother when here she is, clutching her purse in one hand and a rumpled program in the other. "There was a line at the ladies'," she murmurs by way of extenuation, then settles into her seat. The audience quiets. A few latecomers shuffle up and down the aisles, squeeze in over laps, purses, rearranged knees. The man in front of them lets out a nervous ratcheting cough. And then there's an accelerating clatter of applause—apes beating their tight-skinned palms and hard-knuckled phalanges together, she's thinking, no different from the way it was on the savannas of Africa three million years ago, and she's one of them, clap-clap-clapping in affirmation—as the emcee struts briskly across the stage to take hold of the microphone and give the audience a long bemused look till the clapping trails off.

He's a diminutive flesh-challenged man in his forties with limp hair hanging in his eyes and obscuring his ears, and he seizes the moment to deliver an abbreviated pep talk about the series that brings such nationally— and *internationally*—recognized acts as Micah Stroud (applause all over again) to this historic theater in our own little burg of Santa Barbara on a bi-monthly basis and how everyone should feel free to take a brochure and subscribe, because you'll not only be supporting the music you love but getting a real bargain too, and did you realize that series subscriptions can save you up to a hundred and twenty dollars per season? He knows to keep it short, but still there are catcalls from down in front, and someone behind Alma begins chanting *Micah, Micah, Micah* till the crowd picks it up and the man at the mike goes silent. For a long moment he merely stands there giving them an impish look before raising both hands, palms up, until the chant dies down.

"And now," he cries out in a new voice altogether— stentorian, fruity, the voice of the shill, the barker, the advance man—"the moment you've all been waiting for . . . ladies and gentlemen, gnomes and little fishes, I bring you the Cajun Wonder, the Lion of the Bayou, the man with the biggest voice and biggest heart in the business . . . MICAH . . . STROUD!"

Though she's the sort of person who's hyper-vigilant, always aware of her surroundings and open in all five senses to what the world brings her, she doesn't stir or look around her or do anything but tap her foot and nod her head in acknowledgment of the beat till he's three songs into his set, solo, acoustic, the band waiting in the wings because for now, in a reversal of the usual pattern, it's just his voice and guitar. Her mother is there beside her, but Alma's not aware of her, the songs that have become so personal they might have been written for her alone sweeping her up and out of herself to some other place altogether. Which is as it should be. Which is why she's come. Which is why her focus is exclusively on Micah, bent over his guitar till the tight glistening construct of his pompadour breaks loose and the patch of his soul beard shines with sweat.

He opens with "Loggerhead Blues," a slow, walking blues that segues into the syncopated upbeat swing of "Dip and Rise," before bringing it back down to the tragic release of "Minamata," with its images of deformed infants drawn back into the amniotic sea whence they came till the methyl mercury vanishes from the environment, from their mother's eggs and their father's sperm, and they can emerge again, whole and clean and waving their tiny unclenched fingers and toes in a salutation of pure joy. She sways in her seat. She's not thinking, just feeling, because here's a man who understands, who fights for the environment, who if he only knew would rise up in all his power and influence to back her and Tim and everything they're trying to accomplish.

And then she *is* thinking, even as the band slips out of the wings to join him onstage and he ducks under the strap of his electric guitar and the drummer counts off the beat with his two shining sticks, wondering if he's ever visited the islands, if he knows the gravity of the situation and what's at stake. She glances at her mother, who's enjoying herself, or seems to be. Then she's focused again on the stage, the opening chords of "Swamp Savior" coming down like an atmospheric phenomenon, but she's not in the auditorium any longer—no, she's out on the island, Micah Stroud at her side, assessing the pig damage, bending low to gaze in at the captive foxes in the tranquillity and safety of their cages, asking him if he wouldn't maybe write a song for them, an anthem to salvation, and he's leaning in close, hovering over her with the sun caught in his eyes and drawling, *Of course, and I'll go one better and donate the whole proceeds to the cause. How's that? Good enough for you? No? Well, I'm going to write a check too . . . but only if there's a quid pro quo here, because did anybody ever tell you how irresistible you are? Hey, you ever take time off? I mean, would you want to go on the European leg of the tour with me? Stockholm? You ever been to Stockholm . . . ?*

Four songs with the band, then the stage goes dark but for the spotlight. He turns his back a moment, ducking into the shadows to change guitars—back to acoustic—and then sidles up to the old-fashioned standing mike that's become his trademark to wonder aloud if anyone out there's having a good time. Well, they are. All of them. Even Alma's mother, who lets loose with a war whoop right out of the 1960s as the crowd roars its affirmation. "Hot town," he murmurs, wiping the sweat from his face with a limp towel. "And I surely do appreciate that on a cool autumn evening out here on the California coast where a poor boy from the bayou can always wrap himself up in the *heat* you good folks generate"—whistles, applause—"and I thank you from the bottom of my heart."

He bows his head a moment in acknowledgment of the applause, his hair fallen loose in a sweated tangle, and when he straightens up and the light catches his face again, she sees that he's grinning. "But do we have a treat for you tonight, folks, one of your very own"—he raises a hand to shade his eyes and peer out into the audience—"a supremely gifted singer-songwriter who's going to join me on the next number. Anise? You out there, sweetheart?"

That's when everything seems to swirl and rush as if she's caught in a vortex, an open drain sucking her down and taking the whole section of seats with her, her mother an illusion, the sneezing man vanished, hipsters in their trailing coats and scarves and photochromatic lenses all sieving past her as Anise Reed rises from a seat in the front row—how could she have missed her?—in an expanding mushroom cloud of kinked-out hair. But that's not all. Because Dave LaJoy is there too, in the seat beside the one she's just vacated, bringing his hands together in praise as the whole auditorium takes it up, Wilson Gutierrez at his elbow, stamping and whistling, while Alicia lifts her pale expressionless face to the light flooding down off the stage and the woman next to her with the big hair shocked with gray . . . beams with . . . with the pride of a mother. Anise's mother. Anise Reed's. And before Alma can even begin to process that revelation, here she is, *the supremely gifted singer-songwriter* herself, mounting the steps to the stage, her bare feet palpitating, toenails shining, as a lackey darts from the wings with her guitar held aloft in offering.

Nearly sixty years earlier, in September of 1946, when the Lobero was just beginning to fill its seats again after the lean years of the war, Alma's grandmother brought her baby to term at St. John's Hospital in Santa Monica—a healthy girl of seven pounds, seven ounces, who showed no ill effects of her mother's ordeal on Anacapa Island. Beverly was then living with her own mother, having no way to meet the rent on the apartment she'd shared with Till beyond the end of that first catastrophic month when she missed him through every minute of every day as if he'd gone off to war all over again. So they were two widows in that house she'd grown up in, her father ten years' dead, her mother on her feet all day long, working the cash register at a grocery on Lincoln Boulevard though she suffered from varicose veins and her ankles sagged till they were like layer cakes collapsed over the edges of the pan.

At first, when she awoke in the hospital and the nurse brought her daughter into the room, Beverly thought there must be some mistake, so convinced was she that her child would be a boy, Till's son, his reified image come from out of the void to stand in for him—Till Jr., who would grow into a man with both his arms pliable and intact. She hadn't thought of any girls' names. But when her mother, still in her uniform, came straight to her from work and took the baby up in her arms with a look of ecstasy, a new name darted into her head—Matilda, she would call her Matilda, Tillie for short—and she said it aloud, pronounced it for her mother in the echoing room while the woman in the bed beside her looked on with her twin boys and a placid smile. "Tillie, what do you think of Tillie?"

Her mother, staring into the baby's face as if the baby were an embodied message from an unknowable place, clucked her tongue. "Do you really want to live with that for the rest of your life?" she said, without looking up.

"Live with what?"

"If you don't know, then I can't tell you. But think about it. Just think."

She fought the notion through the hushed course of that first day, through the changings and the feedings and the trip in the taxi that came for her next morning, stubborn, seeing Till as he was before the war, Till in his uniform, Till without it, in bed, pressing his urgent body to hers. For the first two weeks, right up to the eve of the christening, the baby was just *the baby*, but finally, sitting there in the rocker by the window of the only house she'd ever known until her husband came along, her daughter sucking placidly at the rubber nipple of the just-warmed bottle and her mother, tired on her feet, shuffling into the room to offer her a cup of tea, she came to herself—she had a daughter, not a son, and Till was a spirit now. In that moment the baby had her name—she would call her Katherine, after the gentle woman with the suffering face and sweet compressed smile who balanced the teacup on its saucer as if it were a feat of legerdemain and never took her eyes from her all the while.

Men came round, men cut from the same mold as Warren, but Beverly never gave them the slightest encouragement, and eventually they stopped coming. There was no question of remarrying, even for the sake of her daughter, because she was a one-man woman, then and always, and she was prepared to die alone at the end of her life to keep herself for Till when they met in heaven. If Katherine (or Kat, as they began calling her because she wouldn't part with her stuffed tabby except in the bathtub, and then only reluctantly) grew up without a father, she wasn't the only one, what with the divorce rate and the toll the war had taken, and she never seemed any the worse for it, at least not while she was in school. Of course, Beverly had no choice but to go back to work within a month after her daughter was born, reversing roles with her mother, who quit the grocery to stay home full-time.

Did her mother spoil the child? Yes, absolutely. There were endless afternoons at the beach with a red plastic bucket and shovel, the seashell collections and the dried starfish, trips to feed the ducks in the canals, cones and sundaes at the ice cream parlor, a parade of toys and dresses and shoes. Children were meant to be spoiled, that was her mother's attitude. And if Kat wanted a story right in the middle of dinner, well, she got it. And another at bedtime and then at breakfast too. In the beginning there were the nursery rhymes Beverly had received from her mother's lips when she herself was a girl, "Goosey, Goosey Gander," "Little Jack Horner" and "Mary Had a Little Lamb," in the very same worn volumes she'd kept on a special shelf in her room till she was old enough to be embarrassed by them and banished them to the garage, and then the narratives stretched out and the three little pigs came to the table along with the three bears, and after dinner each night, before she switched on the radio—and in later years, the TV—she and her mother traded off from book to book and still Kat demanded more. After the nursery rhymes it was "Dick and Jane" and "Winnie the Pooh" and on up the ladder till Kat was already beginning to read on her own by the time she started kindergarten.

School illuminated her. She was an eager student, utterly absorbed in the task at hand, no matter how repetitive or frustrating it might have seemed to her classmates. Her report cards were glowing. And when the achievement tests came round in sixth grade and then again in seventh, she consistently ranked in the highest percentile. She was a happy child. She bloomed. She grew. And then came adolescence, which hit with the sudden impact of a meteor—one day Kat was a little girl with a Minnie Mouse barrette in her hair and the next she was filled out and there were boys mooning round every day after school, junior versions of the men who'd come to the house before them—but Kat never seemed to fall under the spell of one or the other of them and never, even for a day, even for prom, let her school-work flag. Beverly began to hope for college, a scholarship even, because she really felt there were no limits to what her daughter could do.

To that end, she put aside money each week from her paycheck. She hadn't had the opportunity of college herself, graduating from high school in the midst of the Depression and then going right to work in a defense plant during the war, but she'd taken a secretarial course and it had paid off. She'd begun working as a secretary in the main offices of the Santa Monica–Malibu Unified School District when Kat entered first grade, and the work was steady and guaranteed, and since she lived with her mother and her mother owned the house free and clear, what would have gone to rent went into a special savings account. And this was no dollar-a-week Christmas club, this was the real thing. A college fund. For Kat. Kat was her hope. Kat, whose mother was a secretary and whose father was dead and drowned in the roiling waters of the Anacapa Passage, was going to be the first of her family to go on to college and thus have access to all the professions a college degree would open up for her—law, medicine, education, science.

When she was accepted at UCLA on a state scholarship that paid tuition and a modest living allowance, they celebrated—all three of them, though Beverly's mother was by then having difficulty walking and hadn't left the house in months—with a lobster dinner at a hotel on Ocean Boulevard overlooking the sea. The first year Kat lived at home, then went into student housing as a sophomore, so that they saw her only on weekends. After a while she began skipping a weekend now and again, then two in a row, pleading her workload. Sometimes a whole month would go by before she'd come home, and when she did come she brought a duffel of dirty laundry with her, which Beverly was only too glad to wash and fold and stack neatly for her, all the while trying to keep from worrying, from nagging. Because Kat was too thin and she wore her hair long and parted in the middle, like the hippies they read about in the paper and saw on TV, and like the hippies she wore flared hip-huggers with stars and flowers stitched into them and blouses that showed off her midriff, which anybody—not just her mother—would have considered provocative. And what about drugs? Marijuana? Did she use marijuana?

Kat never said a word about it. She never mentioned her grades either, though when the reports came at the end of the semester, Beverly—who would never dream of opening her daughter's mail—couldn't help quizzing her about them. Was everything all right? *Yes*, Kat assured her, *everything's fine*. And added, in a tone Beverly didn't like, *Stop harassing me*. In her senior year, she started dating seriously. She was in love, that was what she told her mother over the phone and on the odd weekends when she came home, but who was the boy? What was his name? What was his family like? What was he majoring in? He *was* a student, wasn't he? He doesn't smoke marijuana or anything, does he? What does his father do? Where are they from? This went on for a whole weekend, from dinner Friday night till Sunday morning at breakfast, the washer churning on the enclosed porch and a pale tired sun smeared like grease over everything in the kitchen. "You can't even tell me his name?" Beverly said, setting a plate of waffles and two poached eggs down before her. "Your own mother? I mean, what's the secret? Is he a dwarf or something"—she let out a laugh—"or a Communist? Or is it us. Your nana and me. You're ashamed of us, is that it?"

"Greg," Kat said finally, her face twisted in sudden fury. "His name's Greg. All right?"

Her mother, who'd been hounding her since she stepped in the door Friday night, looked as if she'd been slapped, and Kat, despite herself, instantly regretted it. "Listen," she said, "I'm sorry, Mom. I've been under a lot of pressure, that's all. At school. I just need some space, okay?"

At the table, her fingers gnarled and her head bent close to her task, her nana peeled shrimp for scampi as if she'd never done anything else in her entire life. The shrimp, gray and denuded, lay mounded in a glass bowl while their translucent shells accumulated on a sheet torn from the *Times*. She never glanced up, though there was revolution in the air.

Her mother gave her a hurt look, bunching her lips over a strip of green pepper she kept shifting round her mouth like a toothpick. She said, "I don't want to pry, but—"

"Then don't."

The next time she came home, for Christmas break, her mother emerged from the kitchen the minute the key turned in the lock of the front door. She was wiping her hands on a dishtowel and her smile of greeting flared and died as she crossed the room to peck a kiss to Kat's cheek before turning to the table in the front hall to retrieve an envelope there and hand it to her. "This came for you yesterday," she said, fixing her eyes on her.

It was from Greg—Kat could see that at a glance. She'd had a late exam in childhood psychology, but he'd finished earlier in the week and gone home to Santa Barbara to be with his parents for the holidays. He was going to drive down to pick her up the day after Christmas for a camping trip to Ensenada they'd been planning for the last month, six days alone on the beach and in the tent at night, in the same sleeping bag, like (Greg's joke) Robert Jordan and his Little Rabbit. She might have blushed when she took the envelope, folded it once and stuffed it in the back pocket of her jeans. She didn't say anything, but her mother was watching her so closely she might have been lasering right through her like in that scene in *Goldfinger*.

"Take-sue," she said, mispronouncing the name, "is that Hungarian? Or Bohunk? Or what? For the life of us, Nana and I couldn't figure it out."

She wanted to say, *You don't have to*, but instead, just to watch the awareness sink deep into her mother's face, she said, "Takesue. Three syllables. And the last one is suey, like chop suey."

"Chop suey?" her mother repeated, looking puzzled. There was the sound of voices carrying down the street and through the glass of the front window, drunks coming back from the bars along the boardwalk. She let out a nervous laugh. "You don't mean—? He isn't *Chinese*, is he?"

This was the moment she'd been dancing around since the day Greg had come up to her in the commons, his hair long and thick and shining—longer than George Harrison's, longer than anybody's in any band she'd ever seen—bent over the table where she was sitting with her girlfriend Pattie and said, *Weren't you in Bieler's class last semester?*

"No, Mom," she said, still standing there in the hallway, the letter tucked safely away, her bag over one shoulder and her peacoat hanging limp at her knees, "he's not Chinese." She took a moment, shrugging out from under the bag and looking her mother square in the face. "Take-sue isn't a Chinese name, it's Japanese."

And then, before her mother could gasp or snort or shout or spin her head around on her shoulders and scream, *Japanese? You're going with a Jap? After what they did to your father?* she was across the room, down the hall and firmly shutting the door to her room behind her.

When Greg came up the steps on the day after Christmas, his arms laden with gift-wrapped packages and his father's maroon Dodge Charger sitting at the curb behind him like a rocket ship at rest, her mother pulled open the door on a vision of beauty, only she didn't see it that way. "Greg!" Kat called out, sailing across the room to him while her mother staggered back in shock, because not only was Greg a hippie, in a tie-dyed poncho, silver-striped pants, scuffed boots and a wide-brimmed hat with an eagle's feather jutting proudly from the band, he was Asian too. Worse than Asian: Japanese. With a Fu Manchu mustache that framed his jaw in two dangling transparent wisps. Kat took his hand, led him into the front hall, saying, "Mom, I want to—" but her mother was gone, retreating into the bedroom at the back of the house.

She'd tried to warn him—*My mother's a little strange, you know, after the war and all, I mean, World War II*—but she knew him well enough to see that he was as shocked as her mother was, shocked and hurt. Older people, the ignorant and the hidebound, with their fat white faces and five-dollar haircuts, might have derided him for dressing the way he did, for being a hippie, but that he could take in stride. Racism was another thing altogether. He was fifth generation, as American as anybody, his family was prosperous, with their own seafood business based out of Santa Barbara, and he was going to take his place in American society whether anybody liked it or not—and if he went out in the street and protested against the war in Vietnam, that was his privilege and his right. As was the way he chose to dress and what sort of records he played on the stereo and the drugs he put in his own body with the freest will in the world. That was Greg. That was the way he felt. And if the world was nothing but combat, so be it. She felt choked. Her mind was jumping from one misery to another like a cricket on a hot sidewalk. "Here," she whispered, and she took his hand and pulled him forward.

Shoulders slumped, eyes down, he followed her stiffly into the living room, where her grandmother was sitting in the armchair, watching one of her soap operas.

She took the packages from him and set them down on the sofa. Then she raised her voice so her grandmother could hear and said, "Let me introduce you to my grand-mother. Nana, this is Greg."

Over the past year her grandmother had slipped into confusion, her face immobile, her gaze dulled, her hands jittery in her lap. With an effort, she raised her eyes and lifted her trembling chin. Greg bent forward, offered his hand. "Nice to meet you," he murmured, but she just stared at the place where his hand was and said nothing in return.

"Greg's my boyfriend, Nana—the one I've been telling you about?" she said, feeling cold suddenly, chilled, as if the house were a glacier that had just split in two, irrepara-bly, forever. Turning to him, she said, "Nana's a little hard of hearing"—a smile—"aren't you, Nana? But my mother, I guess she must be changing into something a little dressier . . . or something. You wait. I'll go get her."

His voice was terse—he was in the chasm of the glacier too. "Don't bother," he said.

She always liked to think it was during the vacation in Mexico that she got pregnant with Alma, but that couldn't have been because Alma didn't come along until October, so it must have been after they got back to school. At any rate, despite the fact that she was on the pill and on a con-scious level didn't have even the slightest inkling of the tiniest fleeting desire to get pregnant, or not yet anyway, she did, and that pregnancy froze her inside the glacier until it split all over again. She couldn't go home. She didn't. She graduated (her mother tearful at the ceremony, without knowing what she was crying over, or the extent of it anyway) and moved in with Greg, in Santa Barbara, and he started working on one of his father's boats, diving for lobster and abalone off the back side of Santa Cruz.

At first they lived with Greg's parents in a house on the mesa, just above the marina, but the house—a big ram-bling craftsman with upper and lower porches and views of the sea out of the south-and east-facing windows—was crowded for all its size. There were Greg's five siblings, all younger than he and perpetually embroiled in their internecine disputes, his father's mother, two bachelor uncles and an assortment of cats, dogs and caged and evilly cackling birds. Though they had a room to themselves, Kat just couldn't feel at home. Her mother-in-law fought off every attempt she made to contribute—she wouldn't let her chop vegetables, wash dishes, even take out the trash, and every time she settled into the sofa or wandered into the kitchen she felt like an intruder, which, in fact, she was. And no matter how utterly without prejudice she felt herself to be, it was nonetheless strange to find herself living in a Japanese household—or Japanese American, as she was constantly correcting herself.

It wasn't that they were all that much different from anybody else—they ate steaks and burgers and hot dogs and all the rest of it, maybe more fish because fish was the family business—but that anything, any other household, even if it had been right next door to her mother's house in Venice, would have seemed disorienting, especially in her condition. She was used to silence and order, a house in which three generations of women lived and worked in peace without the disruptive presence of men, children, pets. But here was chaos, here was the other, a new association and a new regime. The smells were different, the little rituals surrounding meals, where people sat, the noise and confusion of the kids and their mob of friends—even the dogs, a pair of Akitas, were like nothing she'd ever seen, their heads as broad and flat as a bear's, their habits secretive, and where did they do their business? Time and again she'd surprised them in her bed and twice she'd found the blankets suspiciously damp.

Within the month she began pestering Greg to look for a place of their own—a little privacy, that was all she wanted, nothing against his family—and when Alma came along and she was nursing and shutting herself up all day in her room just so she wouldn't have to listen to one more repetition of her mother-in-law's dicta on the subject of child rearing, it became imperative. By spring of the following year, 1969, she got her wish. Greg came home from work one clammy socked-in evening, swept his hair out of his face and announced in a voice that could hardly contain its excitement that they were moving to the harbor, to live on a boat he'd bought for $3,600, one-third down, the rest due after the first year. But for the baby, she would have leapt into his arms. As it was, she took hold of him in one arm while cradling Alma in the other, and the three of them danced round the room till Greg's uncle Billy, who worked nights and slept in the room directly beneath them, mounted the stairs to complain about the noise.

The *Black Gold* was a working boat, a converted thirty-two-foot cabin cruiser with an open rear deck of fiberglass in place of the original wood planking and a compartment for the catch below; the main cabin and sleeping quarters were aft. There was a galley the size of an icebox, an icebox the size of an orange crate, a built-in table that folded up when not in use (which was never), a little upright coffin of a head and a plywood slab, decorated with a disintegrating foam mattress and a sleeping bag that gave off a mélange of festering odors under the bow. Showers, toilets, laundry were available in the marina. Kat liked to joke that the boat gave a new definition to damp. Every garment, every diaper, every towel might as well have been a sponge, and the only relief was when the sun shone and the wind picked up and things could be strung out to dry. On days when she was in harbor, that is. And those days were rare, at least at first.

She'd wake in the dark to Alma's cries, take her to bed with them to feed her, then get up and make Greg his breakfast, fried rice, four eggs, mackerel or abalone or Canadian bacon seared in the pan, toasted cheese, coffee by the vat. And then, when his partner, Mickey Mans, arrived looking hungover, starved and stoned in equal measures, she took the baby and went up the hill to her mother-in-law's for the day, or walked all the way up Ana-capa Street to the library to sit and browse and play with Alma till she was so bored she could barely draw another breath. But they were living on the cheap and they had their privacy and she was waiting for him at the slip each night with a bag of groceries when he chugged in through the mouth of the harbor. She became a genius of the quick but nutritious meal, stir-fry mainly, cauliflower, bok choy, mushrooms, snow peas, bean sprouts—whatever looked good in the market—augmented by the halibut, lobster, crab and rockfish she'd buy for next to nothing from the fishermen when they came in.

And *uni*, though she never really developed a taste for it. *Uni*—sea urchin—was what Greg and Mickey were after, what they were exclusively after, because the abalone fish-ery was taking a nosedive from over-harvesting, ground-fish numbers were down and lobsters seasonal, and Greg's father had found a niche market for the urchins, which he was selling to a distributor in L.A. for transshipment to Japan. They were among the first to exploit the resource, but by the late seventies, when Alma was working her way through fourth, fifth and sixth grade and thinking that living on a boat was the most natural thing in the world, the real boom set in. Urchins, previously considered pests, were suddenly the hottest thing on the market. The Japa-nese couldn't get enough of them. It was the roe they were after—or the gonads actually, tangerine-colored organs arranged in a star shape inside the spiny shell, which were extracted by the wholesaler, packed in ice and flown to Tokyo overnight. Black gold, that was what people called the urchins, though they shaded to red and purple under the sun, and the money was good, the money was boss, out of sight, too good to believe.

By the time Alma was in sixth grade they'd bought their own house on a back street within walking distance of the harbor, and the dampness, the mold, the cramped quarters and the smell of fish so overpowering they might as well have been living in the muck at the bottom of the sea, were behind them. It wasn't perfect—for the first few months Alma slept fitfully, waking in tears because her bed wouldn't move and the floor never rocked or gave or swayed, and when she did sleep it was on the carpet beneath the bed, as if she were still squeezed into her berth under the foredeck—but for Kat it was night and day. Having a house away from the water where you had some space to move around in and didn't have to worry all night about your daughter pitching overboard and drowning and you could walk across the kitchen floor without water squishing under your heels was cleansing, revolutionary, liberating, not to mention what it did for their sex life—she couldn't count the nights she and Greg had had to steal out of the cabin to make goose-pimpled love on the foredeck or on the truncated leather seat in the cockpit so Alma wouldn't hear. And then there was the minor miracle of Mrs. Meehan, the woman they found to watch Alma after school, freeing up Kat to work the boat along with Greg and Mickey.

She became their tender, which allowed them to spend more time harvesting urchins and less hassling with the equipment, and the change brought her back to life after the years spent rotating between the library, the Takesue household and the part-time jobs she took just to drive down the boredom once Alma started school. The first few days were rough, but she caught on quickly—Greg was patient with her, even if his partner, especially in the mornings before the first dive, tended to be a bear—but within a month her confidence began to grow along with the muscles in her arms and shoulders, and if it wasn't exactly feminine to have an upper body made of iron, it felt good. And so did being away from shore, outdoors, under the open sky.

The tender on an urchin boat is responsible for taking care of all the tasks the divers would prefer having done for them, from dropping and setting the anchor over a promising spot, to laying out the wetsuits and hoses, working the winch to bring the catch over the side, keeping an eye on the air compressor when the divers are down in thirty feet of icy swirling water and making a nice hot lunch to fortify them for the afternoon dives. Not to mention digging out the cold beers for the ride home. While they were down, usually in thirty-minute shifts—thirty minutes was about average for filling the steel-rimmed bag with urchins—she would entertain herself as best she could, reading through paperbacks and the piles of out-of-date magazines she got from a friend of Greg's who worked for a dentist, doing pencil sketches of the island bluffs or just staring off into space and dreaming, one watchful eye fixed on the snaking yellow hoses as they cut the surface and plunged into invisibility. Her life, finally, seemed to fit her wanting. She'd never been happier.

Then there came a morning in August, clear and calm, what fog there was bellying across the water out front of the boat only to fall away to nothing as she sliced through it, as relaxed at the helm as a long-distance trucker cruising the interstate, while Greg and Mickey slept below. She was six months in, six months to the day—she and Greg were going to celebrate by going out to dinner and a movie when they got back that night—and she'd reached a confidence level where she did almost all the piloting, there and back, because why should her divers have to waste their energy when they could be collapsed in their bunks on the way out and slumped over their beers on the way back? *Save your energy*, she'd told Greg when she'd been on the job a month, squeezing his arm at the biceps as they stood rocking in the cabin and giving him her best imitation of a sex-starved leer, and he'd leered right back, kissed her deep and run a hand over her breasts and then lifted his other hand too and held them there. *Sure*, he'd said, *why not? You know the routine as well as anybody. Just keep your eye on the gauges and listen to the engine—that's all you need.* And it was. No problem. And if anything did go wrong, she had two mechanics aboard, and she'd let them worry about it. A jolt of coffee in the morning to keep her alert, one beer only at night till they were through the shipping lanes. Watch the depth finder. Fix on a point and never deviate because if you run a crooked line you just waste fuel. Easiest thing in the world.

This morning they were headed for the west end of the island, to the kelp beds at Forney's Cove, where they'd discovered a mother lode of urchins the day before. Alma was with her Grandmother Boyd in Venice for two weeks, all that nastiness over Greg long forgotten, or buried anyway, because when Kat finally brought her daughter home at four months—just herself, just for the day—her mother melted, and there was never another word about Japs or Nips or Orientals, at least not while Alma was around. The haul had been exceptionally good lately, the urchins of primo quality—they were taking in a thousand a day on average—and almost as plentiful as the pitted volcanic stones that littered the bottom. More and more boats were getting into the act, but they couldn't begin to imagine any falloff in the catch—not yet. Not amidst all this abundance. Get it while you can, that was her thinking. Pay down the mortgage. Save for the future.

Greg came up from below, rubbing his eyes, when he heard the engine slow and then clank into neutral. "Here, already, huh?" he said, giving a stretch and a yawn and peering out the window at the kelp fronds spread across the water like so many grasping hands.

"Sure," she said, "life's a treat when you sleep all the time."

"How's the pepperoncini look?" That was his pet term for kelp, because it was the exact color and texture of the little pickled peppers you found in a pint of antipasto at the deli counter.

"I don't know," she said. "There's a lot of it."

He went out on deck to have a closer look—he was watching for the chewed-up leaves that indicated an urchin party was going on down below—and then, after a minute, flagged his arm for her to drop anchor. That was when Mickey crawled up out of the galley, a once-white baseball cap pulled down over his eyes and a mug of coffee clutched like a lifeline in one hand. Like Greg, he wore shorts and a sweatshirt stained with paint, motor oil and the various internal fluids of one sea creature or another. He was short and powerfully built, already balding at thirty, with a winning gap-toothed smile that gave him the look of the class wiseguy, which was precisely what he'd been. If you believed his stories. Unfortunately, he never deployed his smile or any semblance of it before twelve, twelve at least, and when he emerged from the cabin a moment later he was scowling as usual. "Man, I just do not feel like getting in that water this morning," he said, leaning over the rail and staring numbly down into the gently heaving wash of kelp. "Why don't you suit up for me, Kat? And I'll just stay up here and sunbathe. And read what is it—*Cosmo*? Or *Better Homes and Gardens*. That's what we all need, right? Better homes, better gardens?"

"Uh-uh," she said. "We need better hauls." She gave him a grin, then conspicuously checked her watch. "Which means it's time to fire up the compressor and get my divers down there where all the spiny things are."

The compressor—Greg had rigged it up himself—was mounted on the deck just to the rear of the cabin on the starboard side, beneath the gunwale, where it would be protected from the wind and spray. She hated to pull the cord and start the thing up because the racket it made—an endlessly repeating loop of blatting exhaust that sounded like a squadron of leaf blowers pulsing out over the sea—destroyed the peace of the morning and the afternoon too. She wore foam earplugs once the boys went down, but they didn't do much more than dampen the roar so that every word she read in her dog-eared paperbacks and sunbleached magazines seemed to repeat itself, once on her lips and again in the floating dissociated interstices of her brain. The muffler could use replacing, that was for sure, and she'd nagged Greg about it and he'd made the usual promises, but they were getting while the getting was good and at the end of the day everybody felt as if they'd run a marathon and none of them wanted to think about maintenance—maintenance was a concept better suited to the storm-struck days of January and February, when the urchins were spawning and there were whole weeks filled with rotating spirals of nothing.

The motor caught on the first pull—*Vrrrr-rap-rap-rap*—and they had to shout at each other while she paid out the hoses and Greg and Mickey pulled on their wetsuits, flippers, masks and weights. Then they were overboard in a black churn of water, suspended there against the opaque depths for a fraction of a moment before they were gone. For a while, out of habit—or boredom, because what was else was there to do?—she watched their bubbles rise to the surface and then diverge as each went his own way, intent on the clusters of spiny black echinoderms that had only to be pried loose and slipped into the mesh bag that trailed behind them, to the tune of twenty-eight cents a pound.

A breeze had come up as she leaned there over the rail, dreaming, letting her gaze wander across the surface to the white crescent of beach five hundred yards away and the sun-bleached hills that rose beyond it. The boat swung on its anchor. A chop—white-flecked, sudsing—ran before the breeze and erased the air bubbles. The gas motor that ran the compressor missed, sputtered, then straightened out in a high whine, the exhaust flatulating through the pinprick holes the sea air had worked through the muffler. The breeze was cold, sucking the chill from the waves like a giant air conditioner, and she went down in the cabin to get her sweatshirt. On her way back through the galley she stopped to pour a third cup of coffee and make herself a ham and Swiss on rye with a slice of sweet onion and plenty of mustard, which she seared in the pan so it would be nice and gooey, just the way she liked it, and then she was back on deck. They'd been down twenty minutes—perfect—so she'd have time to enjoy her sandwich and linger over her coffee before they came up and she'd have to winch the bags up on deck. And that was always exciting, a break in the routine, the secret shy animals spilled across the boards, their spines waving and coalescing as if to assess the threat of an alien atmosphere, one of poisonous air rather than sustaining water, before she stored them in the darkness of the hold. Which required care—any prick of the spines, no matter how cursory, always got infected, and if one went in deep and broke off, you could kiss twenty-five dollars goodbye because you were going to need the doctor to dig it out and clean up the wound. *Erizos del mar*, hedgehogs of the sea, that's what the Mexicans called them. Or sometimes, just *heriditas*, little wounds.

The boat had begun to roll a bit, nothing serious, nothing out of the ordinary, the weather out here as changeable as can be, and with the sweatshirt on and sitting in the sun she was comfortable and the sandwich was good and the coffee still hot. At thirty minutes, neither Greg nor Mickey had surfaced, meaning the pickings were a little slimmer than they'd thought or that the currents down below were banging them around a bit so the going was slower than usual. She chewed her way around the sandwich, keeping the center for last, then licked the grease from her fingers, wishing she'd thought to tear off a paper towel for a napkin and then finally just wiping her hands on her shorts, which needed washing in any case. When they'd been down thirty-five minutes she got up to look for their bubbles, tracing the lines of the hoses out twenty feet from the boat, but there was nothing to see but the flecks of foam on the wind-driven water. If they weren't up in five minutes more she'd give two quick jerks on the hoses, the signal to surface.

What she didn't know was that the jury-rigged compressor, ratcheting over the steel plate to which Greg had screwed it, had begun, ever so slightly, to work loose. This produced excessive vibration, which in turn caused the muffler to separate at the jointure by a fraction of an inch so that the exhaust began to leach back toward the intake. Because the boat had turned against the wind and because the compressor was located in the space between the cabin bulkhead and the gunwale, the carbon monoxide was trapped there until it began to drift into the intake. Greg wasn't breathing oxygen. Nor was Mickey.

Finally, at forty minutes, she tugged twice—hard—on Greg's air hose and a moment later felt him coming up as she pulled the hose to her, and that was all right, no cause for alarm—the basket must have been full to overflowing and hard to maneuver and she was guiding him in and keeping the hose clear of it. She was watching the water intently now, watching for bubbles, for his limbs beating up out of the depths with the basket she'd have to hook up and winch in, when he suddenly bobbed to the surface like a piece of driftwood, Greg, her husband, her lover, his long silken hair come loose from the grip of his hood and flailing round him like weed, and—this was strange—no bag in sight. Stranger still, he wasn't working his flippers or raising his head from the water to give her a fogged-over grin and a thumbs-up. He wasn't moving at all.

The rest was a blur, a bad dream in which she couldn't move, couldn't react, her feet stuck in quicksand, her hands glued to her sides, but she pulled at the hose till the hose strained and went slack again, and even as she darted into the cabin to radio *Mayday* she saw Mickey rise on the far side of the boat, his limbs splayed and his head down in the water. In the next moment she was over the side and the chill gray slap of the ocean meant nothing to her because she was lifting Greg's face from the water, tearing off his mask, pressing her lips to his, mouth to mouth— but no, she had to get him on deck, that was what she had to do, get him on deck and pump the water from his lungs, because he was drowning, that was it, and Mickey was drowning too. Flailing with all her strength against the chop and the hull that seemed to bob and duck away from her as if it were alive, as if this were a game, she caught hold of the rail in back with one lunging hand and held fast to Greg—to his face, his head, the collar of his wetsuit, any part of him she could grasp hold of—with the other. Frantic, barely able to breathe herself, she tried again and again to get him up and out of the water, but there was no purchase, nothing but the yielding swollen waves and the slick hull, so that finally, wedging his arm awkwardly against the rail on a rising swell, she vaulted up on deck and tugged at the sleeve of his wetsuit, but he slipped back on her, sinking away and then rising again on the next swell that swept in to fill the void.

She was shivering, breathless, but she went in again and again and still she couldn't maneuver the insensate weight of him up on deck. She didn't have the strength. The boat wouldn't cooperate. The waves kept pulling her back, slapping her in the face, scorching her lips and needling her eyes. She panted and strained, crying out in her frustration. Not that it mattered. Not that anything mattered. Because Greg wasn't drowning or Mickey either, and no amount of mouth-to-mouth resuscitation could have brought them back, because they were both dead. Dead of carbon monoxide poisoning long before she'd become alarmed, before she'd tugged on Greg's hose, before she'd gone into the cabin for the sweatshirt or made herself the sandwich. The wind had shifted, the boat swung on its anchor, the muffler worked free at the joint. And before they were down ten minutes they were gone.

Two other boats—another urchin fisherman and a day-tripper—were there in minutes, men shouting and leaping into the water, taking hold of Greg and Mickey and her too and hauling them on deck, the wind crying out and the sun fixed like a rivet in the sky to mark the time, ten-thirty in the morning, August 3, 1984, the moment she became a widow like her mother before her, and Alma, fifteen years old and browning under the sun at Venice Beach while the musclemen spilled out of Gold's Gym and the freaks and punks and street musicians plied their trade along the boardwalk, lost her father forever.

Afterward, after three encores, a valedictory ovation that must have lasted ten minutes and the ritual strewing of long-stemmed roses at Micah Stroud's feet by a sisterhood of squealing fans who made her feel nothing but old, Alma finds herself drifting up the aisle and out the big wooden doors, her mother expanding at her side.

"You were right," her mother's saying as they emerge into the softness of the night and the first diaphanous drizzle of the fall, everything moist and sweet after the arid atmosphere of the theater, of the season, of the parched hills and withered vegetation that put a strain on the whole ecosystem, "he *is* special, really special. I mean, I loved it. And the girl singer he had with him—what was her name? The one he called up out of the audience? She was something too. Not really a Joni Mitchell type, but more maybe Buffy Sainte-Marie—"

"Who?"

"You know—she was a folksinger? From the sixties? I'm sure I played her around the house when you were growing up. Your father liked her, I remember. Or at least at first, before he heard Janis." A laugh, rich with the pleasure of the recollection. "But how could you listen to anybody after you hear Janis?"

The streetlights tease out the mist, droplets elongated to silvering streaks darting toward the slick pavement, and she should feel renewed, exhilarated—Micah Stroud and the first rain of the season, her birthday, her mother, the islands hovering in the mist and everything she's worked and hoped for moving forward to completion—but she doesn't. She feels weak, drained, faintly nauseous—and it has nothing to do with Anise Reed, or at least that's what she tells herself. Of course, the moment she saw her rise from her seat she was seized with hatred and resentment—and jealousy, jealousy too—which had the effect of pulling her right out of the concert and thrusting her all over again into the animus of her life, or at least the life she was leading lately. And Alicia. Alicia there too, complicit with them, a charter member of the gang. Even worse, she had to admit to herself that Anise Reed wasn't half-bad, her voice purer than it had a right to be and something close to magical when she blended it with Micah's. He backed her on two of her own songs and then, incredibly, kept her there onstage in all her barefooted big-haired glory to beat a tambourine against one palm and lean into the mike on the choruses and harmonize with him.

Micah Stroud, Anise Reed, Dave LaJoy, Alicia Penner, Wilson Gutierrez.

They're at the car now, the faint lines where Ed had bent over the hood to erase the graffiti with rubbing compound and a whole lot of elbow grease still showing in evidence of what she's up against, and she feels so sad suddenly, so overwhelmed, that she just drops her arms to her side and stands there in confusion while cars back out around her and her mother catches herself in the middle of a reminiscence about a concert she once attended at the Hollywood Bowl with Alma's father, with Greg, to ask her what's the matter.

But the thing is, she can't answer because she doesn't know.

"Alma?" Her mother's voice is like the soft beating of a wing in the dark. "Are you all right?"

And there it is again, the weakness, the feeling of helplessness and exhaustion, the nausea rising in her as if something's come unstopped, and she's barely aware of opening her arms to her mother's embrace and of holding her there in the rain and the flaring red flicker of the brake lights of a hundred cars while the night passes overhead and Micah Stroud sits alone in his dressing room, bathed in sweat.

In the morning, she feels nauseous all over again, nauseous for no reason, leaning over the toilet till whatever it was—whatever it is—comes up in a quick liquid burn to float there briefly before vanishing in a descending coil of water.

Willows Canyon

$\mathbf{H}$e pays cash for the wire cutters, five pairs, standing in line with an assortment of off-duty housewives, day-time drunks and chipper retirees at Home Depot, the most anonymous place in the world, and nobody looks at him twice. Or maybe they do, because of the dreads, but so what? He's a citizen just like them, a man with ready cash and a need for a particular tool for a particular job and he's waiting his turn without complaint, though all the customers in front of him—seven, to be exact—are leaning into carts piled up like houses on wheels with every sort of crap imaginable, stainless-steel toilet paper dispensers, closet organizers, bug zappers, ceramic garden trolls. The indolent fat woman at the checkout counter lifts the scanner as if it's a set of barbells. The intercom rattles on mercilessly. Jets—the airport is right around the corner—blast overhead at ever-shorter intervals. Everybody wants to stop and chat.

Eighteen minutes. Eighteen minutes to make a simple purchase because customer service is a notion as foreign to these people as paying an honest price for an honest product. He loathes places like this—as a small-business owner, he ought to, what with Costco and Best Buy and all the rest undercutting him twenty-four/seven—and he would have gone to the locally owned hardware store in the upper village instead of driving all the way out here to park in the middle of this paved wasteland except for the fact that they know him there, know him well, and for this purchase what he wants above all else is anonymity. Yes, and *Welcome to Home Depot, shoppers.*

In the car, on the way back to the marina, he's making mental lists, running through the details to be sure he hasn't forgotten anything. The black cap is on the seat beside him, the shades clamped over his eyes, the sunblock in his daypack—along with a sweatshirt in the event it turns cold and a plastic poncho to keep the rain off him because rain is in the forecast, always in the forecast for February, the one month out of the year you can count on it. For food, he's made up three sandwiches, two peanut butter, one Swiss and tomato, and he's got a baggie of trail mix and two PowerBars for energy, plus a liter bottle of water—you can't trust what's out there on the island, especially when you've got pig carcasses rotting all over the place. A compass, though he isn't exactly sure how to use it and won't need it in any case—stick to the canyon and the fence line, that's his plan, and that's what he's going to tell everybody else too. Because whatever you do, don't get lost. You get lost and you'll be swimming home.

He parks in his usual place, across the lot from the close-in spots where people ding your doors and fenders without thinking twice about it and well away from the eucalyptus trees along the fringes, which tend to lose their branches this time of year (that's all he needs, a smashed windshield waiting for him when he comes dragging in off the boat). Wilson has his card key—he didn't want people attracting notice waiting for him outside the gate, so Wilson has already ushered them in—and he flips open his cell to call him as he digs out the daypack and pulls the cap down over his eyes. It's just past ten, the weather holding steady. There's a breeze off the ocean, clouds riding past to eradicate the sun and bring it back again like a bad connection, and he's hitting Wilson's number and thinking rain can only benefit them because it'll keep the pig killers under wraps and mask any boat making its way out to the island, so yes, let it rain. Let it rain like holy hell.

Wilson answers on the first ring: "Yeah?"

"I'll be at the gate in two minutes. Everybody there?"

"Yeah, pretty much."

"*Pretty* much? What the fuck you mean, pretty much? Are they there or not?" He's chopping along, in a hurry now, the sea black and oily-looking, running up the boat ramp at the edge of the lot in a pissing yellow foam, which means it's going to be rough beyond the breakwater. "The reporter, right? Don't tell me—"

"She called. Says she's running late."

"Shit. I told her. I warned her—" And he's just working himself up when he turns the corner by the restrooms and there she is—Toni Walsh, in an Easter-egg-pink slicker and matching sandals, her flayed quasi-red hair beating at her face like sea drift, standing there at the locked gate, looking puzzled. "Hey," he calls out, snatching a quick look round him to make sure no one's watching (nobody is: the place is all but deserted because there's weather coming down and everybody knows it). "Toni, hi." And then, working up a smile as he closes the distance between them, he finds a harmless enough phrase to toss at her: "All set?"

The look she gives him, as if she's never laid eyes on him before, as if they haven't planned all this out on the phone and met twice on the back deck at Longboards to trade information about the progress of the killing and the temporary restraining order Phil Schwartz filed for him (which apparently did nothing more than raise the judge's eyebrows), makes him wonder. The wind whips her hair and he sees she's attached a seasickness patch to the side of her neck, just under her earlobe, as if it's a piece of flesh-colored jewelry. Is she going to be all right with this? Her irises are the color of silt, the sclera cracked and veined, last night's mascara clumped in her lashes. She's clutching her cell phone in one hand, a pink designer bag the size of a suitcase in the other.

For a long moment, she just stares at him, a strand of salmon-colored hair caught in the corner of her mouth.

"You brought your camera, right?" he says, skipping the formalities. "Because you're going to want to take pictures, to document some of this . . ."

"You said we'd be back by seven, isn't that what you said?"

"Yeah, thereabouts. Seven, seven-thirty. I figure we get

there by maybe twelve-thirty or so, you come up the canyon with us and see what's what, snap a few photos—and then we do what we have to do and we're back on board by dark. Then it's two and a half hours across. Give or take."

"Good," she says, "good." No smile, no hello, no thanks for the hot tip, *no hiking boots for Christ's sake*. "Because I have a date"—and here's the smile, finally, a compression of the lips and an erratic flicker of the eyes to suggest there's a brain working in there after all—"like at eight? And I'm going to need to get home and clean up, you know?"

He's wondering what to say to this, coaxing and cajoling not really his strong suits, or being pleasant and making small talk when he's under the gun, but here's Wilson loping up the ramp on the other side of the gate, and in the next moment the gate's pushing open to receive them and they're inside, click, *Boat Owners Only Beyond This Point*. Wilson gives him a thumbs-up, as if pink-slickered reporters with nicotine-stained fingers and open-toed sandals are the usual comrades in arms, and then they're working their way down the ramp to the boat, where the rest of the crew's already hunkered down in the cabin, sipping coffee, lying low. Waiting.

"You know Wilson," he says, making the introductions in the cramped cabin while the boat bobs and weaves underfoot, "and this is Josh, Kelly, Cameron—Cammy, I mean—and Suzanne."

Toni Walsh stands there awkwardly, her shoulders slumped, nodding in turn at each of the crew—the volunteers, as he likes to call them, all of them in their late teens or early twenties, Josh an apprentice tattoo artist and whole-foods advocate, the girls members of the same environmental studies class at City College—before she unbuttons the slicker to reveal a black cashmere sweater, low-cut, with a black bra underneath. "Don't worry," she says, "I won't use any real names."

Josh—he's wearing a wife beater to show off his sleeves, some sort of dragon motif that looks like intertwined earthworms running up both arms—scoots up to the table on the overturned bucket he's been perched on and gives her a long annihilating look. He can't be more than five-six or-seven, pumped but in the stringy way of the body type that's too lean to put on real muscle, and you can see at a glance he thinks of himself as a hard case—which just makes him all the easier to manipulate. "Shit," he says, "I don't care if you blow my name up right across the head-line of the paper, biggest blackest type you got—it's Joshua Holyrood Miller, with two o's—because I'm ready to lay it all on the line to stop the slaughter. We all are. Right, Cammy?"

None of the girls is much to look at, not that he's interested—they're kids, basically, and he's got Anise and Anise is more than enough for him, too much really—but Cameron, Cammy, an emaciated brown-eyed blonde with her hair kinked out to her shoulders and the look of somebody who knows a whole lot more than she's reveal-ing, has her moments. "Right," she says, darting a glance round the cabin, "right. But don't use my name."

And that's it: the cabin falls silent. When they were coming down the ramp, he could hear voices raised in animation, laughter, the giddiness of those about to go into battle, but Toni Walsh has managed to kill it. No mat-ter. They can make their peace on the run out and whether or not they wind up finding common ground is nothing to him—he's no social director and this is no cruise ship. He watches dispassionately as Toni Walsh sets her bag on the table and warily eases herself down on the bench beside Cammy.

"So," he says, "all good, right? Everybody good to go?" And he's on his way up the steps to the cockpit when he catches himself. "Oh, yeah, before I forget"—and here he extracts the wire cutters from the plastic Home Depot bag and fans them out on the table, one to a person, except for Toni Walsh, that is, who's along as an observer only—"put these where you can get at them. And, what? Just kick back—it'll be a two-and-a-half-hour run out there. And if it's rough, you puke outside, right, and not in the cabin . . ."

Of course, given the look of the sky and the way the boats are shifting in their berths, chances are about a hundred percent it will be rough—just how rough becomes apparent as soon as they leave the shelter of the breakwater. The wind's coming down-channel from the west and it's kicking up whitecaps out there as far as he can see, the boat rocking pretty aggressively through the full range of its motion, left to right and back again, and then slapping through the creases with a weightless rise and a hard drop down. For Wilson, it's nothing, because he's off in dreamland before they're even out of the harbor, but the others are looking pretty green around the gills (and where did that expression come from, he's wondering, because people aren't fish and if they were they wouldn't be seasick but wriggling and flapping and happy as clams, and really, how happy can clams be when they just lie there in the mud all day waiting for something to come along and pry them open to get at what they are, which is basically just animated slime?). Anyway, he's got to fight it down himself, the feeling of something alien creeping up his throat while his stomach sinks and sinks lower still, but the good news is that by the time the island heaves into sight the rain has started in, and this is no drizzle but a good gray pelting rain sweeping across the water in rippling sheets that rise up like mythical beings, like gods and angels and devils, to erase everything. Sure. Fine. Anybody want to go pig-hunting today? I don't think so.

The cabin stirs to life when he cuts the engine and drops anchor. They've put in at Willows, on the far side of the island, a place he's picked because it's out of the way and because he knows it as well as any other. It was here that he liberated the raccoons in broad daylight three months back, anchoring the *Paladin* at just this spot and ferrying them across in the inflatable. They'd come to life when he lifted the cage down, thrashing from side to side under the tarp, and thank God it was calm that day or he might have had two drowned raccoons on his hands. They couldn't know what was happening to them, couldn't imagine being at sea or even what the sea was, couldn't know that he meant them no harm and that they were going to virgin territory, mother and son, and maybe they'd breed and start a new genetic line, inbred or not, or maybe, and he had this thought once he'd got the cage ashore and hidden in the willows that lent the canyon its name, maybe he'd trap more. A big male, another female, who knew? That would confound Dr. Alma, wouldn't it? A whole new race of animals out here on the island, and why not? Her precious foxes and skunks and lizards and the three types of snake had got here at random, washed down out of the canyons on the mainland in a storm like this and riding debris out to sea, and it was nothing more than an accident of fate that raccoons hadn't been part of the mix.

He'd pulled back the tarp to see them huddled there, their eyes fastened on him, expecting the worst, and then he flipped open the door of the cage and backed off—actually got behind a bush so as to hide himself—and watched as they put their noses to the air, stiffened, and made a break for it. Two patches of fur, gone so fast and so completely it was as if they'd never been there at all. That was random too. But he—Dave LaJoy, citizen, homeowner, activist, defeated in court and ignored on the picket line—was the deliberate agent of release, nothing random about it. He was a life-giver, that was what he was, the rescuer of these creatures Animal Control had all but told him to eliminate while they looked the other way.

"So, two trips?" Wilson wants to know.

Everybody's out on deck now, the dinghy in the water and jerking at its tether, the rain steady. They're all watching him because he's in charge, he's the captain here, he's got the map showing the fence lines (courtesy of Alicia) and he's the one who knows the way up the canyon. He takes a moment, looking past them to where the beach cuts a dark slash out of the foam, and they all turn their heads to follow his gaze. It's a wild scene: the indented beach cut off at either end by massive pillars of slick wet rock rising up to the ridges beyond, rain riveting the water, the sky fallen in, nothing moving, not even the gulls.

"Yeah, sure," he hears himself say for the benefit of the group, though in his mind he's already leapt ashore and started up the canyon. "Good idea. Don't want to overload the thing, not in this weather."

This is all for show, because he and Wilson worked out the details as they humped round the headland and into Willows Cove. Somebody's got to stay with the boat in weather like this, and that's going to be Wilson because he's the only reliable hand in this group of amateurs. Which means that Wilson will have to ferry them in, three in one group, three in the next, and then haul the dinghy back aboard just in case anybody comes nosing around.

"I'll just tell them I'm sightseeing," Wilson joked while the others were fumbling with their gear below. "Or no, I'm looking for a nice quiet place to commit suicide. What do you think? Think that'll grab them?"

He was too keyed up to play games. "Just keep it straight, all right? And watch for us—I mean, the minute we come back out on the beach you drop that dinghy and hammer it like it's a drill, like every second counts."

"What am I supposed to say, 'Aye-aye, sir'?"

"Don't fuck with me. Not here. Not now."

"You know I wouldn't fuck with you, Dave," Wilson said, doing exactly that. "But no worries, man, every-thing's cool. I want this to happen as much as you do—or did you forget that?"

"All right," he says now, one eye on the beach, where the surf isn't all that bad because the storm's pushing the waves lengthwise down the flank of the island, "Toni, it's going to be you and Cammy and me on the first run, then Josh, Kelly and Suzanne. And when the dinghy hits the beach you jump out and run for those willows over there, see where I'm pointing? Don't worry about getting your feet wet or anything else, just duck out of sight as quick as you can so Wilson can get the dinghy out of there and back on board. I don't have to tell you, if they see us on the water, we're screwed."

Then they're in the inflatable and beating across the waves, the shore coming to them as if pulled on a string, the engine growling, spray spitting in their faces. Wilson brings them in just fine, tipping back the engine and riding in on the surge, but Toni Walsh is a little shaky on the concept of springing lightly from boat to shore and she's already wet to the knees and in danger of getting creamed by the next wave when Dave catches her by the arm and jerks her up the crest of the beach. By contrast, Cammy hits the sand like a Marine and makes for the bushes without breaking stride, her hair wet and streaming beneath the black cap, the transparent rain gear molded to her thighs. She's gone before he can blink.

In the next moment—two minutes, a hundred twenty seconds—he and Toni Walsh are in the willows with her, not even breathing hard. Or at least he's not breathing hard—for her part, Toni seems to be hyperventilating. He listens to her suck air in a choppy smoker's wheeze, water running noisily over the stones, tree frogs shrilling, the rain hissing in the leaves. There's an intense odor of greenery, of muck and rot. Everything seems to be drooping. The sky, flexing overhead, is more black than gray, his socks are sodden and he can feel the cold pelt of the rain leaching through the cap to sponge his hair and slip down his collar, drip by drip.

He's watching the boat through a scrim of rain, Wilson maneuvering the dinghy in against the stern of the *Paladin* while Josh leans forward to take hold of the line. Without thinking, he hoists himself up atop a cluster of water-run boulders for a better view while Toni Walsh, wet through, heaving for breath and fumbling in her big wet pink purse for a cigarette, levels a look of irritation on him. The boulders are slick and ovoid, like the eggs of dinosaurs, and Cammy, long-legged and gaunt and looking satisfied with herself, suddenly appears on the one beside him, but not Toni Walsh. Toni Walsh is standing down there below them, in water up to her calves— flowing water, brown and braided and quick—and he comes to himself long enough to reach down a hand and haul her up like so much baggage, which is what she is. Which is why Anise refused to come, though he blustered and threatened and pulled every guilt trip he could think of on her.

This is when he begins to realize there may be a problem here, a situation he hasn't taken into account—namely, that Willows Creek, normally a gurgling little rill you can jump across, isn't so much a creek as a river right now. Roiled and hissing, bristling with debris and loud with the sucking clamor of dislodged rock, it fans out across the mouth of the canyon in a muddy sheet, carving its way through the sand to send snaking brown tentacles out into the sea. The plan is to take the easy foot trail along the sandbars that wind through the reeds and willows, following it up along the streambed to higher ground where they'll eventually intercept the fence line and cut as much wire as they can while Toni Walsh, with his help, collects photographic evidence of the slaughter, carcasses piled up like dead leaves, like charnel—just follow the ravens and that's where they'll be. That's the plan. But the foot trail is gone and so are the sandbars. And the reeds and willows are neck-deep in a rush of swirling dark water.

No matter. Even as Wilson swings the dinghy in against the beach and the others struggle out into the surf, he's improvising—too late to turn back now, because from the look of Toni Walsh they'll never get her out here again, and if they don't do something soon, the pigs will have gone the way of Anacapa's rats. He swings round to study the canyon walls, thinking they'll have to make their way up at an angle, above the level of the creek, hard going but manageable, not a problem, not a problem at all, because he's up for it, and the kids would jump off the edge of a cliff if he told them to, and Toni Walsh—Toni Walsh is just going to have to tough it out. If she wants her story. And she does, she must, or she wouldn't be here. When he turns round again, the boat is right there and two of the slickered figures—the girls—are leaping out and sprinting across the beach, but Josh, flailing for balance, goes down in the surf, not once, but twice, before he rights himself and starts off after them.

"Here they come," Cammy says, barely able to suppress the excitement in her voice. "And Josh"—she lets out a strangled little gasp of laughter—"look at Josh! Jesus." She's grinning, giddy as a child, and what do they think this is, a reality show? Summer camp? She springs to the rock in front of him, agile as a flea, her eyes lit with the pure joy of the moment. "Guess he decided to take a swim, huh? Hey, Josh," she calls out, "how's the water?"

He's not about to offer explanations or admit he's miscalculated the volume of water washing down out of the canyon this time of year because explanations are for losers and all that matters is getting this done. So when Kelly and Suzanne—short and soft, both of them, pear-shaped and nearly indistinguishable in their matching olive-green slickers—splash up to him, grinning, he just reaches down a hand and hoists first one, then the other, up onto the rock with the rest of the group. And here comes Josh, already shivering, and the only solution to that short of building a fire and drying him out, which is no solution at all, is movement, strenuous movement, as in getting him up out of the canyon to a place where he can manipulate the wire cutters till he works up a sweat.

"All right," he says, lowering his voice conspiratorially though there's no one within miles to overhear him, "the storm's dumping water in the canyon so it's going to be a little bit more of a climb than what it should have been, but everything's going to be fine . . . it just might take us a little longer to get up there, that's all." He snatches a glance down at his wet boots, at the boulders they're perched on, the water sluicing round them—if anything, it seems to have risen in the five minutes they've been here, but that's not possible, is it?

Josh is standing in it, thigh deep, the oversized slicker fanning out behind him in the current. He's trying to look casual, as if pitching headfirst into fifty-two-degree water is the kind of thing he does every day, trying to tough it out though his face gives him away and he's biting his lip to keep from spasming with the cold.

Feeling faintly ridiculous, like the ruck-faced general in an old World War II flick, Dave hears himself say, "All right then, follow me," and then he's down in the water and making for the embankment to the left. It's like trout fishing, that's what he's thinking, like fighting the current in a pair of waders only without the encumbrance of a fly rod and creel, and the water actually gets deeper before they reach the first obstacle—the embankment, which on closer inspection proves to be a thirty-foot-high wall of rock left intact as the stream chewed away the softer strata below it. He makes an attempt to round the corner, pulling himself along with both hands, but the current goes chest deep and he gives it up after a minute and begins to climb.

The cliff—hump, mound—is composed of some sort of volcanic rock, basalt, he supposes, gouged and fissured all the way to the top. The problem is, the stuff is loosely put together and it keeps fragmenting in his hands, bits and pieces sifting down behind him as he flattens his pelvis to the rock and moves from one handhold to the next. "Sorry," he says, peering down at the pale wet melons of their faces, "we're just going to have to get up and over this and then I'm sure it'll be easier . . ."

It's nothing for Cammy—she launches herself at the rock face in a goatish scramble, but the other two girls are a little slower on the uptake. And Toni Walsh, fumbling with the purse, manages to pull herself up as far as the first solid foothold, but then loses impetus. "Josh," he shouts down, "can you give her a boost there?" He knows he should drop back and help her himself, but he's nearly at the top now and he's anxious to see what's on the other side, to see what they're up against.

Though Josh is no woodsman, though he's clumsy and shivering in the wet sack of his clothes and a good three inches shorter than Toni Walsh, he surprises him. He's already given a hand up to the other two girls (Kelly and Suzanne, and it's hard to tell them apart except that Suzanne—or is it Kelly?—sports a blood-red PETA patch on her right sleeve), and he lowers himself, digs his boots in and stretches his full length to hold out a hand for Toni Walsh—and Toni, game at least for now, takes hold of it and pulls herself up to the next handhold and the next one after that, and before long they're all on top and looking down into the brown roil of the canyon.

From this vantage, he can see that the flats are a vast muddy lake fed by a spigot in the distance, a series of spigots that climb up and into the low belly of the clouds—waterfalls, each mounting on the shoulders of the next. When he was here to release the raccoons, there were no waterfalls. The sun illuminated thin threads of water as far as he could see back into the hills, dragonflies danced and hovered, the stream rolled lazily into its shallow pools and trickled through the yellow grasping roots of the willows that were like fingers, like claws. He's angry suddenly. Angry at himself. How could he have been so stupid as to fail to appreciate what canyons were, how they'd come to exist, what rain meant in a state of nature? But then, if they'd waited for a day struck with sunshine when everybody afloat was out cluttering the channel, they might as well have radioed ahead to tell the Park Service goons to come and arrest them. They had to slip out in the rain, no choice. And no choice now but to start down the other side and get this done.

"So, look," he says, "the plan is we're going to have to

work our way around on the slope there, just above where the water is, because the water's up now and it's washed out the trail we were going to take . . ."

They all look out across the valley to where the water races through the distant gap in discolored streaks and chutes. Nobody says anything. The rain is steady, a straight fall, beating at their caps and shoulders, setting the ground at their feet in motion.

"It's going to be steep, it's going to be hell on your ankles, maybe, but it's doable." He turns to Toni Walsh. "You okay with this? Because whenever it gets too much, you just tell me, okay?"

Hunched, pale, a streak of yellowish mud painted across her cheek like a tribal cicatrice, she just shrugs. "I don't know," she says after a moment, and here's that stab at a smile again—a good sign, a very good sign—"I'm afraid I'm more of a city girl. But anything for a story, right?"

And now Kelly speaks up—Kelly, definitely Kelly, with her PETA patch and her moon face and pinched disapproving lips. It comes to him that she looks nothing like Suzanne, at least not facially. "What about mudslides," she says. "I mean, the possibility of a mudslide? You see that depression there, that bowl?" She points to the long scooped-out incline they'll have to traverse to get up-canyon. "That was a massive slide at one time, you can see it."

"Yeah, well, we're just going to have to take that chance, because I've been out in weather like this a thousand times—I mean, haven't you? Haven't we all? And it might put the pig killers off for a day or two, but you know they're sitting back oiling their rifles. Just waiting."

The rain chooses that moment to intensify, a sudden ratcheting up of the ante. His hair hangs limp beneath the sodden cap, drip, drip, drip. He wants to be reasonable, wants to control these people by controlling himself, but that isn't an option, not anymore. "Fuck it. I'm not going to stand around debating. You want to stay here, stay, be

324

my guest. But I'm out of here, right now, right this minute." And he's moving suddenly, dropping down the slope on the other side, riding a sludge of loose stone and mud in exaggerated steps, so worked up he never even bothers to see if they're following him—but they are, he knows they are. They have to be.

Half an hour later, the rain still coming down and the churning dark water in the ravine rising by the minute, he begins to have second thoughts. He's feeling the strain in the long muscles of his thighs, the sleeves of his sweatshirt are mud to the elbow because there's no way to do this without using your hands, and his ankles throb from the effort of maintaining balance on a forty-five-degree slope. And he's in shape. Which is more than he can say for Toni Walsh or the two pear-shaped girls or even Josh. They're all strung out behind him in single file, fifty feet above the waterline, grasping at whatever fixed object they can—whether it has thorns or not—to keep themselves upright, and nobody's saying anything. Cammy's right behind him, pushing him even, followed by the two girls, then Toni Walsh (gray-faced, wet to the bone, looking like one of the risen dead), and Josh bringing up the rear so he can keep an eye on her. They must have gone half a mile— they're almost to the first of the waterfalls, where at least they'll be able to get out of the mud—and they haven't seen any sign of pigs, hunters, foxes, ravens or anything else. They might as well be on the backside of the moon. Except it doesn't rain on the moon. And there's no mud.

The surprise has been Toni Walsh. He's been expecting her to give out ever since they began to work their way down the first hill, but every time he glances back, there she is, head down, plodding along. Still, he's thinking, how much more of this can she take? They need to get up out of the canyon—and soon. Or find a place where she can lie up while he and Josh or Cammy scout ahead, looking for anything that'll make it worth her while to go on. He's scanning the terrain where the canyon begins to narrow three or four hundred yards ahead of them—rock and more rock, everything trenched and gouged and spilling with water—when he spots an overhang projecting from the side of the hill like an outsized awning. Encouraged—*Finally*, he's thinking—he swings round on Cammy and points emphatically before calling out to the others. "Up there," he shouts, watching their eyes lift from the vacancy of their faces. "We'll take a break."

The cover isn't much—a ledge maybe nine or ten feet across squeezed under a dripping lid of rock open on three sides to the weather—but at least it keeps the rain off. It's a bit of a squeeze, everybody wedged in shoulder to shoulder, boot to boot, and the first thing they do, to a man and woman, is dig into their packs for food. There isn't much to say beyond "Scoot over just a little, could you?" or "Did you want the peanut butter or the cream cheese and sprouts?" and for a long moment there's no sound but the hiss of the rain, the crinkle of cellophane and the soft snap of mastication. Then Josh produces a bota bag (vinyl and plastic, no sheep's stomach on *his* conscience) and asks if anybody wants a hit.

"What's in it?" Toni Walsh looks up with interest. She's crouched in a pink heap amidst a tangle of legs and muddy boots, her face fish-belly white, her hair like the stuff they line packing crates with, and she's making no concession to present company, working her way through what looks to be a deli sandwich thick with prosciutto and cheese. "Brandy, I hope?"

"Red wine. A nice sturdy zin. It's good, go ahead."

And then they're opening wide, one by one, for a taste of it. By the time Suzanne passes out the homemade oatmeal cookies, everyone seems to be feeling marginally better. When the wine comes round he takes a hit too—why not? He can use the boost.

"So what do you think?" Cammy says, turning to him.

"Realistically, I mean? Do we have a chance of getting up there and back before dark?" She's slumped against the overhang in a sprawl of limbs, looking about twelve years old. "Because I know you didn't count on this," she adds quickly. "These conditions, I mean."

He shrugs to show it's no big deal and passes the bota bag to Kelly, who's practically sitting in his lap. If there was any adventure in her face, it's long gone, but she lifts the bag dutifully, tips back her head and squeezes a thread of wine into her mouth. She smells of sweat and the orange she's been peeling and her hair frizzes out under the bill of her cap. Absently, he watches her lick the stain from her lips, a dumpy girl, graceless, dull, in desperate need of a makeover if she ever hopes to attract a man and have a life for herself or any life at all beyond a nunnery, before turning back to Cammy. "Yeah, I was thinking maybe I'd go on ahead with maybe two other people while the rest of you make your way back—Toni, I'll take your camera if you want. Maybe I'll get lucky." They're all watching him but he can't tell from their expressions whether they're relieved or not. "But Cammy's right—we just picked a bad day, that's all, and there's no way we're going to be able to do all that much. Or not the kind of scope we'd planned on anyway."

"It sucks," Josh says, his voice gone hollow. He's looking at nothing, cradling his knees to his chest, the depleted bota bag dangling limply from the fingers of one hand. His boots are mud to the laces. He's shivering. They're all shivering. Below them, louder now, loud as static, there's the steady mocking roar of the water crashing through the canyon. No one else seems to have anything to say. They want to go back, want to give up, all of them—he can see it in their faces.

It's a debilitating moment, hopeless, depressing. But there's no way he's giving up—he's going to climb up out of this canyon and snap off one shameful inflammatory picture after another so the *Press Citizen* can run them on the front page and everybody can see for themselves what the killers are up to, and then he's going to cut wire if it takes him all night, if he has to swim back to the boat, if he . . .

And then the wind shifts and everything changes.

"Does anybody smell anything?" It's Kelly, stirring herself. She sits up, arches her back, narrows her eyes. She sniffs audibly, deliberately, making a face. "It's like"—and here it is, they can all smell it now, rank, musty and corporeally sweet all at once—"something *died*."

In the next moment they're back out in the rain, everybody, even Toni Walsh, working their way higher, to the next ledge, the one above the overhang. There's a turning there, a scoop of rock carved out of the high wall of the canyon—sage, coyote brush, coreopsis, and something else, a dark shape wedged like a doormat between two over-spilling rocks in a pale slurry of mud. The footing's bad, horrendous. The odor intensifies, deepens till it's an assault. "Is that—?" somebody says.

They are looking at the remains—the carcasses—of two pigs, one an adult the size of a big overfed dog, the other a juvenile. The eyes of both are gone, reddened pits gouged out of their faces, their jaws gaping, intestines exposed and shading from blue to gray. The hide is a black bristle animated by the maggots feeding there in a frenzy of moving parts.

"Gross," Kelly says.

Josh lets out a curse. "Jesus," he snarls, "what did they ever do to deserve *this*?"

Shivering, hunched, the big pink pocketbook like a withered limb and her face intent on the viewfinder, Toni Walsh moves in to hover over the scene, freezing one frame after another. She doesn't say anything, not a word, because she's at work now, doing her job, recording the scene, making history. The others look awed. Or scared. This is the configuration of death, the thing they've been fighting—the very thing—and here it is, right in their faces, stinking at their feet.

He's trying to sort out his own feelings—horror, pity, sorrow, anger—but there's something else too, a rush of excitement, of happiness even. "Good," he's saying, "excellent—this is just what we want," and he has a stick in his hand now, poking at the carcass of the larger animal, looking for the entry wound, for the bullet, for evidence no one can controvert because these pigs didn't just lose their balance and topple over the rim of the canyon to wash up here. No, they were murdered, *exterminated*— that's the word. "Here, Toni—here, I think this is where they shot him, see? Can you get a close-up on this?"

It's a small space they're inhabiting, no bigger than a hot tub, the stone slick, the creek boiling below, rain in their faces and drooling from the bills of their hats, everyone crowding in for a look and he and Toni at the center of it, ratified, vindicated, the *sons of bitches*, and when Kelly takes a step back to give them space—a single step—he has trouble registering what's unfolding before him. She doesn't cry out. Doesn't clutch at his shoulder or the withered excuse of the pale insubstantial shadow of a bush beside her. She just murmurs *Oh, shit*, as if she's engaged in a private conversation on a subject no one could begin to guess at, and then she's gone.

She goes down headfirst, on her back, both arms spread wide and her hands snatching at nothing, and half the hillside goes with her in a rattling concussion of rock and dirt, a chute opening up before her all the way down to the water a hundred feet below. There's a thunderous splash, her khaki slicker flapping and billowing in the current even as the dark pinpoint of her bare head, the hat gone and her hair spreading like drift, bobs once, twice, three times before she's sucked down the channel and out of sight.

There's no time to absorb the shock of it, no time for curses, exclamations or the strangled shriek that climbs up out of Suzanne's throat to ring impotently through the canyon, because he's already in motion, launching himself back down the rock face, darting beneath the overhang and dropping into the mudfield below, his eyes straining at the place where she went down, expecting at any moment—or no, demanding—to see her there clinging to a rock or log. He can hear the others calling out and fumbling behind him and he can only pray that another one of them doesn't lose their grip and go down with her. There are no handholds. He's made of mud. He can taste something foul in the back of his mouth.

When finally he does get to the water, riding a cascade of rock and mud—and what's it been, five minutes, ten?— it's all he can do to keep from being swept away himself. As it is, he plunges in up to his waist before he can catch hold of the embankment with one hand and the crown of a slick streaming willow with the other and still he can feel the current tugging at him as if it's alive. There are shouts from above. Tumblings of pebbles, sticks, brush. He looks up, outraged, to see that two of them—Cammy and Josh—are working their way down to him. Don't they understand? Don't they realize the danger? "Go back!" he roars, never so furious in his life.

It is then, even as he jerks his legs from the water and lurches upright in the clinging unstable mud that keeps giving way underfoot as if he's on a treadmill, as if he's running in place in a waking nightmare, that the magnitude of what's going down begins to hit him. If she's hurt—Kelly, and all he can think of is the way she went over the side as if she'd been snatched by the collar, help-less, utterly helpless—there's going to be a lot of explain-ing to do. To the Coast Guard. The cops. The newspapers and the membership of FPA and everybody out there who's going to do the hard calculus that measures the fate of the animals against human suffering, human life, and what are they going to do, interview her in her hospital bed? Autograph her cast?

It's a mess. A fucking disaster. And he's moving now, humping low along the waterline, clinging to whatever he can catch hold of, frantic to find her, save her, get her out of this and back to the boat, wrap her in blankets, feed her hot soup, anything, brandy, crank the heater, and the one thing he won't allow, won't even think of, is the darker apprehension that Kelly, with her eager face and pear shape and the patch she wears on her sleeve—*Animals are not ours to eat, wear or experiment on*—is beyond any help he or anyone else can give her.

The rain has slackened to a drizzle, the light fading from the sky, the harsh clawing rush of the river the only thing he's ever known—bone-cold, aching, sick in his soul— by the time they find her. She glows against the dark tumbled backdrop of torn brush and brutalized trees, pale as a mushroom, because what the water has done, the force of it, is strip the clothes from her so that there's no trace left of her sweatshirt, her shorts or the khaki rain slicker either. He's the one fighting the current to reach her while the others form a human chain and pay out the rope somebody found in the bottom of a daypack, and he's the one to touch her, her cold naked flesh, and see the way the rocks have treated her and how her face rides low in the water while a willow branch, caught in the crevice of her underarm, waves back and forth in an imposture of animation.

She's been carried all the way down to where they started, where the resuscitated river undercuts the rock on one side and sweeps wide to fling its refuse on the other—if only they'd known they could have gotten to her sooner. But they didn't know and they had to work their way down-canyon foot by foot, scanning the banks and calling her name till the voices died in their throats. Is there irony in that? He doesn't know. All he knows is the moment and the moment is as bleak and sorrowful as anything he's ever had to live through on this earth. When he takes hold of her, thinking of how Cammy kept saying she knew CPR—she'd been in junior lifeguards when she was in high school and trained on dummies, that's what she kept repeating, her eyes tearing, her breath coming fast— he has to brace himself against the bottom, the heavy freight of the water at his back, pushing him, jerking his legs out from under him, though it can't be more than five feet deep here, and that's another irony. He wraps an arm round her shoulder but can't really get much purchase— she's stuck fast, tangled in the branches, that's what it is— and his impulse is to be gentle with her, but gentle does nothing, and so he tugs, actually tugs at her as if this is a game, a contest of wills, as if she's tugging back. From the bank, Suzanne's voice, thick with phlegm: "Is she okay?"

He is racked with the cold, hypothermic, losing it, but he will not give up, jerking and twisting at the soft obstinacy of her till all at once she breaks free, a disjointed branch of the willow coming with her in a cortege of gently nodding leaves, but he can't hold her, her face revolving to fix a censorious stare on him as the current tears her away. There's a cry from shore, frantic activity, but he's lost his hold on the rope too and what's left of the tree gives way under his frantic clutch. He's adrift. Churning his feet, windmilling his arms, fighting it, but the river has him and the river is going to do what it will. Something clutches at his groin beneath the surface and then there's a hard fist of wood coming up on him to pound the side of his head and then there's another and another and now the river has him by the neck and his face is being pushed down in the murk and for one annihilating moment he can't see, can't breathe, can't find his way up.

Then suddenly the pushing stops and he feels himself flung atop a vast bristling sieve of debris, the current sucking away beneath him. He snaps open his eyes, thrashes his head back and forth to clear it. Kelly is right there beside him, so close he could reach out and touch her. She's on her back, her limbs splayed, her face turned to the sky. Her breasts sag away from her rib cage, her pubic hair smudges her crotch. And her skin, her skin is flayed and raw, the meat showing through in a long scything gash that runs from knee to hip. One foot, the one nearest him, has managed to retain its hiking boot. There's something—a scrap of material, blue, polka dots—cinched round one thigh. Her fingers are clenched. What he wants is to push himself up, up and away from her, to get out of this, to run, but he can't—it's as if his muscles are locked, as if he's had a stroke, as if the sky has fallen in on him and he can't get out from under its weight. And so he lies there for the longest moment of his life, studying the tight twist of her laces, the sock shredded at the ankle, the waffled grid of the sole of her boot that's been washed so clean it might have been new from the box.

He does get up finally, of course he does, and when he gets up Josh and Cammy are there, picking their way through the black tangle of branches while the other two, Suzanne and Toni, look on helplessly from the far embankment. There's the sound of the water, the smell of it. Josh's face is expressionless, his skin the color of lard. Cammy, the slicker gone, her clothes clinging to her like shrink-wrap, her feet bare as a penitent's, is crying, crying still, and she left her shoes behind so she could swim, so she and Josh could swim across no matter the risk and be here to help, to pitch in with her CPR and her red-rimmed eyes.

"She's dead," Josh says, his voice as cold as he can make it because he's on the cusp of breaking down himself, "isn't she?"

"What the fuck you think? Look at her, for Christ's sake."

And here's Cammy, bending to roll her over and pump at her shoulderblades, as if that's going to do any good, and maybe his voice is harsher than it has to be, maybe he should just let her play out the charade and focus on what comes next, but he can't. "Get off her!" he's shouting, yanking at her arm till it feels as if it's going to twist off in his hand, and when she rises under the pressure of it he flings her away from him, his heart slamming at his ribs and every curse he can think of spilling uselessly out of him.

Cammy. The stick girl. The pretty-face. The child. She's as rangy and lean as one of his greyhounds, but she comes at him so fast he can't even get his hands up to protect his face. Her fist is a projection of her will, stabbing at him three times in quick succession till he catches her wrists and she clenches her face to spit at him. "You," she sobs. "It's all you—you killed her. You!"

Josh's voice seems to be caught in his throat. "Hey," he says. Just that—"Hey," soft as a leaf falling.

What are they fighting over? What's the use of it? What's the use of anything?

Cammy subsides. He releases her wrists. The night drops down. The corpse at his feet seems to swell and grow till it sucks in all the available light. The faces of the two people in front of him blur so that Josh could be Cammy, and Cammy, Josh. A squadron of bats materializes from nowhere to ricochet through the emptiness overhead.

"What we have to do," he says finally, because he's rational now, they're all rational, they have to be, "is get her out of here. I mean, wrap her in something"—and though he's wet through and numb in his fingers and toes he's already pulling the slicker up over his head—"and carry her back to the boat. And then we'll see what we can do about, you know . . . whatever it takes . . ." he trails off.

But it's not as easy as all that. While Toni and Suzanne work their way over the hump on the far side on their own—and it's a minor miracle no broken bones come out of that—he and Josh wrap the body in their rain gear and try to secure the ends as best they can with the strap cut from his daypack and an extra pair of shoelaces. The footing is unsteady, the load awkward in the extreme, Josh on one end, him on the other, Cammy in the middle. What's inside—the shuttered flesh, the pooling blood—keeps slipping, loosening, readjusting itself, and to get it—her—up atop the pillar of rock takes all the strength he has in him. There's a suspended moment, each breath a kind of choking for release, and then he's easing her down the far side to where Josh stands barely visible beneath him. "Careful, now, careful—you got her?"

Voices in the dark. The rush of the water, the pounding of the waves. Now he and Cammy are down there too and the three of them form a six-legged monster lurching through the sand, every step impossible, but they manage to haul her to the crest of the beach, just above tide line, and set her down as gently as if she were alive still and sleeping her hurts away. Toni Walsh and Suzanne emerge beside them suddenly, faces floating peripherally in the darkness. *Oh, my God*, Suzanne is saying, over and over. He leaves them there, their voices grating like the rasp of dried-up leaves. The night is absolute. He can't see the boat. He wades into the surf and risks calling out. "Wilson! Wilson, you out there?"

Nothing. There should be a light, at least. He strains to see, looking for the faintest pale faded green hint of the running lights, thinking he needs a flashlight to signal and will anybody have thought to bring a flashlight, any of them? Suzanne, maybe. She thought to bake cookies. She was the one who had the coil of rope neatly braided at the bottom of her pack, the spare laces, gum. He's about to turn back, the waves slapping at him and the shiver running through his body like an electric current, when he thinks he spots something there in the near distance, a deeper, blacker hole cut out of the night. What he doesn't yet realize is that he's fooling himself, because there's nothing there to see, nothing at all.

El Tigre

The morning after the concert—Sunday, thankfully Sunday—she can't quite understand what's happening to her. To push back the covers, to swing her legs to the floor in the stillness of dawn, to feel the carpet alive under the grip of her toes and catch the rich roasted scent of the coffee her mother's already brewing in the kitchen downstairs and then feel that vacancy in her core, that probing deep down that drives her to the bathroom, to her knees, to vomit for the second—or no, the third—day in a row, is wrong, deeply wrong. It can't be a hangover because she had only the two glasses of wine and that wouldn't account for the previous day or the day before that when she'd had no more than two or three *sakes* with her mother and Ed, just to be convivial. Is she becoming hyper-sensitive to alcohol, is that it? Or is it the flu? And then a lyric from one of Micah Stroud's covers pops into her head—*I got the rockin' pneumonia and the boogie-woogie flu*—and the next thing she knows she's pulling on her shorts and a T-shirt and heading down the stairs as if nothing's happened at all.

"You look tired," is the first thing her mother says to her as she shuffles into the kitchen. Apparently Ed isn't up yet, but there's a place set for him at the table—coffee cup and saucer, orange juice, half a grapefruit glistening pinkly under the glare of the kitchen lights, which are up full, and the newspaper laid out beside it in offering. "Did you have trouble sleeping? Because personally I don't think I slept more than five minutes—it's the noise of that freeway. I don't know how you put up with it."

Alma's at the refrigerator, staring without enthusiasm at the milk and juice in their bright cartons, a block of cheese rippling with plastic wrap, something on a plate going brown around the edges, too exhausted suddenly to respond.

"If you want to know the truth, you look like you haven't been getting enough sleep—it's the job, isn't it? It's wearing you down. You always were a worrier, even as a little girl, in way over your head, as if you could personally heal every sick animal on the block and, I don't know, save every mouse and lizard the cat dragged in."

Her mother—a pair of brown-shelled eggs have appeared in her hands and she's separating them over a mixing bowl—doesn't really expect an answer. She's just talking to hear herself, awake and moving around her daughter's kitchen at a lonely hour on a gray-shrouded morning.

"Is this for Ed?" Alma asks, settling into a chair at the table. "The juice, I mean?"

"I can make you eggs—you want eggs? You do eat eggs, don't you?"

"No," she says, irritated suddenly, "I don't want any eggs."

"You don't have to snap at me."

"I'm not snapping at you—"

"Yes you are."

"No," she insists, and she reaches across the table for Ed's juice, sliding the glass to her with a soft whisper of friction. "It's just that I'm not hungry, that's all."

The eggshells are on the counter. The clock on the stove reads 6:17. Her mother sets down the whisk deliberately and turns to study her. Three steps in her clogs and she's hovering over her, laying a hand on her forehead and peering into her eyes. "You feeling all right?"

It is then, just as she's about to confide that in fact she's not feeling all right because she's just been sick in the toilet upstairs and her head feels as if it's about to lift off her shoulders and float across the room, that the truth of the situation comes home to her, the obvious conclusion any biologist who's studied the life processes for the past decade and a half would have drawn in an instant.

"Mom?" She speaks her mother's name aloud, but her voice seems elastic, stretched-out, pulled like taffy. The truth—the fact—is surging up in her in an uncontainable rush but the words to express it seem to be stuck fast in her throat.

Her mother just stares at her. "Yes?" she says. "What?"

"How did you know, I mean, when you first got pregnant?"

In her hurry to get to Longs drugstore the minute they open—eight a.m. on Sundays—she hardly gives a thought to anything but the astonishment of the moment, of what's happening to her, or could be happening to her. It's a walk of three blocks, past the place where she hit the squirrel—nothing there but a stain on the pavement now—then across the freeway bridge and into the long winding strip of the lower village. She takes extra care at the crosswalk, holding herself as if she's already cradling a newborn in her arms, thinking only that she's got to know for sure, though her mother accepted it as a fait accompli. Her mother just hugged her, bending awkwardly to press a cheek to hers in a ferment of heat and emotion. Then she straightened up and let out a laugh. "I had my suspicions," she said, her hands on her hips and her head cocked to one side, beaming, absolutely beaming, "but I didn't want to say anything. And for the life of me I don't know why they call it morning sickness—I must have puked morning and night for six months straight till I thought it would have been easier to scale Mount Everest in a bikini than carry you around a single day more, but your father was sweet about it. He was good that way. Totally supportive. And did he love you from the minute you came out. Doted on you." There'd been more, a whole rhapsody about giving birth at home with the help of a midwife because a sterile overlit hospital room was

338

no place to enter the world—they'd had a birth party that night, did she know that? And they'd filmed it too—"You could see your little head emerging, a soft red little thing so tiny I thought I was giving birth to a mango"—but unfortunately, somewhere along the way the tape had got lost.

It's not till she has her hand on the home pregnancy kit, studying the directions in the too-bright aisle while women whisper by in running shoes and tennis clothes, averting their eyes, that she finally thinks of the prospective father, of Tim. Tim, who's islanded at the moment, beyond the reach of cell phone service, stalking goldens. She can see his face floating there before her as she scans the package (*Accurate Digital Results 5 Days Sooner; 99% Accurate*), see the way he draws down his mouth when he's surprised or puzzled, and he will be surprised, no question about it, because they've never discussed the possibility of having a child, or not seriously anyway. They use birth control, rigorously, and while they gave up condoms for Tim's sake, she never fails—never, no matter how swept away they are—to insert her diaphragm. They're both committed environmentalists. Dedicated to saving the ecosystem, preserving what's left, restoring it. To bring a child into an overpopulated world is irresponsible, wrong, nothing less than sabotage . . .

But then why does she feel so elated? Why does she feel enormous suddenly, dominant, vastly superior to all these other women who aren't weighing pregnancy kits in their hands? Because she's a living thing, that's why, and living things reproduce. The only discernible purpose of life is to create more life—any biologist knows that. She's thirty-seven years old. The clock is ticking. She's a unique individual with a unique genetic blueprint, representative of a superior line, in fact—in cold fact, without prejudice—and so's Tim, with his high I.Q. and mellow personality and his long beautifully articulated limbs, and they have an obligation to pass their genes on if there's any hope of improving the species.

339

The woman at the cash register—post-menopausal, her hair brittle, lines tugging at the corners of her mouth—looks like a mother, albeit one whose pregnancies are long behind her, and she gives Alma a shy collusive smile as she scans and bags her purchase. And Alma, enormous still, towering, locks eyes with her and smiles in return. "You have a nice day," the woman says and the tired phrase carries a whole new freight of meaning. Alma can't seem to keep herself from grinning as she takes up the plastic bag and stuffs her receipt inside. "Oh, I will," she says, "I'm sure I will."

At home, with her mother hovering outside the bathroom door, she tries to concentrate on working up a pee, but for some reason it won't come. She sits there on the toilet a long while, thinking of Tim and how she's going to deliver the news to him, because she's bursting with it, all but certain the test strip she's clutching in her hand will show two bright pink bands of color, proof positive. She could get him on the radio at the field station, of course, but what's she going to say, *How's the weather and by the way I'm pregnant*? He'll be home in four days. She can meet him at the boat, take him by the hand, lead him up the stairs to the Docksider and settle him in a booth with a pint of Firestone and a plate of fried calamari, look him deep in the eye and give him a mysterious smile. *What?* he'll say, grinning in anticipation of the joke. And she'll toy with him a moment, reach under the table to stroke his thigh, lean in for a kiss. Take her time. Enjoy it . . . But then she's getting ahead of herself, isn't she? Because she hasn't peed in the cup yet and hasn't used the dipstick and doesn't know anything at all, not for sure.

"Alma?" She can feel her mother shifting her weight from one foot to the other, the floorboards communicating the movement to her through the tiles of the bathroom floor and up into the soles of her bare feet. And she feels ridiculous suddenly, like a child, a toddler, her mother out there listening for the tinkle of her urine the way she must have all those years ago at the Takesue household or in the cramped little head of the *Black Gold*. Potty training. That's the term for it.

She's drawing in her breath to answer, to say "Not yet" or "Give me a minute," when it comes, hot and sudden. She barely has time to maneuver the cup to catch a portion of it—for a moment there, drifting, she's forgotten entirely the purpose of the exercise—but here it is, her urine, an inch or more of it, captured in the plastic throwaway container the manufacturer has thoughtfully provided. Immediately, even before getting up to wash her hands, she thrusts the dipstick into it and sets it on the tiles between her slim splayed feet. "Alma?" her mother calls, rattling the doorknob now. "Don't keep me in suspense out here."

The seconds tick by. Nothing happens. Heart pounding, feeling feverish and weak, she leans forward to pick up the container and give it a shake—maybe it needs to be stirred, that's what she's thinking, maybe there's not enough contact between strip and solution or she's been doing something wrong—when suddenly the second line appears below the first, as pink as cotton candy.

Her mother insists on celebrating, just the two of them ("And Ed doesn't have to know a thing about it till it's really sunk in because he can just sit in front of the TV and entertain himself with his ball games"), taking her out for the Sunday brunch at the hotel down the street because she's going to have to eat for two now and yes, she can have one mimosa, only one, and that's the last alcohol she'll see for the next nine months. "You won't miss it, honey, believe me, and I just pray you don't inherit my— what would you call it?—*propensity* for morning sickness. Or morning, afternoon and evening sickness," she adds with a laugh. "But everybody's different, every *pregnancy's* different, and I'm sure you're going to be fine."

Sitting there on the patio of the hotel and looking out across the barbered lawn and the strip of blacktop road to where the sea beats immemorially at the beach, the salt scent strong in her nostrils and the symbolic baggage of all that seething oceanic life as apparent as if she were rocking below the waves with her mask clear and her snorkel jutting high, she begins to doubt herself all over again. Does she really want to go through with this? Is there really room for another hungry mouth on this sore and wounded planet? And Tim. What of Tim?

"What are you thinking?" her mother asks, both her elbows propped on the table, one hand languidly revolving the pale orange liquid round the rim of her glass. Her plate is littered with the translucent husks of shrimp and the glistening black shells of mussels, fruit rinds and olive pits, a picked-over salad bathed in oleaginous dressing. "Because it's your decision. And Tim's, of course. But you can make me a very happy woman, honey, because I am ready, let me tell you, loud and clear, to be a grandma. Janis might not have made it or what's her name from the Mamas and the Papas, but I did. And I'm ready to shout it to the world." Grinning, swaying in her seat, she happens to catch the eye of the two women seated at the table across from them. She winks. Mouths: "I'm going to be a grandma!"

On any other occasion, this sort of thing might have been mortifying, especially given the fact that the two women stare right through them and then turn back to their conversation, but today, on this late and glorious morning bathed in autumnal sunshine and scintillant with the rinsed-clean smell of the ocean, Alma lets it wash over her. She's undergoing a process of adjustment, she understands that, hormones percolating up inside her, overwhelming her resistance even as her brain tries to take command, reason, weigh her options, until finally she feels herself giving way. She shrugs. Treats her mother to a smile. Raises her glass. "Yeah," she says, even as her mother leans forward to clink glasses, "I guess you are."

Right. Sure. And then there's Tim.

She's there waiting for him at the slip when the Park

Service boat glides past the breakwater and swings south into Ventura Harbor, the afternoon arching high overhead, the sky a pale feathered blue and the sun a gentle beneficent presence hanging just over the crowns of the palms, so golden and mellow and rich it looks as if it's been painted in. Everything, including the protestors making their endless circuit around the building behind her, seems to glow with an inner light, colors heightened and shadows softened even as their homemade banners and signs—*Stop the Killing!*—fade away to abstraction. She's tested herself three times since the initial trial, investing in a second kit just to be certain there were no anomalies with the first, and just before her mother bundled up Ed and headed back to Arizona yesterday morning, she made an appointment with an obstetrician for Monday of next week. For a blood test. To be sure—incontrovertibly, rock-solid sure.

There are only five people disembarking—two of the college girls working with the captive foxes, an archaeologist studying the Chumash remains, the botanist who's set up a nursery to propagate native plants with the idea of reintroducing them once the star thistle and fennel have been removed or at least reduced, and Tim. He gives her a wave as he comes up the ramp looking thinner than usual, looking tired, wasted, his hair snaking out to obscure the long thin sliver of his face and his shoulders hunched under the weight of his overcrammed backpack. He's wearing a pair of sunglasses she's never seen before—big bug-eyed seventies shades with gilded frames—and how long has it been? Ten days, that's all. It seems like years. She watches the grin lift his jaw and light his face and then he's there, letting loose the backpack and spreading his arms wide to take her in. And when she hugs him to her, feeling the heat of him, the familiar contours of his body, the touch of his lips on hers, she can't let go—or not yet. Not till she communicates her joy in the language that precedes language, flesh to flesh.

"Wow," he says, breaking away from her to bend for the backpack, "I guess you missed me."

Smiling up at him, her eyes roving from the stiffened mud at the cuffs and knees of his jeans to the smooth silken growth of a fledging beard he didn't have the last time she saw him, she just says, "You have no idea."

He's got the backpack slung over one shoulder now and they're heading up the walk, his hand in hers. "So from your body language, I presume you just want to rush home and get it on—or were we going to have a beer first?"

"Beer first."

And it's just as she pictured it: the booth by the window, the fried calamari, the pale pilsner sizzling in the glass, his eyes on hers, the music falling away to a background murmur. "Good news," he's saying, dipping a strand of calamari in a little silver cruet of aioli as if he's trying to thread a needle. "I think we're down to no more than maybe three or four birds."

For the past four days she's been rehearsing what to say to him, running through one imaginary conversation after another. Right now, though, now that the moment has come, she can't do much more than nod and smile and say "Great" in a weak retreating voice.

"By early next year, summer at the latest, because they're pulling us off this for now, till spring anyway when we can see who's nesting and who's not, the goldens'll be gone and you can let the foxes loose." He's gulping beer and putting away calamari as if he's been a castaway all this time instead of bellying up to the big communal pot of whatever's cooking at the field station. "But I tell you," he goes on, waving a chunk of the calamari with the tentacles bunched at the end of his fork, "it's a bitch out there. They're getting wise to us. Hey, but more good news: as of this moment there are three happy and healthy goldens on their way to the Sierras for release, and one, a juvenile whose wing got unfortunately screwed up in the net who's going to find a new home at the Santa Barbara Zoo."

And what does she say? "Great."

"But what about you? Your mother still here?"

"She left yesterday—Ed had some sort of golf tournament or something he had to be back for."

"That was all right, though? I mean, them being there, the concert? How was it?"

"Great."

He takes a moment, craning his neck to flag the waitress for another beer, two hopeful-looking gulls watching him intently from the rail beyond the big table-to-ceiling windows, then turns back to her as if only in that moment discovering that she's there. "But what's the deal—you're not drinking? I thought"—and here he lowers his voice to carry the sexual innuendo, ten days apart and a broad bouncing bed awaiting them at home—"you'd at least have a glass of wine to welcome me home. Aren't you happy to see me?"

It's out before she can stop it: "I can't drink."

Before he can even begin to puzzle that out—she watches the wondering frown spread across his face—the waitress is there to ask if they're ready for another round. "You're having the Firestone, right?" she says, addressing Tim. Tim nods assent. And then to Alma: "Another Diet Coke?"

"No," she breathes, "I'm okay."

"You ready to order, or—?"

"Sure," Tim says, grinning up at the waitress, "as long as you've got any food left back there. You didn't run out, did you?"

The waitress grins back at him and then there's the delay of ordering, "Did you want fries with that or extra coleslaw, the house salad comes with ranch and the soup is clam chowder," and then, finally, the waitress is gone and Tim's staring deep into her, saying, "But seriously, you're on the wagon or what?"

"I'm pregnant."

His grin falters, then comes up again, full-on, as if

he can't control his facial muscles. "What? What are you saying?"

"I'm pregnant."

"You're joking, right?"

"I just found out like four days ago. When my mother was here. I missed my period, I guess, but I didn't—I mean, I didn't think anything about it till I started getting up and puking in the mornings—"

"Puking? What do you mean puking?"

His face has changed, hardening till the pores stand out, the skin dull and worn beneath his sunburn. She doesn't like the look in his eyes, doesn't like the way his mouth draws down around his pursed lips. When she first met him, the first few weeks till he began to relax with her, he used to get that look because no matter how funny he might have been or sweet and caring and genuine, he always held something in reserve. It was because of his ex-wife. Crystal. Crystal had a career of her own—she managed a dress shop in which she owned a half-interest—and couldn't begin to appreciate the sacrifices he had to make in order to pursue fieldwork, which was the only kind of work he was going to do because sitting behind a desk would just kill him, that's the way he felt. *I'm no desk jockey,* he'd said when the subject came up on their third or fourth date. And then he'd backtracked, flushing suddenly, embarrassed, because at that moment he realized what he was saying and he fumbled out an apology, hoping she hadn't taken offense. *I know somebody's got to do it, I'm not saying that, but I'm sorry—and it's what I told Crystal—it's just not going to be me. Not yet anyway. Not till I'm old and decrepit.*

"It's called morning sickness."

"Are you sure? I mean, is there any chance you're wrong about it?"

What's left of the calamari looks sodden and greasy and her stomach flutters at the sight of it. She takes a sip of Diet Coke, reaches across the table for his hand, but he pulls away. She feels a flash of irritation. He's being a child about this. He's being an idiot. "I ran the home test three times," she says in a quiet voice. "And I have an appointment with this obstetrician Paula Meyers recommended—"

"Obstetrician?" The word drops from his lips like a curse.

"—to have her take blood so we can know for sure. But I'm ninety-nine percent positive." And here she is, soaring again, her glands open wide, the blood beating through her veins on a million tiny wings. "Or no: a hundred percent."

He sits absolutely rigid, his hands clasped in his lap, the second beer sitting untouched on the polished wooden surface of the table before him. Freshly poured and set there by the vanishing waitress, the beer gives up its carbonation in a mad delirious rush of ascending bubbles, working its way flat. All around them, people are eating, chatting, laughing. Their voices meld and rise in a muted roar that nullifies the thin throb of the music bleeding through hidden speakers. They're in a restaurant. It's noisy. He's been away for ten days, she's just presented him with the biggest news of her entire clear-eyed life and he's not looking at her. He's looking at the table. Out the window. At his beer. "Well?" she says.

"*Well* what?"

"Don't you have anything to say? Aren't you"—and here she feels herself sinking, as if the legs of the chair were melting and the floor sucking out from under her—"at least, I don't know, *interested*? Engaged? Or, God forbid, *happy*?"

His eyes jump to hers. "Happy? No, I'm not happy—I'm just stunned."

She sees his face as if he's very far away—across the room or out on the boat still—as if she's trying to focus it in with a pair of binoculars. His mouth is clamped shut. His eyes are dull, sheenless, squinted like the eyes of a prisoner in an interrogation cell. Maybe this isn't the time, she's thinking, maybe she should have waited till they got home at least . . . but no, this is their life they're talking about here, the rest of their life, and he's got to understand that, got to wake up and give ground, talk to her, dial it up, lock it in, take her hand and tell her he loves her. "We're going to need to get married," she says, pushing it, and she can't help herself.

"Is that a proposal? Because if it is, isn't it supposed to be me that does the proposing? Isn't that the way it works?" He reaches for the beer, but then stops himself. "What's wrong with the way things are now?"

"Everything," she says, angry suddenly, furious. "Because I am not going to have our son—or daughter, I hope it's a daughter, I really do—grow up with that kind of stigma attached, because let me tell you it was hard enough when I was growing up without a father."

"Don't I get a say in this? I mean, you lay this, this *shit* on me the minute I step off the boat and it's like a done deal—I don't want any kids, okay? I never wanted any kids. I thought you understood that? Aren't you the one always bitching about seven billion people?" He gives her a sour look, pitches his voice high, in mockery: "'We're coming up on seven billion people by 2011 and all the resources are gone and we're all doomed'? Isn't that you? Or am I mistaken? Huh?"

She ignores him. "It's happening. It's a fact. It's life. I'm pregnant."

"Get rid of it," he says, pushing himself up from the table and gesturing angrily for the waitress. The interior of the restaurant rises and recedes again, the waitress there suddenly with a face so shining and bright it's like the big bloated headlight of a locomotive heading for a wreck and he's saying "Forget the food—just bring me the check, will you?" and there's no trace in him of the man she knows, no soothing, no consideration, no love. In that moment, even before he flings down two twenties and stalks out the door without another word, without looking back to see if she's coming or even if she's alive, she feels nothing for him, absolutely nothing.

Four months later, in the descending gloom of February, when each drizzling fogged-in day becomes a soul-killing replica of the last and the windows of the office are so gray and opaque they might as well be cardboard cutouts, things are still unresolved. She hasn't begun to show yet, at least not that anybody would notice, and if she's layering her clothes—loose tops, bulky sweaters—people just think it's because of the cold, because it's winter. Her breasts are tender, there's a tight swollen band of flesh protruding just below her navel that reminds her of the bulge in the gut of a just-fed brown tree snake and half the time she feels as if she's having an out-of-body experience—as if she's floating above herself like a kite in a stiff breeze—but nobody knows about it except her mother, Dr. Chandrasoma and Tim. And Tim isn't around. Because Tim left in December to accept a six-month assignment all the way up the coast in the Farallones to census the murres, cormorants, Cassin's auklets, puffins and pigeon guillemots that were already staking out their ground for nesting in the spring. He had no choice if he wanted to see a paycheck, he told her, ducking his head in shame, guilt, anger and relief. Plus, it was an opportunity to do something with the winter months.

And what about her? What about the baby?

I'll call, he'd said, lamely. *And I'll visit every fourth week. Or fifth. Whenever they rotate us back to shore.*

And marriage? Commitment? Love, support, empathy—friendship, even? All that was on hold. Indefinitely.

That first night they'd wrangled in the car the whole way back from Ventura—thirty minutes that seemed like thirty hours—and by the time he turned into the driveway they weren't talking. He stalked through the door, flung his backpack down in the entryway and locked himself in the bathroom. She could hear the thump of his crusted jeans hitting the floor, the sigh of the smoked-glass door on its abraded hinges and then the wheeze and rattle of the shower. He was washing the grit of the island off him, running water down the drain till it went cold, purifying himself—and for what? If he thought she was just going to dab perfume behind her ears, slip into a see-through negligee and give him what he wanted as if nothing had happened, he was out of his mind. She was so wrought up she was trembling, actually trembling, as she set the teapot on the stove, thinking to calm herself with a cup of herbal tea and maybe one or two of the chocolate-covered biscotti she was always craving yet denied herself because of her waistline, but that didn't matter now, did it? She slammed the pot down on the burner, her elbow kinetic, her wrist snapping angrily. Why did everything have to be such a struggle? *Why?*

The tea was too hot but she drank it anyway, listening to the infuriating hiss of the shower and reminding herself that she hadn't eaten because he'd denied her dinner, created a scene, acted like a cretin. Like a shit. A little shit who refused to grow up, who wasn't a man and never would be. After fifteen minutes—he wasn't showering, he was running the whole of Cachuma Reservoir down the sewer and out to sea—she pushed herself up from the kitchen table, looped her purse over one shoulder and went up the street to Giancarlo's for a pizza margherita and salad. Giancarlo fluttered over her, too delicate to ask after Tim or why she was dining alone, and she had a glass of Chianti, a single glass, that was all, and by the time she left to walk back to the condo she'd begun to feel better, if only marginally. Tim's reaction had been petty, mean, hurtful—inexcusable—but the whole thing had been so sudden he hadn't had a chance to collect himself, to think things through, to think of her, of how she was feeling. He would come around, she was sure he would. Just give him a chance. He was her man. The father of the child growing inside her. She loved him. He loved her. She was sure of it.

She picked up her pace, envisioning him there in the steamed-over bathroom, stepping out of the shower, his muscles lean and work-hardened, a sheen of dampness caught in the hair that framed his nipples, dripping from his chin, his moistened lashes. The lights of the shops and restaurants were suspended in a soft nimbus of mist. The eucalyptus rose white-limbed out of the shadows. Cars eased by. A jogger went up the opposite side of the street in a silent silken glide. She was alive all over again, her arms swinging wide, her heels ringing on the pavement. By the time she got to the front door, key in hand, she was thinking of reconciliation, and beyond reconciliation, seduction—she'd been without sex for ten days herself—and of the negligee tucked in the back of her underwear drawer.

The key turned in the lock, the door swung open. She didn't notice that he'd moved the backpack—that the backpack was gone—not till she called out his name and got no answer. There were two wet towels balled up on the bathroom floor. The closet door stood open and his mud-hardened boots lay there on edge in a spill of dirty laundry. His favorite shirt, the one she'd given him—black with an overlay of tropical flowers in bright slashes of yellow—was missing, as was the jacket he liked to wear with it. Ditto his red Converse.

She stayed up till twelve, watching a movie she barely registered, and then went to bed. He never came home. Not that night or the next night either and she wouldn't call him on his cell, wouldn't give him the satisfaction. To hell with him. He could wither away and die for all she cared. She went about her business as if he didn't exist, cool with Alicia, indifferent to the protestors, driving to work and back in a trance, cooking for one and losing herself in Micah Stroud and mind-numbing made-for-TV movies. When she got home from work on the third day there were signs that he'd been there—the boots were gone, replaced by the Converse, and the dirty laundry had disappeared—but he didn't come home that night either. She called her mother because she had to talk to someone, and her mother, to the accompaniment of ice cubes arhythmically clicking against the rim of her cocktail glass, spent a vodka-fueled hour and a half assailing his character, his looks, his upbringing and intelligence, but all it did was open up the hole inside her till it was so wide she could have dropped all of Santa Cruz Island into it. Finally, on the fifth day, he left her a note pinned to the refrigerator beneath a magnet shaped like a fox in profile. *I'm sorry,* the note read, *I know I'm wrong but I can't help the way I feel. What it is, is I'm just not ready for this.* He'd signed it, redundantly, *Sorry, Tim.*

The next day he was there when she got home and there were flowers on the table and he'd made her a meal and they went straight to bed, both of them starved for it, and he told her he loved her, but still he held back and the next day he was gone again. They talked it out, over and over, face-to-face and on the phone too. Her position was that she was going to have the baby whether he liked it or not and his position was that he wasn't going to be boxed in and certainly wasn't going to bow to any ultimatums. In the end he badgered her into making an appointment at Planned Parenthood—*Seven billion people*, he kept droning, *seven billion*—and he went with her and talked to the counselor and tried to get her to pin down a day for the procedure. She saw his point—she agreed with him—but her body resisted. November wore on. He was staying with a friend—male—downtown. Every few days he was there when she got home and they made love out of desperation, but it was sad and lonely and mechanical and they both held back, resentful, angry, at war, until finally he announced that he was going to the Farallones and she was left to do what she had to do all on her own.

And now it's February and she's sick in the mornings and her body is transforming itself day by day to accommodate the fetus growing inside her and nobody at work knows a thing about it. She's been out to the island three times since the first of the year, twice with Annabelle and once with Fred Sampson, the biologist from UCSB who's overseeing the captive breeding program for the foxes, and if she had to stand in the stern of the boat and lose her breakfast over the rail, it was only to be expected because the channel's notoriously rough in winter, everybody knows that. The good news is that the foxes are thriving. The first six pairs, captured and caged in '02, produced five kits, three of which were released back into the wild, only to fall prey to the goldens. Late that year they brought in another three pairs, which in addition to the two kits held back and the original six pairs, gave them ten breeding pairs. In all, to this point, four years later, they've produced eighty-five offspring, happy enough to breed up their numbers when there's an abundance of fox chow, handpicked berries, freshly trapped mice and quail eggs available and nothing with claws and wings homing in on them from above. With the goldens gone, or mostly gone, and the balds reestablished, it looks as if all the foxes can be released by spring. As for the pigs, Frazier and his hunters—twelve of them, with a lean scrabbling contingent of two dozen dedicated dogs—are working their way systematically through each of the five zones, far ahead of schedule.

Valentine's Day falls on a Tuesday, and she observes it alone, with Chinese takeout and a laptop bristling with work she's brought home from the office, and she's not thinking of Tim, definitely not thinking of Tim, even when the phone rings at ten past nine and she jumps up from the couch to catch it on the second ring only to hear her mother's voice on the other end of the line wondering if she's still having stomach problems. On Friday she has to leave work early for her monthly appointment with

Dr. Chandrasoma ("Everything's normal, not to worry"), and at sunup the following morning she finds herself driving down to Ventura under a stripped skeleton of cloud and a low uncertain sun, on her way to the boat that will take her out to the island for three days of hiking the fence lines and following Frazier on his rounds. As an observer, strictly as an observer. To get a feel for things, check up on the progress, see what it means when you pay somebody else to pull the trigger.

It's the kind of day when the weather could go either way. She was up and out the door before the paper arrived, so she hasn't seen the forecast—not that it matters, since she'll be going out on that boat whether it rains in obliterating sheets or the sun hangs up there in the sky as if she were transported back to the beach in Guam. She hasn't thrown up yet, and that's a positive, but then she hasn't put anything on her stomach either. She's watching the ocean as she drives, the islands fading in and out of visibility through the dirt-spattered windows, whitecaps kicking up as far out as she can see. It'll be rough, rain or shine. And she'll vomit. So what else is new?

Annabelle is waiting for her in the parking lot, her feet propped up on the dashboard of her two-tone Mini, sipping a Starbucks chai latte and leafing through the newspaper. She glances up when Alma pulls in beside her, her face neutral—she must not be wearing her contacts—until she recognizes her, gives a little two-fingered wave and slides out of the car. "All set?" she asks, already smiling in at the window as Alma frees herself from the seat restraint and twists round to extract her backpack from the rear seat.

She's running through a mental checklist of the things she's packed, feeling the first stirrings of the excitement that always steals over her when she has the chance to get out from behind her desk and back into the field, which is where she belongs. Tim might not think so. But then Tim didn't do three years in Guam either. "Yeah," she says, emerging from the car to weigh the backpack in one hand

and slam the door with the other, "I guess I've got everything. Think it's going to rain?"

Ducking one shoulder to readjust her strap, Annabelle winces momentarily before straightening up and arching her spine to readjust the weight. She's wearing her backcountry outfit—a fawn jacket and matching shorts that look like they came off a mannequin at Banana Republic, three-hundred-dollar hiking boots, a red bandanna and a Tilley canvas, also in fawn. "I wouldn't bet against it," she says, as they simultaneously swing round to click their remotes and lock their cars behind them before starting off across the lot for the boat, not a protestor in sight.

"So where're all our friends?" Alma wonders aloud. "In church?"

Long-legged, striding, her hair pulled back in a swaying ponytail that fans out across her lollipop-red High Sierra pack, Annabelle gives her a grin because they're on the same page here, equal opportunity targets. "It's Saturday."

"Right. I guess they must be sleeping off their hangovers then. I mean, what time did you get up Saturday mornings in college?"

"Oh, I don't know—ten?"

"More like noon," Alma puts in.

"Noon? How about one? Or two, do I hear two?"

And this is funny, very funny, at quarter past seven on a forty-nine-degree February morning with the refrigerated scent of the sea riding in off the water and the prospect of three days on the island unscrolling before them, three days free of condo, supermarket, office and car, and as they descend the ramp to the boat, they're laughing. Or no: giggling. Like schoolgirls on a field trip.

The Park Service boat is substantial, no question about it, but it's a whole lot smaller than the *Islander* and doesn't have anywhere near its stability. At first, Alma sits at the table in the main cabin with Annabelle and the three college girls on their way out to relieve the three college girls who've been tending the caged foxes for minimum wage and course credit for the past two weeks, but everything seems closed-in and overheated and she has to go out on the stern and stand in the wind till the nausea passes. It's cold. The sky, which seemed so promising earlier, is beginning to cloud over. Dolphins ride the wake, surfing the swell and leaping up to surf it again. A pair of humpbacks—or are they great blues?—spout off in the distance, wild things in a wild place, the mainland rapidly falling away and the waves gloomily slapping at the hull as if the boat has been hauled out here in the middle of the channel for the sole purpose of intercepting them. After a while she has to choose between nausea and freezing to death, and so she makes her way back into the cabin and sits there rigid at the table, staring off at the horizon and willing herself to think of anything but decks and boats and the sea until she hears the engines decelerate and the long dun pier at Prisoners' comes gradually into view.

Frazier is there to meet them in the battered Toyota Land Cruiser some kind soul donated to the Conservancy and they all cram in for the three-mile run up to the main ranch, where they drop off Annabelle. They sit there in the middle of the dirt drive, engine idling, while she hoists her pack to one shoulder and then leans into the driver's side window to bring her pale pretty face into the sun-blistered orbit of Frazier's as if they're about to compare hat sizes. But no: they're kissing. And this is no mere ritual of greeting between two well-meaning colleagues, no glancing peck to the cheek or coolly affectionate salutation, but something very like the hungry soul kiss of separating lovers. As if that isn't awkward enough, they all have to sit there for an extra sixty seconds so Frazier can watch her sway over her hips all the way across the expanse of the lot and in under the shade of the oaks to where she'll be staying in one of the airy, clean, well-appointed rooms in what was once, before its makeover as a kind of early California ranch-style B and B for the Conservancy's big donors,

356

the bunkhouse of a working ranch. Then he puts the car in gear and they continue another quarter mile on up the rutted dirt road to the field station, where the rooms are not airy, clean and well-appointed, and where they'll all unfurl their sleeping bags and try to stake out a little space for themselves amidst the working chaos of the place.

There's a flurry of hugs, snatches of gossip, truncated hellos and breathless goodbyes as the girls exchange places and Alma ducks into the back room—a single, with a worn but serviceable mattress laid out on a makeshift bedframe—to lay claim to it before anybody else does. She's bent over the bed, smoothing out her sleeping bag and replacing the suspect pillow (who knows how long it's been there and what use it's been put to?) with the one she's brought from home, when she becomes aware that she's not alone. She turns round to see Frazier standing there in the doorway. He's dressed in his bush clothes: khaki cargo shorts and matching shirt, the felt hunting hat with the teardrop crown and a yellowed pair of boar's tusks worked up under the leather hatband, thick-grid hiking boots and Gore-Tex gaiters to keep the foxheads out of his socks. Gaiters, especially, are a necessity out here and she's brought along her own pair, having learned from experience that you can't really cover much ground with half a dozen needle-like seedpods working their way through your socks and into your flesh, and if the foxhead isn't a perfect example of dispersal adaptation, then she can't imagine what else is. Aside from deer ticks, maybe. But there are no deer ticks out here because there are no deer to entertain them. "Well," Frazier says, his smile heating up like kindling set to the match till it's not a smile at all but a kind of maniacal ear-to-ear Kiwi grin, "are you going to take all day or do you want see some pig action?"

El Tigre Ridge lies approximately three miles south of the field station, rising in elevation to 1,484 feet above sea level amidst a tapering wall of eroded peaks that falls away precipitously into the cleft of Willows Canyon to the west. It's a thousand feet lower than the island's highest mountain, Diablo Peak, across the central valley to the northwest, and more than three hundred feet below the top of El Montañon, ten miles to the east, which represents the high point of the barrier ridge between the Park Service and TNC properties. Still, it's a climb, and though there's a bucking lurching potholed semblance of a dirt road winding up and away from the ranch, the Island Healers vehicle—a miniature pickup with a cramped two-person cabin and the steering wheel on the wrong side—can only take them so far. Especially now, in winter, when a succession of storms has rolled in off the Pacific to wash away everything but the rocks so that the road looks as if it's been bombed. Repeatedly. After one especially jarring plunge into a spewing crater and a fishtailing climb up and out the other side, Frazier jerks the wheel hard to the left, pulls just off the road and kills the ignition. "From here, we walk," he announces, flinging open the door to swing his legs out and plant his boots in the mud. If anything, he's grinning wider now, as if all this were a grand joke at her expense, and as she slides out the other side she can't help wondering if he's been hitting the flask already. She steals a glance at her watch: it isn't even noon yet.

The air is burdened with humidity, the breeze cold. What sun there was is gone for good now and though she's never been a betting woman, she'd put everything she has on the prospect—no, the certainty—of rain. "That's what I'm here for," she tells him, shouldering her pack and grinning right back at him. "To get a little exercise." (Unlike Annabelle, who begged off with a wide hypocritical smile, claiming she had too much going on at the main ranch to muddy her boots up in the hills, paperwork, accounts, maintenance issues—*You know, dreary stuff. The worst.*) And then, because of Tim, because Tim's in her mind and she can't get him out, she adds, "I'm not just a desk jockey, you know."

Frazier doesn't answer. He's on the two-way radio he keeps snapped to his belt, chattering away in Kiwi with one of his hunters, part of a two-man team somewhere up ahead of them, apparently closing in on a target. "Royt," he says, "royt," already moving up the road, surprisingly quick for a man who always seems so sprawling and laid back, and how has she missed the rifle he's somehow managed to sling over one shoulder? Her eyes jump to it, to the gleaming stock, the dark rubbed eye of the trigger, the lethal tube of the barrel. The realization comes to her then that this is the tool of his trade, that he's as familiar with it as he is with his cell phone, the gearshift of the Toyota, the corkscrew he carries on his key chain. Why should this surprise her? Electrify her? Rivet her attention? Because she's never fired a gun in her life, never even touched one, and here's the rifle Frazier so casually and routinely employs, riding his back as if it were the most natural thing in the world, as if it weren't for firing high-velocity copper-jacketed rounds into things, as if it weren't for hunting, for killing.

"No," he's shouting, "just go after them if you think you're going to have a shot. We're right behind you." A glance over his shoulder for her, and she's scrambling now to keep up—"I don't think Alma's going to want to shoot them herself anyway." Feet churning, mud kicking up at his heels, he depresses the button for the crackled response, a thin all but incomprehensible Kiwi affirmative snatched from the ether. She can hear him breathing, the air sucked down in quick bronchial gasps. They're moving more rapidly now, leaping puddles, dodging rocks, what's left of the road veering sharply around its hairpin turns and up, always up. "Right, Alma?"

She has neither time nor breath to answer. She grins to demonstrate how good a sport she is, concentrating on moving her legs, matching him stride for stride, though it's an unequal contest because his legs are so much longer. Watching the gun, watching his hat and shoulders and the way his calf muscles ball and release beneath the ties of his gaiters, she follows him at a lively jog up the road to a point where a trail only he can see cuts sharply down through the chaparral to the right. She follows his lead, pitching headlong into the bush, snatching branches to keep her balance, all the while studying her feet so she doesn't step in a hole or turn an ankle. They're angling down—a hundred yards, two—before he cuts again to the right, bearing along the downside of the slope, and all at once she feels the weight lift from her, feeling good and alive and whole for the first time in weeks, taking in the views, the smells, the wet glorious creeping rejuvenation of the flora springing up underfoot and rising around her in a continuous weave of gray-green and bright flowering yellow that reaches to her waist and higher.

She's moving as fast as she can—bushwhacking, that's what this is called—when the rain starts in. It begins as a soft rustling in the chaparral, as if the leaves were coming to life one by one across the hillside, and then it quickens till she can hear the insistent tap of it at the bill of her cap and feel its cold touch on her hands, her bare knees, the back of her neck. Everything smells suddenly of sage, a sweet clean release of perfume wrung out of the careening wet hillside by the force of the downpour. Below them, the sight line to the far side of the canyon softens, thickens, blurs. She's wondering why they call this ridge El Tigre, when certainly there were never any tigers here, not even saber-tooths during the time of the pygmy mammoth, or not that the fossil record shows anyway. There weren't even bobcats—no cats of any kind. But maybe it's a question of perception—maybe the rock formation, as seen from below, suggests a sleeping cat lying stretched out on its side. Or there might have been a vaquero from the old ranching days who hailed from deep in the south of Mexico where the jaguars came out at night to seize the village dogs and maybe he acquired the nickname El Tigre because he exacted vengeance on them before he came to Santa Cruz and ran sheep over this hill. Or died here. In an accident, a slide, in mud like this.

There is no sound but the soughing of the rain and the whisper of leaf and branch giving way as they wade through the chaparral, seeking the path of least resistance. Both her thighs are crisscrossed with abrasions and her forearms would be bleeding too if it weren't for the sweatshirt, which grows heavier and denser by the moment. She's sweating. Fighting for breath. Out of shape because she's pregnant, because she's put on weight, because she's been tired in the evenings and spending her days at her desk instead of getting out for the hikes she used to take with Tim. She startles when a quail bursts out from underfoot, fans its wings and beats away downwind, and it costs her a step or two on Frazier, who's already thirty feet ahead of her. She wants to call to him to slow down, but her pride won't let her.

It is then, just as she's about to give it up and fall back, that the canyon erupts with the frantic baying of the dogs. The sound, ratcheting up in a series of furious yelps till it planes off in a single full-throated ecstatic howl—seems to be coming from somewhere below them, where the ridge falls off into its turnings and declivities. Frazier snatches a look over his shoulder and then he's gone, plunging straight down in the direction of the noise, and before she can think she's following him. Suddenly the vegetation is coming at her in a blind rush, bushes springing up to slam her in the ribs, snatch at her feet, shove her aside, but there's no stopping her. The frenzy of the dogs strikes fire in her and there's no question now of keeping up, her balance flawless, her feet hitting the mark over and over again as she fends off one catapulting branch after another and springs from rock to rock like a gymnast, finally overtaking Frazier as he pauses, hands on hips, to gaze over a sheer drop of forty feet or more. The dogs bay, nearer now.

Bending low in a hunter's crouch, he scoots along the crest until he finds what he's looking for—a debrided chute of rock running with discolored water—and without hesitation he braces himself with both hands, flings his legs out before him and careens down the slope on his buttocks. All at once she's in the water too—forty feet down and a jump at the end, her palms bruised, calves aching—watching for his signal. "Where are they?" she gasps, tugging at his arm as she scrambles to her feet.

Before he can answer, three shots ring out in succession, a quick thin fretful sound like the snapping of a wet towel. The gunshots silence the dogs for a single suspended moment and then they're noising again, barking now, snarling, until the final shot, the fourth, snaps suddenly through the din and they fall quiet once more. She looks to Frazier. He's cocking his head to one side, listening, and his gun, his rifle, is in his hands now and before she can pick up the stealthy patter of advancing hooves the towel is snapping in her ear and the dark hurtling thing coming at them from the cover of the bushes is down and dead as if it's been there all along, switched with the animate pig in some elaborate magician's ruse.

She smells the gun, the rain, the blood, and here come the dogs—a pair of Frazier's prize Australian Bull Arabs, with their straining shoulders and their great wide heads and snouts and the light of the kill shining in their eyes. They break from the bushes in a rush and fall on the hog—a boar, a big boar with meshed white tusks—till Frazier calls them off and strides up to deliver the coup de grâce with the pistol he wears in a holster at his side. One more snap and the dogs sit back on their haunches. There are voices now, Kiwi voices, riding up from somewhere below. "You get him, Fraze?"

"Never miss," he shouts back. "But you lads're getting sloppy. If he gets away, he's going to be one tough hog to hunt down next time."

The rebuke hangs there in the air a moment, and then

one of the voices below—she recognizes it as belonging to Clive Hyndman, a blond twenty-six-year-old with a perpetually peeling nose and legs so good he could have been modeling his khaki shorts for money—comes back at them. "We got the sow and three piglets. Didn't even know the old man was there till he started running up the hill."

And Frazier, cupping his hands to his mouth: "No worries, mate. Just so long as he didn't get away. Now, are you coming up here or am I going down there?"

She can hear them working their way up from below, a scratching and rustling accompanied by the clatter of shingle scattering underfoot. The dogs, slick with wet, settle on their haunches, the pig of no interest to them now— it's the living pig that pushes their buttons, the fleeing pig, the mysterious thing that bolts at the sound of their conjoined voices and never stops till they've got it cornered and the man with the gun is wading in for the finale. She wants to sit down on the nearest rock—her legs are lifeless, numb, too weak to support her—but instead she finds herself standing over the carcass as if she's willed it into existence. It's bigger than she thought it would be, huge really, three or four hundred pounds, its fur brindled and shaggy, more like a sheepdog's than the smooth brushed coat of the domestic hogs she'd seen rooting around the villages in Guam. Frazier's first shot, the one from the rifle, severed the carotid artery and a loop of bright oxygen-rich blood arced away from the wound till the heart stopped pumping and the flow faltered like the choked-off stream of a garden hose. The blood shadows the carcass now, so dark it could be oil, as if the animal had stumbled and fallen in a seep.

Rain stirs the dense tangle of fur, drops silently into the fixed and unseeing eyes, the delicacy of the lashes there, the canthic folds, the deep rich chocolate brown of the irises. She bends from the waist to see more clearly, ignoring the riveting of the rain. The hooves fascinate her. She's never seen a hoof up close before—it's so neatly adapted to

363

its task, a built-in shoe shining and dark with the wet, as impervious as if it were molded of plastic. And the ears, the way the ears stand straight up, like a German shepherd's, to collect and concentrate the sounds that only come to us peripherally. The heavy shoulders, the neat arc of the haunches, the switch of the tail. This wild thing, this perfect creature. She feels the sorrow in the back of her throat, the sorrow of existence, and if she could have brought the animal back to life, restored it to some other ecosystem where it could belong and thrive and live out its time under the sun, she would have done it.

Frazier comes up behind her. "Five down," he says, "and bloody hundreds to go."

She just nods. "It's kind of"—and she feels like an idiot even before the words are out of her mouth—"neat, though. Healthy, I mean. A good specimen."

"Oh, yeah," Frazier says, stepping forward to tap the carcass with the toe of his boot. "He's in his prime, no doubt about it. Probably been out there making all the little piggies he can. But see this?" His boot poking at the jaws now. "These tushes? He could rip the guts out of a dog in a heartbeat with these things and no mistaking it. This is one mean animal. And you can tell by the way he was coming at us he didn't really have any charitable notions in his head."

He's right. Of course he's right. These animals have to be eliminated and if you stop to see them as individuals you're done. How many acorns will have the chance to germinate and grow into trees to shade the terrain and capture mist in their spreading branches because this pig at their feet won't be there to glut himself on them? *Five down. Hundreds to go.*

At that moment Clive emerges from the chaparral downslope, his shorter but just as sturdy and just as sunburned companion following close behind pulled by two more dogs on leashes. The men are dressed identically: gaiters, shorts, ponchos, wide-brimmed hats. Both carry rifles of the same make and caliber as Frazier's. "Jesus, what a day," Clive hollers in his high husky voice that always seems to be going hoarse on him. "I say we're lucky to get what we got because the critters aren't stupid—they'll all be hunkered in cover while it's coming down like this." And then, as if just noticing her, he touches the dripping brim of his hat and says, "Hi, Alma. Nice day, huh?"

The other hunter—he won't look directly at her, not yet—lets go of the leashed dogs so they can rejoin their compatriots in a brief exposition of shoulder bumping and tail wagging. "That's a trophy animal there, Fraze," he says, nodding in the direction of the boar. "Wish you'd left him for me."

"Maybe Alma wants the tusks for a souvenir?" Clive says, giving her a sidelong glance.

"Sure," the second one says, and he looks up now and there's no mistaking the intent of his gaze, a healthy young man out in the bush bereft of the company of women, and he's dissolved her clothes, healed her abrasions and wiped her clean of mud all in an instant, "but as I'm sure she knows that'll require hacking off the head and burying it for a couple weeks so the beetles and worms can get at it. Try to pull those things out otherwise and they'll snap off every time." He looks to the dead animal and then comes back to her. "I'm A.P., by the way, short for Arthur Peter—don't think we've had the pleasure."

She takes the hand he offers—as cold and wet as hers—and murmurs, "I'm Alma. Nice to meet you. But maybe, given all that effort, we ought to just leave this one for the ravens." Turning to Frazier, not for protection, not because the moment is awkward and she can feel the lust radiating like an aura from A.P. and Clive, but because she's feeling good again, or better, and wants desperately to keep from breaking down in front of them, keep from showing weakness in the face of the killing and dying and death they take so casually. The necessary death. The death she's ordered. As boss and overseer. "Right, Frazier?" she says, letting her voice rise in an easy jocular way.

"Royt. But then, and this is always a worry once you start in on these things, you're going to have an artificial blip in the raven population, you know that, don't you?— and nobody can say what effect that's going to have down the road on, say, the island scrub jay or the side-blotched lizard or any of the other species you're trying to preserve."

"Okay then," A.P. chirps, going down on one knee before the carcass, "let me just do some mouth-to-mouth here on this one and see if we can't revive him—"

They're standing unprotected in the rain, deep in a wild canyon on an island off the Pacific Coast on which there can't be more than twenty people total at the moment, discussing the cascading effects of the artificial removal of one species to favor another. In all her years in the library, the classroom, at her desk in her dorm writing papers and dreaming of the outdoors, she couldn't have imagined this. It feels good, though. It feels right. Ignoring A.P., she says, "Of course I'm aware of that. Providing this resource for the ravens is going to increase their numbers exponentially and once the carcasses are gone they're going to starve and die back, but not before robbing every nest they can and predating anything that moves . . . but we've got to take that chance. I mean, that's what this is all about, isn't it?"

Frazier nods. "Just making a point," he says. And adds, as a clarifier, "No worries."

One of the dogs whines. The rain, which has slackened, begins to pick up again. A.P., still down on one knee, still clowning, says, "Nope, there's no bringing this one back." And Clive, hands hanging at his sides and a fountain spouting from the crease at the brim of his hat, says, "What I don't understand, ecologically speaking, is why don't we get out of this rain someplace?"

Lunch, shared round under the canopy of a bright blue plastic tarp Frazier weighted with rocks atop the ledge above them and strung across to the crown of an iron-wood rising up from below, is heavy on jerky, PowerBars and dried fruit, though each of the men produces a foil-wrapped sandwich and Alma contributes half a dozen veggie cheese wraps she made up in her pre-dawn kitchen for just such an encounter as this. They've got a fire going and she's grateful for that, shivering actually, the sweatshirt soaked through and propped up on a stick to dry or at least steam, and no, she's not going to worry about the strict prohibition against open fires out here—not today, not in this mess. Frazier passes round his flask and she fits the cold metal rim to her lips and takes a burning hit like everybody else, feeling it work its way down her throat to ignite in the acid pool of her stomach, fire on fire. From there, it will be absorbed into her bloodstream where it will rise to massage the pleasure centers of her brain and plunge low to sweep through the embryo growing inside her, her daughter, and her daughter better learn to take it, to toughen up, that's what she's thinking. One hit. Half a shot. What harm can that do?

"What're you thinking, Alma?" Frazier asks, leaning in to poke at the fire.

"I don't know. Nothing, I guess."

"Another hit?"

"No," she says, waving away the proffered flask. Then she feels a grin coming on. "Or yes, hell yes—why not?" Another swallow, another burn. She's feeling reckless, celebratory, proven—blooded, isn't that what they call it? Shouldn't Frazier be dabbing a handkerchief in boar's blood and anointing her forehead?

"That's the spirit, girl," A.P. says, and she passes him the flask, conscious now not only of his eyes on her but of something else too, a deferential note to the foolery, as if he were forcing it, as if, despite her passing illusion of solidarity, he—and Clive and Frazier too—can't forget that she's the one paying the bills here.

The rain seems heavier now, if that's possible. All four

dogs, stinking and wet, have crowded in with them, tight quarters. The dead boar, a swollen shaggy heap sinking into its own fluids a stone's throw away, is the only one not invited to the party, though in a way, he's the guest of honor. It's chilly. She edges closer to the fire.

For a long while no one says anything, each occupied with his own thoughts, listening to the rain, the fire, feeling the surge of life all around them—the life of the wild that progresses minute to minute, day to day, in this very spot, whether they're here to record it or not. The brandy is in her brain. She shivers again and leans forward to reach for the sweatshirt.

"So what you think?" Clive asks in a kind of yodel that startles them all. "Should we call it a day? Not much sense in mucking about in this shit. You won't see another pig today, I guarantee you that."

A.P. looks first to her, then Frazier, to see how the proposition is going over, before rubbing his hands together, ducking his head and concurring. "No," he says, "no way."

Frazier, his legs tented before him, his grin in place, leaves it to her. "What do you say, Alma—seen enough?"

Before she has a chance to answer—and she can already see the fire going in the big paneled room of the field station, already feel the dry sustaining warmth of her own showered and talcumed body wrapped tightly in her sleeping bag—two things happen. The first involves the transient appearance, at the far edge of the rough table of dirt and rock on which they're sitting, of a pair of labile snouts and four startled eyes, and the second, the eruption of the dogs in a moil of slashing limbs and frenzied outraged yelps. In an eyeblink, they're gone, the whole business, transient pigs (there were two of them, weren't there? Medium-sized: shoats?) and all four dogs. Frazier leaps to his feet, cursing.

"Aw, shit," A.P. spits, but he never moves. Nor does Clive. "I told you"—to Clive—"we should've kept the dogs chained."

368

"But who would've thought—I mean, the fucking pigs coming right up to us like we had a bucket of slops and it's feeding time?"

"Aw, shit," A.P. reiterates.

The barking—baying—is already fading away downslope when Frazier, who's made no move to shoulder his pack or pluck up the rifle propped against it, begins to break down the fire, separating out the burning brands and kicking dirt over the coals. "Well," he says, glaring first at Clive, then A.P., "aren't you going to get up off your sorry asses and trail those dogs?"

Reluctantly, with exaggerated stiffness, they get to their feet. They look put-upon, angry, stung by the reproach— they don't want to be out in this weather, nobody does, and they were only waiting for her to throw in and say *Yeah, I've had enough, let's go back*. But that isn't going to be possible now. Now they have to follow the dogs because the dogs are on the scent and they can't just leave them out there on their own.

"Alma?" Frazier, who's still poking at the remains of the fire in a shifting robe of smoke that clings to his legs, falls open and wraps itself round again, is watching her. "You up for this? I can take you back, if you want—"

And what's she going to say? Is she going to say *Take me back* like some secretly pregnant pencil pusher, like a woman, or pull the damp sweatshirt over her head, wriggle into her clear plastic poncho and heft her pack like the others? "I'm fine," she says, and then the tarp is rolled up and packed away and the fire stamped out and they're following Clive and A.P. down into the throat of the canyon, rain overhead, mud underfoot.

She's not really keeping track of the time—she's too exhausted for that, too wiped even to lift her wrist and peel back the wet sleeve of her sweatshirt to glance at her watch—but it seems as if they've been walking for hours.

Trudging down one slope and up the next, the world as wet as it must have been when the continents first emerged from the rolling waters and nothing in sight but more hills, more chaparral, more streams, runlets, rills and cascades, it becomes apparent to her that they won't be finding the pigs, not today. They might not even find the dogs. Or the road. Or the truck, for that matter. The hunters are out there somewhere, Clive and A.P., moving like machines, like pistons, up and down, up and down. And she's stuck here behind Frazier, who—and she's acutely conscious of this—is hanging back for her sake, picking his way carefully across the landscape, silent now, grinless, thinking his own thoughts. They're working along the ridge, lower down, much lower—so low she can see the looping brown upper reaches of Willows Creek and hear the deflected roar of it as it blasts its way to the sea, water piling atop water—when she spots something below. Movement. A flash of color. It can't be A.P. or Clive. It can't be the dogs. Or the pigs. Or any pig. Because the color—it's moving, definitely moving—is all wrong. The color, and here she calls ahead to Frazier to stop while she drops her backpack at her feet to retrieve her binoculars from the side flap, is pink.

Crotalus Viridis

There is no boat because Wilson has been scared off by the Coast Guard, who motored up alongside the *Paladin* and by means of a bullhorn ordered him to hoist anchor and quit the premises as the island and its waters were closed indefinitely to all visitors, so that Wilson had no choice in the matter, thinking to head contritely toward Ventura and then circle back after dark, but Dave doesn't know that. All he knows is that things have gone to shit and that he's got a dead girl, three hypothermic would-be saboteurs and one shivering, silent and thoroughly pissed-off reporter on his hands. Beyond that, wet through and with the temperature in the forties and rain still falling intermittently, they could die out here, all of them, if they don't find shelter and build a fire, but a fire's risky—what they need is Wilson and the boat with the heater in the cabin turned up high and dry clothes and a hot Cup O' Noodles or coffee, anything to take the chill off.

"Dave, *Dave*." Someone's calling him in the dark, a suspended face given definition in the thinnest illumination leaching in under the clouds from the distant coast, and he backs out of the water, the foam hissing at his ankles, and sees that it's Josh. "Listen, Dave"—Josh can hardly get the words out he's shivering so hard—"we need to build a fire, all of us, we're freezing—"

"No," he says, freezing himself. "Too risky."

"Yeah, well, risky or not the girls are gathering driftwood and Suzanne's got matches, the strike-anywhere kind, like in a plastic pill container so they're dry? And we're going to light a fire, a bonfire—it can be a signal. For Wilson." He breaks off to sneeze, raising a vaporous hand to his face. "Because where *is* he anyway?"

"Just wait. Give it a few more minutes. He'll be here."

"And then what?"

"Then we go aboard, get dry, get warm."

"What about Kelly?"

"We bring her."

Josh's voice comes back at him, hard, furious, on the verge of cracking: "She's not going to get warm. Not ever."

It's all he can do to hold himself back, trying to fight down his emotions, keep control, because he's the one who's in deep here, he's the one they're going to come after, and he's been trying to think what to do for the past hour now. They could say she fell off the boat, but then he's seen *CSI*—that'd be fresh water in her lungs, not salt. Maybe they were on West Anacapa, hiking, and she slipped and fell down a hill into a rain puddle, a big puddle, deep, a pond really, and by the time they got to her . . . but what about Toni Walsh? Toni Walsh isn't going to stick her neck out. Toni Walsh has her story and the story's going to put it to him and no doubt about that. *Irresponsible behavior. Lawless. Reckless. A young girl dead, and for what?* Finally, he says, "We can't help that. It was"—and he knows how false he sounds—"just one of those things."

"Just one of those things? We're talking about Kelly here. Kelly's dead, don't you get it?" Somewhere in the darkness beyond them he can hear the others gathering driftwood, voices tuned low, feet swishing in the sand. The waves beat and recede. The air smells of rot. "We need the police," Josh is saying, his voice pinched and uneven, as if he's being strangled. "We have to report it to the police. They'll come—they'll take care of, of the body. I mean, radio from the boat."

He doesn't answer. And he doesn't protest when Suzanne, with the scraps of newspaper she's kept dry in a plastic bag, her strike-anywhere matches and a fierce gale of concentrated fanning and blowing, manages to turn a thin searching finger of flame into a blaze and then a bonfire that consumes anything they can throw into it, wet or dry. He stands there with them, as close as he can get to the fire, hugging his arms to his chest, rotating to dry himself, heat the only thing that matters. And when Wilson does come, when the soft sustained hum of the motor rides in over the plangent suck and roar of the waves and the running lights coalesce in the void, he's not even the first to notice. It's Cammy. Cammy shouting out, "He's here! Wilson! He's here!"

As one, they break away from the fire to rush the water's edge and watch the lights maneuver into place, listening to the thin metallic screech of the anchor chain unspooling, the discreet *plunk* of the anchor itself, and then, a moment later, to the muted slap of the inflatable hitting the water. They're picturing Wilson—oblivious Wilson, happy Wilson—lowering himself into the dinghy preparatory to pulling the engine cord and casting off to come and get them out of this, wrap them in blankets, take them home, when there's a shout from down the beach. A man's voice, brutal, roaring, the voice of authority and retribution: "Who's there? Who is it now?" And then, four figures separating themselves from the night, dogs there too, shorts, slickers, bush hats, guns, "Don't anybody move."

The rest is confusion, the dogs nosing up to them, the men with the guns fanning out as if this were some sort of military maneuver, Cammy and Suzanne writhing and flapping their hands and crying out, "Help! We need help here!" like the underage victims in a slasher flick, the fire roaring, the sea pounding, the closing whine of the dinghy's motor cutting through it all like a thin honed blade, and, staggeringly—*How could she have known?*—Alma Boyd Takesue emerging from the shadows to the light, the fiercest hateful unforgiving sneer of triumph sealed into her little sliver of a Gook face. It takes him a moment to sort it out. These are the hunters, the pig killers imported from New Zealand, as if there weren't enough native-born killers to go around. And these are their dogs. And this—the black-haired undersized sneering woman in the mud-spattered gaiters and drooping sweatshirt—this is their boss, the *Haupt*-executioner herself, here to make sure the blood is being spilled with all due haste and efficiency. Alma. Alma Boyd Takesue.

"Just what do you people think you're doing here?" the man in the middle, the beefy one with the cocked hat, the rifle strapped to one shoulder and his hand hovering over the pistol at his belt, the one who'd bellowed at them from fifty feet away like some sort of storm trooper—and why not extend the metaphor if it fits?—wants to know. Demands to know.

Josh looks sheepish, Cammy is fighting back tears, Suzanne holding out her palms and rushing plaintively at the jerk, as if he's some sort of authority here, reiterating in a childish singsong what she's just communicated—"We need help"—while Toni Walsh plants herself in the sand, slumps her shoulders and tries to light a cigarette. That leaves it to him. And what does he say? He says, "Who the fuck are you to order us around?"

The man takes a step forward till there's no more than ten feet separating them. His eyes are a cold feral glitter in the firelight. "I'm the man with the gun," he says. And pauses to let that sink in, the belligerence of it, the implied threat, the stone-cold arrogance, gazing slowly from face to face, taking his time, before his eyes come back to settle on Dave. "And you're the trespassers. Worse—you're vandals. Here to interfere with—"

"Bullshit. You've got no authority here." Swinging round savagely to point a shaking finger at Alma. "And you either, *Dr.* Takesue. This isn't even Park Service property."

The inflatable is on the strand now and Wilson, blinking, running a bewildered hand through his hair, steps into the firelight. "Jesus," he groans, as if to himself, "what the shit is going on here?" And then, to the big killer, the one with the mouth and the boar's tusks shoved up under his hatband as if he were some sort of aborigine (and why not stick them through his nose, Dave's thinking, wouldn't that be more appropriate?): "Who are you people?"

Alma, ignoring them, turns to the big man. "Call the Coast Guard," she says. "And the ranger station."

"What," Dave breaks in, "Ranger Rick to the rescue? Again?" He can't believe what he's hearing. "I told you— you've got no authority here. None. Zero. Zilch. And you"— raking the loudmouth with his eyes—"you want to start giving orders, let's see your badge. Where is it, huh? You're not even an American citizen. You're just some hired gun, some shithead with about as much respect for life as, as—"

"Shut it," the man says, and now the gun, the pistol, is in his hand.

"I'm making a citizen's arrest"—Alma glances round the circle of faces, her mouth set, eyes hard. "Until the proper authorities get here and we can—"

It's Suzanne who cuts her off. She throws back her head and shrieks, all the misery and frustration and horror of the day pouring out of her in a long shattering fusillade of helplessness and rage. "Don't you understand? There's been an accident!" she cries, her shoulders heavy with the burden of it, all her facial muscles pulled tight till she could be wearing a latex mold of her own face. "Somebody got hurt, a girl, she, she—"

"She's dead." Toni Walsh, the cigarette at her lips, finally adds her voice to the mix. She's come up silently to stand beside Dave, her shoulders hunched, strands of salmon hair laminated to the side of her throat just above the seasickness patch. She shoots him a look of impatience— worse: of hate, of doom—then addresses Alma. "You're going to need to call the coroner."

The night is like the first night the island ever saw, still, enveloping, silent but for the regular thump of the waves, the sky close and breathing out its moisture, life-giving and sustaining. Wild night. Night apart. Night on the island. They've all had a look at the motionless form encased in the wrapped-up tube of the poncho like a nymph in its chrysalis, a nymph that will never emerge, death come down to sit amongst them and quiet them. Wilson passes round a thermos of hot coffee overloaded with sugar, the big man's radio crackles at his lips, people recede into the gloom and emerge again with gnarled lengths of driftwood to toss on the fire. Ten minutes have sifted by. The hunters—almost human—have shared around their energy bars and jerky with Cammy and Suzanne, whose chewing muscles work greedily in the firelight despite their shock and grief, and while Dr. Alma and the big man stand apart with their radio, Dave gathers Wilson and Josh to him on the far side of the fire, out of hearing, because his mind's been racing the whole time, the fury in him, the rage, held in reserve for just this moment, the moment of decision, of extraction, of getting the fuck out of here before the Coast Guard shows up and damn the consequences.

"I don't care," he says, spitting it out, "they can shoot me if they want. I dare them to. I tell you, they've got no right to hold us here." He kicks angrily in the sand at his feet. "It's kidnapping, you know that? Forcibly detaining somebody. You know what a court of law would do to these clowns?"

Wilson, the faintest shade of the barrio creeping into his voice: "But it looks bad. I mean, who would've thought? This girl—Kelly, right? The one with the PETA thing?"

"Yeah, it sucks," he says, staring into the darkness out beyond them. "No, worse than that. It's a disaster. A tragedy. And we all feel it, don't we? But it's our problem—right, Josh? You with me?—and it's for us to deal with it. An accident, that's all. We were hiking and there was an accident."

Josh says nothing. He's there, though, compact, gleaming, his face buttery and soft in the glow of the fire, the tough guy reduced. The thing is, can he be counted on?

"You know what we're going to do? We're going to take Kelly to Cottage Hospital, that's what we're going to do.

She died in an accident, it's nobody's fault. And what we were doing out here today is nobody's business but ours, am I right?"

The fire cracks and hisses. Smoke, a dead stinking pall of it, runs at their faces, then sweeps back to chase away on the breeze. After a moment, sotto voce, Wilson says, "I'm with you, man. We don't have to listen to these *pendejos*, I mean, who are they?"

"Exactly."

Then they're moving, he, Wilson and Josh, downwind of the fire and across the short stretch of sand to where the body lies wrapped in its dark winding sheet. They have it—her—in hand, him in front, Josh in the middle, Wilson at her feet, the weight staggering, concentrated, enormous, and they actually make it across the beach to the inflatable before one of the hunters shouts out, "Hey, what're you doing?" and everybody's shoving in all over again, even the dogs.

His wet boots are wetter suddenly, socks squelching, surf foaming at his shins. It's hard to keep hold of her, hard to see what they're doing, the black rubber bottom of the dinghy like a hole cut out of the earth—like a grave, that's what he's thinking—but he never hesitates. "What do you think you're doing?" the hunter elaborates, but the three of them, wet all over again, ignore him, laying their burden in the bottom of the boat while Wilson takes hold of the line to drag the boat into the water.

This is not a matter of reason, reflection, debate. He's had it, stacked right up to his ears with it, and when one of them puts a hand on his arm he flings it off so violently he has to stagger to keep his balance. "Get your fucking hands off me," he says, and his voice is low and even because he's ready for anything now, beyond threat or calculation or even caring. "What are you going to do, shoot me? Go ahead, you motherfucker. Because this is our problem, this is our"—he hesitates, wanting to say comrade but thinking better of it—"friend here. Kelly. And we're going to do what we were going to do before you"—he slashes his arm in Alma's direction—"and your hired goons butted in."

"You can't—" she sputters, and she even takes a step toward him, toward the surf, but whatever the prohibition is she can't seem to find the words to frame it.

"Can't what?" he throws back at her, shouting now, enraged. "Live, breathe, save the lives of innocent animals, get in our own boat with the body of this girl you've never laid eyes on in your life? What, leave your stinking fucking island?"

They're ranged round him in silhouette, the bonfire leaping behind them. The surf is like ice. The dinghy scrapes at the sand, the line tight, Josh pitching in now to get her afloat. He doesn't bother to say *Try me* or repeat that they have no authority here because whatever he might have to say is just wasted breath at this point. "Get in the boat, Josh," he says. "And anybody else who's coming."

The surf sucks out. He's thigh deep now. "Cammy?" he shouts into the darkness. "Suzanne? You coming?" He gives it a beat, two. "Okay then," he announces, "it's your choice. We're out of here."

And when one of the hunters, he can't tell which in the dark, comes for him, he's ready, more than ready, the son of a bitch, the blind stupid pathetic interfering excuse for a human being, wrestling him down in the surf till they're both soaked through, and in that crucial moment when one or the other of them is either going to have to relax his grip or drown, he breaks free to heave himself up onto the lip of the inflatable and kick the lurching white ball of the man's face with every particle of hate he can summon. They're cursing him. He's cursing back. "Go ahead and shoot!" he screams. "Go ahead!" And then the engine catches, the boat swings round, and the sea rushes in to take all the burden out from under him.

The release is short-lived. As soon as they shove off they're in trouble all over again. The seas are up because of the storm, the dinghy lifted and pounded in the breakers and a furious keening wind rising up out of nowhere to rake them down the length of the beach and away from the receding lights of the boat. The shoreline is black, the water blacker still. There are rocks out there, shoals, channels where the current can suck you in and flip you end over end in a heartbeat. Dave knows it and Wilson knows it too. Wilson's fighting the tiller, the engine straining in a high continuous whine, and it's as if they're dead in the water. Minutes stretch out and snap, one after the other, until at long last they're heading into the wind and the lights of the *Paladin* stabilize on the horizon and then begin to rush up on them. No one says a word, though Dave is seething, half a beat from shoving Wilson aside and taking the tiller himself, and when they get there, when finally they're alongside the boat, the dinghy keeps lurching away from the stern while the *Paladin* rises and pitches at exactly the wrong moment till his nerves are stripped raw, and it's all they can do to haul Kelly up on deck and stow the dinghy without killing themselves.

It's all bad. He's in a panic to get under way before the Coast Guard shows up, and how he's going to avoid them out in the channel—or worse, back at the marina, where they'll be sure to be waiting—he doesn't know . . . but then, he keeps telling himself, he hasn't done anything wrong. A girl dies tragically out in the middle of nowhere and you bring her back, isn't that the way it's supposed to be? You don't stand around with your hands in your pockets listening to Alma Boyd Takesue, you drag her out of the water and rush her to the hospital so they can pronounce her dead and take it from there. Maybe he does want the Coast Guard, after all. Definitely, once they're at sea, he's going to have to put out a distress call. Make it official. Do things by the book. Show that they're not trying to hide anything whether they were trespassing or not because the only thing that matters here is getting medical attention for this girl . . . right? But why is he making speeches to himself? And why isn't the anchor up? Why isn't he at the helm? Why, for shit's sake, aren't they under way?

All three of them are dripping wet, that's why, shivering, banging into each other like zombies as they fling themselves around the cabin, stripping off their wet clothes and tearing through the locker for anything dry—a blanket, a sweatshirt, shorts, socks, a windbreaker so stained with oil it's translucent. Their faces are drawn. They won't look each other in the eye. The cabin has never seemed so cramped and inadequate. "We need to get out of here," he keeps saying but he can't seem to stop shivering. The electric heater's up full. Wilson's already at the stove, boiling water for tea. "Or hot cocoa, man, what do you want? Josh? Dave?"

Then, finally—it can't have been more than ten minutes, fifteen at the outside—he's at the helm, the anchor's up and he's nosing the bow out to sea. Everything lurches, the waves hitting them broadside, then they're stern to the wind and cruising east along the atramental flank of the island, nothing before them and nothing behind, not even the glow of the bonfire. Warmth trickles up from below. He's in dry clothes now, wearing a sweater over a flannel shirt buttoned right up to the collar, but his hair, wet still, chills the back of his neck like a cold dead hand laid there, like Kelly's hand. After a while the scent of hot chocolate begins to waft up the stairs and he swallows involuntarily, suddenly aware of how hungry he is. In the next moment Wilson and Josh are in the cockpit with him and he's got a mug of hot chocolate cradled between his thighs and a handful of saltines smeared with peanut butter vibrating on the seat beside him.

"Shit," Wilson offers, "what a day, huh?"

"Worst day of my life," Josh says in a hollow monotone. "I still can't believe it."

"Me either." Wilson's leaning forward over his knees, adulterating his cocoa with a splash of no-name scotch out of a pint bottle. "Josh?" He hoists the bottle, gives it a wag.

"Sure," Josh murmurs, holding out his cup even as the boat bucks and half the liquid rides up out of it to slosh over the deck. And carpet.

"Dave?"

"No, not for me. I've got to keep my head clear here, because we're in the shit now—in so many ways I can't begin to tell you. Soon as we're in cell phone range I'm calling Sterling."

"What, the lawyer?"

He's picturing Sterling sitting down to dinner with his dried-up stick of a wife, droning on in his dead-and-buried court voice about whatever case he's on—or maybe he's telling jokes, mixing a shaker of martinis, getting down in some dance club with a woman in a low-cut top with her boobs hanging out who definitely isn't his wife, who can say? He doesn't know a thing about the man, except that he bills like an extortionist.

"Yeah," he says, "I need to find out where we stand. I mean, I don't really feature the Coast Guard boarding us, you know what I mean? We've got to put out a Mayday at some point, but I'm thinking that's when we see the lights of the harbor in about"—he checks his watch—"two and a quarter hours maybe. And then they can do whatever they want, take our statements, unload the body, bring in the detectives and the coroner and whoever else. In fact, I want Sterling there. On the fucking dock."

"But we're not in trouble"—Josh's voice is so reduced it's barely audible over the thrash of the waves and the steady throb of the engine—"are we?"

Wilson shakes his head. "No way. They're going to want a statement—we're witnesses, right? Or you are. You saw her die, right? So it's like a car accident or something, where you witnessed it and the cops want to know who, where, when and why, that sort of thing."

There's a sudden punch at the bow, a rogue wave moving out of sync with the prevailing seas, and they're weightless a moment before slamming down into the trough and rising back up again, the boat shivering along its length. And then once more, the slap, the rise, the plunge, only this time, on the way down something slams at the cabin door and it takes them all a moment to realize what it is.

"We got to bring her in," Josh says, staggering to his feet.

"Leave her," Dave says, thinking of the mess, of the sand and the wet and whatever fluids might be leaking out of her at this point. Aren't you supposed to loose your bowels when you die? Didn't he read that someplace?

"Leave her? This is a human being we're talking about."

"A former human being."

"You son of a bitch. Fuck you. Cammy's right. If it wasn't for you—"

He's on the cusp of getting up out of the chair and laying into this baby-faced whining kid who might as well be in diapers he's so pathetic because who does he think he is—who the *fuck* does he think he is—to talk to him like that, when Wilson, the voice of reason, intercedes. "What if she goes overboard?"

"She's not going anywhere."

"But if she does—"

They're right. Of course they're right. Lose the body and it looks as if they're covering up, as if there's been foul play, murder even. Suddenly he's ashamed of himself for even thinking this way. Until today he's never seen a dead person in his life, and here he is, plotting like a criminal, like one of the killers themselves. "Yeah, okay," he says finally. "Bring her in. But don't lay her on any of the bunks or the couch either. Just on the deck, okay?"

The door flings open on a smell of the open sea and in the next moment Josh is backing his way in, dragging Kelly along with him, but he can't manage it all on his own and Wilson gets up to help. Dead weight. The expression comes home to him in a way it never has, never could have, until now. She's half-in the door, half-out. The boat dips, rises. There's a smell of something else now, of feces, urine. And then the poncho, a cheap rubberized thing not worth the cost of it, already peeling in places, splits down the side as Josh, bending to the task, tries to get a purchase on it, and there she is, Kelly, sprawled across the stain-resistant carpet, staring up at him all over again.

The digital display on the dash of the car reads 2:15 by the time he swings into the driveway and flicks the remote to roll back the gate. He's so exhausted he can barely turn the wheel, headlights raking over the lawn and nothing there, no humped-over thieves of the night or overfed housecats on the prowl, just grass, lush and deep and evenly cut, and when he pulls up to the garage and kills the engine he can only sit there, incapable of mustering the strength to push open the door. He can picture the entry hall, the steps up to the bedroom, his bed with its cool sheets and over-stuffed pillows and the off-white bedspread his mother crocheted for him, but he remains where he is, frozen there, listening to the heat ticking out of the engine till the motion sensor over the garage abruptly kills the light. Thinking of Anise—he's got to call her, no matter how late it is—and then of the dogs, locked up all this time in the house, he pushes open the door and the light clicks back on again. Then he's out on the pavement, standing in his own driveway, at his own house, safe behind the locked gate. He breathes in the night air, lets his head roll back on the fulcrum of his neck so that the sky comes to life above him, the stars on full display and the rain blown out to sea. If it even rained here. Everything is silent, but for the faint muffled whimper of the dogs at the front door.

Of course, there's shit in the entry hall but he's got no one to blame for that but himself—he thought he would have been back six or seven hours ago. The dogs are there to greet him, thrashing round his legs before slipping guiltily out into the night, and he leaves the door ajar and goes into the kitchen to see if they need food. Their kibble bowl is empty. Ditto the water bowl. He pours dry food out of the bag, refills the water bowl from the tap, and then leans back against the counter, utterly drained. His mouth is dry, his lips cracked. He pours himself a glass of water and then, unbidden, the idea of food steals into his head— there's Asiago in the reefer, tomato, avocado, half a loaf of oatnut bread—and right after, the thought of liquor. A shot of something to deaden him. The liquor cabinet gives up its glints of glass, brown, clear and green, and he thinks first of tequila before he remembers the white rum in the freezer. The first shot clears his head, the second starts up his heart again. The sandwich is in the microwave and the dogs clacking their nails on the tile floor and noisily lapping water when he picks up the phone and punches in Anise's number.

It rings three times and goes to her voice mail. There's a maddening pause followed by a repeated guitar figure and her strong soaring soprano singing distantly in the background before her recorded voice delivers the standard greeting: "Hi, this is Anise. I'm not here right now. Please leave a message at the beep. Or tone. Or whatever."

He dials her home phone and lets it ring, seven, eight, nine times, then hangs up and tries the cell again. Finally, just before the recording clicks in, she answers. "You know what time it is?" Her voice is drugged, sleep-thickened.

"I just got back."

A pause. "Just?"

"It was a fucking nightmare. The worst. You can't imagine—you're lucky you weren't there, you were the smart one."

"You didn't get caught, did you?"

"Worse, much worse."

"What?" All the lethargy is gone from her voice now. He can picture her sitting up in bed, her eyes squinted and her lips pursed in concentration. "Did you wreck the boat or somebody fell overboard or what?"

"Somebody died."

"Died? What do you mean died?"

"Kelly." He's angry suddenly, angry again. All this because of some spastic uncoordinated overweight college girl who couldn't keep her balance to save her life, literally. Carrying a placard around in a parking lot is one thing and going into the backcountry is another. He doesn't know what he was thinking. He should have stuck with Wilson. Just him and Wilson. And no reporters either. "She's dead," he says. "She fell"—and he's seeing her all over again, the drained flesh and disarranged limbs, flat white where everything else was dun and gray and green—"out on the island. At Willows. There was nothing we could do . . ."

There's a muffled exclamation on the other end of the line, a self-reflexive curse, muttered low. "Were the police—? Or the Coast Guard?"

He doesn't want to get into it, doesn't even know why he called. Or no: he called because he needs to hear her voice, needs comfort—needs, above all, to get this out of him, because no matter how exhausted he is he won't be able to sleep, he knows that already. "I want you to come over."

"Come over? I can't come over. I was in the middle of sleeping, I've got work tomorrow. I'm singing at Cold Spring, don't you remember? The early gig? Five p.m.?"

There were two cop cars waiting at the marina when he pulled into the slip, lights revolving as if they'd just made a traffic stop, and it was the Coast Guard escorting him in for good measure. An ambulance was there too, its own lights chopping up the scene in alternating slices of amber and red, and a rotating cast of gapers and gawkers and half-dead bums roused from the bushes by the prospect of a show. Sterling, looking alert and dressed officially in three-piece suit and tie, kept the police at bay—and kept him from spending the night in jail on a report of criminal trespass radioed in by Alma Boyd Takesue, through Ranger Richard Melman, on behalf of her colleague

Annabelle Yuell of the Nature Conservancy. All three of them, even Wilson, were cited and released on their promise to appear in court, at the same time Sterling, a fine sheen of bluster and outrage on his face, insisted on their filing a police report citing Alma and the foreign hunters on the grounds of assault and battery, false imprisonment and intentional infliction of emotional distress in preventing them from taking the injured—that is, dead—girl to the hospital. Alma was on the island. Sterling was right there standing at the desk in the police station, immovable, his face carved of stone. The report was filed. Josh went home. Wilson went home. Dave went home.

"I need to talk to you," he says.

"Tomorrow."

"You don't understand—we're screwed, it's over. Toni Walsh—you should have seen the look on her face. She's going to crucify me."

There's a silence on the other end of the line.

"Come over," he says.

"Sleep on it, Dave."

The finality in her voice infuriates him. "No"—he's shouting suddenly, and the dogs, alarmed, back away from their dish in a scramble of frantic clacking paws—"you fucking sleep on it! I need you. Don't you hear me?"

A pause. Then, utterly unruffled, calm as a sedative, her voice seeps back to him in a slow drip of unforgiving syllables: "Good night, Dave. See you in the morning."

He wakes, embittered, just after noon. At what hour he finally did fall off to sleep after lying there staring at the ceiling and listening to every least crepitation of the house as if it were amplified ten times over, he can't say, but the moment he blinks open his eyes, all the misery and dislocation of the previous day rush in to repossess him. The morning's gone. If Anise called—or Wilson or Sterling or anybody else, the AP wanting a statement, the *Hog Butchers'*

Journal, Harley Meachum telling him all four stores burned to the ground simultaneously—he didn't hear the phone ring. And he's too sore, mentally and physically, even to think about checking his messages. Fuck them, that's what he's thinking. Fuck the world. Fuck them all.

Barefoot, in a pair of shorts and a flannel shirt, he goes to the door to let the dogs out and continues on down the drive, walking gingerly, to retrieve the morning paper (which will have nothing in it yet, he knows that, Toni Walsh stuck out there on the island till it was too late to do anything about it, but he can't help scanning the thing nonetheless). No, no mention. But tomorrow will be a different story. Tomorrow the shitstorm starts in all over again, a hurricane of it, Force 10 winds, and he's wondering vaguely if he should write up his own version of events and post it on the FPA website as a counterweight to whatever Toni Walsh is going to lay on him, when he hears the phone ringing in the depths of the house.

He's up the front steps and back inside, snatching up the phone in the living room on the fourth ring—and wincing, wincing too, because he must have pulled every muscle in his body out there yesterday, a pure searing jolt of pain rocketing from his left knee to his groin so that he has to fling himself down in the nearest chair and grab hold of the inside of his thigh and squeeze till it passes. "Hello?" he snaps, expecting Anise.

"Is this Dave I'm talking to?"

He doesn't recognize the voice, a man's voice, low and whispery, jangling with some sort of unreconstructed redneck accent. "That's right," he says. "Who's this?"

The name means nothing to him. It flies right out of his head. He needs coffee, eggs, toast, something substantial on his stomach. It takes him a moment to register what the man on the phone, a friend of an associate of a friend of Wilson's, is trying to communicate. "I can git you what you want," the man says. "As many as you want. Only question is price. Thirty apiece? That sound okay to you?"

What he's talking about, and it comes to Dave in a flash, is rattlesnakes—the western rattlesnake, *Crotalus viridis*, to be exact. He's too surprised—or no, overwhelmed by the timing—to respond.

"You there? Can you hear me? I say this is Everson Stiles, from Wellspring? In Texas?"

"Yeah," he says, recovering himself. "Yeah, okay. Yeah, I hear you. I'm interested. Very interested."

It was months ago, around the time he'd gone out to the island with the raccoons, that he'd asked Wilson to put out some feelers for him, and this was the contact he'd come up with. Everson Stiles, formerly pastor of an evangelical Christian church that believed in bringing the serpent right into the house of worship. Every year there would be a rattlesnake roundup and the parishioners would show up with burlap sacks of them and roll around on the floor in their midst, speaking in tongues and prevailing upon the Lord to keep them from harm. But the Lord, apparently, let them down, and people were bitten—one, a ten-year-old girl, fatally. There was a lawsuit and it went against the church and that was the end of the practice and the church too.

"Plus expenses. Travel, I mean. Gas money."

"What, all the way from Texas?"

There's a brief snort of laughter on the other end of the line. "No, all that's done with. Now I'm in Ojai. Right up the street from you. And I tell you, this is the time to get 'em, when they're denned up for the winter? Big balls of 'em, all wound up together. You wait till they emerge in spring and it's basically one snake at a time, and then the price's going to go up."

He's trying to envision it, snakes in a bag, flexing and roiling, three bags, four, laid out on the concrete floor in the garage, and he's going to want other things too—more raccoons, rabbits maybe, gophers, what about gophers? "Sounds fine," he says, feeling himself expand with the exactitude of that vision, rabbits in cages twitching their noses, thumping their feet, giving him a wide anxious walleyed look. And not the white ones you get as a kid at Easter, but jackrabbits, big rangy wild-hearted things honed for survival. "No, the price is fine, and I want them, I do. Definitely. But listen, this isn't a good time—can I get back to you?"

The instant he hangs up the phone rings, startling him out of his reverie. It's Anise, asking if he slept well, and his mood comes crashing down all over again.

"You know I didn't. And no thanks to you."

"Look, why don't you pick me up for lunch and fill me in on the details, then we can go up to the gig together, all right?"

He says nothing, hating her.

"I can make an announcement," she offers, and he can picture her in her kitchen, chewing on the end of a pencil or a breadstick, everything in its place, gleaming and safe. "About the girl and what happened, what we're up against. Or flyers, we can do flyers, if you want."

"You don't know what I've been through," he says finally, sounding soft and self-pitying in his own ears, giving in. "You can't begin to imagine."

•

The Wreck of the *Anubis*

W hen she gets off the phone with Maria Campos, the lawyer Freeman Lorber recommended, she's so wrought up she has to go directly into the kitchen and pour herself a glass of *sake* just to keep from collapsing like a vacant suit of clothes. She takes a long steady drink, staring out into the sodden pit of the yard, the ferns bowed by the recent storm, the lawn a swamp, the eucalyptus shedding bark in long tattered strips. The sun is shining, at least there's that, but the condo feels alien and sterile and everything in it, from the woodblock prints her grandmother Takesue left her to the forest-green leather couch with the cherry frame that cost her a month and a half's salary to the stereo and the potted Dracena and even the Micah Stroud CDs stacked on the bookshelf, seems as if it belongs to someone else. Tim is gone. And without Tim, the place is empty, abandoned, useless. For a moment she feels as if she's going to cry, and she doesn't want to cry, not over Tim or Dave LaJoy or anybody else, and she has to press the cold glass to her forehead, hold it there right between her eyebrows like a compress, till the moment passes.

What Maria Campos has just told her is so outrageous she can't process it—a joke, a crazy sick perverted joke made all the worse because it's no joke at all but the hard truth of what the world is and what she's facing. Personally. Not as Projects Coordinator and Director of Information Services of the Channel Islands National Park who's only doing her job and fighting day and night to improve things and give the ecosystem a chance to recover, flourish, bloom, but as an individual before the law. In the morning—tomorrow, Monday morning, her trip to the island cut short because of the incident at Willows so that she got only the single day in the field, as if that isn't punishment enough—she has to report to the Santa Barbara County courthouse on a warrant stemming from what happened out on the island or have the police come get her. Incredibly. As if she were the criminal and the true criminals the law-abiding citizens. Even worse, arrest warrants have been issued for Frazier, Clive and A.P., meaning that they'll have to be pulled off the hunt for a day at least, maybe more—and just at the most crucial time.

"You can't be serious," she'd said, the phone like a grenade about to explode in her hand.

"I know it's upsetting," Maria returned, her voice firm, business-like, as if all this were nothing, the commonest thing in the world, "but you have to appear on this warrant whether the charges are legitimate or not. But believe me"—and her tone hardened—"we'll get these charges dismissed and see that the bad guys get what's coming to them. All right? Don't you even think about it. Just put it out of your head."

"But I've never—I mean, I've never even had a speeding ticket."

"I know, I know. But just let it go. I'll take care of everything, okay?" She paused, waiting for Alma to protest, then, in a softer tone, she said, "Listen, why don't you go take a walk on the beach, go to a movie, anything. What about Tim? Have Tim take you out to dinner."

There was so much wrong here Alma couldn't begin to put the pieces back in place. All she said, her voice dropping to a murmur, was "Okay."

"It's nothing, I'm telling you. Just a desperate maneuver on their part. You'll see. Trust me."

And now, the phone back in its cradle, the dry cold rumor of the *sake* lingering on her palate and her mind drifting out of focus, she lifts the glass to her lips and then abruptly sets it down again. What is she thinking? She can't drink. Not at all, not a drop. And she had alcohol yesterday, only yesterday, as if she were some out-of-control knocked-up teenager in the ghetto. She upends the glass in the sink, thinking fetal alcohol syndrome, cognitive impairment, mental retardation, and her hand is shaking when she sets it down again. She's got to get a grip. Got to be strong. In command. The only thing is, she doesn't feel anything but weak and confused and hurt.

It's just past ten in the morning. Though she slept in the boat on the way back, it was a hazy intermittent sleep, and every time she opened her eyes Toni Walsh and the two girls were staring at her as if she were their jailer and they were only watching for the chance to make their escape, as if they could fly or walk on water, and now she can feel the tiredness seeping into her, an exhaustion so complete it deadens her legs till they feel as if they're detached from her, and she has to pull out a chair at the kitchen table and sit heavily. For a long while she just sits there staring out the window, and then, inevitably, humiliatingly, uselessly, she reaches for the phone and dials Tim's number.

She's expecting nothing. He's on the Farallones, in the field, where there's no cell service—she knows that as well as anybody. But then maybe he's gone into San Francisco, for supplies, for R & R, and he's just arrived, just stepped off the boat, which is why he hasn't called her yet, and he'll answer, he's got to answer, because she wants to hear his voice, has to hear it . . . Her stomach turns over. One knee begins jittering under the table. But she's expecting nothing and nothing is what she gets. The phone rings twice, there's a distant faint click, and then the line goes dead.

In the morning she puts on her navy blue suit over a white silk blouse fresh from the cleaner's, slips into her stockings and heels, and appears in court, Maria Campos at her side, and nothing much happens, except that she wastes an entire morning sitting there listening to one case after another until she gets her two minutes in front of the judge, who barely glances at her before releasing her on bond to appear again the following month. When she finally does get to the office, Alicia is nowhere to be seen—an emergency came up and she's taking one of her personal days, that's what Suzie Jessup, in the adjoining office, tells her—and there's a sea of paperwork to get through and a string of e-mails half a mile long. Work. It's what she needs—it's what absorbs her—and it isn't until half-past two, when she's beginning to feel the urge for a tall iced tea with lemon and maybe a bite to eat, that she leaves her desk and heads down the stairs to the walkway along the marina, thinking to get something at the Docksider. She's strolling along absently, trying to clear her head, when suddenly she catches herself. There's something different here, something out of the ordinary, but what is it? She scans the walkway (tourists, strolling), the Park Service building (tourists, milling, passing in and out to gape at the relief map of the islands and the other first-floor exhibits) and finally the broad expanse of the parking lot (sunshine glinting off the glass and chrome of the cars parked in their neatly aligned rows) before it hits her: the protestors are gone.

It's astonishing. As if she'd awakened in her concrete hut in Guam to step outside and see the jungle vanished overnight. *The protestors are gone.* No more chants, no more defamatory signs, no more graffiti. Have they given up? Finally? At long last? The thought comes to her—the happy thought, rushing through her in a surge of exhilaration—that they're gone because their motive force is gone. Because Dave LaJoy is behind bars or out on bail or lurking in an alley someplace pulling the hood of his sweatshirt up over his head like a mafioso or a disgraced senator. He's made the fatal misstep. He's done. Finished. And the pig hunt is progressing so far ahead of schedule that by the time he does surface again the project will be over and done with and he'll have nothing to protest. Won't that be sweet?

The idea fills her with light. Everything around her seems to glow as if it's been re-created from dross, new and shining and bright. The mood carries her all the way up the walk to the Docksider, and she finds herself nodding at people she vaguely recognizes and pausing to smile over a young mother and her toddler sharing a floating pink cloud of cotton candy, but then, mounting the stairs, she feels the heaviness creeping over her again, the weight inside her as immovable as a brick—how she'd love to tell Tim the news, radiate her joy, share the sweet taste of victory and vindication. But there is no Tim and the lunch crowd has gone back to work and the place feels vacant and vaguely depressing. She's just one for lunch, just one, thanks, and when the hostess tries to steer her to an undersized table in the middle of the room, she insists on a booth by the window that's usually reserved for parties of four or more, and why not? She's tired of being pushed around. Tired of everything. Just tired.

Staring at the menu, trying to decide whether she'll have a cup or bowl of the clam chowder with her crab Louie, it takes her a moment to realize that the Korean woman from the variety store downstairs is standing there beside the table. Mrs. Kim. She has a newspaper in her hand, the *Press Citizen*, and she's holding it out in offering. "You have seen this yet?" she asks.

Alma hasn't seen it. She was in such a state this morning, what with the tension of having to get to court and worrying whether she could leave the blouse untucked so as to hide the fact that her jacket would no longer button across her midsection, that she'd forgotten all about it. Half the time she runs right over the paper anyway, remembering it only when she pulls into the driveway at night to see it lying there scuffed and torn. Which doesn't really matter because it's a rag in any case, blustering and cocksure and half-competent and on the wrong side of just about everything she believes in. Tim used to call it the *Press Critizen*.

"No," Alma says. "No, why?"

Mrs. Kim, an erect tall woman in her mid-seventies who once startled Alma by remarking, after a casual exchange of greetings, *You Nihon-jin, eh?*, lays the paper on the table and with a smile of complicity gently pushes it to her. "You going to like what they print today. Free copy. You take."

Before the thank-you is out of her mouth, she fastens on the headline: *Death on Santa Cruz.* And below it: *Questionable Tactics on Part of FPA Lead to Death of City College Sophomore* by Toni Walsh.

Mrs. Kim backs away slowly, giving an abbreviated bow, which Alma, seated, returns as best she can. "No more protestor, eh?" the old woman says, winking. "Bad for business anyway. You business, my business too."

Alma, heart pounding, smiles up at her. "You can say that again."

The article isn't everything she could have hoped for, but clearly, for the first time since all this began, the newspaper of record in Santa Barbara is attempting to distance itself from LaJoy and his gang of crazies. He's still seen as a crusader and TNC and the Park Service as the enemy, but Toni Walsh—muddied, bloodied and thoroughly provoked—cuts him loose, sounding more like an editorialist than a reporter:

Activist and local businessman David Francis LaJoy, 47, of Montecito, founder and president of the animal rights organization For the Protection of Animals, was arrested late Saturday evening after a bizarre and tragic incident on Santa Cruz Island. Mr. LaJoy led a group of his followers in an alleged attempt to sabotage the Park Service's campaign to exterminate the island's feral hogs after the failure of a last-minute injunction to stop the hunt. Members of the party claim that he proceeded recklessly despite the severe weather conditions that struck over the weekend. In attempting a dangerous climb at the direction of Mr. LaJoy in an area of extensive flooding, Kelly Ann Johansson, 19, of Goleta, fell to her death.

Mr. LaJoy was charged with criminal trespass, vandalism and conspiracy. The parents of the deceased, Ronald and Eva Johansson, also of Goleta, contacted by phone, had no comment, but a family friend, who asked to remain anonymous, states that they are planning to file a wrongful death suit against Mr. LaJoy.

She reads the article twice through, feeling better now, much better. When the food comes, she leaves the newspaper spread out before her so she can run her eyes over the headline and the murky file photo of the pier at Prisoners' Harbor they've dug out to accompany it. The chowder is delicious, rich with clams, potatoes, butter, the crab Louis the best she's ever had. She finds herself wiping the plate clean with chunks of the hot sourdough bread the management prides itself on and she winds up eating too much, or it feels that way anyway. When finally she looks up, it's well past three, and despite the lift the iced tea gave her, she can barely push herself up from the chair. She's sleepy, exhausted, but even as the idea of taking off early comes into her head, she dismisses it.

Once she's outside, she forces herself to pick up the pace, snapping her knees in a martial stride and taking in great lungfuls of sea air, the marina tranquil, the parking lot just a parking lot once again. The breeze is soft and fragrant, wafting up out of the south in a hint of the season to come, and she takes a moment to stand there on the patch of lawn out back and turn her face to it while the custodian emerges from the rear door to shake out his mop and a half a dozen starlings squabble over a spill of French fries on the walk. Then it's back to work, her mood darkening again when she sees Alicia's empty chair, and she settles in at her desk thinking that when Alicia comes up for evaluation, she's going to have to act on her conscience. That's all there is to it. And she's sorry if she's going to hurt anybody's feelings.

She winds up working till six, trying to make up for wasting the morning in court, though of course she would have been out on the island still if it weren't for what happened at Willows, so she can't be too hard on herself. She's thinking about that, about the scene on the island, about the dead girl, as she locks the door behind her, makes her way down the steps and crosses the deserted lot to her car. Coming up the beach with the men and the dogs, she'd felt powerful, in charge, and at first, seeing the humped and useless form flung down there in the sand beneath the wet poncho, she'd thought it was a pig, one of the dead pigs they'd pulled out of a ravine and were planning to spirit back to the coast and put on display. Her blood sang in her ears. Removing anything from the island, animal, vegetable or mineral, was a crime, and here they were, caught out at it, and it wasn't enough that they were trespassing and trying to interfere with a project that had already cost taxpayers millions of dollars, but they were trying to possess wildlife as well, steal it, own it, use it, when as anybody knows all wildlife throughout the country, on public or private land, is the property of the government. She was savage, worked up, thrilling with the joy of nailing them, finally nailing them, when a knot flared in the fire and the form beneath the poncho became something else altogether.

Traffic is heavy along the darkened freeway, an undulating river of soft rubicund taillights carrying her along in its flow. She flicks on the radio, listening first to the news, then switching to music, trying not to think of the dead girl, of Tim, of the child growing inside her and what she's going to tell people when she can hide it no longer. A song she loves comes on, one they hardly ever play on the radio—"I Came So Far for Beauty," a Leonard Cohen song in the Jennifer Warnes version—and she tries to sing along, but the words tumble past her and after the second chorus she falls silent.

Her first stop is at the grocery in the lower village—after that big lunch she doesn't need much: a piece of salmon (farmed, color added) and a bag of spinach to pop in the microwave—and then the video rental. It takes her a long while to pick something out, working her way through the current releases, most of which she and Tim saw in the theater when they came out, and then the comedies, which are uniformly puerile and funny by definition only, before finally drifting into the classics section and settling on an Ernst Lubitsch movie she's seen at least twice or maybe three times but not recently. The idea—the theme of the evening—is to keep it light, a little distraction, that's all, and then crawl up to bed and let the oblivion wash over her like a dark tide of nothing.

Fine. Super. But when she gets to the front door and inserts her key in the lock, she finds that it's already open. Which is strange, because she's not the sort of person who forgets to lock up. Not ever. For a moment, mentally retracing her steps from the time the alarm clock went off and she'd lurched out of bed in a panic till she left the house with a stale bagel smeared haphazardly with cream cheese, she tries to visualize herself at the door and turning the key in the lock, but the image won't come. All at once, she's afraid. There's been a series of break-ins in the neighborhood recently, in one of which a woman on Olive Mill Road—not three blocks from here—was attacked on surprising the thieves while they were rearranging the furniture so as to get at her oriental carpets. Very slowly, silently, like a thief herself, she turns the knob and reaches in a hand to flick on the hallway light.

She's poised on the doorstep, ready to bolt if need be, but when she gradually pushes the door open—all the way to the wall to be sure there's no one flattened behind it—she sees nothing but the familiar entry hall, the table there piled with outerwear, umbrellas, unread magazines and the three purses she's most tired of. "Hello?" she calls. "Anyone here?" And then, heart leaping, she thinks of

Tim. He's the one who can never remember to lock the door behind him—half the time he doesn't even know where his keys are. "Tim?" she calls, already foreseeing a reunion, Tim come back to surprise her, and wouldn't it be just like him to pop out of a dark corner and scare the wits out of her? "Tim, is that you?"

It isn't until she's inside, until she's made her way through the kitchen and living room and into the bedroom, that she begins to understand. Tim has been here, but he's here no longer. His things—everything, his bicycle, his books and video games, even his underwear and his T-shirt collection—are gone. Empty drawers, that's what he's left behind. Dust bunnies. An old pair of hightops with broken laces and soles worn through at the heels.

She has an impulse to pick up the sneakers, to touch them, lift them to her face, but she can't. Her legs go weak on her and she has to sit down right there where she is, on the corner of the bed. She folds her arms across her breasts and holds tight to her shoulders. She can't seem to lift her head. After a while, her hair begins to slip loose, the force of gravity teasing it away from her ears strand by strand till her face is in shadow. How long she sits there in that posture, she doesn't know, hopeless, slumped over, staring at her own two knees locked together in the navy blue twill of the suit she wore to court, the knees he stroked and caressed, the thighs, and where was he? He couldn't even call? Leave a note? Anything? Anything to acknowledge that they meant something to each other, that they'd slept in the same bed for five years? It was obscene. A joke. And wrong, deeply wrong.

Later, much later, when she finally does push herself up from the bed, she wanders the rooms like a patient on the surgical ward, shuffling her feet, brushing her fingers idly over the tables and chairs, looking for some trace of him. The note is there, has been there all along—she finds it in the kitchen, pinned beneath the whetstone on the cutting board. A single sheet of paper, folded over once. Inside are two keys—his house key and the spare key to the Prius. The note consists of three sentences:

> Alma:
> I love you, I'll always love you, but if you want to do this, you're on your own. You can keep the car because I won't be needing it—after the Farallones thing I'm thinking of going up north for the summer to work with this bird guy from the U. in Fairbanks. After that, we'll see.
> Tim

The smell of the salmon nauseates her but she forces herself to eat, the kitchen overlit, cheerless, absolutely still. Afterward, she puts on the movie to distract herself, but she can't follow it. It's just noise and motion. She hates Tim, that's what it is—she's just glad she found out what he's really like before it's too late. And she hates the baby inside her too—the embryo, the thing he implanted there, the life, always more life. She goes to bed when the clock tells her to but she can't sleep. She can't call her mother. She won't call Tim.

In the morning, it's worse. She must have dozed, must have dreamed, but all she can remember is lying flat on her back and staring at the ceiling while daylight came creeping into the room as if ashamed of itself. It's a workday, Tuesday, but she isn't going in to work. What she's going to do—what she has to do—is force herself out of bed so she can evacuate her bladder, go through the morning ritual of vomiting, washing her face and brushing the sourness out of her mouth, then pull on her clothes and drive downtown. To the clinic. She's twenty weeks pregnant, second trimester, and she hasn't been to the clinic, hasn't even driven past it, since Tim forced its existence on her back in November. She doesn't even know when they open or if anybody there will see her. Or more to the point: if they perform late-term abortions. What she does

400

know is that for an abortion at this stage—or procedure, as they call it—the fetus will have to be removed with instruments, with forceps, and then they'll use the suction device and finally a curette to scrape the lining of the uterus to make sure all the remaining tissue is removed. Her uterus is stuffed full, that's the problem, pressing at her abdomen, swelling it, pushing and puffing and shrinking her clothes, and they—whoever they are, somebody, a doctor in surgical scrubs—will empty it, make everything go away. That's the point of the procedure. That's the plan.

All she can think of as she swings out into traffic on the freeway is just that—making it all go away. She's put nothing on her stomach, not even coffee or dry toast. The nausea is there, scratching at the back of her throat as if to claw its way out. Cars bristle around her. The morning is bright, charged with sun, and the rains have greened the vegetation along the roadway, but she hardly notices. She sees the concrete, the steel and chrome of the cars, exhaust rising poisonously as the traffic inevitably stalls and brake lights flash up and down the line. Trucks. Minivans. Trash strewn along the median. And then, just as she's turning off the freeway, nature reasserts itself in the form of a gull sailing past toward the rippled brightness of the ocean, its wings as inevitable as the sea itself and the first creature that crawled out of it.

But the thing is, she can't find the place. And where is it—on Haley? Ortega? Or no: Garden. It's on Garden, isn't it? Angry, frustrated—not tearful, not yet—she tugs at the wheel, stymied by one-way streets and lights that seem to change randomly as if the whole city were in league against her, bicyclists careening across her field of vision from every direction, pedestrians throwing up a wall of human flesh at one intersection after another. She goes too fast, then too slow. Someone honks behind her. She's shuffling through her maps, none of which seems to show downtown Santa Barbara, and at the same time trying to prise her cell phone from the side pocket of her purse—she'll call them, that's what she'll do, call and ask directions, but she won't give anything away, won't ask for an appointment or to talk to the counselor she and Tim saw last time, just directions, that's all—when a woman in a tiny silver car shaped like a hair dryer edges out of a driveway right in front of her and she finds herself rolling into her, softly, sweetly, their bumpers meeting as gently as two pool balls kissing in the middle of a green felt table.

There's another honk behind her, a sudden startled screech of brakes. She snatches a look at the woman's face, a woman not much different from her, a woman in her thirties on her way to work with her hair brushed out and her eyes freshly made up. They study each other for an instant, the woman's expression running through its permutations from shock to embarrassment and then annoyance, anger and resignation, before they both simultaneously push open the doors of their cars and step out into the light. It is only then that Alma notices the two children in the backseat of the car—two small girls in school uniforms, belted in and craning their necks to see what the fuss is all about.

The *Anubis*, out of Santa Barbara, a thirty-seven-foot fiberglass cabin cruiser with twin Volvo diesel engines capable of doing fifty-two miles an hour on a flat sea, was purchased new in 2005 by a local couple trading up. Todd and Laurie Gilfoy, both in their late twenties, were experienced boaters, Todd having spent his summers aboard his father's boat, the *Dreamweaver*, for as far back as he could remember. They'd married on graduating from UCSB, he with a degree in business and she in elementary education, and he'd been co-managing his father's GMC dealership ever since, while she taught second grade at a private school in Hope Ranch. They had no children and liked to spend their weekends on the water, often in the company of other young couples. Santa Cruz Island was one of their favorite destinations, particularly the south shore, where there were fewer boaters to spoil the scenery. Both liked to drink. And when they drank, they often fell into a kind of competition for attention that could make things uncomfortable for their guests, particularly when those guests were trapped on a boat in the middle of the channel with nowhere to go.

On a clear Saturday in September, just a month after they'd purchased the boat and renamed it the *Anubis* (Laurie's idea—she was a devotee of Egyptian mythology and hoped someday to visit the great pyramids along the Nile), they invited two other couples to spend the weekend with them at Coches Prietos. Jonas and Sylvie Ryerson were close friends from their undergraduate days; Ed and Lucinda Cherwin, who were ten years older and lived next door to Jonas and Sylvie, were new acquaintances. They met at the marina at ten in the morning, the day perfect, temperatures in the mid-seventies with a light to moderate offshore breeze and swells of two to three feet. Laurie was there at the gate in a leopard-print bikini and pink Crocs to lead them to the boat, where Todd, wearing only a pair of cargo shorts, was waiting with a pitcher of margaritas. "Hey, you lubbers," he shouted. "I thought you'd never fucking get here. Come on, what are you waiting for?"

Before they were out of the harbor, Todd was pouring a second round of drinks, and when Lucinda Cherwin demurred with a smile, pointing out that it was only ten-fifteen in the morning and they had all day—and night, for that matter—Todd's face darkened. "Pussy," he snapped. And then, for the benefit of the group: "All pussies and lubbers go below. Right?" He leaned into Jonas, grinning tightly. "Am I right?"

What can be forgiven and what cannot? By the time they were five miles offshore, all four guests were in the cabin and Todd and Laurie were on deck in the cockpit, which was open to the sun, the canvas sides and hardtop having been stowed away, and they were arguing about something. Loudly. Violently. There was a punishing thump from the deck above and then Laurie came down the steps to the cabin, bleeding at the corner of her mouth. She was crying—at least Sylvie Ryserson claimed she was, but that was in retrospect—and she went into the head and locked the door and wouldn't let anyone in. In the meanwhile, Todd was gunning the boat, swerving tightly to port and then jagging to starboard for no reason except that he felt like it, and things started to rattle in the lockers and slide across the cabin floor. Lucinda Cherwin began to feel nauseous and her husband, Jonas at his side, went up on deck to try to reason with Todd, but Todd just sat at the helm, his face frozen, ignoring them.

"Will you listen to me?" The veins stood out in Ed's neck. He was a contractor, used to giving orders. "I tell you this is bullshit and I don't care what's going on between you and your wife but I want you to turn this thing around and take us back. Lucinda's sick. We're all sick. Do you hear me?"

Todd never even looked up. He just jerked at the wheel as if he were towing a water skier and threw them both against the rail.

"Todd, come on, man, this isn't right," Jonas pleaded, fighting for balance. They were old friends. He was trying to be reasonable. "You know it isn't. Now you're going to have to either straighten out or take us back—I mean, you've got Lucinda terrified—"

The upshot was that Todd finally did nose the boat around—at speed, in a savage looping turn that very nearly swamped them—and he didn't say a word all the way back to the marina. When they'd unloaded their bags, the engines running, the air blistered with the reek of diesel and the boat still rocking on its dying wake, Jonas, who was furious at this point, stepped off the boat and shouted up at him, "You can be a real fucking jerk, man, you know that?" Todd looked up from the console then—he had a drink in his hand, another drink—and gave them all the finger. "You're pussies," he roared so that people on neighboring boats swung round to stare at him, "pussies, that's all. All of you!"

No one looked back. If they had, they would have seen that Laurie was out on deck and that she was flying at him, cursing, her hair cartwheeling in the air and her fists drumming at his naked shoulder with its tattoo of a cartoon skunk wrapped round it, even as he shoved her away. What the point of contention was, no one ever knew. But the *Anubis*, on autopilot, went aground at China Beach ninety minutes later with no one aboard. Speculation has it that at some point in the crossing the violence escalated and the couple, locked together in a rage, tumbled overboard, while the boat, under speed, receded in the distance. The husband's body, without a mark on it aside from abrasions on both forearms, was recovered that evening in the vicinity of where the couple was presumed to have gone overboard. The wife wasn't found until the following winter, when her body, face up and still clad in the bikini, washed ashore at Prisoners' Harbor.

Alma would have missed the story, but for her mother. Her mother found it on the Internet, printed it out and mailed it to her without comment, the headline—*Body Found at Santa Cruz Island*—underlined in red.

Winter lingered through the end of March, but the rain fell off abruptly and the snowpack wound up being just eighty percent of normal, which meant water woes down the road. Meteorologists talked of the effects of global warming, as if any one season was reflective of anything other than itself, and the *Press Citizen* ran a number of alarmist articles about the shrinking polar caps, the rising sea level in the Seychelles and the threat of tsunami along the California coast—and all to the good if it got people thinking. Then it was April, a steady swelling sun climbing higher each day, and though Alma knew she should be praying for a last good soaking storm, she couldn't help feeling uplifted by the opportunity to walk the beach and get some sun on her face and legs. It felt especially good after the grimness of the winter and all she'd been through, the court business over with now, dissolved like a tablet in water, as if it had never been there at all. Maria Campos had proven true to her word—the judge dismissed all charges, not only against her but Frazier, Clive and A.P. too. And why? Because they had no merit, because they weren't real, and the district attorney saw that, knew that, and declined to prosecute.

April was followed by a gray May, and now, in the first week of June, the sun has vanished and the real gloom has set in. June gloom. That's the prevailing weather pattern this time of year, the marine layer lingering throughout the day, sometimes clearing in late afternoon, sometimes not at all. It's the time of seasonal affective disorders for people living along the coast, and she can relate to that, absolutely. This is a La Niña year, so the water is colder than usual, which results in a thicker soup hanging over the condo and the beach and most of downtown, not to mention her office and all of Ventura and Oxnard. The way she's dealing with it is to get out of the office as much as she possibly can, and for that the island has become her refuge—especially the main ranch, which gets more sun than Scorpion.

She's there now, lying down in the back room at the field station, trying to close her eyes. Just for a minute. It's six-thirty in the evening and dinner is about ready, judging from the inescapable scent of sizzling garlic, ginger and green onions arising from the kitchen where the two remaining fox girls—Marguerite and Allison— are concocting a tofu and rockfish stir-fry. She can hear the murmur of voices in the main room, laughter, somebody strumming a guitar. There'll be a dozen or so for dinner—Frazier, Annabelle, an assortment of hunters (pig boys and fox girls, they've been pairing off for the past year now and who could blame them?), the odd biologist, archaeologist, maintenance man, the whole thing very collegial, catch as catch can, tonight you cook, tomorrow I cook.

They'll be drinking wine. Wine is the sacrament here, and after tramping the backcountry all day, it's a necessary sacrament. She can picture them there, sprawled around the room, tipping the bottle over a makeshift assortment of glasses, joking, buzzing, gossiping, talking field biology, talking politics and scandal and sex and anything else that comes into their heads in the absence of TV and cell phones. Her friends. Her family. The people who've worked with her and under her to pursue rigorous lines of scientific inquiry and not coincidentally eliminate 5,036 feral pigs in just fifteen months, with no sign of a single survivor detectable anywhere on the island. In a minute, she'll push herself up and go out to join them. She'll eat—she can't remember ever having been so ravenous as she's been the past few weeks—but she won't join them in a glass of wine, not even the smallest most innocuous little drop.

It's a struggle, elbows, arms and wrists as weak as if they've been deboned, but she works herself into an upright position and in the next moment her feet are finding their way into the sandals, though the Velcro straps are too much for her and for now at least they'll have to remain unfastened. She sits there a moment watching the flies gather at the window, their world turned alien on them, the sweet generous air that floated them on its wafting currents to soup pots and trash cans and tender bits of carrion gone as hard and impermeable now as rock, and how could this have happened, what mystery has intervened? They can't know. They can only fumble and buzz and die, paradise right there before their eyes and unattainable for all that. If she were in Guam still, there'd be a gecko to climb the wall and feast on them, but here the reptiles are more circumspect. But dinner's ready, definitely, and in the next moment she's on her feet and moving across the parched floorboards, through the doorway and into the main room, where everybody looks up as one and everybody seems to be grinning.

"Jesus, Alma," Frazier roars out, his face red and getting redder, "we thought you'd gone and given birth to triplets back there—just toughed it out and bit off the umbilical all on your own." He mugs for the others, shifting the glass from his right hand to his left as he crosses the room to her, spreads his fingers wide across the swell of her abdomen and crows, "Nope, they're still in there, folks. And I don't blame them—what baby in his right mind would want to come out and face this bloody bunch of drunks and bush crazies?"

"Speak for yourself," somebody says, and the laughter is general.

Annabelle floats in to intercede, playfully pushing Frazier away from her and holding up a bottle for Alma's inspection. "Sparkling cider, non-alcoholic. Thought you might want a glass—do you?"

"Yes, that would be nice," she says, her voice soft and delicate, a flutter in her own ears. "If anybody left me a clean glass, that is."

A hoot from A.P., who makes a show of throwing back his wine in a gulp, then getting up to wash the glass at the tap and elaborately dry it with the one semi-clean corner of the dishtowel before handing it to her with a flourish. Annabelle is right there on cue, moving in with the bottle to fill the glass and call for a toast. "To Alma," she says. "And the baby!"

"Or babies," Frazier puts in.

"Easy for you to say"—Annabelle bends to refill her own glass from the nearest bottle of pinot grigio—"but you're not the one who has to carry all that weight around." She pauses, reconsidering, and reaches out to pat his midsection. "Though on second thought . . ."

"Not me, I swear I'm not pregnant."

"Sextuplets!" A.P. shouts. "Anything less is, is"—he's weaving, grinning, trying to drink from the neck of the bottle and make sense at the same time—"insupportable. Or unsustainable. Or, or—whatever."

She's due in two and a half weeks. Everyone's aware of that, even Freeman Lorber, who tried his best to assert his authority over her and for the first few weeks after she began showing kept insisting he'd be best man at the wedding till she let him know that there wasn't going to be a wedding and it was none of his business in any case. *All you need to worry about*, she told him, and she'd let her voice harden till there was no coming back, *is who's going to look after things when I'm on maternity leave—which is only going to be a week, five working days, so don't get that look on your face*. If there are any surprises—if she should go into early labor and she happens to be here on the island—there'll be plenty of time to get back to the mainland, if not by boat, then helicopter. But that's not going to happen because she'll be back at home for the last week and her mother will be there with her. And Ed. Ed, with the car gassed and tires inflated, already primed to floor it all the way to the hospital.

After dinner, she takes a chair outside to sit and watch the light change over the rise behind the bunkhouse. Her book is back on her bed, but she doesn't need a book, not here, not tonight. Everything is still, the swallows back in their nests, the grasshoppers that the foxes so love to crush between their teeth settling down in the high yellow grass, the colors of the buildings and the fields and the chaparral shifting and melding in exactly the way of the Diebenkorn paintings hanging in the main house—and Diebenkorn stayed here, right here, walked this very ground, a friend and guest of Carey Stanton in the time

409

before all this became public land, or at least held in trust for the public. She's thinking about that, about capturing this scene, the sweep and solace of it, in oils or even pencil, how very nearly impossible that must be, and of her last attempts at figurative art, in the seventh or eighth grade, which wound up looking more like abstract expressionism, when one of the fox girls, Allison, comes out to join her.

The light has begun to fade, bats careering across the open spaces, a cool current of sea air creeping up the pass from the ocean. Allison—a smoker—settles in on the ground beside her, resting her back up against the rough stucco wall. "Do you mind?" she asks, waving the unlit cigarette at her.

"No, go ahead," she says, but she can't help feeling the slightest tick of annoyance. Couldn't she smoke out back? Up on top of the ridge? On one of the buoys in the channel? Anywhere but here?

"I mean, I'm downwind of you, I'm pretty sure." There's the flare of the match, the pursed lips, the sharp assaultive odor of charred weed, and then it's gone, drifting along the base of the house like a spirit summoned and dismissed.

For a moment they're silent, Alma staring off across the expanse of the yard to where the compost bin rises up like a building itself, Allison absorbed in her cigarette. The bats ricochet off nothing, the shadows go one degree denser. Then, just to say something, to be gracious and welcoming instead of merely old, pregnant and bearish, Alma says, "Dinner was great. You guys really outdid yourselves."

"You like it?"

"I think I ate too much."

"Yeah, I mean, when Marg and I saw the rockfish A.P. caught we figured bread it, flash-fry it and then set it aside so it won't get soggy, then the rest was easy, your standard stir-fry with brown rice. And wine." She lets out a laugh. "Enough wine and anything tastes good." Allison's a blonde, what Alma's mother would call a dirty blonde, thin-faced and pretty and no older than the girl Dave LaJoy brought out here to die.

"Well, whatever," Alma says, "you were inspired tonight. Really, you guys should open your own restaurant."

But Allison doesn't respond. She's looking off in the direction of the compost bin. "What's that," she says in a whisper, "a fox? Or no, that can't be a fox, can it?"

The foxes, used to a free handout when they were caged, are common around the ranch now, even in daylight. Alma has identified six different individuals making the rounds of the compost every night, delicately gourmandizing on the leftovers, which tonight would feature a certain irresistible quantity of rockfish skin, guts and bone. But Allison—she's a fox girl, after all—is right. Even without her glasses, Alma can see that. This is no fox. The movement is all wrong, too humped and discontinuous, not nearly fluid enough. "Skunk," Alma says, rising from the chair in the same moment Allison unfolds herself from the ground to stand there beside her. "What else could it be?"

And that's when things become interesting, the two of them advancing cautiously across the drive and up the slight rise where the seasonal grasses have been scythed to yellow stumps and the occasional eruption of hacked fennel shows itself like a clenched green fist, the going unsteady, the fading light playing tricks with their eyes. Both are trying to minimize their movements as in some children's game, red light–green light, keeping their arms at their sides and freezing in place after each step. The bin is no more than fifty feet away now. They're squinting their eyes to focus against the descending screen of the night, but even in the diminished light it becomes apparent to both of them that this creature, working its paws like a peasant woman bent over her wash on the banks of a nighttime river, is neither fox nor skunk. For one thing, it's too big. And the movement is all wrong. The fur. The way it sits back on its haunches while it eats. For an instant, puzzlement giving way to outrage, Alma sees a dog there before her, a ragged stinking disease-spreading mongrel some idiot boater set loose without a thought to the consequences, to the disaster canine distemper or parvovirus could wreak on the fox population, but then she sees that this is no dog either. Amazingly, bewilderingly, it seems to be something else altogether. Something with a mask and articulated fingers and a long striped bushed-out tail.

The Separation Zone

So it's June finally and the channel's full of boats and all the pigs are dead and nobody knows and nobody cares. His approach is he's not going to be bitter, not get himself worked up where it's not going to do any good. FPA is defunct, just a sad joke now, every last nickel in donations evaporated in the face of Toni Walsh's assault and the way the national papers picked up on it. Not to mention the blogs. Where what they'd been doing once seemed heroic in the eyes of a certain demographic, now they've become a symbol of willfulness and excess—and worse, of a kind of clownish incompetence that makes him ashamed to hold up his head in public. Even Marta, fat-assed pathetic Marta, who's in the kitchen right now making damn sure his eggs are over easy and his toast is at least malleable, referenced the situation one bleak early morning when the café was full to bursting and everybody—right down to the greasy-pantsed apprentice bum who shuffled in each morning for his take-out coffee—was listening. "Looks like you got yourself some trouble, that right, Dave?" she said, making sure her voice was pitched loud enough for them all to hear, though she was careful to let the pouchy folds of her face droop in a simulacrum of sympathy. Burning with rage and humiliation, he'd looked past her to sweep the room with his eyes—just let anybody crack a smile—and then, in a controlled voice said, "Nothing I can't handle."

He's sitting in a window seat brooding over that little scene, over all the unfortunate scenes of his shit life in the course of the past four months, watching the traffic ease past on the slick streets, the fog so dense it seems to create each successive car out of nothing. What he wants is a second cup of coffee and his eggs and toast, but Marta has been moving as if the floor's made out of flypaper and it's been at least five minutes since she disappeared into the kitchen, probably for a smoke or maybe a blood transfusion or better yet, a new brain. Does he hate her? No. He tolerates her, that's all, the way he tolerates all the other half-wits and incompetents of the world. Does he want to find another café, one with better food and better service? No. Because he's a creature of habit, for better or worse, and he'll be the first to admit it—even to Anise, who wouldn't set foot in a place like this. Especially to Anise.

At least the court business is behind him, or mostly. The civil suit's a joke—Kelly was an adult and went along willingly, in service of her own needs and beliefs—and it'll never get past summary judgment. And Sterling has got the criminal charges reduced to a single misdemeanor count of trespass, to which Dave will plead guilty—proudly, and puff it up in his blog on the FPA website for whoever's still out there—and pay the fine and move on. Which is what today is all about. When he's done with breakfast, if Marta can ever drag herself through the swinging door and actually deliver it, which, if he's not mistaken, is what she's paid to do, he's going to go to the supermarket, stock up on some sandwich things, tofu, cherry tomatoes, red peppers, mushrooms and sweet onions for kebabs, a couple bottles of nice local wine, and then he's taking Anise, Wilson and Alicia out to Coches for the weekend. To relax. Do some snorkeling. Catch some sun. And the radio did promise sun by noon, all appearances to the contrary.

He shoots a savage look at the motionless slab of the kitchen door, with its greased-over wire-glass window and the smudged push plate, then turns back to the fog and the reborn cars. Is it his imagination or does it seem a degree thinner? Because a minute ago he couldn't see that fire hydrant across the street, could he?

This is the moment at which a woman appears out of the fog, sidesteps the hydrant, gives a quick glance in both directions and crosses the street as if she's coming directly to him. She's thirty-five, forty maybe, wearing a skirt, dark hose, slick black vinyl boots that rise to her knees, her face round and sweet and generous, big soulful eyes, all made up at six-thirty on a Saturday morning and with a white beret cutting a sharp mysterious line just above her eyebrows. A quick little hop and she's up on the curb, the walk, coming right up to the window, and she's nobody he knows, is she? Her pupils are dilated, hugely, dark planetoids rimmed with a corona of cola brown, making her appear vulnerable, soft, receptive—isn't that the look of love? Or is it just myopia? She's right there, inches away, but she's not looking at him, hasn't come for him at all. She's peering past him, scanning the interior, the counter, the booths, looking for somebody, until all of a sudden she realizes he's there and flashes him a wide teetering smile of surrender.

Normally, at this hour in the morning, interrupted in his own booth—caught out—he might have scowled. But not today. Today's different. Today's the start of something, of relaxation into the world, of acceptance, joy and forgiveness, and so he smiles right back at her, and that smile, though he has Anise and she has somebody too, somebody who'll show up at any minute and breeze into the place with her on his arm, says that he is willing and able and ready for anything.

There are lines at the supermarket, though everybody should be sleeping still, shouldn't they? He can't help feeling a stab of the old familiar impatience as the checkout woman calls futilely for a checker at checkstand three— *Randy? Randy, checkstand three?*—and no one shows up so that he has to wait for the old man moving like an undersea diver who's forgotten his Vons card and can't remember his phone number and the three women buying a year's supply of groceries each, as if they were going straight home to lock themselves in their bunkers, before he can finally get some service, and though the checker is all caffeinated and chattery he responds to every idiotic word out of her mouth in monosyllables until he's out the door with a *You have a nice day now* ringing at his back.

At home, he leaves the groceries in the car, taking a moment to shift the perishables into the cooler in the back, then going on into the house to let the dogs out in the yard. He's arranged with the maid, Guadalupe, to come over in the evening and look after their needs and then again tomorrow morning, so there's no worry on that score. The dogs—they've already been out once, at dawn, when he woke and went to fetch the paper—slink across the lawn to do their business in their hunched skeletal way. They've been abused, imprinted with pain, running all their fine-boned lives, from the puppy mill to the track to the kennel and back to the track until they're too old to run and along comes the man with the needle—from whom he's saved them, these two at least. Still, they're timid, skulking beasts, ghosting around the house as if they were ashamed to be seen. He watches them for a moment, then checks the time and whistles them back to the house. It's eight-thirty and Stiles is due at nine.

At nine precisely there's a buzz at the gate and then Stiles's acid-etched tones leaching through the intercom like a message from a distant planet. "It's me, Stiles," he says. "I got your goods."

If Dave was expecting some sort of Southern carica-ture in overalls and a reversed feedlot hat driving a hard-used pickup with bales of hay and neck-craning goats in back he's surprised. Stiles is driving a freshly waxed GMC Yukon, same model as his own, only newer, and when he pulls up in front of the house and steps out into the paved drive to take Dave's hand in his own, he's dressed no dif-ferently from a suburbanite at the mall. And he's young, much younger than Dave would have guessed from hear-ing his voice over the phone—Stiles can't be much older than he is himself.

"Yeah, well, thanks for coming," Dave says, dropping the man's hand.

An awkward pause follows, Stiles just staring at him as if awaiting a speech of praise and deliverance. After a moment he says, "This your place?"

"Yes."

"Pretty pricey, I'd guess."

Dave shrugs. "It's California."

"Tell me about it." Another pause, longer this time. "But I'm a man of my word, no matter, and the price we agreed on if I'm not mistaking, is thirty apiece. That right?"

"That's right. How many did you wind up—?"

"Ten. Each one in their own separate burlap bag," he says, moving to the back of the SUV now and pulling open the rear hatch.

Dave peers in. There's the same interior light he's got on his car, the same gray carpet and hard vinyl storage compartments. Atop the carpet, a sheet of plastic, and atop the plastic, distributed like sacks of onions or potatoes, are the burlap sacks. Look closely and you can see movement there, a flex and release of muscle like a wave rippling and breaking across the dull tan surface of the material.

"You put 'em separate so you don't get 'em biting each other. They're not immune to their own poison, you got to know that. I seen it where they get so mad they bite their own self, like suicide. You don't want that. Not at thirty per."

Until this moment he hasn't really considered the lethality of the things—they're snakes, that's all, rattle-snakes, and if Santa Catalina has them, why shouldn't Santa Cruz, and so what if Dr. Alma happens to step on one some blissful sunny morning? That's nature, isn't it? But now, looking at the mute brown sacks and the living presence lurking inside them, he can feel a thrill run through him, no different from the thrill of fear and excitement he felt the first time he ever saw a gun, a pistol, an inert black metal object lying casually on a kitchen counter in a neighborhood kid's house. It was just there, dully gleaming beside the sugar bowl and the cookie jar, but it had the potential to come fatally to life. "How do I handle them? I mean, will they bite through the bag or what?"

Stiles reaches in and slides one of the bags out, hefting it by the knot on top. His arm strains. The shape shifts inside the bag, going heavy at the bottom. "Might. But they like the bag, like the dark. They don't want to bite what they can't see—or fix on with their radar."

"Radar?"

"That's what I call it. Heat sensors. For detecting warm-blooded prey when they come out slinkin' at night. Mice and such. Rabbits." He holds out the bag. "Here, you want to hold it? No?" A smile now, ungenerous, pinched down at the corners. "You want a look at least, see you're gettin' your money's worth?"

"No," he hears himself say, waving the flat of one hand. "That's okay."

A silence. Stiles is watching him, that uncharitable look on his face still. "All right then, have it your way. That'll be three hundred. Cash. And forget the gas money. You want me to put 'em in the back of your vehicle for you?"

"Yeah, sure," Dave says, trying to extract his wallet from his pocket and flip open the rear hatch of the Yukon at the same time. "Am I going to need plastic like you have?"

A shrug. "They might shit, I guess. It's a wicked smell once it's in the carpet. But you can have this sheet here if you want. I got no use for it."

And that's it. Stiles flips back the plastic sheet like a waiter changing tablecloths and spreads it across the floor of Dave's car, smoothing out the wrinkles with a brusque stroke of one hand. Then he hoists the burlap sacks, two at a time, laying them in gently on top. When he's done, Dave hands him the money, three hundred-dollar bills. Stiles takes a moment, fanning them out in his hand before folding them once and stuffing them in his right front pocket. Then he tips an imaginary hat and climbs into the cab of his truck. The door slams. The engine turns over, smooth as a vacuum cleaner. One final thing, his head craning out the window, his smile so tight it's almost a grimace: "Nice vehicle you got there." There's a soft mechanical thump as he eases the transmission into drive. "I do like your style."

Dave is aboard the boat nearly an hour before he told the others to show up, stowing things (the snakes he intends as a surprise, sort of like the capper to the day, and he lays them gingerly below, one at a time, careful to keep the sacks away from contact with his body) and generally making ready to go to sea. There's a stop at the fueling dock, then back to his berth to prepare the sandwiches and marinate the tofu and veggies for kebabs. The wine is in the cooler, beer too—Wilson's a real beer hound—and the rabbits are in their cage under the table, with plenty of newspaper spread underneath to catch their droppings. To this point he never realized just how much food rabbits process, as if they evolved on the earth for the sole purpose of producing little balls of crap, infinite crap, and having them in the garage for the past two weeks was a real trial. It was Guadalupe's husband who got them for him—cottontails, not the big lean jackrabbits he'd been hoping for—but it was the only avenue open to him. Salvador had trapped a pair of wild rabbits that had been raiding his garden three years back and he'd kept them in a pen and bred them for food, quite a thriving business, according to Guadalupe. Well, these five would be spared anyway, and cheap at five dollars apiece. The girls—both Anise and Alicia—cooed over them and fed them slivers of carrot, lettuce and whatnot for the first week, till they lost interest and left the custodial duties to him. But they're hot to release them, that's for sure. "We'll have a little ceremony on the beach," Anise said, squeezing his biceps. "A coming out party, *Rabbits in Bunnyland*. Won't that be cool?"

As for raccoons, he struck out there. The traps yielded nothing but the same cat three nights in a row and then nothing at all. Ditto opossums, though he spotted two of them on the street out front of the house late one night a couple weeks back and he's keeping the traps set and baited just in case. Gophers he's given up on. They moved in within weeks of the raccoons' departure, fanning up great conical mounds of dirt like miniature calderas all over the new lawn, and he consulted with his gardener over the problem. "Can you catch them—alive, I mean? Unhurt." The gardener looked at him for a long while. Then, very slowly, measuring out his words, he said, "Poison or Macabee trap. Either way, they're dead. You want pets, go to PETCO."

Anise is the first to show. She's wearing clogs and a crotch-high jumper kind of thing, in yellow, like the playsuits little girls used to wear when he was a kid, with the exception that she's no little girl and her playsuit is cut deeply in front to show off what she has. Her bag is slung over one shoulder and she's got a bottle of wine in each hand, one red, one white. "Cambria, honey. Martha's Vineyard. My favorite." She tips back her straw hat to peck him a kiss and then wrinkles up her nose. "What's that smell?"

"The rabbits. Don't you remember? This is their big day."

Then she's down on hands and knees, making kissing noises at the cage under the table and talking baby talk to the brainless nose-twitching things backed up against the wire mesh as if wire was all there was in the world. "Oh, the poor little bunnies, all stuck in that awful cage. Little bunnies, look at you. Nobody's going to eat you now, don't you worry. Uh-uh, not with Mommy here."

He watches with real interest, the fringe of her skirt thrust up in back and her breasts gone heavy with gravity— *Doggie-style*, that's the term that comes into his head—and how long has it been since they've had sex? Was it last weekend? Seven whole days? Three steps and he's hovering over her, bending from the waist to peer into the cage, one hand seeking out the heat of her, right there where the flap of skirt rucks up and the tight silken material of the crotch takes over. "Mmm," she murmurs, pushing back against his hand with a revolution of her hips, "that feels nice."

They're in a deep clinch, mouth to mouth, groin to groin, Anise pressed up against the bulkhead and everything in him strung tight as a bow, when Wilson's face appears in the doorway. "Hey, hey, now, none of that," Wilson crows in the voice of the class clown, which is exactly what he was and is, "or we'll never get out of port." And then, to Alicia, whose face slides in place next to his as if they're looking down a well, "You see what's going on down there? They're doing a porn movie only they forgot the camera."

Alicia has wine too, a wicker basket crowded with the necks of bottles, and she's all legs coming down the steps in a pair of tight white shorts. Wilson has a case of Dos Equis propped up on one shoulder, a grocery sack of avocados and tortilla chips in his free hand. "Got to have chips and guac," he announces, setting his burden down on the table, "or it's not a party. And this is definitely a party, am I right, Alicia?"

Before she can respond, before she has a chance to hand the basket to Anise or even say hello, Wilson has her in a simulated clinch, thrusting his hips in parody. "Can't let nobody show us up, huh, baby?"

Dave is feeling loose, or as loose as he's able to feel because relaxation is not his long suit, and instead of shutting Wilson down he just lets him go. Smiling, one arm around Anise's waist, he says, "We'll see about that—knowing you, you'll be snoring about ten minutes after we pass the breakwater."

Wilson's in motion suddenly, swinging away from Alicia to take the basket, set it down on the table and then spread his arms wide in an elaborate palms-out shrug. "Maybe so, Captain, but when the time comes"—a wink for Alicia—"I'll be ready to report for duty."

And everything's fine, sparkling, beautiful even. They're all smiling, all the way around, and he's thinking how great it is to be able to do this, to get away, kick back, slow down, let life come to you instead of chasing after it all the time. Ever since he was a kid he's been going out on trips like this, and for his money there's nothing that can compare with the excitement of coming aboard with your arms laden and taking your sweet time to stow your gear and provisions in the ingenious motion-proof lockers designed specifically for that purpose—"Making everything shipshape," as his mother used to say—and then starting the engine, casting off the lines in a solid pillar of sun or even a cold dripping mist or a rain that taps on the roof of the cabin like a thousand separate fingers and motoring out of the harbor with nothing but anticipation ahead. When he was in school and the tedium of routine and term papers and pop quizzes got him to the point where he felt as if he were buried in layers of mud like one of the hibernating frogs in the tricolor illustration of the winter pond in their biology text, his parents would take him and a friend of his choosing—Barry Butler, Joe Castle, Jimmy Mastafiak—out to the islands for the weekend.

Casting off was like settling into your seat on the jet to Hawaii or strapping your longboard to the top of the car to drive down to Baja, only better, far better, because the trip was part of the adventure and when you got there it was like you had your own house with you and not just a suitcase or a gym bag. And yes, he's seen the mile-long motor homes out on the freeway with the reanimated corpses propped up behind the wheel, spewing out the fumes while they drag their earthly belongings with them from Toledo to Butte and back again, but sitting on a concrete strip in a pall of smoke with ten thousand other idiots can't compare with being at sea, where every day, every hour, every minute, there's something new to get your mind around and you can just flick the wheel with one little finger and go anywhere you want.

Wilson, quick on his feet and with the makings of a sailor in him if he ever wanted to go there, casts off and then joins him at the helm. The girls are down in the cabin, glasses of cold clear viognier balanced delicately in their hands while the bottle beads in the antique ice bucket Anise found in a junk shop somewhere. They motor down the long double row of berths, the *Chez When*, the *Mikado* and the *Isosceles II* showing them their sterns, the fog so dense they can barely make out the letters of their names. "It's supposed to be clear around noon," he says over the sound of the engine, "and, I don't know, it should be nice out there the rest of the weekend. That's what they're saying on the radio anyway."

"You joking or what?" Wilson has a beer cradled between his legs. He's dressed in an oversized T-shirt, baggy shorts, sandals. On his head, canted back, a baseball cap—not black, not this time—but the tomato red of the Anaheim Angels of Los Angeles. "I picked up Alicia down at her apartment on Bath? I couldn't even fucking see the house." The beer comes to his lips, his throat works, it sinks again. "Noon? If it clears by six we'll be lucky. Shit, if it clears at all."

The long looming multi-pillared structure of Stearns Wharf, with its restaurants and trinket shops and tramping lines of tourists, suddenly breaks through the mist like a giant centipede humping across the water, and then it vanishes again and they're through the mouth of the harbor and out onto a sea as flat and scoured as a stainless-steel pan. "At least it's calm," he says, thinking of how the channel can look so placid when you get up in an airplane or you're coming down San Marcos Pass on a sunny day, as if it's nothing, as if you could paddle across it in twenty minutes.

"At least. But I'd trade calm for some sun any day."

That's the last thing Wilson has to say because within minutes, given the gentle rocking of the boat and the somnolent thrum of the engine, he's gone. The beer, still clutched between his thighs, is in no danger of spilling, and at this point it's mainly suds and backwash anyway. His head tips forward till his chin is resting on his chest. Very lightly, he begins to snore. For the next hour, Dave lets him be, content to focus on the task before him, keeping an eye on his instruments, staring out into the fog till the fog is all there is, heaven and earth and sea swallowed up and spat out again and still no sign of clearing. He's thinking his thoughts, but those thoughts are greatly reduced, until eventually he's thinking nothing, his mind gone free of his body the way it always does at sea. He's just alive, that's all. His heart's beating. He's breathing. And the fog props him up on a smooth cool sheet of nothing as if he's floating—or no, flying.

They've just passed midpoint when Wilson wakes with a start. "Oh, shit," he murmurs. "What'd I do, doze off?"

"More like deep R.E.M. time. You've been out almost an hour."

From below, the tremolo of the girls' voices, giggling, a snatch of music fading in the background. Wilson, adjusting himself to his surroundings, discovers the bottle clamped between his legs, raises it experimentally and lowers it again. "You want a beer? I think I need another one at this point."

"Not till we get there."

"Right. Steady on, Dave." There's a silence, nothing but the soft wash of the bow, the engine, chatter from below. "At least the girls are having a good time, sounds like. But shit, this stuff is thick. How in Christ's name are you navigating through it—I mean, I wouldn't know the middle of the channel from the back end of the island. Or the rocks. Or the cold briny bottom, full fathom five and all that. You going to keep us off the bottom, Dave?"

"That's my intention. Here, just look at the chart on the screen—here, yeah, this one."

After a moment, Wilson says, "Yeah, but I still don't like it if I can't see where I'm going."

"You don't have to."

"This is what I like, this kind of chart here"—he leans forward to pull one of the laminated sheets out of the rack to his left. "Old school, you know what I mean? Something you can hold on to. But what's this yellow thing here in the middle?"

"What, you need glasses now?"

Wilson squints, holds the chart out at arm's length. "Only when I'm on the job," he says. "But I can make it out: 'East Santa Barbara Channel Weather Buoy.' But you already knew that."

"We just passed it. We're like halfway to the island, then we've another bit to get around the west side and all the way out to Coches."

"So we're in the"—quoting—"'Northbound Coastwise Shipping Lane'?"

"No, see here, on the GPS—we just left it. We're in the zone in between."

"The Separation Zone."

"Right. And once we cross the southbound lane, in about five minutes, we're home free. Until we get to the western tip of the island and head into the Santa Cruz Channel, which is where the rocks are, since you're asking. So no beer, no cocktails, nothing, not for me. Not till we drop anchor and I can relax, because you know as well as I, you don't want to fuck around out here. Especially in conditions like this."

"I hear you. But your copilot, he can drink himself into a coma—in fact, isn't that required, I mean, by regulation? Unless you have a heart attack. You're not going to have a heart attack on us, are you, Dave?"

The wash of the waves, the stray giggle from below. No birds, not even shearwaters. The strained half-light of the sun up there somewhere trying to break through. And the calm. The calm you can't buy. Or maybe you can, because isn't that what they're doing?

"You know something I didn't tell you—or Alicia or Anise even?"

Grinning now, leaning over his knees, the hat pushed up high on his crown with a quick nervous flick of his fingers, Wilson awaits the answer. He likes surprises, likes parties. "What?" he says and the grin expands.

"It's not just rabbits we're setting loose today. You know that guy from Texas, the one your friend or uncle or whoever knows? The snake man?"

"Get out of here."

"Yeah, we've got ten primo condition rattlesnakes down there in the hold in burlap sacks. And that's just the start—guy says he can get as many as we want."

"Can I see them?"

"Not till we get there."

"Aw, come on, what are you afraid of? *The Sequel: Snakes on a Boat.* I can see it now. Come on, man, I used to handle snakes when I was kid. I had like six terrariums, with a rubber boa, a racer, couple of gopher snakes, kings and rattlers, rattlers too. Did you know that the ones in the San Gabriels, down in L.A., are going through a whole weird evolutionary change where the snakes with the smallest rattles get to mate more because the big ones, the noisy old pissed-off *cascabeles*, are all getting killed off?"

"I don't know. I wouldn't doubt it. But these ones are going to be just fine." And this is his vision—he can see it right there before him—coming to fruition, because the snakes he's bringing out here where nobody's going to bother them can grow till their rattles drop off, and if that isn't conservation, he doesn't know what is.

"Come on. Just one. Just let me see one." Wilson's eyes—he's never noticed this before—palpitate ever so slightly, nerves jumping under the whites like the snakes moving silently in the loose grip of their bags.

"I said no. Can you hear me? Am I talking loud enough for you?"

Wilson's shoulders go tight and his mouth draws down. He smoothes his goatee a moment, as if thinking things through, then pushes himself up from the bench, jamming the chart back in its rack and swiping up the empty bottle in the same motion. "All right, fuck it. But I'm going down there—to get a beer—and if I happen to take a look then that's my business, right?" And then he turns, puts both hands on the rails and disappears down the steps.

He's calm. He's been calm all day, all week. But this just turns his burners on high because Wilson can be such a jerk sometimes, and what is he anyway but just a carpenter and a wiseass who thinks he can rain on anybody anytime he wants, and before he can stop himself Dave is up from the controls and hammering down the steps shouting, "No, you're wrong—it's my fucking boat and it's *my* fucking business!"

The *Tokachi-maru*, a twelve-thousand-ton freighter out of Nagoya, bound for Long Beach with a load of Chinese-made textiles and machine parts, was one of the oldest ships still flying a Japanese flag. She'd been commissioned in the late 1960s and except for brief spells in port or dry dock had been at sea continuously ever since. She was etched with rust from the waterline all the way up her six decks to the bridge, and though paint had been applied belowdecks and above in various eras (elephant-gray and dirt-adherent white for the most part), she tended to stand out in any harbor as an eyesore, if not a derelict. Still, she was a moneymaker for her owners, who intended to sail her until it was no longer economically feasible—or better yet, till she went to the bottom in some fortuitous South Sea typhoon, fully insured, of course, and with all hands spared. There had been surprisingly few accidents aboard, given the miles she'd logged and the years she'd been at sea (the usual broken bones, heart attacks and cases of alcohol poisoning, and just one man overboard, off the coast of Georgia in the late 1980s, who was, regrettably, never found), but for all her unsightliness and the problems the crew had with doors that rusted shut and the galley that still relied on the original four-burner gas range and three antiquated microwave ovens, her instruments were state of the art and her captain, Noboru Nishizawa, nephew of the ship's first commander, was among the most reliable and cautious in the entire fleet.

On this particular day, a Saturday in June, the ship encountered dense fog on entering the Santa Barbara Channel from the north and Captain Nishizawa himself appeared on the bridge to oversee operations. As a precaution he cut the engines to three-quarter speed and ordered the ship's horn to sound at intervals. Beyond that, he relied on his instruments, his experience and the sheer mass of the ship to keep them from harm. He was right dead center in the middle of the southbound lane and nothing was showing on the radar up ahead of him. If there was an emergency, the *Tokachi-maru* would take two miles and three and a half minutes to come to a stop. The tightest turn of which she was capable was nearly a mile across. And at seven stories above the surface, even in the clearest conditions, the crew on the bridge would have little chance of sighting any small craft below in any case.

That was the way it was. That was what the shipping lanes—and the Separation Zone—were meant for. Was the system perfect? Of course not. The Separation Zone functioned like the median on a freeway, but there were no lines drawn on the water to delineate the lanes and no concrete bumpers, palms or oleanders to separate north- and southbound traffic. Were there accidents? Of course there were. But in most cases the crew of a freighter or tanker never saw, felt or heard a thing when a small craft was unlucky enough to blunder across its path. Think of it this way: a heavyset woman, heavier even than Marta at the Cactus Café, a real monument of flesh and bone and live working juices, plods out to her car on aching feet after a double shift and can't begin to know the devastation she wreaks on the world of the ant, the beetle and the grub.

Wilson is fast, he'll say that for him. By the time he bolts down the steps Wilson's already got the hatch in back of the table open and manages to grab one of the sacks from it before Dave can get there and slam it closed. The girls—the second bottle of wine, Anise's chardonnay, is half gone and they're eating something now, helping themselves to the sandwiches he's made without even having thought to offer him one—look up in amusement as if he and Wilson are playing some sort of game, but this isn't funny, not at all. It's stupid is what is. Idiotic. And he won't have it, not on his boat. The table is between him and Wilson and Anise is wedged in on the bench, right there in his way. "Put it down," he says.

And Wilson, all teeth, bright as a toothpaste commercial, wags the sack out front of him. "No way, man. I'm just going to"—he drops his eyes to pull loose the cord at the neck of the bag even as Dave snatches for it and draws back all in the same instant, afraid of the dark shape within, of the fangs, and didn't Stiles say they can bite through the bag?—"loosen this and show the girls . . . the, ta-da, surprise!"

In that moment, the moment at which the neck of the bag falls open and Wilson, so quick of reflex it's as if the bag has never been there at all, thrusts his hand in and comes out with the thing itself, his hand clamped behind its flat triangular head and its body twisting on itself like a hard sure slap to the face, Dave can't remember ever having felt more powerless. And hopeless. He's frozen there, both girls erupting with choked-back little shrieks of horror and amusement because that's what girls are supposed to do in a situation like this and Wilson flashing that smile and brandishing the snake as if he's given birth to it, and all he feels is that things have gone terribly wrong.

There it is, the snake, his snake, the one he's bought with his own private funds to possess it and free it again because that's his pleasure and it's not secreted in a bag anymore, not wrapped in burlap and hidden from sight, but right there in his face, coiling and uncoiling, rattling its tail in a high furious buzz like a stirred-up hive of bees, thick, potent, menacing, revealed in its essence. A snake. A rattlesnake. *Crotalus viridis.* Its mouth is open in outrage, the fangs yellow-white and slick with wet, with venom. The cabin closes in. The sea moves. And he understands, for the first time, how wrong this is, how wrong he's been, how you have to let the animals—*the animals*—decide for themselves.

Then the ship's horn sounds, loud as a cannon blast.

Then the crash comes.

Then nothing.

Scorpion Ranch

She's never seen the channel so smooth. There isn't even so much as a bump coming out of Ventura Harbor and at ten in the morning it's as warm as midday. As far as she can tell there's no hint of a breeze, nothing at all—it's dead calm, the surf flat, boats fixed in place, the kelp fanned out limp on the water. There won't be many sailboats out today, but the weekend sailors are just going to have to suffer, that's all, because she doesn't mind being a little selfish here—even if she had the ability to arrest the planet on its axis, she couldn't have ordered up better weather for the occasion. Amazing, really. Though the *Islander*'s full to capacity with Park Service and Nature Conservancy people and campers and day-trippers alike, everyone's just standing around as if they're at a cocktail party in a crowded apartment with unconquerable views. Nobody's looking green, nobody's got their head down and there's no Bonine or Dramamine in evidence. It's so flat that when Wade brings her a cup of tea in the recycled cardboard container, he's able to walk from the galley and down the length of the cabin without flailing his arms or lurching like a tightrope walker—and he doesn't spill a drop. "It's not water out there, it's glass," he says, leaning into the table where she's sitting with Annabelle and Frazier. "We're not sailing, we're just skating. And will you look at that sun."

"You're right," she says. "It couldn't be more perfect." She's thinking of the last end-of-project celebration, the one out on Anacapa three years ago, and so is he.

"Nobody's going to freeze today," he says, "that's for sure. And the paper cups and plates and all the rest—shit, even the cake—aren't going to blow out to sea either, right, Fraze?"

Frazier and Annabelle are dreaming over their coffee,

431

their faces soft and content, their posture so relaxed they might have been in a trance. He's cradling his cardboard cup in his left hand and she's got hers in her right. They're sitting very close, hip to hip, and their two otherwise unoccupied hands are interlocked and resting casually in Annabelle's lap. Alma is thinking how serene and pretty Annabelle's looking—she's wearing an aquamarine jacket and yellow blouse set off by the dangling boar's ivory earrings Frazier gave her and gazing soulfully off across the water to where Anacapa and Santa Cruz rise up in the distance like the original Eden, the one before Eve, before Adam, before names.

Frazier looks up, distracted from his thoughts. "I wouldn't know, mate. I wasn't here for that one"—he gives first Alma, then Annabelle a look—"because you people didn't think to get us out here to put holes in all those scampering little rats . . . at, oh, I don't know, a bargain rate of let's say fifty dollars per. Do I hear fifty?"

Wade gives him a quizzical look, as if he's not quite sure whether he's joking or not, then ducks his head and announces that he's got to get back and make sure everything's in order. "No screwups this time, right?" He flashes a nervous smile, rubs his hands together as if he's personally molding the dough for the wood-fired pizzas. Alma can see he's worked up. The party's his to worry over, beginning to end—his and Jen's. Jen is her new secretary and factotum, a month on the job now, and she's a rock—a computer genie with two years of biology courses at SBCC under her wing. Jen can handle anything. And so can Wade. They'd better. Because she's taking the day off herself. She didn't even bring her laptop.

There's an interval, Wade gone, people milling, the boat moving forward so imperceptibly they might have been at anchor for all anyone knew, and then Frazier takes a sip of coffee, glances up casually over the folded lip of his paper cup, and says, "So, this'll be Beverly's first sea voyage then? Or have you had her out already?"

This is Annabelle's cue to roll her eyes and release his hand to give him a playful shove. "She's only nine weeks old, Fraze, what do you think?"

The weight of the baby against her shoulder, her breast, the whole right side of her body, is like the weight of a comforter on a fogged-in night, light, reassuring, indispensable, nothing at all like the immovable lump growing inside her that had made her feel as if she were about to sink through the earth with every step she took. Beverly. She has Tim's eyes, two bright flecks of green like forest leaves touched with sunlight, though Tim doesn't matter, not anymore, and she's got the strong ever-so-slightly bowed legs of the Takesue clan. She's a greedy insatiable feeder. She gurgles. She laughs. Her smile could stop traffic. Alma says, "Uh-huh, yeah. First time."

"She's a good little traveler, I'll say that for her. I haven't heard a sound out of her."

"Wait'll she wakes up and realizes she's hungry. My mother says she's got the lungs of a prima donna."

"Don't sell her short—the way she's going now she could be the first baby to sail solo around the world. What do you think? Asleep at the wheel?"

Beverly stirs. The green eyes flash open and don't particularly like what they see. Two or three heaves for breath and then the encapsulated wail breaking free to startle the cabin, everybody looking her way now, some in annoyance, some in the fondness of reminiscence, and then they look away and there's the maneuver with the blouse and the nursing bra and the baby's at the nipple, the flow of milk commencing and conversation starting up again.

"I don't know about you," Frazier says, looking to Annabelle, "but I'm ready for a beer. Anybody want one? Alma?"

"She's nursing, dummy." Annabelle gives him a look, her eyebrows knitting, her lips clenched in mock exasperation.

"So? A little beer in the system just makes the buggers stronger. I mean, look at me. My mother put away four or five pints a day her whole life—and nobody can tell me she was about to take a holiday just because she had a baby hanging off her teat."

Annabelle cuffs him lightly on the meat of his arm. "Oh, come on, Frazier—be civilized, will you? Pretend you're an American."

"You expect me to dignify that with a response?" he says, pushing himself up. "Beer—that's the universal language." He's hovering over the table, Annabelle sliding out to make way for him. "Annabelle?"

"Yeah, I guess so. Why not? We're celebrating, aren't we?"

"Alma? You sure?"

She shakes her head. "I'm okay. Really."

They both watch him make his way up the aisle between the tables to the concession stand–galley, where, Alma sees, any number of people seem to have the same idea, beers universal, though it's just past ten in the morning. "It's going to be one heck of a party," Alma says.

Annabelle nods, grinning. "And that one"—indicating Frazier with a nod of her head—"is going to make sure it never stops, not till we're back in Ventura and they kick us off the boat anyway."

The celebration—and it's not premature, not at all, because miracles do happen and they need to be consecrated when they do—is in recognition that no pig sign has been found anywhere on the island since the last pig was shot in the spring. They might have waited a year to avoid the potential embarrassment of having an old sow with six piglets show up somewhere in time for the six o'clock news, but pigs make a real mess of their environment, rooting things up in great wide swaths you can see from the air, and everybody's about ninety-nine percent sure they're gone—though of course they'll go on monitoring the fences for two more years yet before removing them permanently. Besides which, Frazier and his crew

434

won't be here in a year—or maybe Frazier will, judging from the way she's seen him gaze at Annabelle when he thinks no one's watching.

No, for her money—for all intents and purposes—the pigs are gone. And this day—mid-September, sun high, seventy-three degrees out on the water and maybe eighty at Scorpion—has been created in PR heaven for just such an occasion as this, and because Freeman Lorber has a conflict, she herself will stand before the gathered party-goers and the news camera from KNBC and deliver her speech with Beverly in her arms, declaring Santa Cruz Island free of invasive fauna.

Except for a single inconvenient specimen of *Procyon lotor*, that is, observed feeding at the compost bin at the main ranch three and a half months back. Or perhaps there were two—the ground was too hard to give up much in the way of prints—but certainly the animal was there. She saw it and so did Allison, unmistakably. And that—the appearance of the raccoon as dusk fell on that June night—is either one of the greatest coincident finds in the history of island biogeography or a disaster in the making. Or both.

No one believed them at first, and of course by the time everybody rushed out there in confusion the animal was gone. *It must have been a fox*, everybody said, *or a skunk; maybe a crippled fox, with a broken leg or something* (which would account for the odd movement), but she wouldn't be swayed. They were all out there the next night, and they saw the evanescent figures of foxes and skunks going about their rounds, but no raccoon. People began to look at her as if she were suffering from some sort of ramped-up hormonal delusion—and they dismissed Allison because Allison was very young. And she'd had a lot to drink that night.

On the third night she and Allison hauled out one of the fox traps and baited it with a healthy smear of pea-nut butter and half a can of questionable tuna some-body dug out of the back of the refrigerator, while the others—Frazier and Annabelle included—drank wine in an atmosphere of elevated sarcasm. *Raccoons, yeah, right, and what have you two been smoking?* Though she felt as if she weighed at least as much as Konishiki, the celebrated sumo wrestler—Konishiki and his brother too—Alma was up at first light and making her way across the blistered lot to where the cage stood hidden behind the compost bin. It was very still, the birds not yet fully roused, the western sky wrapped in darkness and a spatter of penetrant stars. When she got within fifteen feet of the trap she saw that there was movement inside, an animal there, a mammal, its features cloaked in fur. And when she was right there, right on top of it, the animal's head and shoulders swung round and the hard brown unblinking eyes fixed on her from deep in the black robber's mask.

Frazier wanted to exterminate it. "I tell you," he said, enormous in the boxers and T-shirt he wore to bed, all that skin, the plump bare feet and toes clutching at the dirt, "you let these things go and they'll take over. I've seen it with innumerable species on too many islands to count. And this is an omnivore. It's got to impact negatively on the foxes you just spent—and don't look at me—seven million dollars to preserve."

"What if it rafted here?" Alma said, staring down into the cage while everybody crowded in, sleep in their eyes, hair mussed, sinking into the grab bag of their clothes. "During the winter storms maybe. There was a lot of debris washing down out of those canyons on the mainland—we could be looking at something like a minor miracle here. The first colonist."

"So bring it back. Take blood. Test it," Annabelle said.

"It couldn't have been here all along, right?" Frazier put in, a look of impatience pressed into his features, as if he had a bus to catch. "There's no way, what with the documentation of this island and the way we combed it for those hogs—"

"They're nocturnal," Alma countered, "holing up all

day in burrows or downed logs, so they might have escaped notice. But do we know how long they've been here? No. Certainly it's got to be recent. Again, I'm telling you, we're looking—probably, I mean, possibly—at the first natural transplant in what, sixteen thousand years?"

"What if somebody brought it here?"

"Who?"

"As a joke."

She just glared at him. "Who's going to trap a raccoon and bring it all the way out here for a joke? What kind of joke is that? It doesn't even make sense. No, this animal got here the way the skunks and the foxes and the mice and the fence lizards and all the rest did and we have a clear duty not to interfere with it. Tag it maybe. Collar it. But nature's got to take its course." She looked round at them all, her eyes sweeping from face to face, all but pleading. "Isn't that what we're doing here in the first place?"

In the end, after keeping the animal confined for three days in the lee of the field station and consulting by radio with Freeman Lorber, Annabelle's boss at TNC and half a dozen mammalogists, they sedated it, weighed and measured it and drew two vials of blood for comparison with coastal populations. On the third night, somehow—and this is a very bright species, very dexterous—the door of the cage fell open and the animal was gone.

By the time the boat butts up against the dock at Scorpion Bay, Beverly's asleep again and stays asleep, thankfully, as Alma works her limbs into the Kelty pack and zips it up. Annabelle—she's never seen her so solicitous—holds the baby up so Alma can slip her own arms through the straps and wriggle the pack into position on her shoulders, and then they're out on deck in a line of people waiting to climb the ladder to the dock while the *Islander*'s captain, with the precision born of long experience, keeps the bow nose into the dock with just the minimal thrust of his engines. When it's choppy, it can be quite a trick getting hold of the ladder, which, of course is fixed, while the boat is not, but today it's not a problem. Even for the elderly and slow of foot. Even for people with babies.

On the dock—and it's so purely beautiful it always takes her breath away, with the tower of rock rising up right there to reduce her and the boat and every human thing to insignificance, the air alive with seabirds, the view to the east along the cliffs so jagged and wild and ancient you could almost picture the great flying reptiles of the Cretaceous crouched there over their cluttered nests—the group divides in two. The Park Service and TNC people head off for the ranch house around the corner, while the campers and day-trippers are held in check by one of the Park Service volunteers, who's there to recite the rules for them, rules meant for their own protection and which most people tend to observe, though there are always screwups as there always will and must be when you're dealing with the public. People fall from cliffs, people drown, people get drunk and do violence to one another, bones break, hearts give out, and it's all in a day's work for the Park Service. Alma almost resents these people, the public, tramping all over everything and leaving their trash behind, stealing artifacts, chasing birds off their nests, though she knows she shouldn't—and yet how much better would it be if nobody ever came out here and the islands could exist in the way they always had. Or should have. Before the Aleuts got here and killed off the otters, before the sheepmen and the cattlemen and all the rest.

Just as the captain reverses engines to take the remnants on board up the coast to Prisoners', the volunteer— an eager middle-aged man in shorts and a tipped-back cap with an elaborately carved walking stick in hand— delivers the all-important injunction: "Be back at the dock by three-thirty for a four o'clock departure." A pause to search out each face. "Or you'll be staying overnight whether you're planning on it or not." The campers and picnickers and hikers exchange smirks—they'll never miss the boat, that's what they're thinking, but of course half the time somebody does.

It's then, in the moment when Wade and Jen and the others are off-loading the supplies for the festivities and Alma's just standing there taking it all in—her first trip to the islands since Beverly was born!—that she happens to catch the eye of a woman standing just to the right of the volunteer. The woman—she looks to be her mother's age—is staring directly at her, and does she know her? She's pretty enough, for a woman of sixty or so, she supposes, with her great bush of graying hair flaring out from under one of those worked straw hats the Mexicans wear and the overall impression of trimness and fitness she exudes, her youthful clothes—Levi's jeans and jacket, a black T-shirt with some band's logo, cowboy boots—and the guitar slung over her back. She's still staring—and Alma's staring too, trying to place her—when Wade appears in her line of vision.

Wade is smiling. He's got a bottom-heavy canvas bag full of provisions hanging off each shoulder and the muscles in his legs are flexed tight under the burden. "Come on, Alma," he says, "what're you standing around here for? Don't you know there's a party going on?"

And so there is. The day washes over her like a bath. She sits there surrounded by friends in the shade of the old adobe ranch house while the grill sends up its festive aromas and people come up, one after another, as if she's a dignitary, a potentate, the Queen of the Island seated on her throne, to make small talk and coo over the baby. When the time comes she gets up and delivers her speech, Beverly clutching at the microphone in high baby spirits, and she feels so relaxed and natural she might have been talking to herself in the mirror. She praises Annabelle, praises Freeman and Frazier and all the dedicated men of Island Healers, praises New Zealand, praises the fox girls, and finally, when she's done thanking everybody she can think of and rattling off every statistic in support of the ongoing recovery she can summon, she raises a glass—of cider, pure sparkling apple cider, still dripping from the cooler—to the foxes, present and future. And the applause? The applause comes down like rain on the parched hills above, where the pines are sprouting in the duff and the oaks hang heavy with acorns.

As for Rita, she knows that something's going on, some sort of Park Service foolery that's going to keep her off the grounds and out of the ranch house she came here to see and dwell in if only for the day, but she doesn't know what the event is all about or what it's meant to commemorate. She can smell the smoke of the barbecue and it brings her back, though it won't be lamb they're roasting, she can bet on that. What, then—pig? Or what's left of a pig once it's gone through the mill and been ground up, bone, anus, eyeballs and all, and repackaged as hot dogs. And beef, of course. Beef is safe. None of the conservationists have to see it other than as some sort of bloodless lump of protein in a plastic-wrapped tray in the supermarket, and then probably half of them are vegetarians in any case. So tofu, falafel, eggplant—aubergine, they call it—red bell peppers, summer squash, the sort of thing Anise used to like, used to insist on once she grew up and got out of the house.

There's the noise of a microphone, a blurred voice swelling and receding on the whim of the electronics, and she skirts the house, the place of memories, keeping her distance from all these people and their wants and needs, and then climbing up into the floodplain of the creek to get a little elevation so she can look down on it and see it the way it was. All the way out on the boat she kept thinking about where the ashes should go, where Anise would have wanted them. She thought maybe the front corner of the house where it looked out on the bay or maybe in back where she'd had her vegetable garden, but now, given the intrusion, given what's going on there, she's not so sure. She keeps walking, the ground dry and cracked, the washed-down rubble of stones turning under her boots. She can feel the sweat starting up under her armpits, rimming the brim of her hat. It's a clear high day, the sky cupped overhead like the lid of a bell jar. Grasshoppers chirr and take to the air. The world jumps at her in a hundred shades of brown and gray and the parched pale seared-out green of the plants that won't see any rain till the fall runs its course.

It was two fishermen, partners on an urchin boat, who found Anise's body, not far off Scorpion, as if she'd been trying to get home. She'd been down nearly a week and must have traveled twenty miles in that time, judging from where they thought the wreck occurred. Things had been at her. And to have to look at her, what was left of her, when the coroner pulled the sheet away from her face and shoulders and you could see the stained and twisted weed that was her hair and the flesh that wasn't flesh anymore was a criminal thing, so hard and so wrong Rita thought she'd never walk out of that place but just die right there on the floor in that cold, cold room. The rest of them—Dave, Wilson, the other girl—they never found. Not a trace. Nothing of the boat either, except the scrap or two that washed ashore. And what did they tell her? They told her there were boats on top of boats down there.

Her legs are carrying her up the wash, going higher and higher till the banks begin to narrow and there's a trickle of water running in and out beneath the rocks as if trying to hide itself. There's a place up ahead, a grove of trees on the opposite bank where one of the hundred runlets that feeds the creek in winter chews its way down into the canyon, and she realizes now that she's heading for it. There's peace there, she knows there is, and though things would have changed over the course of the years, trees gone and trees come up, cliffs sheared and great blinding

441

caravans of boulders flung down, she thinks she can find it still. And she has her legs under her and her legs know the way.

She's sweated through, even to her underwear, by the time she gets there, and her breath isn't what it once was. But the place—a high seep where the sheep liked to come to lick at the rock, both for the water and the minerals—looks pretty much the same as she remembered it. A clutch of oaks, bigger now, thick around as her shoulders, and a slow easy drip of water that falls away from the rock face and into a shadowed pool alive to the dance of water striders and the other things, the smaller ones, the boatmen. The boatmen are there. And a single frog, disappearing with a soft musical plop under a hover of electric-blue damselflies.

The ashes are in a metal canister, with a screw top, not an urn. Or not a clay urn anyway, which is how she thinks of the term, something in it that speaks of antiquity and continuance. But this isn't an urn, it's a canister. And she settles down by the shaded dark pool no bigger than a washbasin, extracts it from her daypack and sets it beside her. Then she unhooks the guitar from her shoulder, cradles it in her lap and begins to strum, listening, pausing to tune it, getting it right. The first song she sings is one she used to do with Toby, a blues lament, key of E-flat, so sad she can barely get the words out, then her fingers find the chords of "Carrickfergus," a tune Anise made her play again and again when she was a girl—"Carry me over where, Ma?" she used to say. "Carry me over where?" And then the songs for Anise, just for Anise, the ones she made her own and the ones she wrote herself. The songs. The sun. The island. And she won't scatter the ashes till dark, till they're all on the boat and gone away, and the only sounds are the sounds of the night.

Somewhere there's a fox, its eyes stealing the light. This isn't one of the foxes that's been caged or collared or even captured. He's a survivor, a fighter, the flange of his nose torn in a forgotten dispute over territory and healed and torn and healed again. There's movement in the nighttime grass—crickets will be out, scorpions, things with the juice of life in them. He's alert and listening. And somewhere, in the deepest shadow of the hacked yellow grass, something else moves in a slow sure friction of scale and grasping vertebrae—a colonist, a rafter, a survivor of a different kind altogether. Picture the stripped-back slink of muscle, the flick of the tongue, the cold fixed eyes that don't need to see a thing. And hush. The grass stirs, the moon sinks into the water. Night on Santa Cruz Island, night immemorial.

AVAILABLE FROM PENGUIN

BY T.C. BOYLE

 PENGUIN BOOKS